R. W. Miller, R. W. Miller

Life in the new diamond diggings

R. W. Miller, R. W. Miller

Life in the new diamond diggings

ISBN/EAN: 9783742848475

Manufactured in Europe, USA, Canada, Australia, Japa

Cover: Foto ©Andreas Hilbeck / pixelio.de

Manufactured and distributed by brebook publishing software
(www.brebook.com)

R. W. Miller, R. W. Miller

Life in the new diamond diggings

Vol. V.   MARCH, 1873.   No. 5.

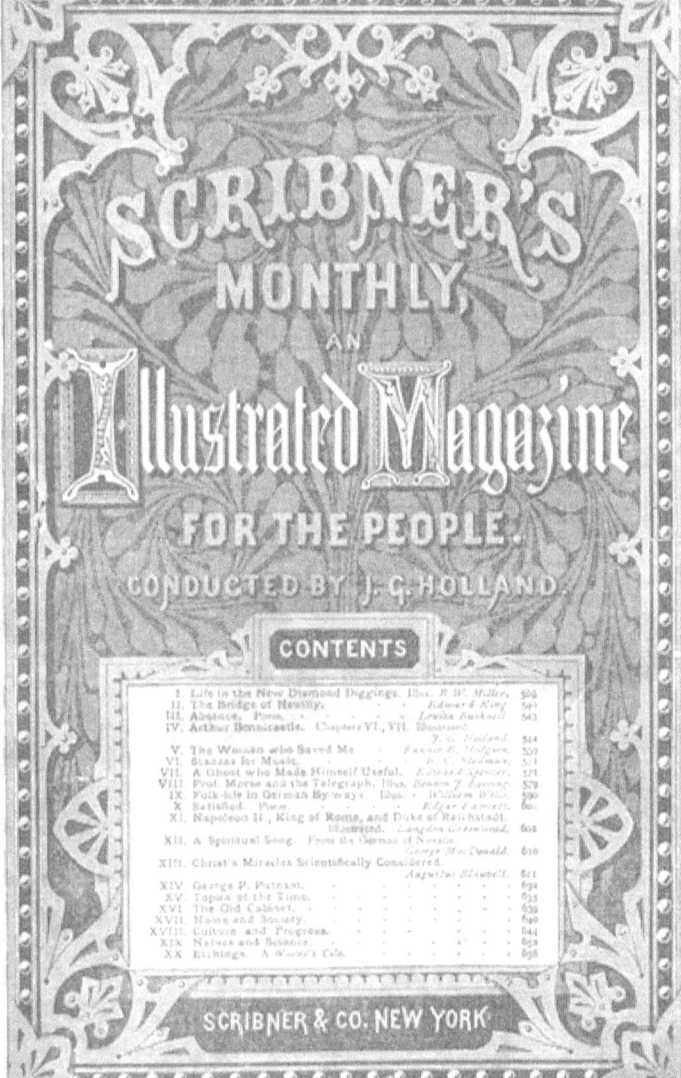

SCRIBNER'S MONTHLY,
AN
Illustrated Magazine
FOR THE PEOPLE.
CONDUCTED BY J. G. HOLLAND.

CONTENTS

SCRIBNER & CO. NEW YORK

FOR SALE AND SUBSCRIPTIONS RECEIVED BY ALL BOOKSELLERS.
COVERS FOR BINDING SENT POSTAGE PAID FOR 50 CENTS EACH.

Scribner's Monthly.

CONTENTS FOR MARCH, 1873.

WHERE TO BUY.

MINERAL WATERS.

CONGRESS & EMPIRE SPRING CO., 94 Chambers St., Proprietors of the Congress, Empire & Columbian Springs, Saratoga. Gen. Mineral Water Depot.

MIRRORS.

W. A. WILLARD, 117 Canal St., bet. Mulberry and Mott Sts.
WHOLESALE AND RETAIL.

MUSICAL BOXES.

M. J. PAILLARD & CO., 680 Broadway. Manufacturers and Importers of Musical Boxes. Agents for Leon Schneider's Cornets & Band Instruments.

OFFICE FURNITURE.

T. G. SELLEW, 111 Fulton Street.
FINE CYLINDER DESKS.
Banks and Offices fitted up.

PERFUMERY & TOILET ARTICLES.

S CLOFT, PLAUT & CO., 111 Broadway.
The largest and most complete assortment at prices 20 per cent. less than the usual trade.

PHOTOGRAPHY.

W. KURTZ, 872 Broadway.
RECEIVED FIRST PREMIUM
for its exhibit at the Paris Exposition, 1870.

PIANOS.

G EO. STECK & CO., Manufacturers of
GRAND, SQUARE, and UPRIGHT PIANO FORTES.
Warerooms, Nos. 11 East 14th St., near Union Square.

PICTURE FRAMES.

W. A. WILLARD, 117 Canal St.,
bet. Mulberry and Mott Sts.
WHOLESALE AND RETAIL.

F RANCIS HART & CO., 12 & 14 College Place.
BOOK, JOB, AND NEWSPAPER PRINTERS,
STATIONERS AND BLANK BOOK MANUFACTURERS.

PRINTING.

RAILROAD BONDS.

C HAS. W. HASSLER, 7 Wall Street.
WRITE TO HIM
"Whether you wish to buy or sell."

RESTAURANT.

J. H. BAKER'S DINING ROOMS,
Cor. Thirteenth and Greene Streets.
For Ladies and Gentlemen. Neat, Quiet, First-class.

RUSSIA LEATHER GOODS.

C ULBERT & CO., 24 Maiden Lane.
Traveling Bags, Dressing Cases,
Pocket Books, Writing Desks, Card Cases, &c.

SEEDS.

J. M. THORBURN & CO., Seedsmen,
15 John Street.
CATALOGUES ON APPLICATION.

SEWING MACHINES.

"F AMILY FAVORITE."
WEED SEWING MACHINE CO.,
613 Broadway.

SILVER WARE.

F ORD & TUPPER, 1190 Broadway,
Manufacturers of
STERLING SILVERWARE.

SHIRTS.

J. W. JOHNSTON, 260 Grand Street.
Shirts, Hosiery, and Men's Furnishing Goods.
See advertisement on another page.

STEAM ENGINES.

T HE BAXTER STEAM ENGINE, from 2 to 10
Horse Power. Perfect Mechanism, Safety & Economy.
For Circulars, address, W. D. Russell, 18 Park Place.

STEAM & HOT WATER FURNACES.

F OR WARMING DWELLINGS, GREEN-
HOUSES, &c.
CHARLES R. ELLIS, 180 Centre Street.

STEREOSCOPES & VIEWS.

E. & H. T. ANTHONY & CO., 591 Broadway,
Chromos and Frames, Albums, Graphoscopes,
Photographs, Megalethoscopes.

TILES & CHIMNEY-TOPS.

M ILLER & COATES, 279 Pearl St.,
MINTON'S TILES,
Glazed & Chimney Tops and Vases.

TOOL CHESTS.

J AMES T. PRATT & CO., 53 Fulton Street.
FIRST-CLASS MECHANICS' TOOLS AND CUTLERY.
Send for descriptive circular.

TREES & PLANTS.

R. B. PARSONS & CO., Growers of Ornamental Trees
and Shrubs, Rhododendrons, Camellias, Roses, &c.
Flushing, N.Y. Catalogues at 91 Broadway.

TRUSSES.

P OMEROY & CO., 744 Broadway. The "Finger Pad,"
"Adjustable" and of "N___d" Trusses, Elastic Stockings,
Crutches, Shoulder Braces & other Surgical appliances.

WATCHES & JEWELRY.

V R J. MAGNIN, GUERIN & CO., 672 Broadway,
Importers of Clocks, Bronzes, Jewelry, Musical
Boxes, and Fancy Goods. Agents for Nardin Watches.

Railroad Bonds.

WHETHER YOU WISH TO

BUY OR SELL

Write to

HASSLER & CO. BANKERS,
No. 7 Wall St., N. Y.

AT THE WELL.

WHAT visions of undiscovered Koh-i-noors, Braganzas, Orloffs, and the like, led me to this far-away country, — what hopes that I might be their lucky finder, — i n n a t e modesty forbids me to 'tell. It keeps down, too, any desire I may have to hint how far those hopes and visions have been realized. Suffice it to say that I have picked up diamonds, genuine diamonds; my luckier neighbors have picked up more; and we have all added largely to our stock of rough experiences. Perhaps some of my American friends, who are contemplating a visit to this new South African world of adventure, may be pleased to share a portion of my writings in this last and most abundant commodity of the diamond-bearing country: diamond-iferous is the word here, but as that is also our chief superlative, applied equally to picks and shovels,

Kaffirs and cattle, hats and boots — everything, in short, from a Kopje to a capital friend, a diamondiferous good fellow — I will stick to the old-fashioned combination, diamond-bearing.

By the way, speaking of Kopje, I might as well explain at the outset a couple of words of frequent use in this region, Kopje and pan. The first, pronounced "Koppie," is Dutch; Kop, hill or knoll; Kopje, little hill; Spitz Kop, hill with a pointed top, cone-shaped. The second may be Dutch or English. A pan is a shallow depression, evidently the bed of a dried up pond. The ground is usually incrusted with salt earth, impregnated with niter. In rainy weather these pans frequently form natural reservoirs of rain-water. I write at Du Toit's Pan. From a distance the Pan reminds one of a monster gravel-pit, or a gigantic colony of ants at work. Eager, earnest, cheerful labor is going on everywhere in orderly confusion : digging, sifting, loading, carrying, sorting, with men, women, and children moving about with no apparent system, crossing, mixing, zigzagging here and there like laboring ants, yet there is method underlying all the seeming disorder. As far as one can see with in the camp there is but a succession of pits and mounds mainly occupied by workers busily intent on finding the precious gem. Here and there are pits that have been worked out, or perhaps abandoned by owners discouraged by lack of luck, or attracted elsewhere by the glittering promises of some "new rush." The perseverance and temper of the drifted diggers are shown by the depth of their deserted pits ; some are but three or four feet deep, some forty. Frequently a patient digger will find nothing for the first twenty feet, then his luck will change and he will turn out a handsome stone, a fortune in itself, and go on discovering a stone or two a day, the quality improving with the depth ; or he may become thoroughly discouraged and abandon his claim, or sell it for a few shillings, and have his ill luck aggravated by hearing that his more fortunate successor has turned up a twenty, maybe a fifty-carat stone before he has had time to pack up his tools to start for a new claim.

At the bottom of the working pits are naked Kaffirs digging and throwing up the earth ; others carry it to the *baas*, who, perched high on the up-turned soil, is busily engaged in sifting or sorting the gravel.

The claims are limited to thirty feet square, for which a license fee of ten shillings a month is exacted. As there is no opportunity to cast away the upturned earth and surplus gravel,—no space being left for roads, and encroachments on neighboring claims being punishable by a fine fixed by the committee, —all the earth must be handled on one's own claim. The usual plan is to work out half the claim, piling the sorted gravel on the other, then fill up the hole and proceed with the remainder of the claim in the same way.

For sifting the gravel an apparatus is prepared in this wise : two posts about seven feet long are driven into the ground, four feet apart, and across them ropes are loosely fastened so as to hang in an ample curve. On these ropes are suspended two large sieves of wire or perforated metal. The soil is thrown into the upper and coarser sieve, and the sieves are shaken to and fro. The larger stones stop at the top, the gravel is retained by the finer sieve, the dirt of course passing through to the ground. As the soil is limy and much of it very fine, the dust is terrific, the camp being usually enveloped in a cloud of this irritating, eye and lung destroying substance, which is so penetrating that the best hunting watches are clogged up with it in "no time." The editor of the *Diamond News* classes it " with plague, pestilence and famine, and if there is anything worse, with that also ;" which is somewhat more mildly than the average digger would state his disapprobation of this pest of the diggings.

The sorting is done rapidly ; at first sight it would seem carelessly. When "new chums" begin this branch of the business they are apt to waste a good deal of time looking at and testing all the pretty stones, especially the clear crystals, which are numerous. After they have once picked up a diamond, however, they find no difficulty in deciding at a glance which are and which are not the objects of their search. Under the bright clear sky of this region the diamond is sure to shine out among the worth-

SIFTING THE GRAVEL

KLIP DRIFT.

less gravel in a way that there is no mistaking.

When such a find is made, the shout of joy rings out and loud *hurrahs* go circling through the camp. Picks and shovels are dropped, the sifter is left at rest, and every dirt-pile is dotted with eager lookers, anxious to see who is the lucky man, all giving the diggings the appearance of a prairie-dog village, or a colony of meerkats perched on their mounds.

If the cheer is loud enough to indicate an extra find, a diamond-buyer or two, perhaps half a dozen, are quickly on the spot to bargain for it, while everybody is asking, "How big is it?" "What's its shape?" "Who found it?" and other questions in regard to its quality and color.

This is a "dry digging," the wet diggings being along the now famous Vaal River, where the first discoveries were made. The story of the discovery of diamonds here may be summed up in few words. The first one was found in the Hope Town Division of Cape Colony, near the Orange River, by the child of a Dutch Boer, or farmer. Ignorant of its value, the children used it as a plaything until one Schalk van Niekerk, a neighboring farmer, saw it, and, struck by its luster and weight, offered to buy it. The child's mother laughed at the idea of selling a stone, and gave it to him. The stone passed through several hands, reaching at last a Dr. Atherstone, of Grahamstown, who on examination pronounced it a veritable diamond. Its weight was 22 carats. Soon after an 8-carat stone was found in the same Division, and more extensive search was begun. No particular stir or excitement resulted, how-

ever, until the famous Star of South Africa became known, in 1869. This rare gem of 83 carats was bought from a native sorcerer by the quasi-discoverer of the first-found diamond. Search for others was increased, and with such success that a "rush" set in from all quarters in the early part of 1870, and in a short time the banks of the Vaal, the north branch of the Orange, were covered with busy diggers. The year after, the richer and more extensive dry diggings were discovered in the open, almost desert country between the Vaal and the Orange, and since then new diamond-bearing localities have been found almost daily.

The river or wet diggings center at Klip Drift and Pniel, two small towns opposite each other on the hill-slopes overlooking the Vaal, which at this point is an extremely beautiful river, five or six hundred feet wide. The Vaal would be a lovely stream anywhere; but in South Africa it is a peculiarly charming and novel thing to see a broad flowing river, with wooded banks and numerous islands covered with verdure. A fine view of the river is to be had from the Church property at Pniel. In the way of river scenery there is nothing to equal it in South Africa. Toward the south as far as the eye can reach are hills and dales, beautifully broken, with clumps of deep green camel-thorn, which grow luxuriantly and contrast admirably with the red hill-sides. Along the river many trees, especially the native willows, grow to a great height, casting their thick shadows on the shining surface of the water. Back from the stream are wide expanses of bush-land, which furnish plentiful fuel for the miners.

The Pniel diamond claims lie along the slope of the hill, or kopje, between the town and the river. The ground being very valuable, as little space as possible is left for roadways to the river, where all the gravel is carted to be washed, and communication is intricate and sometimes dangerous, especially as the roadway is seriously encroached on sometimes by eager diggers, and there is constant risk of pitching headlong, oxen, cart, load and all, into the deep pits on every hand.

Diamond-digging is hard work here. The gem-bearing gravel lies amongst huge basaltic boulders, the removal of which makes the work heavy, slow, and expensive. Besides, the diamonds are scattered with great irregularity and are less numerous, though of slightly better quality, than in the dry diggings. The washing-cradles are generally at the river-side, it being cheaper to cart the gravel to the stream than the water to the gravel. After the first rough washing the gravel is shovelled into the cradle,—a strong frame work carrying sieves and resting on two stout rockers,—and the owner "rocks the cradle;" his native helpers pour water over the gravel until it is thoroughly cleaned and sifted. After a hasty glance at the large stones in the upper sieve for a possible big diamond, the contents of the finer sieves are transferred to the sorting-table. If this has legs, the sorter sits at his work; if it rests on the ground, he has to work in a reclining posture. This is a pleasanter place for sorting than the dry diggings, owing to the absence of dust; still it has its objections. The sorters suffer severely from cold sometimes, and, at best, sitting with one's feet in wet gravel all day is far from comfortable.

The gravel is spread thinly over the level surface of wood or metal that serves as a table. The sorter detects at a glance any diamond or other stone that he may wish to preserve, then strikes off the rest with a straight-edge of wood or metal, usually a short piece of hoop iron. Occasionally a valuable ruby or a sapphire is found in these riverside diggings. Some do their washing on their claims, especially when working alone or with a single partner, or when too poor to own a cart and team. The washing is done in a couple of tubs made by sawing a wine cask in two, and filled with water from the stream. If the earth is tolerably dry the gravel can be cleaned in part by dry-sifting; it is then placed in common hand-sieves and twirled in one tub until tolerably free from dirt, and rinsed quite clean in the other. When the tubs become too muddy they are refilled from the river and the washing goes on. The claims at this place are worked to the depth of thirty or forty feet, turning the hill-slope upside down and covering it with heaps of quarried stone.

The work goes on in much the same way at Klip Drift, on the opposite side of the river,

and at the numerous camps up and down the river,—Good Hope, Laversages, Hebron, Robinson's, Bad Hope, Gong Gong, Union Kopie, Kersikamma, Blue Jacket, Maynard's Rush, Delport's Hope, Hart's River, etc. In the Kopjes the same sort of digging is found as at Pniel; but in some of the other camps mentioned exceedingly rich claims have been found on the flat, as the diggers call the old bed of the river. In fact, many prefer the flat to the Kopjes, and I believe they have turned out some of the very best stones that have been found. Long-toms are used for the gravel of the flat, which is a mixture of pot-clay and gravel, and many diggers are working deeper than was at first thought necessary, and with great success.

The advantages of the river-side diggings are mainly in the direction of health and comfort. First of all there is an abundance of good water for drinking and bathing. Then there is the absence of dust, the great scourge of the dry diggings, and the presence of wood, almost as great a rarity on the plains as water. The disadvantages are the severer character of the work, the inferior richness of the gravel and the irregular distribution of the gems, and the need of a cart and team as a part of the miner's outfit.

There is a good deal of black sand in the river gravel, in which small particles of gold may be seen without very close examination. It may be paying dirt, for all I know; but just now no one can think of anything less valuable than diamonds. I should not be surprised if the search for gold proved in the end more uniformly remunerative than the lottery of diamond digging.

The dry diggings are wide, almost treeless and waterless, plains covered with calcareous soil, which from its dusty nature adds immensely to the miner's discomfort. The earliest finds away from the river were made in 1870, at Du Toit's Pan. At first the claims were worked only two or three feet below the surface; after this surface-earth was worked out and the diggers were looking about for "pastures new," some one had courage to penetrate the bottom rock, and was rewarded by finding the diamonds more numerous and of larger size as he descended. A rush then set in, and Du Toit's Pan soon became the largest and richest diamond camp in the world; no other place up to this writing has afforded so large a number of stones of so many of large size. Gems of a hundred carats and upward are by no means uncommon. An immense area is being dug over here, and there are rich diggings all around.

RIVER WASHING CRADLING.

This is a good place for a beginner with small capital. Living is comparatively cheap, supplies are easily obtainable, and labor uniformly remunerative.

There are a number of good stores here, several hotels, and an excellent market every morning, to which the Dutch boers bring cattle, sheep, and farm produce to be sold at auction.

The following are the quotations for to-day: meal $12 to $12.50 a bag; mealies (Indian corn) $5 a bag; Kaffir corn $5 a bag; potatoes $12 a bag; onions $2.50 a bucket; butter 43 cents a pound; eggs 63 cents a dozen; bacon 30 cents a pound; hams 36 cents a pound; turkeys $3 each; fowls 60 cents each; spring-boks and bles-boks (antelopes) $2 each; wildebeestes $4 each; soap 14 cents a pound; boer tobacco 16 cents a pound; meat 8 to 12 cents a pound; bread 24 cents a loaf (size of a six-cent loaf at home); blatcham 48 cents a bottle; brandy $30 a keg, of 14 gallons; light Cape wine $11 a keg; walnuts 37 cents a hundred; figs 52 cents a pound; raisins 20 cents a pound; oranges and naartjes $4 a hundred; oat-hay 25 cents a bundle; fire-wood $15 a cord; plank (yellow-wood) $5 each; joists $5 each. All trades and industries are pretty well represented at the Pan. Some of the best finished houses and stores were brought ready made from the Cape. They are of wood, with corrugated iron roofs, and have a very finished appearance, with suitable doors and windows.

Joining Du Toit's Pan is Bultfontein, originally a cattle farm. Diamonds were found here in 1871, and a number of rough diggers took possession of the ground, in spite of the boer's protests, and began to work. They were expelled by the Free State Police; but the owner of the farm, fearing the return of a stronger force of miners, wisely threw the ground open to diggers on the customary terms—that is, a monthly license-fee of ten shillings a claim. This farm has yielded a very large number of diamonds, none of which, however, have been of considerable size.

Another similar farm called Alexandersfontein joins Bultfontein, making with Du Toit's Pan one large community, with regular streets and other beginnings of a great city. Two miles to the other side of Du Toit's Pan is a picturesque camp known as De-Beers, where many large stones have been found. Workings began here in May, 1871, and in a few months a large population had come together, making quite a town.

In September the following advertisement appeared in a Cape paper. I copy it in evidence of the rapid development of this "diamondiferous" region.

"NEW TOWNSHIP AT DEE BEERS.

"The proprietors of the farm 'VOORUIT ZIGT,' commonly known as Dee Beers, beg to intimate to the Public that they have laid out a town on the above farm, the Erven of which will be offered at public auction on the spot on Saturday, the 21st October next, at 11 o'clock in the forenoon.

"The site is eligibly situated on a gentle slope, contiguous to the TWO RUSHES which are now yielding such LARGE FORTUNES to the diggers, and the Erven will be sold with all the PROPRIETOR'S RIGHTS to THE DIAMONDS which may be found on them.

"*The Pniel Road will pass through the Town, which is situated within easy walking distance of* 'DU TOIT'S PAN,' 'BULTFONTEIN,' *and* 'ALEXANDERSFONTEIN' *diggings.*

"In selecting the spot for this Township, the Proprietors have specially regarded the healthiness of the situation ; the fact of GOOD WATER being found at moderate depth, and the proximity to the several digging camps.

"*Ample space has been provided for a Market, and eligible allotments reserved for churches and schools.*

"It is scarcely necessary for the Proprietors to point out the advantages that will accrue to the possessors of Erven in this Township, so conveniently situated in close proximity to all the successful diamond diggings, either as a center of Business or Healthy Residence."

This has become quite an aristocratic camp, the English element predominating, and many of the diggers bring their wives with them. Prices were so high at first that only men of capital could purchase, and these, being able to employ plenty of help, have made the excavations larger and deeper than those of the adjacent old camps.

An early rival to Dee-Beers was Colesberg Kopje, a mile farther to the left of the Pniel road, where a thriving town grew up in a very short time. The Kopje is a hillock about 250 acres in area, surrounded by a reef of hard rock. In a fortnight after the discovery claims were selling from twenty to a hundred pounds sterling apiece, and within three months a good claim could not be bought for less than £2,000 ; some sold as high as £4,000, and part claims in proportion. Bringing such high prices, the claims were generally sold in half and quarter sections ; and as every miner was anxious to get through his ground as fast as possible, many native laborers were employed and the work was pushed with ceaseless energy. The chunks of limestone and other rock too hard to be broken with a shovel were carted away at first and dumped on the "veldt" or plain without the camp. It happened that one of those pieces fell from the front of a cart and was crushed by the cart-wheel, setting free a 20-carat diamond. After that no more stones were thrown away before they were carefully broken up with mallets ; and some claimless diggers have made a very good living out of the refuse stuff carted away from the claims. Many fine diamonds have been found in the rock, and in one instance a 33-carat stone was found embedded in a block of solid quartz.

Last November (1871) diamonds to the value of $250,000 were being taking weekly from this small hill, counting about a thousand claims. In one week 657 stones were reported, ranging from 103 carats downward, and including stones of 102, 84, 83, 82 carats. Diamonds are found at all depths, and in some claims from the surface down : a fine 10-carat stone has been found at the depth of 96 feet, while sinking a well. Sixty feet is not an uncommon depth for claims to be sunk, and sometimes twenty feet of red sand has to be removed before the diamond-bearing soil is reached. The best diamonds are said to have been found at the depth of twenty five feet or thereabouts. The noise and dust and heat at Colesberg Kopje are fearful, the work being carried on with the utmost vigor and at a rate that will exhaust the Kopje in less than a year. Still prices keep up and buyers are eager. The Cape Town *Standard and Mail* reports in its issue of Dec. 5th, 1871, the sale of half a claim for £1,000 ; and the next day the buyer sold it for £1,600, on condition that after that sum had been realized by the purchaser the seller should have a half-share of the finds.

Rich diggings have since been discovered four miles from this Kopje, and the price of claims is going up throughout the whole neighborhood, especially on and near the "reef," a ridge of rock and shale running round nearly all the rich tract constituting the dry diggings. The claims nearest this reef are generally the most productive, and turn out the finest stones.

It is impossible to estimate the extent of the diamond-bearing country ; new fields are being discovered almost daily. The more intelligent people here are of opinion that the surrounding country is as likely to be rich in diamonds as the claims at present worked. A rush has lately been made to a farm on the Orange River, a hundred miles from this place, where diamonds of 50, 47½, 11, 10, and 8 carats have already been found, besides numerous smaller ones.

On the whole, the prospect of the diggings is very favorable, and, with a few companies having sufficient capital to send out prospecting parties, I think that the way will be opened for thousands of fresh diggers, who will be able to find paying fields of labor without having to pay exorbitant prices for their ticket in the great lottery.

Here, as elsewhere, the capitalist has a great advantage, since he can employ numbers of laborers properly over-looked by trustworthy men, move them from place to place as discoveries are made, and, if he is scientific, bring to his aid all the help that science can lend to the matter, which, however, is not much. The finding of diamonds is simply fortune: nothing on the surface can tell you where to dig. Muscle and patience are the winning cards. Those who have been longest here and have had the most experience are no wiser than those who came yesterday as regards the selection of a claim. Success is a question wholly of time and perseverance and good luck, the last being the principal item, since many have worked long and faithfully with little profit, while others have made splendid finds almost with the first stroke of the shovel. To come here without money, in the hope of making a fortune, is absurdly hazardous. Opinions may differ; but I should say, let no man come here with less than $1,000 or $1,500 available on the field, and let his time be not less than six months. Such a man *with good health* may be successful: he probably will be if in other matters he is resolute and plucky. To make success morally certain, two conditions are necessary; unlimited time and independent means of subsistence, presupposing of course physical and moral vigor. The farms in this neighborhood have a high reputation, and justly; and to any one determin-

ed to come out, I should counsel a sojourn on one of them, although the banks of the Vaal offer a much more comfortable home in the summer; that is, during the months of November, December, January, and February.

I believe that the right men would find it worth while to give the fields a trial; but let those who think of coming understand that they come for diamonds, and not comforts, and that they must be able to endure disappointments, persistent hard work, and be steady in their general habits. That enormous wealth is to be gained in the diggings is beyond dispute; that an occasional white man working alone has exceptional success is equally true: but that general emigration to the fields should be encouraged I very much doubt. The first requirements of the diamond-digger are robust health, already inured to hot climates, ability to withstand constant exposure to all kinds of weather, and a thorough capacity for "roughing it;" yet-how few of those drawn hither by the rumored wealth of the fields have even one of these qualifications! Many sink under the work, many more succumb to fever, but most of all to that fatal curse, drink. The incessant thirst induced by heat and dryness, the temptations held out by the canteen-keepers, and the fatal absence of restraint, are almost irresistible incentives to drinking; and the young man who drinks on the fields is lost. I do not say all drinkers die, but they do become wrecks of their former selves. Hard drinking is peculiarly incompatible with this climate, and many a man who might have gone home with health and wealth has been brought by it to a nameless grave.

The climate here is by no means the worst,

DU TOIT'S PAN—MARKET SQUARE.

yet it is extremely trying to new-comers, especially to those unused to an exposed life. During the summer months the thermometer frequently registers 100° Fahr. in the shade, and there is very little shade to be found at the dry diggings. There is almost always a hot wind blowing at this season, with the attendant clouds of acrid dust already described. Thunder-storms occur almost daily, and are frequently preceded by dust-storms of the most violent character. I have already quoted the opinion of the editor of the *Diamond News* in regard to these visitations; perhaps I cannot do better than to copy his description of a storm that played havoc with these camps in the early part of last summer:

"On Sunday evening week the Du Toit's Pan, De-Beer's and New Rush camps were maddened by a dust-storm from the northward, which lasted nearly a couple of hours. We have been asked to write an article descriptive of the event; but as we had to shut ourselves up within our small cabin, to prevent ourselves from being blown away, and to ballast the cabin itself, and as during the said two hours our eyes in common with the eyes of all the camp were clouded with dust, and our ears deafened with the flapping of canvas and the roar of thunder, description is impossible. All we can say from personal observation and experience is, that the dust was the finest, the most searching, the densest, the most pervading, and the most irritating we ever had the bad fortune to see, smell, taste, or feel. It was not only moving about in the air, on the plain, and in the Pan, but it entered into tent, shanty, and store, and penetrating broadcloth, flannel and linen, plugged up the pores of the skin and dried up the very source of life. The dust of the dry diggings is to be classed with plague, pestilence, and famine, and if there is anything worse, with that also.

"The wind was very willful and did a deal of damage. Half the population in the fields had to hold on to poles and ropes like grim death during the time the storm lasted. In some cases holding on was of no use. Bell-tents went after bell-tents by the score, especially at the New Rush and De-Beer's. . . . A little rain followed the dust, but scarcely enough to make the ground damp."

Whirlwinds are frequent at this season and cause great annoyance. In their errant course through the camps, every moderately light article is snatched up and whirled away, and if a tent door is caught open, woe to the tent!

All the more active operations of diamond-digging are usually committed to Kaffirs during the severe hot weather, and those who can get away find it much to their health and comfort to spend a month or two at the wet diggings along the Vaal. Autumn begins in February, and with it an improvement in the weather, and a waking up of all sorts of mining activity.

But work goes on most merrily during the delightful months of winter,—May, June, and July. The nights are cold and frosty, ice making to the thickness of half an inch, but during the day the weather is positively charming.

In consideration of the vast numbers brought together here, the health of the camp is exceedingly good. The hard work does not hurt a man if he keeps from bad company and abstains from drink. The hot months are naturally most unfavorable to health, and the heat is aggravated by the scarcity of good water and the deficiency of sanitary arrangements. The principal diseases are a sort of low fever, diarrhœa and dysentery, colic, inflammation of the lungs, and sore eyes from the glare of the sun and the all-pervading dust. This same dust is also very poisonous to scratches and slight wounds, which are apt to become festering sores, especially on the hands. In some cases these sores appear to come spontaneously where the skin is perfectly sound, and are thought by some to be a mild form of scurvy.

The population of the diggings is rather mixed, but on the whole well disposed and law-abiding. The English element predominates, yet a good number of Americans are here, some Germans, and a sprinkling of Frenchmen, Italians, and Spaniards. The Dutch boers of course predominate in the surrounding country and are numerous at the diggings. As a rule they are not favorites; the English especially hate them heartily, and their regard is returned with interest. The Germans are more apt to be diamond dealers than diamond diggers. Native laborers, Kaffirs, Korannas, and Hottentots swarm at the fields. The "Zulus" are the most trustworthy, and the fresher they are from the up-country Kraals, the better. The native women about the camps are chiefly Hottentots and Korannas. They find ample

and profitable employment as washer-women, household servants, etc.

A large number of trades and professions are represented in the camps; carpenters, tent-makers, and blacksmiths find constant employment at remunerative rates. Butchers make rapid fortunes, the demand for meat being enormous. Bakers and confectioners find quick market for their wares at exorbitant prices. Photographers are already on the ground, and Du Toit's Pan has a matrimonial agent! There are also doctors, lawyers, watchmakers, and jewelers. Hotel-keepers, store-keepers and auctioneers are plentiful, the last finding all the business they want, and as they get 10 per cent. of the sales their profits are very large.

The hotels do a rushing business: three meals a day are furnished; breakfast at eight, 2s., tiffin (lunch) at one, 2s., dinner at six, 2s. 6d. A bed costs 2s. or 2s. 6d., a "shake-down" 1s. or 1s. 6d. Some diggers board and lodge regularly at the hotels, but it is a bad practice. The food supplied is abundant but of small variety—mutton and beef, venison, a few vegetables, white and brown bread of indifferent quality, and plenty of tea and coffee. There is no style,—the rough digger in his shirt-sleeves elbows the gorgeously-arrayed diamond dealer, or the clergyman of the camp,—one man is as good as another, and all are free and easy.

Sunday is generally observed as a day of rest, and the churches are well attended. The Church of England has regular chaplains at all the camps, with stated places of worship

DE-BEERS' RICH CLAIMS.

ON THE ROAD TO THE DIGGINGS.

at all the older stations. The Methodists are well represented, and so are the Roman Catholics. The boers are generally members of the Dutch Reformed Church, but their religious feeling is not apt to be very fine, or strong enough to prevent their being what the Yankee diggers call "mean cusses." Collections have been made for the erection of permanent church-buildings, and substantial structures are everywhere taking the place of the insufficient and unstable church tents heretofore in use.

Amusements are well provided for. We have already a Theatre Royal (at Du Toit's Pan), where appreciative and paying audiences are regularly gathered. A grand Ballad Concert, with the comedy of "Delicate Ground" and the farce of "Box and Cox," was the first performance, by gentlemen amateurs. The price of seats is usually 2s. 6d., 3s. 6d., or 4s. for reserved seats. A company of actors and vocalists make regular tours of the diggings and find it profitable. We have had a circus stationed here for some time, and it was well filled with merry diggers. Billiard-tables are numerous in every camp, and several bowling-alleys are doing a roaring business. A young man named Rogers has gained considerable local fame for his comic singing and banjo-playing. Here is one of his songs, which has been extensively sung among the diggers. Its chorus shows its origin to have been at the river-side diggings:—

DIGGER'S SONG.

Six months ago to the fields I came,
   I was a heavy swell,
My clothes were brushed, my boots the same,

My coat it fitted well;
I wore a collar then, of course.
Alas! that day's gone past;
And stockings too my feet did grace;
Oh dear! I've seen my last.

Chorus.

Rocking at the cradle, sifting all the day—
   That's the life we diggers lead.
Rocking at the cradle, sifting all the day—
   That's the life for me!

I had some notions in me left
   I really thought were good;
But here there's no such thing as theft,
   Though jumping's understood.
Beware your morals, diggers dear,
   And don't let them decay;
If jumping's winked at, soon you'll hear
   Your character's jumped away.

Chorus.

Now straying cattle and wayward "boys,"
   And diamonds never handy,
Have brought me down, and all my joys
   Are centered in Cape brandy;
I wear a shirt and trousers now,
   And smoke a dirty clay;
My feet are cased just anyhow;
   This hat I "jumped" to-day.

Chorus.

Bad luck, however, cannot last,
   A turn must come some day;
A ninety-carat would change the past
   And make the future gay.
May every digger's luck be this,
   Who to these fields has come,
To take back health and wealth and bliss
   To those he's left at home!

Chorus.

Cricket matches, rifle-shooting, running and walking matches, and athletic games, are the chief out-door sports. Hunting at no disagreeable recreation; and along the Vaal and the Modder, fishing gives not only sport, but a welcome change and variety to the digger's diet.

The scarcity of water at the dry diggings has already been noticed. It is one of the great privations of the digger's life. Each camp has a large dam where water collects during the rainy season for the supply of the cattle, and sometimes for drinking-water for the miners; and a smaller reservoir set apart for washing, constantly surrounded by a chattering crowd of native washer women of every shade of color. But the busiest scenes are at the public wells. The payment of £1 a month entitles a digger to two buckets a day, which he must fetch or send for with his own buckets and ropes. There is room for twelve or fourteen people round a well, but scarcely ever less than fifty trying to draw. Buckets have to be lowered a dozen times before a pailful of water can be obtained, the constant drawing making the water low and muddy. There are some private wells, having a limited number of subscribers at 4s. a month. Four buckets a day are allowed at these wells, which are fitted with a windlass and rope, and the water is usually very good. Well-digging is profitable work, whether done for the camp committee or as a private enterprise; the committee pay handsomely for the work and the digger gets all the diamonds he finds. Occasionally a digger strikes water in sinking his claim, then boards it up and makes a good thing selling the water by the bucketful or letting it out to subscribers.

Since the fields have been "annexed" by the British government, a great deal is being done to improve the sanitary condition of the camps; but much more needs to be done toward increasing the supply of good water, and in doing away with nuisances which offend the eye and endanger the health of the community.

I have said nothing of the different routes to the diggings, my design being to give rather a picture of camp life, and such a description of the diamond fields as may enable my American friends to form some estimate of their character. Still, perhaps a word or two in regard to modes of getting here may not be out of place.

When time is no object, and the coming digger is fond of country travel, the bullock-wagon route via Grahamstown offers some inducements. The wagons are drawn by ox trains numbering from twelve to sixteen, according to the weight of the loads and the state of the road. The wagons carry from eight to nine thousand pounds weight of goods. There is a tolerable supply of grass and water along the route, and game is plentiful. These slow, old-fashioned colonial conveyances, however, are becoming a thing of the past, except for the transportation of heavy goods. To gain time, mules and horses are substituted for oxen, but the expense is largely increased. A quicker passage can be made by the wagons of the Inland Transport Company, or the Diamond Fields Transport Company, from Cape Town to the diggings, 700 miles; time, from seven to nine days; fare, £12. Forty pounds of baggage are allowed each passenger, all excess being charged at the rate of a shilling a pound. From Port Elizabeth, Algoa Bay, the traveler has the choice of mule-wagons making the trip in fifteen days, or Cobb & Co.'s stage coaches, coming in five days, the fare proportionately less than by the other route. These coaches are of American manufacture, built of wood calculated to stand the climate—strong, light, and admirably suited for their purpose. The tent is covered with American water-proof cotton; at the back of the wagon is a space for luggage, covered in the same way; the body of the coach rests on stout leather bands instead of springs, and has an easy swaying motion that contrasts favorably with the heavy jolting of the colony wagons. The ride by this route is 456 miles. Another quick line of passenger wagons is promised from Natal. Ere many more years are numbered with the past, the snort of the iron horse and the whiz and whir of railway travel will doubtless disturb these newly-awakened solitudes of South Africa, and passengers will breakfast at the coast, dine at the new Golconda, and in the evening lave their weary limbs in the waters of the limpid Vaal.

THE BRIDGE OF NEUILLY.

"THE Avenue of the Grand Army!" How like a satire it sounds,—the sonorous name of the glittering street which runs from the Triumphal Arch to the Porte Maillot, in Paris,—how like a sneer! For there is no grand army now, and the very limbs of the great figure of "Departure" on the Arch seem nerveless. Lutetia can now count a disgrace, a defeat for every fête-day, and her anniversaries are filled with mourning.

The Maillot Gate is the outlet in the fortifications for the "Avenue of the Grand Army," which, as it wanders over the Seine on the massive stone bridge not far from the walls, becomes the "Avenue of Neuilly." From the Triumphal Arch you can see as far as Courbevoie—nearly three miles in a straight line—a hard, white road, bordered two-thirds of the way by elegant houses. Neuilly is a suburb much affected by the Parisians, because the flavor of the great city is there combined with a few rustic charms, and it cost them a hard struggle to come inside the walls, and leave their pleasant mansions, when the siege began. High up on Courbevoie's hill stands a pedestal, formerly occupied by a bronze statue of Napoleon the Great. As you look from the Triumphal Arch this pedestal stands out, black, against the horizon, a land-mark for miles around. And it became a very notable land-mark to us in Paris in Commune-time, for around it and just beyond it were planted many of the batteries which were engaged in shelling the Maillot Gate, the Avenue of the Grand Army, and the Triumphal Arch.

The Communists, as Americans have been taught to call them, had made very ample preparations against the enemy on all that side of Paris toward the Bois de Boulogne, St. Cloud, and Versailles. The great gates were doubly and triply barred, and the bastions were thoroughly manned by the uncouth but resolute soldiery. In the clear crystal weather of April, thousands upon thousands of people poured out of the great avenues of the city to see the fight, and to watch, from carriages posted on convenient eminences, the bombardment of the forts in the distance. America was amply represented every day, and the fair daughters of Gotham, Boston, Chicago, and San Francisco often braved danger for the sake of recounting adventures over dinner in the evening.

The old bridge of Neuilly was the scene of many a bloody combat during the Communal sway. The adventurous scout was daily stricken down there, but no record was made of his death in the official journal. It will be impossible ever to estimate the losses at this dread point. Dombrowski, the rebel general, handsome, light of foot, and fearless, sauntered very near to the dreary belt of waste country which led to the bridge on the Parisian side many times by day and night, and walked unharmed among seemingly deadliest rain of shells and bullets. At night the Versailles batteries always kept up a tremendous rain upon the bridge, fearful lest some attempt to take it might be successful. The weary watchers at the gates were often hurled into fragments by the sudden arrival of a huge death-messenger, and their mangled and dissevered corpses were found heaped upon the ramparts or strewn in the ditches in the morning. A poor woman arrived one noon with her husband's dinner-pail. "He will need it no longer, citoyenne," said a sergeant; and, as she stooped above the corpse of her dearest, a shell splinter carried away one of her arms and opened a ghastly seam in her face. Two marines were firing a long-range cannon at the batteries around Courbevoie one bright day. One man was blown away from his post; the other, sailor-like, leaped on the gun, and defied with rude gestures the far-off enemy. Presently a well-directed shot killed him also. Two more marines took the dead men's duty, and the fight went on as sternly unyielding, as grimly, grotesquely terrible as before.

One fair April afternoon, when the Seine rippled in gleaming beauty past the great palaces and under the noble bridges out into fields which had put garments of loveliest green over their breasts, torn and wounded by the shock of contending armies,—when the long walks in the Champs Elysées were odorous with perfume from the thousand shrubs, and the great Arch rejoiced in the magnificent sunshine, there came a series of crashing detonations from the Courbevoie batteries, and from many others on the high table-lands, miles away, which indicated that a general attack had begun. It was not long after the desperate conflict over the bridge, in which Gen. Besson bit the dust, and hundreds of brave men in both armies went down in a few brief hours. On this occasion the attention of those Parisians who had no sympathy with the insurrection was arrested by the extraordinary activity at the Communist headquarters, and the signs of trepidation and alarm manifested. Members

evening, and the thunders of the rebel forts awoke, the wagons, loaded with household goods and with half-starved fugitives, were hurrying forward, regaining the fortifications amid a rain of death-dealing missiles. Some people left the houses which for twenty days had been under fire to meet their death before they had reached the Maillot bastions. Towards eight o'clock in the evening the spectacle was thrilling and horrible. It was a vast mob, fleeing before a nameless and indefinable terror, yelling, praying, cursing, trampling each other in the dust, and crying out that the Communists had broken faith and opened fire before the appointed time. It was not until long past midnight that the sentinels at the gates were relieved of the laborious duty of searching the heavily-laden wagons, anxiously looking for spies or infernal machines. The Versailles troops had established their lines half-way between the Neuilly bridge and the batteries at Courbevoie, and were visited during the day by thousands of people who begged them to desist from the struggle and return to Versailles. But the lines maintained a sullen and dogged demeanor, and answered all entreaties with an imperative movement of the bayonet, which caused a lively retreat. There were some very affecting incidents during the period of the armistice. One old man, who was removed from a species of infirmary where, in the care of suffering fellow-creatures, he had spent the better part of his life, refused to be carried away of his own will and preferred to remain and perish with his house. A little baby was found in the cellar of one of the mansions, tightly clasped in the arms of its mother. Both had been dead many days.

It was on the day that Dombrowski undertook his famous movement against the Versailles troops beyond the bridge at Neuilly that the following tragic incident occurred. A raw battalion of artisans from Belleville was stationed at a certain point not far from the bridge, and, under the unaccustomed rain of missiles, but illy held its ground. Dombrowski arrived, radiant, audacious as ever. He leaped from his horse and approached the barricade behind which the battalion was wavering. "You are afraid!" said he scorn-

fully; "look at me—I am not fearful." And he mounted the barricade, although bullets were flying thick as hail around him. He took off his cap. "Give me a cup of wine," said he, "and I will drink confusion to the enemy." A tin cup filled with wine was brought, and at that very moment a shell splinter struck the wine-bearer, and laid him dying behind the barricade. Dombrowski leaped down and took the man in his arms. "We were not afraid, thou and I," he said, and the rough fellows around shed tears.

Dombrowski was always planning movements which his raw and sometimes cowardly troops could not execute. He would have carried all that stretch of country held beyond the Bridge of Neuilly at one fell swoop, had his men had ordinary military experience. Even the Versailles officers admitted the genius of his movements. His headquarters were not far from the old bridge, and directly under a heavy fire. He never wavered, and was as unconcerned when shot and shell were flying around him as when he sang Polish songs, and conversed with us at the headquarters of the city forces in the Place Vendôme. He knew the struggle was hopeless from the very first; he went to it willingly, and died in it bravely.

Finally, one clear day, the Versailles troops poured over the old Bridge of Neuilly, through the deserted Maillot Gate, and along the broad avenue towards the Triumphal Arch. The tricolor floated from the windows of the battered mansions; the gay hussars galloped noisily over the fallen barricades; and the dead men who so thickly strewed the waste ground near the bridge were hastily buried. There was slaughter at Neuilly; there was slaughter at the Maillot Gate; death and destruction everywhere; and the May breezes bore flame-breath and blood scent to the nostrils of the incoming victors. Cannon were placed upon the old bridge, and stout artillerymen grimly waited there the order to throw shells into the center of the subjugated city. Dombrowski had been at the bridge on the very morning of his defeat, and had despairingly admitted that the enemy would soon take the bridge, as his men would not arrange themselves according to his orders. And when the bridge is no longer ours, he said, Paris is lost to us!

ABSENCE.

Through'out azure realms of loneliness
  Sails the hot sun; no cloudy fleet
Convoys him o'er the trackless waste,
  Or cools his path with snowy sleep,
  Becalmed upon that tropic deep;
Or scuds, by freshening breezes chased,
Dropping swift shadows down to bless,
  And make the sunlight doubly sweet.

Earth's upturned face is glad no more.—
  Expressionless beneath the noon;
The listless winds in covert lie,
  Nor hunt in lightsome companies
  Through whispering grain and sighing trees;
The sea sends inland no reply
To the dumb yearning of the shore,
  But ebbs away in weary swoon.

A bird in yonder thicket sings,—
  And if so be his song tells true,
In miles and miles the only bird;
  For ne'er such plaintive monotone
  Of heart companionless and lone
Was in a summer noontide heard;
Tight folded are his **useless** wings,
  His **mate is lost beyond the** blue.

.

Gone is the nameless charm that finds
  The outer world in kinship blest,—
The interchange, the light refrain;
  And 'twixt our souls, that once were near,
  Lie leagues of stirless atmosphere,
Asleep upon a silent main:
Nothing to-day its heart-mate binds,
  Nor any answer to its quest.

One kiss of shadow or of air
  The world to lovelier life would stir;
Or might I clasp that distant hand,
  Then love would grace for me the whole;
  So light a touch on hand or soul,
So light a touch on sea or land,
Makes all things one and all things fair,
  Wake, wind! and blow a touch from her!

ARTHUR BONNICASTLE.

BY J. G. HOLLAND.

"WHY THIS IS LIKE A BOOK, ISN'T IT?" SAID SHE.

CHAPTER VI.

WHILE Henry was a guest at my old home, Mr. Bradford resumed his visits there. That he had had much to do with securing my father's prosperity in his calling, I afterwards learned with gratitude, but he had done it without his humble friend's knowledge, and while studiously keeping aloof from him. I never could imagine any reason for his policy in this matter except the desire to keep out of Mrs. Sanderson's way. He seemed, too, to have a special interest in Henry ; and it soon came to my ears that he had secured for him his place as teacher of one of the public schools. Twice during the young man's visit at Bradford, he had called and invited him to an evening walk, on the pretext of showing him some of the more interesting features of the rapidly growing little city.

Henry's plan for study was coincident with my own. We had both calculated to perfect our preparation for college during the winter and following spring, under private tuition ; and this work, which would be easy for me, was to be accomplished by him during the hours left from his school duties. I made my own independent arrangements for recitation and direction, as I knew such a course would best please Mrs. Sanderson, and

left him to do the same on his return. With an active temperament and the new stimulus which had come to me with a better knowledge of my relations and prospects, I found my mind and my time fully absorbed. When I was not engaged in study, I was actively assisting Mrs. Sanderson in her affairs.

One morning in the early winter, after Henry had returned, and had been for a week or two engaged in his school, I met Mr. Bradford in the street, and received from him a cordial invitation to take tea and spend the evening at his home. Without telling me what company I should meet, he simply said that there were to be two or three young people beside me, and that he wanted Mrs. Bradford to know me. Up to this time, I had made comparatively few acquaintances in the town, and had entered, in a social way, very few homes. The invitation gave me a great deal of pleasure, for Mr. Bradford stood high in the social scale, so that Mrs. Sanderson could make no plausible objection to my going. I was careful not to speak of the matter to Henry, whom I accidentally met during the day, and particularly careful not to mention it in my father's family, for fear that Claire might feel herself slighted. I was therefore thoroughly surprised when I entered Mrs. Bradford's cheerful drawing-room to find there engaged in the merriest conversation with the family, both Henry and my sister Claire. Mr. Bradford rose and met me at the door in his own hospitable, hearty way, and, grasping my right hand, put his free arm around me, and led me to Mrs. Bradford and presented me. She was a sweet, pale-faced little woman, with large blue eyes, with which she peered into mine with a charming look of curious inquiry. If she had said: "I have long wanted to know you, and am fully prepared to be pleased with you and to love you," she would only have put into words the meaning which her look conveyed. I had never met with a greeting that more thoroughly delighted me, or placed me more at my ease, or stimulated me more to show what there was of good in me.

"This is my sister, Miss Lester," said she, turning to a prim personage sitting by the fire.

As the lady did not rise, I bowed to her at a distance, and she recognized me with a little nod, as if she would have said: "You are well enough for a boy, but I don't see the propriety of putting myself out for such young people."

The contrast between her greeting and that of Mr. and Mrs. Bradford led me to give her more than a passing look. I concluded at once that she was a maiden of an age more advanced than she would be willing to confess, and a person with ways and tempers of her own. She sat alone, trotting her knees, looking into the fire, and knitting with such emphasis as to give an electric snap to every pass of her glittering needles. She was larger than Mrs. Bradford, and her dark hair and swarthy skin, gathered into a hundred wrinkles around her black eyes, produced a strange contrast between the sisters.

Mrs. Bradford, I soon learned, was one of those women in whom the motherly instinct is so strong that no living thing can come into their presence without exciting their wish to care for it. The first thing she did, therefore, after I had exchanged greetings, was to set a chair for me at the fire, because she knew I must be cold and my feet must be wet. When I assured her that I was neither cold nor wet, and she had accepted the statement with evident incredulity and disappointment, she insisted that I should change my chair for an easier one. I did this to accommodate her, and then she took a fancy that I had a headache and needed a bottle of salts. This I found in my hand before I knew it.

As these attentions were rendered, they were regarded by Mr. Bradford with good-

natured toleration, but there issued from the corner where "Aunt Flick" sat—for from some lip I had already caught her home name—little impatient sniffs and raps upon the hearth with her trotting heel.

"Jane Bradford," Aunt Flick broke out at last, "I should think you'd be ashamed. You've done nothing but worry that boy since he came into the room. One would think he was a baby, and that it was your business to tend him. Just as if he didn't know whether he was cold, or his feet were wet, or his head ached! Just as if he didn't know enough to go to the fire if he wanted to! Millie, get the cat for your mother, and bring in the dog. Something must be nursed of course."

"Why, Flick, dear!" was all Mrs. Bradford said, but Mr. Bradford looked amused, and there came from a corner of the room that my eyes had not explored the merriest young laugh imaginable. I had no doubt as to its authorship. Seeing that the evening was to be an informal one, I had already begun to wonder where the little girl might be, with whose face I had made a brief acquaintance five years before, and of whom I had caught occasional glimpses in the interval.

Mr. Bradford looked in the direction of the laugh, and exclaiming "You saucy puss!" started from his chair, and found her seated behind an ottoman, where she had been quietly reading.

"Oh, father! don't, please!" she exclaimed, as he drew her from her retreat. She resisted at first, but when she saw that she was fully discovered, she consented to be led forward and presented to us.

"When a child is still," said Aunt Flick, "I can't see the use of stirring her up, unless it is to send her to bed."

"Why Flick, dear!" said Mrs. Bradford again; but Mr. Bradford took no notice of the remark, and led the little girl to us. She shook hands with us, and then her mother caught and pulled her into her lap.

"Jane Bradford, why *will* you burden yourself with that heavy child? I should think you would be ill."

Millie's black eyes flashed, but she said nothing, and I had an opportunity to study her wonderful beauty. As I looked at her, I could not think of nothing but a gypsy. I could not imagine how it was possible that she should be the daughter of Mr. and Mrs. Bradford. It was as if some unknown, oriental ancestor had reached across the generations and touched her, revealing to her parents the long-lost secrets of their own blood. Her hair hung in raven ringlets, and her dark, healthy skin was as smooth and soft as the petal of a pansy. She had put on a scarlet jacket for comfort, in her distant corner, and the color heightened all her charms. Her face was bright with intelligence, and her full, mobile lips and dimpled chin were charged with the prophecy of a wonderfully beautiful womanhood. I looked at her quite enchanted, and I am sure that she was conscious of my scrutiny, for she disengaged herself gently from her mother's hold, and saying that she wished to finish the chapter she had been reading, went back to her seclusion.

The consciousness of her presence in the room somehow destroyed my interest in the other members of the family, and as I felt no restraint in the warm and free social atmosphere around me, I soon followed her to her corner, and sat down upon the ottoman behind which, upon a hassock, she had ensconced herself.

"What have you come here for?" she inquired wonderingly, looking up into my eyes.

"To see you," I replied.

"Aren't you a young gentleman?"

"No, I am only a big boy."

"Why that's jolly," said she. "Then you can be my company."

"Certainly," I responded.

"Well, then, what shall we do? I'm sure I don't know how to play with a boy. I never did."

"We can talk," I said. "What a funny woman your Aunt Flick is! Doesn't she bother you?"

She paused, looked down, then looked up into my face, and said decidedly: "I don't like that question."

"I meant nothing ill by it," I responded.

"Yes you did; you meant something ill to Aunt Flick."

"But I thought she bothered you," I said.

"Did I say so?"

"No."

"Well, when I say so, I shall say so to her. Papa and I understand it."

So this was my little girl, with a feeling of family loyalty in her heart, and a family pride that did not choose to discuss with strangers the foibles of kindred and the jars of home life. I was rebuked, though the consciousness of the fact came too slowly to excite pain. It was *her* Aunt Flick; and a stranger had no right to question or criticise. That was what I gathered from her words;

and there was so much that charmed me in this fine revelation of character, that I quite lost sight of the fact that I had been snubbed.

"She has a curious name, any way," I said.

At this her face lighted up, and she exclaimed: "Oh! I'll tell you all about that. When I was a little girl, ever so much smaller than I am now, we had a minister in the house. You know mamma takes care of everybody, and when the minister came to town he came here, because nobody else would have him. He stayed here ever so long, and used to say grace at the table and have prayers. Aunt Flick was sick at the time, and he used to pray every morning for our poor afflicted sister, and papa was full of fun with her, just to keep up her courage, I suppose, and called her 'Flicted,' and then he got to calling her Flick for a nickname, and now we all call her Flick."

"But does she like it?" I asked.

"Oh, she's used to it, and don't mind."

Millie had closed her book, and sat with it on her lap, her large black eyes looking up into mine in a dreamy way.

"There's one thing I should like to know," said Millie, "and that is, where all the books came from. Were they always here, like the ground, or did somebody make them?"

"Somebody made them," I said.

"I don't believe it," she responded.

"But if nobody made them, how did they come here?"

"They are real things: somebody found them."

"No, I've seen men who wrote books, and women too," I said.

"How did they look?"

"Very much like other people."

"And did they act like other people?"

"Yes."

"Well, that shows that they found them. They are humbugs."

I laughed, and assured her that she was mistaken.

"Well," said she, "if anybody can make books I can; and if I don't get married and keep house I shall."

Very much amused, I asked her which walk of life she would prefer.

"I think I should prefer to be married."

"You are sensible," I said.

"Not to any boy or young man, though," responded the child, with peculiar and suggestive emphasis.

"And why not?"

"They are so silly;" and she gave her curls a disdainful toss. "I shall marry a

ward speaks of an altar inscribed to Love and Home. And when it ceases to burn, it is because the altar is forsaken. Bread is the symbol of that beautiful ministry of God to human sustenance, which, properly apprehended, transforms the homeliest meal into a sacrament. What wonder, then, that when the bread of life and the fire on the hearth meet, they should interpret and reveal each other in an odor sweeter than violets—an odor so subtle and suggestive that the heart breathes it rather than the sense!

This is all stuff and sentiment, I suppose; but I doubt whether the scent of toast has reached my nostrils since that evening without recalling that scene of charming domestic life and comfort. It seemed as if all the world were in that room—and, indeed, it was all there—all that, for the hour, we could appropriate.

As we took our seats at the table, I found myself by the side of Millie and opposite to Aunt Flick. Then began, on the part of the latter personage, a pantomimic lecture to her niece. First she straightened herself in her chair, throwing out her chest and holding in her chin—a performance which Millie imitated. Then she executed the motion of putting some stray hair behind her ear. Millie did the same. Then she tucked an imaginary napkin into her neck. Millie obeyed the direction thus conveyed. Then she examined her knife, and finding that it did not suit her, sent it away and received one that did.

In the mean time, Mrs. Bradford had begun to dispense the hospitalities of the table. She was very cheerful; indeed, she was so happy herself that she overflowed with assiduities that ran far into superfluities. She was afraid the toast was not hot, or that the tea was not sweet enough, or that she had forgotten the sugar altogether, or that everybody was not properly waited upon and supplied. I could see that all this rasped Aunt Flick to desperation. The sniffs, which were light at first, grew more impatient, and after Mrs. Bradford had urged half a dozen things upon me that I did not want, and was obliged to decline, the fiery spinster burst out with:

"Wouldn't you like to read the Declaration of Independence? Wouldn't you like to repeat the Ten Commandments? Wouldn't you like a yard of calico? Do have a spoon to eat your toast with? Just a trifle more salt in your tea, please?"

All this was delivered without the slightest hesitation, and with a rapidity that was fairly bewildering. Poor Millie was overcome with the comical aspect of the matter, and broke out into an irrepressible laugh, which was so hearty that it became contagious, and all of us laughed together except Aunt Flick, who devoted herself to her supper with imperturbable gravity.

"Why, Flick, dear!" was all that Mrs. Bradford could say to this outburst of scornful criticism upon her well-meant courtesies.

Just as we were recovering from our merriment, there was a loud knock at the street door. The girl with the toasting jack dropped her implement to answer the unwelcome summons. We all involuntarily listened, and learned from his voice that the intruder was a man. We heard him enter the drawing-room, and then the girl came in and said that Mr. Grimshaw had called upon the family. In the general confusion that followed the announcement, Millie leaned over to me and said: "It's the very man who used to pray for Aunt Flick."

Mr. Bradford, of course, brought him to the tea-table at once, where room was made for him by the side of Aunt Flick, and a plate laid. The first thing he did was to swallow a cup of hot tea almost at a gulp, and to send back the empty vessel to be refilled. Then he spread with butter a whole piece of toast, which disappeared in a wonderfully brief space of time. Until his hunger was appeased he did not seem disposed to talk, replying to such questions as were propounded to him concerning himself and his family in monosyllables.

Rev. Mr. Grimshaw was the minister of a struggling Congregational church in Bradford. He had been hard at work for half a dozen years with indifferent success, waiting for some manifestation of the Master which should show him that his service and sacrifice had been accepted. I had heard him preach at different times during my vacation visits, though Mrs. Sanderson did not attend upon his ministry; and he had always impressed me as a man who was running some sort of a machine. He had a great deal to say about "the plan of salvation" and the doctrines covered by his creed. I cannot aver that he ever interested me. Indeed, I may say that he always confused me. Religion, as it had been presented to my mind, had been a simple thing—so simple that a child might understand it. My Father in Heaven loved me; Jesus Christ had died for me. Loving both, trusting both, and serving both by worship, and by affectionate and helpful good-will toward all around me was religion, as I had learned it; and I never came out from hearing one of Mr. Grimshaw's sermons without finding it difficult to get back upon my simple ground of faith. Religion, as he preached it, was such a tremendous and such a mysterious thing in its beginnings; it involved such a complicated structure of belief; it divided God into such opposing forces of justice and mercy; it depended upon such awful processes of feeling; it was so much the product of a profoundly ingenious scheme, that his sermons always puzzled me.

As he sat before me that evening, pale-faced and thin, with his intense, earnest eyes and solemn bearing and self-crucified expression, I could not doubt his purity or his sincerity. There was something in him that awoke my respect and my sympathy.

Our first talk touched only commonplaces, but as the meal drew toward its close he ingeniously led the conversation into religious channels.

"There is a very tender and solemn state of feeling in the church," said Mr. Grimshaw, "and a great deal of self-examination and prayer. The careless are beginning to be thoughtful, and the backsliders are returning to their first love. I most devoutly trust that we are going to have a season of refreshment. It is a time when all those who have named the name of the Lord should make themselves ready for his coming."

Aunt Flick started from her chair exactly as if she were about to put on her hat and cloak; and I think that was really her impulse; but she sat down again and listened intently.

I could not fail to see that this turn in the conversation was not relished by Mr. Bradford; but Mrs. Bradford and Aunt Flick were interested, and I noticed an excited look upon the faces of both Henry and Claire.

Mrs. Bradford, in her simplicity, made a most natural response to the minister's communication in the words: "You must be exceedingly delighted, Mr. Grimshaw." She said this very sweetly, and with her cheerful smile making her whole countenance light.

"Jane Bradford!" exclaimed Aunt Flick, "I believe you would smile if anybody were to tell you the judgment-day had come."

Mrs. Bradford did not say this time: "Why, Flick, dear!" but she said with great tenderness: "When I remember who is to judge me, and to whom I have committed myself, I think I should."

"Well, I don't know how anybody can make light of such awful things," responded Aunt Flick.

"Of course, **I am** rejoiced," said Mr. Grimshaw, at last getting his chance to speak, "but my joy is tempered by the great responsibility that rests upon me, and by a sense of the lost condition of the multitudes around me."

"In reality," Mr. Bradford broke in, "you don't feel quite so much like singing as the angels did when the Saviour came to redeem the world. But then they probably had no such sense of responsibility as you have. Perhaps they didn't appreciate the situation. It has always seemed to me, however, as if that which would set an angel singing—a being who ought to see a little further forward and backward than we can, and a little deeper down and higher up—ought to set men and women singing. I confess that I don't understand the long faces and the superstitious solemnities of what is called a season of refreshment. If the Lord is with his own, they ought to be glad and give him such a greeting as will induce him to remain. I really do not wonder that he flies from many congregations that I have seen, or that he seems to resist their entreaties that he will stay. Half the prayers that I hear sound like abject beseechings for the presence of One who is very far off, and very unwilling to come."

This free expression on the part of Mr. Bradford would have surprised me had I not just learned that the minister had at one time been a member of his family, with whom he had been on familiar terms; yet I knew that he did not profess to be a religious man, and that his view of the matter, whether sound or otherwise, was from the outside. There was a subtle touch of satire in his words, too, that did not altogether please me; but I did not see what reply could be made to it.

Aunt Flick was evidently somewhat afraid of Mr. Bradford, and simply said: "I hope you will remember that your child is present."

"Yes, I do remember it," said he, "and what I say about it is as much for her ears as for anybody's. And I remember too, that, during all my boyhood, I was made afraid of religion. I wish to save her, if I can, from such a curse. I have read that when the Saviour was upon the earth, he took little children in his arms and blessed them, and went so far as to say that of such was the kingdom of heaven. If he were to come to the earth again, he would be as apt to take my child upon his knee as any man's and bless her, and repeat over her the same words; and if he manifests his presence among us in any way I do not wish to have her kept away from him by the impression that there is something awful in the fact that he is here. My God! if I could believe that the Lord of Heaven and Earth were really in Bradford, with a dispensation of faith and mercy and love in his hands for me and mine, do you think I would groan and look gloomy over it? Why, I couldn't eat, I couldn't sleep; I couldn't refrain from shouting and singing."

Mr. Grimshaw was evidently touched and impressed by Mr. Bradford's exhibition of strong feeling, and said in a calm, judicial way that it was impossible that one outside of the church should comprehend and appreciate the feeling that exercised him and the church generally. The welfare of the unconverted depended so much upon a revival of religion within the church—it brought such tremendous responsibilities and such great duties—that Christian men and women were weighed down with solemnity. The issues of eternal life and death were tremendous issues. Even if the angels sang, Jesus suffered in the garden, and bore the cross on Calvary, and Christians who are worthy must suffer and bear the cross also.

"Mr. Grimshaw," said Mr. Bradford, still earnest and excited, "I have heard from your own lips that the fact that Christ was to suffer and bear the cross was at least a part of the inspiration of the song which the angels sang. He suffered and bore the cross that men might not suffer. That is one of the essential parts of your creed. He suffered that he might give peace to the world, and bring life and immortality to light. You have taught me that he did not come to torment the world, but to save it. The religion which Christendom holds in theory is a religion of unbounded peace and joy; that which it holds in fact is one of torture and gloom, and I do not hesitate to say that if the Christian world were a peaceful and joyous world, taking all the good things of this life in gratitude and gladness, while holding itself pure from its corruptions, and not only not fearing death, but looking forward with unwavering faith and hope to another and a happier life beyond, the revivals which it struggles for would be perpetual, and the millennium which it prays for would come."

Then Mr. Bradford, who sat near enough to me to touch me, laid his hand upon my shoulder, and said: "Boy, look at your father, if you wish to know what my ideal of a Christian is,—a man of cheerfulness, trust, hope, under discouragements that would kill me. Such examples save me from utter infidelity and despair, and, thank God, I have one such in my own home.' His eyes filled with tears as he turned them upon his wife, who sat watching him with intense sympathy and affection while he frankly poured out his heart and thought.

"I suppose," said the minister, "that we should get no nearer together in the discussion of this question than we were used to get when we were more in one another's company, and perhaps it would be well not to pursue it. You undoubtedly see the truth in a single aspect, Mr. Bradford; and you will pardon me for saying that you cannot see it in the aspects which it presents to me. I came in, partly to let you and your family know of our plans, and to beg you to attend our services faithfully. I hope these young people, too, will not fail to put themselves in the way of religious influence. Now is their time. To-morrow or next year it may be too late. Many a poor soul is obliged to take up the lament after every revival: 'The harvest is past, the summer is ended, and my soul is not saved.' Before the spirit takes its flight, all these precious youth ought to be gathered into the kingdom."

I could not doubt the sincerity of this closing utterance, for it was earnest and tearful. In truth, I was deeply moved by it; for while Mr. Bradford carried my judgment and opened before me a beautiful life, I had always entertained great reverence for ministers, and found Mr. Grimshaw's views and feelings most in consonance with those I had been used to hear proclaimed from the pulpit. The fact that a revival was in progress in some of the churches of the town, had already come to my ears. I had seen throngs pouring into, or coming out of church-doors and lecture-rooms during other days than Sunday; and a vague uneasiness had possessed me for several weeks. A cloud had arisen upon my life. I may even confess that my heart had rebelled in secret against an influence which promised to interfere with the social pleasures and the progress in study which I had anticipated for the winter. The cloud came nearer to me now, and in Mr. Grimshaw's presence quite overshadowed me. Was I moved by sympathy? Was I moved by the spirit of the Almighty? Was superstitious fear at the bottom of it all? Whatever it was, my soul had crossed the line of that circle of passion and experience in whose center a great multitude were groping and crying in the darkness, and striving to get a vision of the Father's face. I realized the fact then and there. I felt that a crisis in my life was approaching.

I could not say a word. The eyes of the minister still haunted me. The spell of a new influence was upon me. What Mr. Bradford had said about Mr. Bedlow only increased my desire to hear him, and to come within the reach of his power.

"Well, children," said Mr. Bradford, "for you will let me call you such, I know; I have only one thing more to say to you, and that is to stand by your Christian fathers and mothers, and take their faith just as it is. Not one of you is old enough to decide upon the articles of a creed, but almost any faith is good enough to hold up a Christian character. Don't bother yourselves voluntarily with questions. A living vine grows just as well on a rough trellis of simple branches as on the smoothest piece of ornamental work that can be made. If you ever wish to change the trellis when you get old enough to do it, be careful not to ruin the vine, that is all. I am trying to keep my vine alive around a trellis that is gone to wreck. I believe in God and in his Son, and I believe that there is one thing which God delights in more than in all else, and that is Christian character. I hold to the first and strive for the last, though I am looked upon as little better than an infidel by all but one."

A thrill, sympathetically felt by us all, and visible in a blush and eyes suffused, ran through the dear little woman seated at his side, and she looked up into his face with a trustful smile of response.

After this it was difficult to engage in light conversation. We were questioned in regard to our past experiences and future plans. We looked over volumes of pictures, and a cabinet of curiosities, and Millie amused us by reading, and at an early hour we rose to go home. Millie went to her corner as soon as we broke up, giving me a look as she passed me. I took the hint and followed her.

"Shall you go to hear Mr. Bedlow?" she inquired.

"I think I shall," I answered.

"I knew you would. I should like to go with you, but you know I can't. Will you tell me what he is like, and all about it?"

"Yes."

I pressed her hand and bade her "good-night."

Mr. Bradford parted with us at the door with pleasant and courteous words, and told Henry that he must regard the house as his home, and assured him that he would always find a welcome there. I had noticed during the evening a peculiarly affectionate familiarity in his tone and bearing toward the young man. I could not but notice that he treated him with more consideration than he treated me. I went away feeling that there were confidences between them, and suffered the suspicion to make me uneasy.

I walked home with Henry and Claire, and we talked over the affairs of the evening together. Both declared their adhesion to Mr. Bradford's views, and I, in my assumed pride of independent opinion, dissented. I proposed to see for myself. I would listen to Mr. Bedlow's preaching. I was not afraid of being harmed, and, indeed, I should not dare to stay away from him.

As I walked to the Mansion, I found my nerves excited in a strange degree. The way was full of shadows. I started at every noise. It was as if the spiritual world were dropped down around me, and I were touched by invisible wings, and moved by mysterious influences. The stars shivered in their high places, the night-wind swept by me as if it were a weird power of evil, and I seemed to be smitten through heart and brain by a nameless fear. As I kneeled in my accustomed way at my bed I lost my confidence. I could not recall my usual words or frame new ones. I lingered on my knees like one crushed and benumbed. What it all meant I could not tell. I only knew that feelings and influences which long had been gathering in me were assuming the predominance, and that I was entering upon a new phase of experience. At last I went to bed, and passed a night crowded with strange dreams and dreary passages of unrefreshing slumber.

CHAPTER VII.

I HAD never arrived at any definite comprehension of Mrs. Sanderson's ideas of religion. Whether she was religious in any worthy sense I do not know, even to-day. The respect which she entertained for the clergy was a sentiment which she shared with New Englanders generally. She was rather generous than otherwise in her contributions to their support, yet the most I could make of her views and opinions was that religion and its institutions were favorable to the public order and security, and were, therefore, to be patronized and permanently sustained. I never should have thought of going to her for spiritual counsel, yet I had learned in some way that she thought religion was a good thing for a young man, because it would save him from dissipation and from a great many dangers to which young men are exposed. The whole subject seemed to be regarded by her in an economical or prudential aspect.

I met her on the morning following my visit at the Bradfords', in the breakfast-room. She was cheery and expectant, for she always found me talkative, and was prepared to hear the full story of the previous evening. That I was obliged to tell her that Henry was there with my sister, embarrassed me much, for, beyond the fact that she disliked Henry intensely, there was the further fact—most offensive to her—that Mr. Bradford was socially patronizing the poor, and bringing me, her *protégé*, into association with them. Here was where my chain galled me, and made me realize my slavery. I saw the thrill of anger that shot through her face, and recognized the effort she made to control her words. She did not speak at first, and not until she felt perfectly sure of self-control did she say:

"Mr. Bradford is very unwise. He inflicts a great wrong upon young people without position or expectations, when he undertakes to raise them to his own social level. How he could do such a thing as he did last night is more than I can imagine, unless he wishes either to humiliate you or offend me."

For that one moment how I longed to pour out my love for Henry and Claire, and to speak my sense of justice in the vindication of Mr. Bradford! It was terrible to sit still and hold my tongue while the ties of blood and friendship were contemned, and the motives of my hospitable host were misconstrued so cruelly. Yet I could not open my lips. I dreaded a collision with her as if she had been a serpent, or a furnace of fire, or a hedge of thorns. Ay, I was mean enough to explain that I had no expectation of meeting either Henry or my sister there; and she was adroit enough to reply that she was at least sure of that without my saying so.

Then I talked fully of Mr. Grimshaw's call, and gave such details of the conversation that occurred as I could without making Mr. Bradford too prominent.

"So Mr. Bradford doesn't like Mr. Bellow," she remarked; "but Mr. Bradford is a trifle whimsical in his likes and dislikes. I'm sure I've always heard Mr. Bellow well spoken of. He has the credit of having done a great deal of good, and if he is coming here, Arthur, I think you cannot do better than to go and hear him for yourself."

Like a flash of light there passed through my mind the thought that Providence had not only thus opened the way for me, **but** with an imperative finger had directed me **to** walk in it. God had made the wrath of woman to praise him, and the remainder he had restrained. Imagining myself to be thus directed, I should not have dared to avoid Mr. Bellow's preaching. The whole interview with Mr. Grimshaw, the fact that, contrary to my wont, I had not found myself in sympathy with my old friend Mr. Bradford, and the strange and unlooked-for result of my conversation with Mrs. Sanderson, shaped themselves into a divine mandate to whose authority my spirit bowed in ready obedience.

Mr. Bellow made his appearance in Mr. Grimshaw's pulpit on the following Sunday; and a great throng of excited and expectant people, attracted by the notoriety of the preacher, and moved by the influences of the time, were in attendance. The hush of solemnity that pervaded the assembly when these two men entered the desk impressed me deeply. My spirit was thrilled with strange apprehension. My emotional nature was in chaos; and such crystallizations of opinion, thought and feeling as had taken place in me during a lifelong course of religious nurture and education were broken up. Outside of the church, and entirely lacking that dramatic experience of conversion and regeneration which all around me regarded as the only true beginning of a religious life, my whole soul lay open, quick and quivering, to the influences of the hour, and the words which soon fell upon it.

The pastor conducted the opening services, and I had never seen him in such a mood. Inspired by the presence of an immense congregation and by the spirit of the time, he rose entirely out of the mechanisms of his theology and his stereotyped forms of expression, and poured out the burden of his soul in a prayer that melted every heart before him. Deprecating the judgments of the Most High on the coldness and worldliness of the church; beseeching the Spirit of All Grace to come and work its own great miracles upon those who loved the Master, moving them to penitence, self-sacrifice, humility and prayer; entreating that Spirit to plant the arrows of conviction in all unconverted souls, and to bring a great multitude of these into the Kingdom—a multitude so great that they should be like doves flocking to their windows—he prayed like a man inspired. His voice trembled and choked with emotion, and the tears coursed down his cheeks unheeded. It seemed as if he could not pause, or be denied.

Of Mr. Bedlow's sermon that followed I can give no fitting idea. After a severe denunciation of the coldness of the church that grieved and repelled the Spirit of God, he turned to those without the fold—to the unconverted and impenitent. He told us that God was angry with us every day, that every imagination of the thoughts of our hearts was only evil continually, that we were exposed every moment to death and the perdition of ungodly men, and that it was our duty to turn, then and there, from the error of our ways, and to seek and secure the pardon which a pitying Christ extended to us—a pardon which could be had for the taking. Then he painted with wonderful power the joy and peace that follow the consciousness of sin forgiven, and the glories of that heaven which the Saviour had gone to prepare for those who love him.

I went home blind, staggering—almost benumbed, with the words ringing in my ears that it had been my duty before rising from my seat to give myself to the Saviour, and to go out of the door rejoicing in the possession of a hope which should be as an anchor in all the storms of my life; yet I did not know what the process was. I was sure I did not know. I had not the slightest comprehension of what was required of me, yet the fact did not save me from the impression that I had committed a great sin. I went to my room and tried to pray, and spent half an hour of such helpless and pitiful distress as I cannot describe. Then there arose in me a longing for companionship. I could not unbosom myself to Mrs. Sanderson. Henry's calm spirit and sympathetic counsels were beyond my reach. Mr. Bradford was not in the church, and I could only think of my father, and determine that I would see him. I ate but little dinner, made no conversation with Mrs. Sanderson, and, toward night, left the house and sought my father's home.

I found the house as solemn as death. All the family save Claire had heard Mr. Bedlow, and my mother was profoundly dejected. A cloud rested upon my brothers and sisters. My father seemed to apprehend at once the nature of my errand, and, by what seemed to be a mutual impulse and understanding, we passed into an unoccupied room and closed the door. The moment I found myself alone with him I threw my arms around his neck, and bursting into an uncontrollable fit of weeping, exclaimed: "Oh, father! father! what shall I do?"

For years I had not come to him with a trouble. For years I had not reposed in him a single heart-confidence, and for the first time in his life he put both his arms affectionately around me and embraced me. Minutes passed while we stood thus. I could not see his face, for my own was bowed upon his shoulder, but I could feel his heart-beats, and the convulsions of emotion which shook him in every fiber. At last he gently put me off, led me to a seat, and sat down beside me. He took my hand, but he could not speak.

"Oh, father! what shall I do?" I exclaimed again.

"Go to God, my boy, and repeat the same words to him with the same earnestness."

"But he is angry with me," I said, "and you are not. You pity me and love me. I am your child. You cannot help being sorry for me."

"You are his child too, my boy, by relations a thousand times tenderer and more significant than those which make you mine. He loves you and pities you more than I can."

"But I don't know how to give myself to him," I said.

"I have had the impression and the hope," my father responded, "that you had already given yourself to him."

"Oh, not in this way at all," I said.

My father had his own convictions, but he was almost morbidly conscientious in all his dealings with the souls around him. Fearful of meddling with that which the Gracious Spirit had in charge and under influence, and modest in the assertion of views which might possibly weaken the hold of conviction upon me; feeling, too, that he did not know me well enough to direct me, and fearful that he might arrest a process which, perfected, might redeem me, he simply said: "I am not wise; let us pray together, that we may be led aright."

Then he kneeled and prayed for me. Ah, how the blessed words of that prayer have lingered in my memory! Though not immediately fruitful in my experience, they came to me long years after, loaded with the balm of healing. "Oh, Father in Heaven!" he said, "this is our boy,—thy child and mine. Thou lovest and pitiest him more than I can. Help him to go to Thee as he has come to me, and to say in perfect submission, 'Oh, Father, what shall I do!'"

I went home at last somewhat calmed, because I had had sympathy, and, for a few moments, had leaned upon another nature and rested. I ate little, and, as soon as the hour arrived, departed to attend the evening service, previously having asked old Jenks to attend the meeting and walk home with me, for I was afraid to return alone.

A strange and gloomy change had come over the sky; and the weather, which had been extremely cold for a week, had grown warm. The snow under my feet was soft and yielding, and already little rivulets were coursing along the ruts worn by the sleighs. The nerves which had been braced by the tonic of the cold, clear air were relaxed, and with the uncertain footing of the streets I went staggering to the church.

In the endeavor now to analyze my feelings I find it impossible to believe that I was convinced that my life had been one of bold and intentional sin. A considerable part of my pain, I know, arose from the fact that I could not realize my own sinfulness as it had been represented to me. I despaired because I could not despair. I was distressed because I could not be sufficiently distressed. There was one sin, however, of which I had a terrified consciousness, viz., that of rejecting the offer of mercy which had been made to me in the morning, and of so rejecting it as to be in danger of forever grieving away the Spirit of God which I believed was at work upon my heart. This was something definite and dreadful, though I felt perfectly ignorant of the exact thing required of me and impotent to perform it. If I could have known the precise nature of the surrender demanded of me, and could have comprehended the effort I was called upon to make, I believe I should have been ready for both; but in truth I had been so mystified by the preacher, so puzzled by his representation of the miracle of conversion, which he made to appear to be dependent on God's sovereign grace entirely, and yet so entirely dependent on me that the whole guilt of remaining unconverted would rest with me; I was so expectant of some mighty overwhelming influence that would bear me to a point where I could see through the darkness and the discord—an influence which did not come—that I was paralyzed and helpless.

I was early in the church, and saw the solemn groups as they entered and gradually filled the pews. The preachers, too, were early in the desk. Mr. Bedlow sat where he could see me and read my face. I knew that his searching, magnetic eyes were upon me, and in the exalted condition of my sensibilities I felt them. In the great hush that followed the entrance of the crowd and preceded the beginning of the exercises I saw him slowly rise and walk down the pulpit stairs. I had never known anything of his methods, and was entirely unprepared for what followed. Reaching the aisle, he walked directly to where I sat, and raising his finger pointed it at me and said: "Young man, are you a Christian?"

"I suppose not," I answered.

"Do you ever expect to become one?"

"I do," I replied.

At this he left me, and went to one and another in the congregation, putting his question and making some remark. Sensitive men and women hung their heads, and tried to evade his inquiries by refusing to look at him.

At length he went back to his desk, and said that the church could do no better than to hold for a few minutes a season of prayer, preparatory to the services of the evening; and then he added: "Will some brother pray for a young man who expects to become a Christian, and pray that that expectation may be taken away from him."

Thereupon a young man, full of zeal, kneeled before the congregation and poured out his heart for me, and prayed as he had been asked to pray: that my expectation to become a Christian might be taken away from me. He was, however, considerate and kind enough to so far modify the petition as to beg that I might lose my expectation in the immediate realization of a Christian experience—that my hope to become a Christian might be swallowed up in my hope of a Christian's reward.

This kindness of the young man, however, to whose zeal and good-will I give hearty honor, could not efface the sore sense of wrong I had suffered at the hand of Mr. Bedlow. Why he should have singled me out in the throng for such an awful infliction I did not know, and why he should have asked anybody to pray that all expectation of becoming a Christian should be taken away from me I could not imagine. I felt that I was misunderstood and outraged at first, and as my anger died away, or was quenched by other emotions, I found that I was still more deeply puzzled than before. Was I not carefully and prayerfully seeking? And was not this expectation the one thing which made my life endurable? Would I not give all the world to find my feet upon the sure foundation? Had I not in my heart of hearts determined to find what there was to be found if I could, or die?

No; Mr. Bedlow, meaning well no doubt,

and desiring to lead me nearer to spiritual rest, had thrust me into deeper and wilder darkness ; and in that darkness, haunted by forms of torment and terror, I sat through one of the most impressive sermons and exhortations I had ever heard. I went out of the church at last as utterly hopeless and wretched as I could be. There was a God of wrath above me, because there was the guilt of unfulfilled duty gnawing at my conscience. It seemed as if the great tragedy of the universe were being performed in my soul. Sun, moon, stars, the kingdoms and glory of the world—what were all these, either in themselves or to me, compared with the interests of a soul on which rested the burden of a decision for its own heaven or hell ?

As I emerged into the open air, I met Jenks at the door, waiting for me, and as I lifted my hot face I felt the cold rain falling upon it. Pitchy darkness, unrelieved save by the dim lights around the town and the blotched and rapidly melting snow, had settled upon the world. I clutched the old servant's arm, and struck off in silence toward home. We had hardly walked the distance of a block before there came a flash of blinding lightning, and we were in the midst of that impressive anomaly, a January thunderstorm. It was strange how harmoniously this storm supplemented the influences of the services at the church, from which I had just retired. To me it was the crowning terror of the night. I had no question that it was directed by the same unseen power which had been struggling with me all day, and that it was expressive of His infinite anger. As we hurried along, unprotected in the pouring rain, flash after flash illuminated the darkness, and peal after peal of thunder hurtled over the city, and rolled along the heavens, and echoed among the distant hills. I walked in constant terror of being struck dead, and of passing to the judgment unreconciled and unredeemed. I felt that my soul was dealing directly with the great God, and under the play of his awful enginery of destruction I realized my helplessness. I could only pray to him, with gasps of agony, and in whispers : "Oh, do not crush me ! Spare me, and I will do anything ! Save my life, and it shall be thine ! "

When I arrived at the house I did not dare to go in, for then I should be left alone. Without a word I led Jenks to the stable, and, dripping with the rain, we passed in.

"Oh, Jenks," I said, " I must pray, and

you must stay with me. I cannot be left alone. I should die."

I kneeled upon the stable-floor, and the old man, touched with sympathy, and awed by the passion which possessed me, knelt at my side. Oh, what pledges and promises I gave in that prayer, if God would spare my life ! How wildly I asked for pardon, and how earnestly did I beseech the Spirit of all Grace to stay with me, and never to be grieved away until his work was perfected in me !

The poor old man, with his childish mind, could not understand my abandonment to grief and terror ; but while I knelt I felt his trembling arm steal around me, and knew that he was sobbing. His heart was deeply moved by pity, but the case was beyond his comprehension. He could say nothing, but the sympathy was very grateful to me.

And all this time there was another arm around me, whose touch I was too benumbed to feel ; there was another heart beside me, tender with sympathy, whose beatings I was too much agitated to apprehend ; there was a voice calling to the tempest within me, " Peace ! be still ! " but I could not hear it. Oh, infinite Father ! Oh, loving and pitying Christ ! Why could I not have seen thee, as thou didst look down upon and pity thy terror-stricken child ? Why could I not have seen thy arms extended toward me, and thy eyes beaming with ineffable love, calling me to thy forgiving embrace ? How could I have done thee the dishonor to suppose that the simple old servant kneeling at my side was tenderer and more pitiful than thou ?

We both grew chilly at last, and passed quietly into the house. Mrs. Sanderson had retired, but had left a bright fire upon the hearth, at which both of us warmed and dried ourselves. The storm, meantime, had died away, though the lightning still flapped its red wings against the windows, and the dull reverberations of the thunder came to me from the distance. With the relief from what seemed to be the danger of imminent death, I had the strength to mount to my room alone, and, after another prayer which failed to lift my burden, I consigned myself to my bed. The one thought that possessed me as I lay down was that I might never wake if I should go to sleep. My nervous exhaustion was such that when sinking into sleep I started many times from my pillow, tossing the clothes from me, and gasping as if I had been sinking into an abyss. Sleep came at last, however, and I awoke on the morrow, conscious that I had rested, and rejoicing at least in the fact that my day of probation was not yet past. My heart kindled for a moment as I looked from my window into the face of the glorious sun, and the deep blue heaven, but sank within me when I remembered my promises, and felt that the struggle of the previous day was to be renewed.

This struggle I do not propose to dwell upon further in extended detail. If the record of it thus far is as painful to read as it is to write, the reader will have tired of it already. It lasted for weeks, and I never rationally saw my way out of that blindness. There were literally hundreds in the city who professed to have found a great and superlatively joyous peace, but I did not find it, nor did it come to me in any way by which I dreamed it might come.

The vital point with me was to find some influence so powerful that I could not resist it. I felt myself tossing upon a dangerous sea, just outside the harbor, between which and me there stretched an impassable bar. So, wretched and worn with anxious waiting, I looked for the coming in of some mighty wave which would lift my sinking bark over the forbidding obstacle, into the calm waters that mirrored upon their banks the domes and dwellings of the city of the Great King.

Sometimes I tired of Mr. Bedlow, and went to other churches, longing always to hear some sermon or find some influence that would do for me that which I could not do for myself. I visited my father many times, but he could not help me, beyond what he had already done. One of the causes of my perplexity was the fact that Henry attended the prayer meetings, and publicly participated in the exercises. I heard, too, that, in a quiet way, he was very influential in his school, and that many of his pupils had begun a religious life. Why was he different from myself? Why was it necessary that I should go through this experience of fear and torment, while he escaped it altogether? All our previous experience had been nearly identical. For years we had been subjected to the same influences, had struggled for the same self-mastery, had kneeled at the same bed in daily devotion; yet here he was, busy in Christian service, steadily rejoicing in Christian hope, into which he had grown through processes as natural as those by which the rose-tree rises to the grace of inflorescence. I see it all now, but then it not only perplexed me, but filled me with weak complaining at my harder lot.

During these eventful weeks, I often met Millie Bradford on her way to and from school. I have no doubt that, from her window, she had made herself familiar with my habits of going and coming, and had timed her own so as to fall in with me.

In communities not familiar with the character and history of a New England revival, it would be impossible to conceive of the universality of the influence which they exert during the time of their highest activity. Multitudes of men neglect their business. Meetings are held during every evening of the week, and sometimes during all the days of the week. Children, gathered in their own little chambers, hold prayer-meetings. Religion is the all-absorbing topic, with old and young.

Millie was like the rest of us; and, forbidden to hear Mr. Bedlow preach, she had determined to win her experience at home. It touches me now even to tears to remember how she used to meet me in the street, and ask me how I was getting along, how I liked Mr. Bedlow, and whether he had helped me. She told me that she and her mother were holding little prayer-meetings together, but that Aunt Flick was away pretty much all the time. She was seeking to become a Christian, and at last she told me that she thought she had become one. I was rational enough to see that it was not necessary for an innocent child like her to share my graver experiences. Indeed, I listened eagerly to her expressions of simple faith and trust, and to her recital of the purposes of life to which she had committed herself. One revelation which she made in confidence, but which I am sure was uttered because she wanted me to think well of her father, interested me much. She said her father prayed very much alone, though he did not attend the meetings. The thought of my old friend toiling in secret over the problem which absorbed us all was very impressive.

Thus weeks passed away, and the tide which rose to its flood began to ebb. I could see that the meetings grew less frequent, and that the old habits of business and pleasure were reasserting themselves. Conversions were rarer, and the blazing fervor of action and devotion cooled. As I realized this, and, in realizing it, found that I was just as far from the point at which I had aimed as I was at the beginning, a strange, desperate despair seized me. I could hope for no influences in the future more powerful than those to which I had been subjected. The stimulus to resolution and endeavor was nearly expended. Yet I had many times vowed to the Most High that before that season had passed away I would find Him, and, with Him, peace, if He and it were to be found. What was I to do?

At last there came a day of ingathering. The harvest was to be garnered. A great number of men, women, and youth were to be received into the church. I went early, and took a seat in the gallery, where I could see the throng as they presented themselves in the aisles to make their profession of faith and unite in their covenant. When called upon they took their places, coming forward from all parts of the audience in front of the Communion table. Among them were both Henry and Claire. At sight of them I grew sick. Passage after passage of Scripture, that seemed applicable to my condition, crowded into my mind. They came from the North and the South and the East and the West, and sat down in the Kingdom of God, and I, a child of the Kingdom, baptized into the name of the Ineffable, was cast out. The harvest was past, the summer was ended, and my soul was not saved! I witnessed the ceremonies with feelings mingled of despair, bitterness, and desperation. On the faces of these converts, thus coming into the fold, there was impressed the seal of a great and solemn joy. With-in my bosom there burned the feeling that I had honestly tried to do my duty, and that my endeavors had been spurned. In a moment, to which I had been led by processes whose end I could not see, my will gave way, and I said, I will try no longer. This is the end. Every resolution and purpose within me was shivered by the fall.

To what depth of perdition I might be hurled—under what judgment I might be crushed—I could not tell, and hardly cared to imagine. Quite to my amazement, I found myself at perfect peace. What did it mean?

Not only was the burden gone, but there thrilled through my soul a quick, strong joy. My spirit was like a broad sea, alive all over with sunlit ripples, with one broad track of glory that stretched across into the unfathomable heaven! I felt the smile of God upon me. I felt the love of God within me. Was I insane? Had Satan appeared to me as an angel of light and deceived me? Was this conversion? I was so much in doubt in regard to the real nature of this experience, that when I left the house I spoke to no one of it. Emerging into the open air, I found myself in a new world. I walked the streets as lightly as if wings had been upon my shoulders, lifting me from point to point through all the passage homeward. Ah, how blue the heavens were, and how broad and beautiful the world! What a blessed thing it was to live! How sweet were the faces not only of friends, but even of those whom I did not know! How gladly would I have embraced every one of them! It was as if I had been un-clothed of my mortality, and clothed upon with the immortal. I was sure that heaven could hold no joy superior to that.

When passing Mr. Bradford's, I saw Millie at the window. She beckoned to me, and I went to her door. " How is it now?" she said.

" I don't know, Millie," I replied, " but I think it is all right. I never felt before as I do now."

" Oh, I was getting so tired!" said she. " I've been praying for you for days, and days, and days! and hoping and hoping you'd get through."

I could only thank her, and press her little hand, and then I hurried to my home, mounted to my room, shut and locked the door, and sat down to think.

(To be continued.)

THE WOMAN WHO SAVED ME.

PART I.

THE medical man was holding my wrist and talking, and I was not listening. In the first place, I knew more about myself than he could tell me; in the second, I should scarcely have understood what he was saying if I had listened; and in the third, I was in so listless and indifferent a condition of mind that I did not care to listen—did not care to answer—did not even care to look, as I was half unconsciously looking at the dead brown leaves twisting in the eddying wind that whirled them down the street.

How dull it all looked! how dull the dragging days were! how I was beginning to hate the big, obtrusive stone houses, and dread the long gray patch of November sky showing itself over the roof, and alternately drifting leaden clouds and drizzling leaden rain that made the wide flagged pavement wet and shining with the slop of passing feet! I had always disliked the English winter, but I had never lost spirit in any other winter as I had during this one. Three months of its slow, dull birth had added a hundredfold to the listless misery which had become almost a part of myself, and more than once I had almost hoped that its ending would end my life. If during that wretched autumn I had hoped for anything, I had hoped for this, however vaguely; but the time had often been when I had been so utterly indifferent to life or death that I had not even cared to wish for either.

I was in one of the worst of these moods to-day, and when the doctor came it was at its strongest; so, as he talked to me I scarcely listened, but looked out at the whirling leaves and dust in silence. But, though I was not listening, I could not help hearing his last words.

"And as I told Mr. Leith," he was saying, "I cannot be responsible for the result if you do not go."

I began to listen then, though I scarcely knew why.

"Go?" I repeated, "where am I to go, and why?"

"Anywhere," was his emphatic reply. "To the seaside—to some country place—to Yarmouth—to Swansea—to Switzerland—anywhere away from London."

"But why?" I asked again, beginning to wonder if the man did not, after all, know something more than I had fancied.

"Because," looking at me steadily, "if you remain here you will die in two months, and Mr. Leith will blame me."

"Will he?" I muttered, half unconsciously—"would he blame anybody?"

Doctor Brainard looked at me again—keenly this time—but he said nothing.

"And I may go anywhere out of London?" I said, after a short pause.

"Anywhere," he answered—"though I should advise the sea-side."

"And you have spoken to my husband about it?"

"Yes."

"What did he say?" I asked this unwillingly.

"He said that he hoped the change would improve your health."

I looked out at the leaves in the street again. It was so like him. I knew what it meant. I must decide for myself. He did not care. I might live if I cared for life—die if I chose.

"I have a friend in Bamborough," I said after a while, "I will go there."

Dr. Brainard rose and took his hat.

"Do," he advised—"Bamborough is just the place I should have chosen for you, had I not thought it best to let you choose for yourself. There is plenty of strong sea-breeze on the Cornish coast, and your friend will improve the tone of your nervous system if she is anything of a woman."

So he left me, and so I turned to the street again and stared blankly at the dead leaves and the patch of gray November sky. But I could not watch it long. For the first time in many long months a certain quiet excitement crept upon me, brought about by the thoughts that drifted into my mind concerning my friend at Bamborough—concerning Lisbeth Grant.

We had been girls together and we had loved each other. We had been to each other what girls seldom are—we had been faithful, though for four years Lisbeth had been a wife, and though she was the mother of three children. I knew she was faithful to me still, notwithstanding that since her wedding-day we had never seen each other.

"My hands are full, Gervase," she had written to me once.—"and my heart is full too—to the brim. Hugh and his children fill it as they fill the hands. They give me no time to stagnate. They keep the hands at work and the heart at work too—loving, hoping, thinking for them—and I am sure the beating is more in time for the work the children bring. But they have not crowded you out, Gervase, you may be sure of that. There is all the more room because they have made it larger. The children have made me love you more than ever."

" Yes," I said to myself as I got up from my chair—"yes, I will go to Lisbeth. If I am going to die, better die with Lisbeth than here."

I did not love my husband—I had never loved him, I told myself. It was not even love that had made us happy in the first months of our marriage. It had only been a weak mockery after all, and we had both learned the truth too late. Even the little child that had scarcely drawn a breath could not soften **our** hearts towards each other. And, worse **than** this, out of my wretchedness had grown a shadow of sin and despair. I looked backwards sometimes to a fancy I had long left behind—to a fancy that I thought my husband had long blotted out, and looking backward so, I fell into a wonder at what now seemed my blindness. That man would have loved me; there would have come no bitter words from him,—that man would have been true to me through life and death; *his* love would never have died, burning out the more rapidly for the very strength of its first flame.

I did not often wait for my husband, but I waited for him that night. I wanted to tell him of my decision. Not that I fancied he would care for my absence or presence,—he was past that; we were both past it. Still I would show just so much grace as to make a pretense of consulting him.

"I am going to Bamborough," I said to him, "to visit Lisbeth Grant. Doctor Branaird advises me to do so." And I glanced at him carelessly.

He had just come in, and tossed his hat upon a sofa in his careless fashion, and now he was standing upon the hearth looking silently into the fire. He did not raise his eyes.

" I hope you will find your health improved," he said.

" I hope so," I returned briefly.

But he was not quite easy, I could see, and I must confess to some slight surprise. The old black lines came out on his forehead, but they were not angry lines; they were something new to me in their changed expression. He was so fidgety too, and even more taciturn than usual. But I took no notice of the change until after we had supped and he had been reading for half an hour, when he suddenly broke the silence by flinging his book upon the sofa after his hat and speaking to me abruptly :

" You are not worse than usual," he said, " are you ? " I did not look up this time, but went on working steadily. " I think not," I answered; " I am sure not."

I would not tell him the truth. He should have had sight clear enough to discover it for himself.

He got up, and coming to the side of the hearth upon which I was seated, caught hold of my netting silk, so stopping my work.

"That is not true," he said—" it is one of your fables."

"One of *my* fables ? " I returned quietly.

He took hold of my hand and held it up so that my loose sleeve fell back from my arm.

" Yes," he said, " it is a fable. Look at your arm—look at your wrist, see how your bracelet fits it. It was as round as a baby's before"—and here seeming to recollect himself, he let my hand drop.

I looked at it myself as I settled my sleeve again, and as I looked I smiled faintly. My beautiful arms had been my pride once, and now the heavy gold bracelet slipped loosely up and down over a white surface that was little more than delicate skin and slender bone. Perhaps after all Doctor Branaird was right—I had better leave London.

So the next day I went to Bamborough and Lisbeth. But early in the morning, as I stood before the mirror in my dressing room, my husband came to me. I was surprised again, for of late there had been so little pretense at sentiment between us that I had scarcely expected he would care to make any farewells. But I discovered in a very few moments that this was what he had come for, and I felt myself excited and nervous. This surprised me too. If we had loved each other I might have understood the feeling : but since we did not love each other, what could it mean ? He stood by my toilet-table, looking pale and agitated for a few minutes after his entrance, and then he broke the awkward silence :

" You will need money," he began.

I interrupted him.

" No," I said, " you mistake. I do not need any. Thank you."

" Very well," he answered, " if that is the case I suppose it is useless to offer you any. But if you should require anything—wish anything—I hope you will write to me about it."

"Thank you again," I replied. " I will write to you once a week whether I wish anything or not."

He lingered a few minutes longer and then turned to go.

"Then as I shall not see you again I will bid you good-bye," he said; "you will not return until—"

"I recover or die," I interrupted. "If Rumborough agrees with me no better than London has done, Doctor Brainord says I shall die in two months; so good-bye."

I scarcely knew what feeling of desperation prompted me to make a speech so reckless, but it was a feeling desperate enough.

"Gervase!" he exclaimed.

I would not look at him, but in the mirror I saw reflected on his face a pallor as ashen as the pallor of death. Sometimes in after months I wished that I had looked at him more straightly.

But he said nothing more—only waited a moment and then came to my side.

"Good-bye," he said.

"Good-bye," I answered. And the next moment he had touched my cheek lightly with his lips and was gone.

It was late when I reached Rumborough, and the tide was running in under a red, fog-obscured sun. I looked out of the carriage window as I drove from the station through the narrow streets, and looking I saw little more than an immense expanse of sea, and a dry and wet brown beach where fishermen were lounging, fishermen's children shouting and playing, and fishermen's boats drawn up and fastened upon the sand with chains. I had always felt drawn towards the sea with a curious sense of fascination, and this evening the fresh salt air blew so coolly upon my cheeks that I had a quiet, half-defined feeling that I was not sorry I had come to Rumborough.

And at her open door Lisbeth stood ready to welcome me, and my first glance showed me the same handsome womanly face and handsome womanly figure, neither face nor figure a whit unfamiliar or a whit less perfect for the crown of comely matronhood. Two of her children clung to her flowing skirts, her handsome baby clasped her neck, and as she stood there smiling, I thought of Cordelia, and my heart warmed,—Lisbeth's strength and beauty always warmed it.

She caught me in the one arm her child left free, and drew me into the hall, pressing her warm red lips to mine.

"My dear!" she said, "my dearest!" and it seemed as though she had for the moment no other words to utter. Her very voice warmed me and put life into my veins. I clung to her, enjoying her tender caresses, but scarcely speaking a word, for at least

Lisbeth understood what my silence often meant and would not reproach me with it. She did not ask me any questions. It seemed that in an instant she comprehended everything, for she carried me to my room and took off my wrappings as if I had been a child and she my mother. I could not help noticing the mother touch in her strong, gentle hands, and the mother tone in her voice.

"I will show you my children as soon as you are rested," she said, "but you must rest first, Gervase. Your husband's telegram did not prepare me for seeing you look so changed."

I felt a sudden pulsation of the heart.

"My husband's telegram?" I said—"did he send one?"

"Yes," she answered, "very early this morning, to say that you were coming."

I answered not a word. Why had he done this? If we had loved each other, I should have known that it was because he could not brook the thought of my meeting even the momentary chill of an unexpected reception; but now the news only startled me.

But though she spoke no word, Lisbeth's eyes lost nothing. I knew that she was searching me even when she spoke of other things, and I knew that she was searching me when, after she had called her children into the room, she stood near me in her royal mother pride, with her little one in her fair, strong arms.

"This is Hugh's boy," she said, touching the crumpled brown curls of her eldest. "Look up, Laurence. See, Gervase—Hugh's eyes."

They were magnificent children. Lisbeth's perfect, healthful nature had dowered them, and her unwarped, fearless soul shone out of their childish eyes. A desolate aching filled my breast as Lisbeth stood near me with them. Her life was so full—mine so empty. I had never loved children very much—had seen very little of them—and of my own baby I had seen nothing but the poor little cold body I had for one moment caught a glimpse of as Roger bent over it, shaken with a man's terrible weeping. I thought of this when I looked at Lisbeth's children, but no tears came into my eyes. I was wondering vaguely if I were a wicked woman, and if my faded, empty life were my punishment. I do not think I had ever loved my baby or wept for it—Roger had ceased to love me long before its birth, and I had learned to know what a mistake I had made.

But I lived again that day as I talked to Lisbeth. We sat by the fire after tea—she with her child on her breast, and I on a lounging chair near her, until the heavy fog had crept over the sands and up into the little town, hiding even the red lights. We had so much to say, and we were alone together for the first time since we had parted four years ago. Hugh was absent on business, and the children had gone to bed, so we went over the four years again—but until the close of the evening Lisbeth said nothing of my husband. At length, after a silence, she lifted her eyes from the fire and looked at me tenderly—searchingly—sadly.

"And you are happy, Gervase?" she said. I could not answer her at first, but after a silent struggle the words came. I could not tell a lie to Lisbeth.

"Happy! no, I am wretched."

She looked at me for a moment longer and then spoke again.

"Gervase," she said, "if your little child had lived—" I broke in upon her, losing all self-control in a wild, sudden passion of uncontrollable weeping.

"No—no!" I cried out. "Better as it is—far, far better as it is."

She moved her seat nearer to me and drew my head down upon her lap with that tender mother touch.

"Gervase," she said softly, "you think you do not love your husband."

How did she know? for she seemed to understand me in an instant. I cried out again in the midst of my passionate sobs.

"I have never loved him," I said—"he has never loved me. It was a mistake—it was all wrong from first to last, and he is wretched too."

It was all told then—the miserable secret that had grown to its full strength in my own heart alone. It was all told in one brief rash speech—no, not quite all. The rest would be a secret forever even from Lisbeth.

But I had wept myself into calmness at last, and we had been talking together again, though with longer silence between our words than there had been before, when in one of these silences I heard the front door open, and felt a great rioting rush of the boisterous sea wind, and there were sounds of a man's footsteps in the hall, and a man's voice flung out a scrap of song :—

> "I am come, its deeps are learned—
> Come, but there is naught to say :
> Married eyes with mine have met,
> Silence! Oh ! I had my day,
> Margaret, Margaret?"

I was trembling from head to foot.

"The rush of night wind has made you shiver," Lisbeth said.

But I scarcely heard her.

"Who is it?" I asked breathlessly, though I knew so well—

"It is Hugh's cousin," was her answer. "I forgot to tell you. It is Ralph Gwynne."

PART II.

I HAD been nearly a month at Rumborough and my health was improving slowly. As Doctor Brainard had prophesied, Lisbeth had strengthened my nerves. Her perfect health and spirits roused me as nothing else would have done, and I found myself growing stronger from their force of example. It might be, too, that since I was relieved from my husband's presence a pressure was removed that had been too heavy for me. But, though I was so much better, I was creeping towards the goal of health very slowly, and it seemed that a breath of renewed pain would undo all.

"You do not gain color fast enough," Lisbeth said to me one morning. "You do not get enough of the sea breeze. You must go out with Ralph again to-day, Gervase."

I had often been out with Ralph.

He looked up first at Lisbeth and then at me.

"I am entirely at Mrs. Leith's service," he said, "and I think you are right, Lisbeth; she needs more air." I got up and walked to the window, so that my back was turned to both of them, but Ralph Gwynne followed me and looked out over my shoulder.

Rumborough looked better than usual this morning. An adventurous ghost of sunshine was casting a clear bright light over the brown sands and gray waves, and over the huts and boats and sturdy brown-legged children. It gave to Rumborough in November a pretense of fresh animation that three times as much sunshine could not have been able to give to London. So I carelessly remarked to Ralph Gwynne.

"Is it bright enough to tempt you out—with me?" he said in a low voice.

He knew I was not strong enough to refuse. He had not changed. He was the very Ralph Gwynne who had led me, years before, into a girlish romance that was like a dream of heaven, and had only ended when Fate separated us and put between us and our untold love a whole world. But now it was different. There was more than a whole world between us; there was the past, the present, and the future. I at least had suffered since we bade each other an indefinite farewell—I at least could not love as I had once loved. Sometimes before the very thought of love my whole nature rose up and battled fiercely. At first I think that I was only indifferent; but in the end I fancied that this man understood me a little, and sorrowed a little over the woman's blunder I had made.

"Let us ask no questions of each other," he had said to me once. "We have both suffered. Let us trust each other."

It was just what I needed. I should never have told him what I felt, but I was not sorry that one human soul understood the misery the dragging days held for me. So this morning as we walked along the beach we were both silent. It was our custom to be oftener silent than inclined to speak. We both listened to the moan of the breakers and watched the long line of foam out at sea; and at last both by one accord stopped where a cluster of rocks sheltered us from the wind. I sat down, but Ralph Gwynne remained standing, with his back against a rock and his arms folded. At length he spoke to me.

"It is three years to-day," he said, "since you were married."

The sudden, hurried beating of my heart almost suffocated me. I had forgotten until this moment, and the rush of old memories overpowered me. I remembered the very day—just such a day as this, with sunshine warming even the leaden November sky, and whitening the piled edges of the clouds. I had thought it bright then. I remembered too how the day had closed in as I stood at the window of my new home with Roger's arms folded about me and his heart beating against mine. I could scarcely speak steadily, but I managed to do so at length.

"So long?" I said coldly; "yes, I believe you are right. Where were you? How did you learn it?"

He did not look at me; his eyes were fixed steadily on the far-away white line of foam.

"I was in Calcutta," he answered. "The news had been a long time on its way and reached me on this very day—the day that was to be your wedding-day. I shall not forget it easily."

I dropped my glove, and as I stooped to pick it up a sudden recollection flashed across my brain. One day, three months after our marriage, Roger had come home with a budget of news from Calcutta, and among other things had referred to the intense heat and the prevalence of sunstroke among the foreign inhabitants.

"My informant is one of the travelers for Amboyse & Derig," he said, "and he tells me that the very day he left—the day we were married, Gervase—one of the salesmen was struck down with it. He was talking to one of our clerks who had just arrived from England—talking about our wedding too, Hegblase says—and he saw the young fellow change color and stagger, and in a minute more he fell like a shot. Gwynne his name was, I believe—Ralph Gwynne."

So one man had suffered for me at least—one man's love had not died a natural death in a few brief months.

Ralph put his hand into his pocket and drew forth a letter.

"This was handed to me last night," he said. "It bears a London post-mark."

I did not offer to take it for a moment. I knew he had searched me to the core, that he had seen every fruitless pang and bitter humiliation of the past two years. My letters to my husband had been regularly sent, but his answers had been few and far between, and my pride had forced a fresh sting upon me even while I was otherwise indifferent to the neglect. So I hesitated now, and the next moment Ralph Gwynne came to my side as if drawn there by an uncontrollable impulse. A gleam of light shot over his dark face.

"You do not care to take it," he said. "The very sight of it is a new torture. Let me throw it into the sea, Gervase."

His vehemence actually startled me into self-control. "That would be a new reading of old laws," I said. "No, give it to me."

He submitted without a word. But I did not read the letter. It had come too late for perusal, I said to myself. So I held it in my hand carelessly, making a show of an ease I could not feel.

It was in my hand when we returned and I sat down before the fire in Lisbeth's room. The sea breeze had done me no good this morning. I was tired and worn out, and drooping into a chair before I removed my wrappings, sat silent, resting my chin upon my hand and holding the letter loosely.

Lisbeth came in to find me sitting thus, and at her first glance at me I saw a strange shadow cross her face.

"Tired, Gervase?" she asked.

"Yes," I answered briefly.

She crossed the room to the fire and knelt down, on pretense of brightening the hearth a little with the brush she held in her hand. The next minute she turned her fair, gracious face full upon me.

"And you have not read your husband's letter?" she said. "Why, Gervase?"

"Because I am not going to read it," I replied, and then, ruled by some sudden wretched impulse, I flung it into the fire.

But Lisbeth said nothing. I wondered at the time whether it was possible for her calm, healthful nature to comprehend the morbid misery that possessed me. I fancied not. The broad, even current of her life's affection had swept on undisturbed, bearing on its smooth surface many flowers. She could not understand me and my weak miseries and weaker regrets.

I hid my face in my hands when she left the room, and abandoned myself to thought. I could not explain why it was that during this month at Bamborough I had scarcely once thought of returning to London and my husband. If ever my mind had recurred to the thought, I had shrunk from it with a misery almost intense. I felt that I could not go back now unless, as I had hoped, in a coffin, shut out forever from his sight.

As I sat by the fire I was wondering vaguely how he would meet me if treated thus—whether he would be touched for a moment with some remembrance of those first days of our marriage, when we had at least fancied we loved each other.

Two hot tears falling upon my hand startled me from my reverie just in time to hear Lisbeth coming down stairs with her child in her arms, and singing to it softly. Should we have loved each other better— Roger and I—if my baby had not died,—I asked myself with a pang.

Lisbeth came in and sat down near me again, still singing softly, still holding her baby upon her shoulder as she rocked her chair. O how I envied her her strength and happiness! She was so strong and happy; her handsome baby was so light a burden in her arms; her quietly busy ways so womanly gracious. I looked at her lovely, clear-browed face, and at the coronal of thick light-brown braids across her stately head; I looked at her peaceful eyes, and the soft mouth that seemed made for children's kisses, and, remembering her girlhood, gave the palm to the beauty of her mother life.

Her calm, radiant face struck me to the heart's core. Often during the last year I had told myself that I was only one of the many, that my mistake was only the mistake all women suffer from—the mistake of hoping for a happiness the world cannot hold. But Lisbeth broke down my theory.

I did not write to London again. The correspondence had only been a matter of courtesy at first, and a shadow of neglect could end it.

Ralph Gwynne did not go away, as Lisbeth had told me he intended doing. He had changed his mind, he said. Bamborough agreed with him, and the India house had prolonged his furlough in consideration of his past services and present ill health. He did not look ill, I thought, and I told him so. But he stayed at Bamborough from day to day, and the longer he stayed the more strongly his old power reasserted itself. Not that I loved him. I was past that. Love could not come back to me, but I had loved him once with all the fervor of a girl's romance, and at least he loved me and had not forgotten the past. One tithe of such love as he poured at my feet, in actions that were unspoken words, might have won me back to my husband and peace.

I did not repulse him. The listless wretchedness that ruled me would have prevented that, even if there had not been a faint fascination in the miserable aggrandizement of feeling that at least one man had been true to me, and was true to me yet. I used sometimes to wonder that Lisbeth never guessed at the truth. She rarely spoke to me of my husband—never of Ralph Gwynne —and yet I was always conscious of a restraining influence in her simple presence. A glance from her would check my recklessness. She held me back by a thread when nothing else on earth could have controlled me.

And so the days drifted by, and I strolled upon the sands with my old lover, and sat in the shelter of the rocks with him, and let him say what he would, scarcely listening, as I watched the waves and the incoming and outgoing boats and dipping sea-gulls.

After my husband's letters ceased coming I did not grow better, even slowly. I grew nervous and restless—even more nervous and restless than I had been in London. The old red spot came back upon each cheek, I did not sleep well, and when night came on I often spent hours at my window watching the driving clouds, and listening to the chanting of the fishermen in the late-returning Bamborough boat.

I was sitting thus one night when I heard a low knock at my door, and opened it to find Lisbeth standing there, shawl-wrapped and without a light.

"May I come in, Gervase?" she asked.

I opened the door wider that she might pass.

"Of course," I said; "you know that. What is it, Lisbeth?"

"It is nothing," she answered—"only that I heard you moving and thought I would come and sit with you. Hugh is out."

We both went back to the window, and she knelt down in a girlish fashion of hers, resting an arm upon the window-ledge and turning her fair face up to the night sky and the starlight.

"I hope you are wrapped up well, Gervase," she said after a while.

"I am quite warm enough, thank you."

"You must take care of yourself, you know," she said in her sweet, even voice, "for your husband's sake."

I smiled.

"For my husband's sake," I said, "yes."

"When he wrote to me last," she began, taking no notice of my words.

I started a little.

"When he wrote to you!" I exclaimed. "When did he write to you?"

"Yesterday," she said; "last week, the week before—every week since you have been here. He was afraid you would not speak quite freely of your wants, and he was anxious to hear all about your illness, and to be quite sure that no wish was left ungratified."

I leaned back in my chair, and held to the cushioned arms for support. My breath was coming quickly and a sudden heat had flashed to my face. I could not understand this, but a strange feeling of joy took possession of me—though I told myself that I did not love this man and had never loved him.

"Your illness has been a great anxiety to him, Gervase," Lisbeth went on still, with her face turned upward in the twilight—"and it has troubled him more since you came here. He has felt your absence deeply."

I did not speak in answer, but I was weak woman enough to feel another thrill of mingled pain and pleasure. Lost as the past irrevocably was, it had yet a strong power over me. As there never was a husband colder than mine, so there had never been a bridegroom more impassioned in affection; and, even in this winter of indifference, I could remember days in the dead summer when his untiring love had wakened me to a happiness almost divine, ephemeral as it had proved. Glancing at Lisbeth, the thought struck me that under her quiet speeches and quiet manner there lay a deeper thought for me than I had fancied, and then there flashed across my mind a remembrance of times when she

had silently stood between me and the man who was my evil genius.

At this moment I recognized the man's power for evil over me as I had never done before, and a curious sense of repugnance came upon me with my recollection of something I had sometimes seen sleeping in his quiet persistence. I could not understand the influence that stung me to anger and roused my pride, but I never failed to succumb to it, nevertheless, and it invariably roused me to some fresh rashness of speech or action. But though I said little to Lisbeth, the pang of remembrance softened my heart, and before she left me I had made up my mind to write a few words to my husband, at least; and when she was gone I drew my desk towards me and wrote them—only a few words.

"Your wife Gervase."

I had not ended a letter thus for two years, and I hesitated a moment before I wrote the signature. But despite the lingering of pen over paper they were written at last, and as I looked at them I felt the warm blood beat into my cheeks, and my head drooped upon my clasped hands. Should I send them or not? I thought of Ralph Gwynne, and of what I had suffered, and my letter's fate was almost sealed. But even as I paused, a soft little cry from Lisbeth's room broke upon my ear. It was hushed the next moment, but the tiny voice had turned the scale.

I put the letter into its envelope and sealed it with a new resolution. I would try to retrieve something of the past, at least. I would do no new wrong. I would cherish no bitterness against my dead child's father. If I could not be happy I would endeavor to be patient. It might not be for long—it could not be for long, I knew.

"I will give it to Ralph Gwynne to post in the morning," I said aloud—"it will show him that——"

I did not finish my sentence, because I dared not, even in the silence of my room. Even to the readers of this record I have not told all that my reckless misery drove me to. I could not justify my weakness, and otherwise had better be silent.

The sun was shining bright and warm into the breakfast-room when I went down with my letter in the morning, and the salt sea wind blew fresh through the open window up from the beach. As I had lain awake in the night a change seemed to have come over me, and under its influence I forgot the dull November days and pitiless November skies in this one rare chance of morning warmth and sunlight.

Ralph Gwynne was alone in the room, his stubborn persistency showing itself as it always did in his waiting for my coming.

I went to him at once, holding my letter in my hand.

"I have a letter here I am anxious shall reach London to-night," I said, looking straight into his face. "I thought I would give it into your charge at once, as you generally go into Bamborough earlier than any one else. Will you post it for me?"

He held out his hand and took it from me, slipping it into his vest pocket with scarcely a glance, but I knew that he had seen the superscription by the instantaneous change in his face. It was a very slight change, almost an imperceptible one in fact, but I saw it notwithstanding and caught its meaning.

"I envy your husband," he had said to me once—"I pity him—I hate him."

And just at the moment this abrupt, passionate speech, which was only one of many such, was embodied in the faint change that passed over his dark face, as he leaned upon the window ledge and looked out calmly enough at the fishermen working upon the beach.

He did not even refer to the letter in the commonplace conversation we drifted into. The momentary shadow left him so entirely that I found myself wondering if he had altogether forgotten it. But though he did not refer to the letter, before Lisbeth came in he spoke of my husband.

"I did not know," he said, after an interval of silence—"until yesterday I did not know that your husband had ever visited Bamborough."

The words were so unexpected that I glanced up quickly to see what they might signify, but to judge from his careless, averted face, they might have held no significance at all.

"I did not know," I said coldly, "that my husband had visited Bamborough at all. If he has been here I have been kept in ignorance of the fact."

"He has been here," he said indifferently, "often."

I did not make any reply. I knew well enough that he intended to force me to questioning him, but I was not in the mood , to question, and so was silent. If my husband had been to Bamborough in secret, whatever his motive might be, he had hidden it from me, and the mystery was only a new thread in the web of his distrust, so it might pass. It was only a fresh sting, but I felt it at the time all the more deeply because of my last night's

resolve and the three words with which I had ended my letter. I made no comment, I did not even speak of it to Lisbeth when she came. I buried it in my own heart, as I was prone to bury my miseries.

When breakfast was over I wandered out on the beach alone. I did not often walk alone, but this morning even Lisbeth herself would have been unwelcome.

Down upon the sands where the rocks clustered together, and where the boats oftenest came up to the little cove, was my favorite resting-place, and there I took my seat as usual upon a large flat stone. The brawny fishermen knew me, and the barelegged, shouting children knew me too, and as I sat there there were few who passed me without a good-natured greeting. I had amused myself with watching them often, but they did not amuse me now. I was dull and wretched again. It was a trivial thing to be wretched about, this slight concealment, which might have had no motive, but it had dampened my spirit and made me indifferent and miserable once more. The brown, bare-legged fishermen passed to and fro, mending their nets in the sun, and wading in and out of the water, but I scarcely saw them; the children shouted and chased each other like happy, uncouth young savages, but I did not notice their play. I saw nothing but the sea and sky, and a boat whose tiny sail seemed growing larger as it neared the shore, until a shadow fell before me, and I glanced up half impatiently and saw Ralph Gwynne. He took a seat at my side, and then spoke to me carelessly.

"I thought I should find you here," he said.

"You did not go to Bamborough, then," was my cold comment.

"No," hesitatingly and slowly; "I thought I would see you first."

I looked out at the boat again absently; it was coming nearer to the land, and I felt a faint sort of interest in it, because I saw a woman at the prow, and the woman had a child thrown over her shoulder.

"Why?" I asked.

He did not answer me at first, but turned on his elbow, and spoke to one of the net-mending fishermen who sat not far from us.

"Who is coming in, Gunnle?" he asked; "your women don't fish, do they?"

The man touched his hat good-naturedly.

"Some on 'em does," he said; "this un doent though, this un 'ats comin in. She's bin o'er to Bambro' fur work. It's Janey—Janey an 'th child, little Roger."

I moved impatiently, though I scarcely knew

why. The boat was almost upon the beach, and the next minute the man who was in it jumped out and waded up, dragging it in by its chain with a great splash of the sea water, and then the woman turned her head, and as she got up I saw her distinctly. She was a handsome young creature, tall and straight and shapely, and very unlike the rest of the Hamborough women, with her long violet eyes, and thick curling red brown hair.

"Look at her, Gervase," Ralph Gwynne whispered, "and look at the child."

He had no need to tell me to do so, for I was looking at them both. There was a certain proud, steadfast sadness which attracted my attention in the girl's face, and I could not help noticing that she did not look at any of the bystanders when she replied to their friendly greetings. But as she passed the place where I sat my eye caught hers, perhaps because I had looked at her so steadily, and I observed that the instant she saw me a hot deep color ran up to her forehead, and she walked on hurriedly, holding her child more tightly.

As soon as she was gone Ralph Gwynne turned again to the old fisherman, and spoke to him just as he had spoken before.

"She's a handsome creature," he said, "and the child is handsome too. Who is her husband?"

The old fellow glanced up at me.

"Savin' the lady's presence," he said in a low voice, "she haint got none—Janey haint. We're all sorry for her here. There haint one of us but is sorry for Janey. She never was a bad 'un, but she was handsome an' unfortnit, and she's seen a sight o' trouble. She doent say much to none on us, because she doent like to face us, but she knows we feel friendly to'rds her, Janey does, and she knows we feel friendly to'rds little Roger."

"Roger?" I broke out abruptly, scarcely knowing what I said.

The old man looked up at me, rubbing his weather-beaten forehead as if I puzzled him by my vehemence.

"Yes'm," he said, "his name it's Roger Leith, and its named fur—"

I did not stop to hear the rest. For a moment the whole horrible truth flashed upon me, and I staggered to my feet blindly, clinging to Ralph Gwynne, who had risen too. "Come away," I said; "take me away somewhere—farther down the beach—anywhere out of sight."

He did not speak to me, nor I to him, until he had half carried, half dragged me to the very rock shelter where we had sat the day

he handed me my husband's letter, and there I dropped upon the sands, hiding my wretched face in my hands.

"Tell me the truth," I panted; "tell me—You knew this!"

He looked down at me with some vague pity in his eyes, and though I knew that he would have forged a lie to suit his purpose, I knew that this was no lie, and that he believed it even more steadfastly than I did.

"Yes," he answered, "I knew it."

"And came to prove it to me?"

"Yes."

I knew then what I had never known before. I knew that even in my misery I had mocked myself with a delusion. I knew that I had never loved this man, even as I fancied I did, through the contrast of his warmth with my husband's coldness; I knew that through all I had been weaker than the weakest of women, for I had loved my husband and I loved him still.

I broke into a low, wretched, hysterical laugh.

"You might have spared me this much," I said. "If my ignorance was not bliss, it was folly to be wiser than I was—to know more of my humiliation than I did."

"It would have been folly to let you add to the humiliation by relenting towards the man who has trampled you in the dust," he said passionately. "I swore that you should not send this letter—am I to keep my oath?"

I held out my hand for it.

"No!" I cried out sharply, "give it to me."

He handed it to me, and as I touched it the remembrance of what it contained and how I had been duped rushed upon me with the force of a whirlwind. I tore it into a hundred pieces and scattered it on the sand.

"There," I said, "it is gone—forever."

He came and bent over me, a little later, as I sat with my face buried in my hands, and he touched my shoulder, for I did not look up at him.

"And you will listen to me, Gervase!" he said.

I shook his hand off quickly, for his touch angered me—but I had made up my mind.

"Yes," I answered him, "I will listen."

.   .   .   .

I sat crouched before my window, feeling cold and sick and weak, but still with my mind full of my desperate resolve. I had written my farewell letter to my husband, and it lay upon the table. I had written my

farewell letter to Lisbeth and told her all, in
the faint hope that Lisbeth would believe
what no one else on earth would believe—
in the faint hope that Lisbeth would believe
my solemn word, when I told her that even
at the worst I should not be so utterly lost
as the world would deem me. I had laid
my things all back into my trunks, even to
the merest trifle. The very dress I wore
was one I had myself purchased. I had not
retained in my possession a single thing my
husband had ever given to me—not even the
sapphire ring that had been the pledge of
our betrothal. And now that all my preparations were made. I was waiting at my opened window for the signal that was to come
to me from the beach below. I had thrown
myself adrift on the broad ocean of chance,
and the waves might fling me upon what
shore they would, for the momentary passion of misery had settled into passive despair.

"When women lose all, as I am doing,"
I had said to Ralph Gwynne that night,
"they generally have something at stake,
some love or hope, but I have none; I had
risked all I had to risk, and lost all I had to
lose. You are clinging to a mad hope if you
think to win me even in the course of time.
I tell you I shall never love you. I will
leave England with you, not because I love
you, but because I love my husband and cannot bear to see his face again. I will be
honest with you. I take all to give nothing.
If you love me enough to help me, well and
good; if not, leave me here and I will go out
into the world alone."

And he had held to his purpose and agreed.
Of course he did not believe me strong enough
to battle against his stubborn persistence,
and of course he was false in professing to
be honest; but I knew my own steady strength
of obstinate endurance, and he did not.
And here, in the dim moonlight that streamed
through the curtain of sea fog into my window, I was waiting for his signal, and Lisbeth
was sleeping in the next room with her baby
on her breast and her little children near her.
I thought of the abasement I had seen in the
handsome girl-face a few hours before, and I
thought of the child who had looked at me
over his mother's shoulder in his fearless
baby way.

"Roger's baby—Roger's!"
I hid my face in my hands, stifling the low
cry that burst from me. I remembered the
one moment, on the night of my baby's birth,
when the delirious mists had cleared away
from my brain, and I had seen my husband

bending over the tiny form that lay upon
the white pillow.
"If my baby had lived," I said aloud. "if
my baby had lived I might have been like
Lisbeth."

I got up after this and walked across the
floor and back again a dozen times. I was
wondering what he would say when Lisbeth
gave him the letter, and whether there would
be a shadow of self-reproach in his memory
of the past. I did not ask myself how my
life was to be spent. I had a vague feeling
that it could not last long, but I asked myself a hundred times how my husband would
spend his. He would not mourn for me, I told
myself, and some better woman might make
him happy; but even in this my worst and
most reckless mood, my heart cried out aloud
at the thought. I had ceased pacing the
floor and gone back to the window again.
I had even waited in the chill moonlight an
hour when the signal came, and I rose with a
fierce pulsation of the heart to obey its summons. I took up my shawl from the bed
and folded it around me; I went to the table
where my husband's letter lay and I bent over
and kissed it—my last farewell. I caught a
glimpse of my face in the glass as I did so,
and saw that there was a great hollow purple
ring about my eyes and a deathly pallor on
my cheeks. I laid my husband's letter back
and crossed the room to the door; as I laid
my hand upon the key I heard a light foot-
step in the corridors, and as I turned the
handle and stepped out I started backward
with a low cry, for I stood face to face with—
Lisbeth.

We looked at each other breathlessly for
an instant in dead silence—I at her with
a wild intense, unreasonable longing for some
hope that might rescue me even at this late
hour—she at me with nothing in her tender,
dilated eyes but pity and wonder and love.
Then she broke the strange stillness in a hurried, terrified voice.

"Gervase," she said, "Gervase, what does
this mean?"

I met her gaze steadily. I do not think I
was in my right senses.

"I am going away," I said, and my voice
sounded strange and unnatural even to myself.

Another moment and she caught me in her
arms as if I had been a child, and so drew me
into the room and closed the door.

Her face was white as death. She was woman enough to read at a glance how matters
stood, but her purely healthful nature could
not at once comprehend a recklessness so desperate.

"What do you mean?" she demanded—"I cannot believe—where are you going?"

I answered her as steadily as before.

"I am going away," I said, "where I do not know—I do not even care. I am going away from England with Ralph Gwynne. I am going away with him that I may be lost to my husband forever. You think I am a wicked woman, Lisbeth, and so I am, but God has laid his hand upon me and I am under a curse."

She gazed at me as if she believed I had gone mad indeed.

"You are going away?" she cried out—"You! Gervase! Gervase!"

Nothing more; but the fullness of divine pity and passionate appeal in her voice, in her face, even in her clasped hands, overpowered me. I sank into a chair, holding to its arms to steady myself.

"Lisbeth," I said, feeling as though I had turned to ice, "I saw a woman upon the beach to-day—a woman with a little child in her arms—and the child's name is Roger Leith. You cannot save me, Lisbeth—let me go."

She caught me in her arms and held me. She thought that I was dying—I thought I was, myself, and it was only the sudden flash of comprehension in her face that helped me to retain my consciousness.

"Who told you that the child's name was Roger Leith?" she cried out—"Who could be so cruel as to lead you astray with that? My poor Gervase, tell me!"

I rested my face upon her bosom, panting for breath in the darkness.

"It is true," I gasped; "Ralph Gwynne was with me and he knew. One of the fishermen upon the beach told us the child's name and its mother's history."

"Listen," she said, and her voice rang out like a command, "listen to me. Some one has told you a lie. *I* can tell you the girl's history—no one knows it better than I, Gervase, as no one knows better that the truth should prove to you the wrong you have done your husband. It was not through him that this girl was lost—it was through him that she was saved. He found her in London, wandering in the streets with her child in her arms, and he saved her from despair and death. He brought her here—back to her home—and helped her in her wretchedness so mercifully that she prayed from him upon her knees that her child might bear his name, since it could claim no other. He has guarded her ever since; he has saved two human souls—one for the sake of the little child who died, Gervase—his little child and yours."

In an instant it flashed upon me that I had not waited to hear the end of the fisherman's explanation. And he would doubtless have cleared away my misery with the next word, for they must all know the story, even the roughest of them—the story of my husband's generous deed. And then the thought that I had not been deemed worthy to hear it struck me to the heart.

"I did not dream of this," I said; "how could I? he has told me nothing. He has never loved me even well enough to trust me so far."

"He has loved you always," Lisbeth said, "though you have both been wrong; he has loved you better than you have loved him, and he has been wretched through your distrust and coldness. It was his despair that made him seek me when he brought Janey to Bamborough. He knew that you had loved me, and so came to me for comfort and help. And you would go away—you, with the past all unredeemed, and your husband's love unsought,—you, with your little child's white soul to hold you to purity and faith! Gervase! Gervase!"

There was a moment's silence in which I crouched shuddering in my chair, my face buried in my hands! And then there came beneath the window the sound of a man's footsteps, and the sound of a man speaking in a low voice. His words might have been an echo of Lisbeth's but that the one voice was the voice of the tempter, and the other the voice of the rescuer.

"Gervase! Gervase!"

It was Ralph Gwynne.

My strength was ebbing away fast. I could not have spoken to him if I would; but Lisbeth rose and went to the window, as calm in her womanly strength of purity as ever she had been in her calm woman's life.

"Ralph!" she said, her grave, pure-toned voice dropping upon the still night air like the voice of a spirit, "Ralph, Gervase is here—with *me*."

He did not reply, and not another word was uttered between them. She came back to me as his footsteps died away in the distance, and found me shivering from head to foot, yet burning with sudden fever.

"Better to have let me go, Lisbeth," I said weakly, "better to have let me go away and die, for I should have died, Lisbeth—I am dying now." And as she caught me in her arms again the dark room seemed to blaze up into sudden light and then fade out, and as the shadows closed around me I felt that the end of life had come.

.   .   .   .

Weeks of interminable wanderings in some mysterious, barren land of misery,—weeks of interminable watching hideous panoramas that seemed to pass and repass and pass again,—weeks, nay, it appeared ages, of suffering through old wrongs, and loves and hates,—and weeks of waiting restlessly with frantic impatience for something which never came and never would come—for some stopping-place or shutting out of the crowding faces I did not know and was constantly scanning and striving to remember—weeks of such suffering, with now and then a blank or a dim sense of struggling consciousness, and then one day a long blank ended by my opening my eyes heavily, and dimly seeing Lisbeth bending over the bed upon which I lay.

I did not speak to her—I could not. My weakness was so great, nay power over my languid limbs so utterly lost, that I gazed up at her without even trying to address her, only thinking half unconsciously of stories I had heard of people who had fallen into trances and retained the spirit of life without the power of motion. Was I in such a trance? No, for Lisbeth was speaking to me and I could hear her quite distinctly, though I could not reply.

"You must not try to speak, Gervase," she was saying—"you must not try to think, even. You are getting better and you must sleep."

I heard her first words plainly enough, but as she ended her voice seemed to die away into the distance, and as my eyes drooped she was lost to me.

This was my first awakening after the night I had fallen into her arms, and after this first awakening there were no more of the interminable wanderings, though I seldom was strong enough to open my eyes. But as I lay there with my eyes shut I grew strong enough in a day or two to listen to the hushed voices of the people who were in my room, and in the end to distinguish them one from another. I heard Lisbeth's voice often, calm and low and sweet. I heard Hugh's softened until it was like a woman's. I heard a voice I knew to be the doctor's. I heard other voices strange to me, but first of all and before all I heard my husband's. I did not hear it once or twice, or at stated intervals: day and night without an hour of absence. I felt Lisbeth's touch often: I felt Hugh's. I felt hands that were kindly and tender enough, but there was one hand that never touched me without drawing me farther from the grave and nearer to life, and this hand was my husband's.

And at length I found myself awake again, far into the night, and this time my eyes fell first upon my husband seated at my bedside, and when I made an effort to speak I found strength enough to utter a single word:

"Lisbeth."

He brought her to my side with a gesture, and as he turned towards the light his haggard face was a wonder to me; but I had only power, when Lisbeth bent over me, to say to her one thing, in a whisper so weak that I scarcely could hear it myself.

"If I live," I said, "he must know. If —I die, it—cannot matter. Let him love —me—if he will."

The weak tears began to roll down my checks, and I could not stop their flow, and I saw that Lisbeth's tears were falling too.

"You will not die," she said; "you will live to retrieve the past. He knows all—he read your letter. Roger, speak to her."

He laid his haggard face near mine upon the pillow, and the old glow of our bridal days was in his eyes.

"You shall not die," he said, "you cannot die—you are mine—I love you. I have followed you down to the valley of death, and brought you back, and I claim you, as God is merciful. I have loved you through all our misery, but I was not fit to understand your woman's heart. The blame was mine, not yours. God forgive me for the wrong I did your tenderness. You love me —yes, you love me. You must love me—you cannot help it. Do not try to speak. This shall be my first sacrifice, that I will deny myself the bliss of hearing your voice, since to speak might fatigue you. Do not try to speak, but if you love me and would give me hope, lay your hand upon my cheek."

Not a word of the wrong I had done, not a word of the misery I had wrought for him, not a word of distrust or reproach: I had come up from the grave and the gates of Heaven seemed opening to me. I tried to speak, but could not, for my soul was full and overflowing with the passion of a joy too divine for human words to express. But I found strength at last to move, and stirring a little in the very faintness of happiness, I laid my hand upon my husband's cheek, my head upon his arm, and so was clasped to his breast.

He loved me—he had loved me always, though he had tortured himself with the belief that my love for him had died. He was unlike most men, as I was unlike most women; he could not speak in common words of what lay so deeply locked in his heart. But tortured as he was, he had hoped as I never hoped.

He had come to beseech her comfort because she loved him, and he told you it to him that I knew that I did not know myself, that it was my mistake, and now that was so impenetrable, and under such woman because she wished and testimonial the time I was unconscious of his power.

I did not see Ralph Gaynor again until three happy years had passed, and in passing I

had made my life like Lisbeth's. Then, as I stood one night in the brightly-lighted hall of our home, holding my child in my strong arms, as I greeted my husband a man passed by upon the pavement and looked in at us. As the light from the hall-lamp fell upon his face I saw it was Ralph Gaynor, and that he knew me.

STANZAS FOR MUSIC.

(FROM AN UNFINISHED DRAMA.)

Thou art mine, thou hast given thy word;
　Close, close in my arms thou art clinging;
　Alone for my ear thou art singing
A song which no stranger hath heard:
But afar from me yet, like a bird,
Thy soul, in some region unstirred,
　On its mystical circuit is winging.

Thou art mine, I have made thee mine own;
　Henceforth we are mingled forever:
　But in vain, all in vain, I endeavor—
Though round thee my garlands are thrown,
And thou yieldest thy lips and thy zone—
To master the spell that alone
　My hold on thy being can sever.

Thou art mine, thou hast come unto me!
　But thy soul, when I strive to be near it—
　The innermost fold of thy spirit—
Is as far from my grasp, is as free,
As the stars from the mountain-tops be,
As the pearl in the depths of the sea,
　From the portionless king that would wear it.

A GHOST WHO MADE HIMSELF USEFUL.

"But why should we suppose such things?" cried Lightbourn, impatiently; "what need is there for them? what good do they do—or evil? Did you ever hear of one of these new-born spirits disclosing anything not before revealed, telling you anything you didn't know, doing anything not to be done by ordinary means and common hands? Where is the *proof* that their claims to supernatural importance and consideration have any ground whatsoever? What excuse have the spirits for disturbing us? What can they effect, not reached already? What do they give us as a compensation for the drivel they compel us to put up with? Is it not a pitiful farce, all of it?"

Lovelace gently shrugged his shoulders. "Did you ever hear Madam Philarete lecture?" said he.

"No," quickly answered Bertha; "but I consulted her once—"

"Consulted her!" cried Lightbourn, looking sharply at his wife.

"Why not? She is a fortune teller—bah! She told me my age, less five years of the fact, and my fortune—it was not possible.

Test-medium, she called herself, and—I tested her. A poor pale thing, who was ashamed
to look me in the eyes lest her face should
confess its fraud. Why I could beat her
guessing, myself!"

"Strangely eloquent, on the rostrum," said
Lovelace.

"O yes! a well-written lecture, well
memorized, some skill in the commoner elo-
cutionary tricks, some passion and fervor of
her own, some of that strange fury that is
born in the hearts of most actors when they
come before an audience—it is all easy
enough to understand. But the fact stands,"
added Lightbourn, "that the spirits know
nothing, accomplish nothing, are of no
earthly use, and therefore differ so entirely
from all other created things, that, to my notion, we would have no right to believe in
their existence, even were it brought palpably
to the conviction of our senses."

"They are not like ghosts, these thin and
flimsy spirits," struck in Knox. "Ghosts
are very useful creatures; somewhat strange
and startling in their ways, perhaps, but highly
serviceable, when they choose. I have known
a ghost to save a man's life; and, by the bye,
that same amiable specter was the means of
introducing me to practice, thereby saving
another life, perhaps, for I was half-starved
and had no credit."

"Do tell us about it, Mr. Knox!" cried
Bertha; "I've read ever so many ghost-
stories, but never heard one told in all my
life, and I know you can do it nicely." And
the little lady settled herself in an attitude
for listening.

"Yes," said Knox, jauntily, "I intended
to tell it, and I have the reputation of telling
the best story on our circuit. The judge
always sends for me when he has the gout:
nothing puts him into such prompt and balmy
slumber as one of my tales, he says."

"'William the Trumpeter was a good
waterman!'" quoted Lovelace.

"St!" cried Bertha, lifting a finger, and
Knox began:—

I had only been at the bar a few months,
but they had seemed weary, long ones.
It had taken all my money to furnish my
office and its shelves, and pay the first six
months' rent. Then, I knew that Charlotte
was waiting for me, and, if practice didn't
come soon, my clothes would become intol-
erably shabby. My best coat was very shiny
about the elbows, anyhow, and where the
next one was to come from I could not imagine. In a county court there is always a

little help for juniors, however, and I had
made enough, by battery and larceny cases,
and by collections, to pay for a meager sort
of board. That was all; and you may fancy
how my heart thumped up into my throat
when one day Grandison asked me to assist
him in a murder case! He was our "great
gun" in those days, before politics had made
him so fat and lazy, and was indeed, barring
some small defects of manner, a great lawyer
and a noble-hearted gentleman. "Knox,"
said he to me in his pompous way, as he put
his fat white hands on my shoulder, "you do
not push yourself enough, my young friend.
I have been observing you, and I perceive
you lack the essential quality upon which a
bright forensic career depends. Get impudence, friend Knox; increase your store of
that indispensable attribute of success, or prepare to be written down a failure! How
would you like to aid me in Jake Moore's
case? There—say no more—I see how it is
with you. Come to my office to-night and
talk it over with me."

Jake Moore's case! A real murder, and
the only one that had been committed in our
county for years! The most important case
on the docket: one that would be reported in
all the city papers, too!

"O, I am not such a charitable fellow as
you think," said Grandison, as I began to
thank him at his office that night. "I am
busy, and—lazy. I haven't time to study up
this case, and it needs study, for there's some
mystery about it, or my instincts are at fault.
You have application and ambition, and it is
profitable to us old lawyers to serve ourselves
by means of you youngsters with your keen
eyes. I'll get all the glory of it, and you'll
have the work to do. Fact is, I took the
case for you, and for that murderous rascal's
little girl—curious force of entreaty in her
pathetic wide blue eyes! By the way, will
have to work for a ridiculously small fee—
don't tell anybody—and let's divide. It's the
preliminary process in every partnership case,
as you'll find by and by. Ahem!—there's
half of it." And he pushed fifty dollars across
the table to me.

I did not know, until years after, that this
came out of his own pocket, and that Jake
Moore had not paid him a cent of fee. Few
people know the big heart that beats within
the huge body of our fat and insolent Senator,
after all.

"Never hem nor haw about fees, young
man!" cried he; "it is fatal to yourself and injurious to the whole profession. No good lawyer ought to think himself well paid, no mat-

ter what the fee. Good service ought to be always invaluable. Now, to the case."

And he briefly detailed to me the circumstances under which Jake Moore had been arrested, and the grounds of suspicion against him.

Jake Moore was a shoemaker in the village of Humberg, in the western part of the county,—a worthless, drunken fellow, who worked at his trade about two days in the week, to get money for making himself drunk the other five. He had drifted into the village some dozen years before that, with a slattern, red-haired wife, a puny, sickly baby, a cow, a pig, his tools, and a wagon-load of broken-down household gear. His worthless ways were thought to be his chief fault, for he was a good-natured happy-go-lucky, who did not even beat his wife, indeed, was reputed to be beaten by her. When the Mexican war was about half over, Jake took a halt, a patriotic fever, or an overdose of rum,—it was never rightly known which,—and enlisted, coming back after it was over with a saber-cut on the head and a pension. The wound, or something else, had changed his temper, and while he drank as much as ever, he was sullen, morose, and not talkative, even in his cups. He and his wife quarreled savagely, and when she died, a year or two later, Jake transferred his ill-temper to his daughter, a frail, timid girl, whom he beat sometimes so severely that the neighbors had to interfere.

Such were the antecedents of Jake Moore, when, on the 5th day of August, 1850, the body of the unknown stranger was found in a ravine near the little stream—"Potts' Level," it was called—that flowed through the meadows and woods about a mile to the east of Humberg. It was stiff and cold when discovered by two screaming school-children straggling among the bushes after blackberries—stiff and cold, and frightfully disfigured with a wound across the throat nearly from ear to ear, from which blood had poured so copiously as to stain the body from head to feet, and bespatter bushes, leaves, and grass for several feet around. The alarm soon spread; and the constable, magistrate, doctor, and all the population of Humberg speedily gathered around the unwonted ghastly spectacle. The body was that of a noticeable elderly man, thought to be about fifty-five years old, short and stout, very neatly clad in a suit of sober drab, cut Quaker fashion, and was at once recognized by several persons as the stranger who had been seen in the village a day or two before, a quiet-looking yet well-to-do pedestrian, whose broad-

brimmed gray beaver, and brown gaiters, and respectable cane, had been remarked by all. Broad brim and cane were near by, but the man was dead, and nothing about his person gave any clue to his identity. Who killed him? A shoemaker's knife, bloody on blade and handle, was found in the bushes near by, and identified as Jake Moore's property. The magistrate, acting coroner, issued a search-warrant; Jake was found in his house stupidly drunk, the girl scared and incoherent, and in a drawer in the living-room a pocket-book was discovered containing seventy or eighty dollars; and the stranger was known to have carried one like it, for he had paid for a pound of cheese and some biscuit at one of the stores in the village. Jake was at once committed to jail, his daughter being permitted to go with him, and the coroner's jury rendered a verdict against him of wilful murder of the unknown. Then followed the indictment, and now the trial was to come off, the murdered person, meantime, having been buried without being identified.

"Of course, it will be conviction as the case now stands, and the fellow very likely is guilty," said Grandison; "but it is our business to get him off. I want you to visit Humberg, view the locality, and sift the witnesses. If we can can get a clue to the Quaker we may find that some one else was interested in his end, or at least we may persuade the jury so."

"But the pocket-book," said I,—"isn't that a circumstance which brings the thing right home?"

"O no! The pocket-book may not be positively identified, and, if it should be, is proof of robbery only. It may have been lost, and found by Jake; or Jake may have robbed the man after death; or, in short, the pocket-book proves very little. If Jake could furnish an alibi, there'd be no trouble; but the drunken brute can furnish nothing—says he don't recollect, and don't care—is as good dead as alive."

"What does the girl say?"

"Well—her testimony's worth nothing, and of course she is not any help. She says that the stranger gave her the pocket-book, after asking her for a drink of water—a very likely tale, of course! However, he was seen by several to go into the house."

"I don't see how we are to defend him, Mr. Grandison."

"Neither do I; but if we go about it right we will see, before the case is called. We have a week to prepare in, and a good deal can be done in a week. To-morrow morning we'll have a talk with Jake and the girl; the next day you'll take my horse, ride over to Humberg, and ascertain all the facts. If you find a clue, follow it up regardless of time or money. I've a shot in the locker if there's need, and interest enough with the court to get a postponement should there be any occasion. That's all. Here are some references to authorities which it will be well for you to overhaul between this and the trial. Young lawyers are always expected to spout text-books to the court and jury, you know."

I made little by my visit to the prisoner. He was careless, taciturn, and refused to assist either Grandison or me to a knowledge of the circumstances. "I don't know anything about it—drunk all that week—drunk when they fetched me in here—wish I was drunk now—or dead! It don't matter a wax-end, only for Sally there."

Sally sobbed, wept, wiped her eyes on a dirty apron, and whispered: "He is always that way, since he could not get any whisky. It is no good to talk with him. But he did not kill the strange gentleman—no, indeed!" added she, looking up into my face.

A dirty, puny, unhappy-looking, sallow girl of thirteen was Sally,—yellow hair wild and uncared for, clothes tattered and filthy,—yet what a pleading innocence and convincing frankness in her wide, straightforward eyes.

Grandison beckoned her after him into the corridor. "Now, Sally," said he, "tell this gentleman what you told me."

"Pappy was drinking harder than ever that week; he'd got paid for some work, and his jug was full on Monday. On Wednesday it was empty, and he setting on his bench, savage-like, so that I was afraid of him, half. He didn't sleep none the night before; and Mrs. McCausland wouldn't trust me for the pint he sent me for, you know, and that made him mad. Then it was after dinner, only I had none,—pappy wouldn't eat, and I had only a piece of cold corn-bread for my share,—then the strange gentleman come in——"

"That was Wednesday afternoon?" asked Grandison.

"Yes, sir, Wednesday, after dinner, he came in,—such a nice, neat-looking old gentleman, and stands by the shop counter, and lays his hand on it, and says, 'Friend, will thee let thy little girl fetch me a drink of cool water from thy well?' and pappy, he don't look up, but cusses the strange gentleman, and tells him to git out of there! So the strange gentleman was going to say something more, only I beckoned to him to be

quiet, and he went out; and I took my mug and went out the back door, to the well, and drawed him a drink, and took it round to him, just as he was going through the gate. And he said, 'Thank thee,' and took the mug. And while he was drinking I says to him, 'That's my pappy's shoe-knife you've got in your hand, mister, aint it?' And he says, 'Verily, it is, but I have need for it more than thee, and I pray thee let me keep it.' And I says, 'Pappy'll 'most cut my liver out when he misses it, so you can't have it.' And he says, 'I did not mean to rob thee of it, but to take it at a fair price, and I will give thee the money to buy a dozen like it.' And with that he takes out his pocket-book and studies over the notes like, then says, kinder to himself, 'Nay, her needs seem to be great, and mine are none any longer. Here, child, take and keep it all, and may the Lord bless thee!' And so he walked away, and I didn't see him no more, only heard he was found with his throat cut. But pappy didn't do it, for he kept the house all that day, and raved so all night I couldn't sleep, and early in the morning I took a dollar out of the strange gentleman's purse, and run to Mrs. McCausland's, and got the jug filled for him, and that quieted him; and he was home the same way, drinking and stupid, until Friday night, when Mr. Bent, the constable, came and took him. And that's all I know about it, gentlemen, only that poor pappy hadn't anything to do with killing the strange gentleman!"

It was agreed between Mr. Grandison and me that I should make Sally's straightforward yet very improbable tale the basis of my inquiries at Humberg, and, if I could in any way verify it, I was then to push the search after the old Quaker's antecedents. "But you will fail," said he; "who ever heard of a Quaker committing suicide, much less stealing a knife to do it with!"

"If there is anything to be found out, I will find it," said I, confidently; and the next morning I rode over to Humberg.

This forlorn place was a mere fringe of houses on either side of a turnpike road, at a cross-roads, and did not deserve the name of village. There were first Mrs. McCausland's store, and opposite it, Joline's; on the left again, a couple of dwellings and another store, kept by Yingling; on the right, the house of Bent, the constable; next below, the residence of Stehlmann, coachmaker, and his shop. Still on the right, the next house was the old dismantled tavern, with its broken windows and creaking gibbet of a sign-board;

below that came Dr. Beard's, a long, low house, as shabby as its owner ; next, still on the right, was the house attached to the toll-gate, kept by Holmes ; then, in the middle of the road, at its fork, the weather-beaten log-house occupied by Jake Moore ; on the left of it, the comfortable domicile of Williams, a carpenter ; on the right, the little cottage occupied by Miss Strait, seamstress and gossip. The fork of the road to the left from the turnpike led straight to the stream, Potts' Level, near where the body was discovered.

My inquiries established that, about noon of Wednesday, August 5th,—it was very hot, still, and sultry,—the stranger was first seen, coming down the road, dressed as I have described ; and all who saw him noticed his white cravat, neatly tied, but with the bow a little awry, and almost under the left ear. He went into Mrs. McCausland's, bought cheese, showing the pocket-book that was identified, rested, asked a few questions, then crossed the road to Joline's, where he bought half a pound of biscuit ; from there he went down the road. He gave no name, asked for no person, and no one had ever seen him before. He was seen by persons in Bent's family, by Stehlmann's hands, and by Yingling's clerk, to try the pump at the old tavern, but, it being dry, he could of course get no water. He passed through the toll-gate, and was seen by Beard and his wife, by Holmes, by Miss Strait, by Williams and his wife, and by several others, to open Jake Moore's gate, go in, presently come out again, and turn down the left-hand road. On Friday afternoon, after five, the body was found by two children, coming up the lane on their way home from school. Dr. Beard was convinced, by indubitable signs, that the stranger had been dead not less than forty-eight hours when his body was found. The knife was positively identified ; there were several witnesses to identify the pocket-book ; and Bent, the constable, was satisfied, from the position of the dead man when found, that he could not possibly have inflicted with his own hand the wound of which he died.

The case seemed perfectly made out against Jake Moore. Miss Strait was willing to swear she saw light in his house late that night, and motions of his shadow against the wall, as if of a person washing clothes. Mrs. Williams thought she had seen him, on Thursday evening, coming rapidly from the direction of Potts's Level branch, and looking around him uneasily, as if to see if he were watched. There was apparently a perfect

and inexpugnable harmony in the evidence. I rode on through the village, and a mile or so along the turnpike, pondering the case, and grieving over its hopeless aspects. There was absolutely no chance that I saw, either to save Jake Moore from the gallows, or to gain attention to my own merits as a lawyer. It was a perfectly blank wall, up which climbing was impossible.

" Hallo dere, mein freind !" I looked up to see who called in such a harsh and broken base. It was a German, a tall, broad-shouldered fellow, with a heavy stoop in the back, who stood under the porch of a little tavern by the roadside. He beckoned to me, and I rode up to him.

" Ja !" said he, in his raucous tones, " I see you up dere shoost now, didn't it ?" pointing towards Humberg.

I nodded assent.

" So ! I tink so, den. Lawyer, eh, vrom court ?—coom for Shake Moore's pisness—ah ? So den! I tinks so ! Shump down a leetle, und dake a class bier mit me ; I dells you sometings about um, I tinks ! Ja ! I see um ! I see um ! Mein Himmel, ja ! Heinrich, dake de shentlemench's horse a leetle beet ! Coom, das bier is goot !"

I dismounted, followed my German friend into his little bar-room, and drank a glass of bier with him. He pushed me a cigar over the counter, came out with a couple more glasses of bier, and shouldering me to a chair by a little table in a corner, sat down, and made me do likewise.

" So den !" said he, after giving me a light, " I dells you sometings ! I dink Shake Moore not kill das Quaker. Ja ! I dells Shon 'Pent so, de gonstaple, unt he dells me I vas a pig fool ! Maype I vas, bot I tink Shake Moore not kill das Quaker."

" What do you mean ?" I asked, in great excitement.

" I dells you. I see das mann, mein self. I vas go py de school-house pack from Humperg on de evening, pout dusk vrom mein bruder's, unt ven I goes py te Potts' Lefel pranch I see das mann sit py de fence in de dusk, unt he peckon mit me to go 'vay ; unt I dry to ride close mit him on mein horse, to see vat he vas if I know him, unt vat de matter vas mit him ; unt you tink der fertarnt horse will not coom to him, bot prance, unt go pack, unt schweat, unt drimple, unt dum unt runned avay ; unt ven I goes pack dere mit de horse bimepy, vhat you tink ! das olt mann bin gone ! He vas pale like das wall, unt I tink it vas his own throat he vas cut, not Shake Moore."

"When was that?"

"Vat I dells you, mein friend. It vas Durstay efening."

"Impossible! You mean Wednesday?"

"I means vat I dell you, mein friend. It vas Durstay in de efening! Vensday I vas thrash mein wheat, unt dat Durstay I vas go to mein bruder's to get some butter unt eggs mit him—I vas go to market dot night. I reckon I don't go mit de market on Venstay night, mein friend. Dot is mein pisness, to de market. Ja!"

"Who else saw him on Thursday?"

"I don't know, mein friend! I dells you vat I **saw** unt vat I tink, unt Shake Moore vas not kill das mann, oder I bin der pig fool vat Shon Pent vas call me. Bot I tink dat Mees Straidt, she dell you sometings about dat—she bin on de look out der ten year past, unt see all vat go py! Ja! ja! Unt das Holmes, mit de voodten leg, he dells you sometings, I tink. I pin nicht ein lawyer, mein friend, bot I tinks Shake Moore ish not put das oldt Quaker's light out dis time! Ja!"

In half an hour I was riding back towards Humberg in a very different mood. Observing great caution, I pushed my inquires in every direction, and in the course of two days I had collected a mass of evidence, which, when I had analyzed it and laid it before Mr. Grandison, on my return, surprised that gentleman amazingly, and made him say, as he grasped my hand, "Knox, if you can prove the half of that, our man will be acquitted!"

"I will prove it all, Mr. Grandison," I answered.

When the case of the State *vs.* Jacob M. Moore was called, the next week, it was in the presence of a large and curious audience. For a wonder, both State and prisoner were ready for trial, the witnesses were all present, and a jury was impaneled at once. Jake Moore sat in the box, stolid and impassive as ever, but something improved in looks by a clean shirt and the use of a hair-brush. Sally, by his side, looked like another child. She was washed and combed, and had on a neat new frock and apron which Grandison had bought and the jailer's wife made for her. All the spectators were interested in her, and the hearts of most of them softened towards the prisoner for her sake. The State's officer made a brief statement of the law of murder, spoke of what he should prove, and claimed a verdict of felonious homicide of the highest grade. Then Mr. Grandison arose, and, after accepting the prosecutor's

law, and saying that he would leave the facts to speak for themselves, informed the court that he was suffering from a severe headache, that would prevent him from doing more than passively watching the case; but that he had no scruples about it, since his client's interests were perfectly safe in the hands of his able and ingenious associate, whom he was proud to have as a colaborer, etc. etc.

"Aha!" whispered the State's officer to me; "the old fox knows he has no case, and wants you to take all the odium of a failure."

"We'll see," I returned, oracularly, my face glowing and my heart throbbing with gratitude towards Grandison for his evident intention to let me have all the credit of our singular defense.

The case went on; the facts were proved as I have already told you; and, as witness after witness gave in his statement, without any cross-examination by me, I could see that the District Attorney was beating his brains in a puzzled endeavor to find out the line of defense I meant to adopt. But this was precisely what I did not choose he should do. I asked but very few questions. I made all the witnesses give assurance that it was positively on Wednesday that the stranger had come into Humberg, and had been seen to go into Jake Moore's. I made them assure the jury that the body was found on Friday evening. I carefully and plainly established, by exhaustive questioning of Dr. Beard, that the body, when found, could not have been dead less than two days. I established also, by Mrs. McCausland, that she had refused Jake Moore credit for whisky on Wednesday, and had sold his daughter a gallon for cash, early on Thursday morning. This fact, so damning, had not been elicited by the prosecuting attorney, and when I brought it out plainly, he stared at me full of wonder.

"Which side are you on?" asked he.

"You'll see, presently," retorted I, glancing towards Grandison, who smiled benignant approval.

The case for the State was closed, and I rose to open for the defense.

"May it please your Honor, and Gentlemen of the Jury," I said, "as there are mysteries in nature, no matter on what side you view it, so there are things in evidence which are inexplicable, which it is folly to attempt to explain. We follow no theory of defense in this case; we do not pretend to account for either the facts already adduced, nor for those which we shall adduce. We simply give you those facts, in order, by their own showing, to make it clear that, whether the unknown

was murdered or not, he was not murdered
by the prisoner at the bar, and *could* not
have been murdered by him. I have to re-
quest that the witnesses, both for State and
defense, be removed, in order that all suspicion of collusion may be avoided."

It was so ordered.

"Call Johann Ammermann."

My friend of the lager-bier tavern took the
stand, and made the statement I have already
given. I insisted upon his giving an unmistakable description of the person he had seen
on Thursday evening, and he swore graphically to the white cravat with the bow a little
awry.

"*Thursday?*—he means *Wednesday* evening,
of course,' said the State's attorney, correcting.

"No he don't!" said I; and Ammermann
was splutteringly positive that he knew Wednesday from Thursday.

"But, your Honor," said the State's attorney, "this is palpably a mistake. The murder took place on Wednesday—it *could* not
have taken place later; how then could the
man be seen alive on Thursday? It is an
absurdity!"

"That is our defense!" I said, quietly.
"We cannot prove an alibi for the prisoner,
your Honor; but we *can* show, by his daughter, that he was at home all day and night
Wednesday and Thursday, up to the arrest—"

"Much her testimony is worth!" sneered
the prosecutor.

"And in order to corroborate and strengthen
her testimony, your Honor," I went on, "we
propose to prove an alibi for the deceased.
We propose to prove that he was alive, and
was seen several times, after the time when
you have shown that he *must* have been
dead."

"Absurd!" said the State's attorney.

"Your witnesses must needs be good ones,
Mr. Knox, to show that," said the Judge, sig-
nificantly.

"Wait and hear them, your Honor, if you
please," said Grandison.

"Call John Coan."

Coan, a well known farmer, took the stand.

"Mr. Coan, where were you on Thursday,
August 6th, about 4½ o'clock in the afternoon?"

"At the gate-house, in Humberg, talking
to Holmes."

"How do you know it was that day and
hour?"

"I asked Holmes the time o' day, as for
the date, my cousin was buried that day, and
I was just returning from the funeral—here's

Vol. V.—38

a paper with the notices and dates; she died
on Wednesday, and was buried o' Thursday,
on account of the heat. I can't be wrong."

"Well, while you were talking with Holmes,
what did you see at Jake Moore's gate?"

"I saw a little old Quaker come out, shut
the gate, latch it, stand a minute, then walk
slowly off down the lane towards Potts' Level
branch. He wore a drab sort of suit, a white
broad-brim hat, and his cravat was a white
one, tied up under his ear, like. It was the
same man as was killed, for I saw him on
Saturday morning, during the inquest."

There was a sensation in court.

"Well, what else?"

"Holmes asked me something; I turned
to answer him, and when I looked back the
old man was out of sight. I went on home,
down the lane, and just by the branch, sitting
on the fence, who should I see but the Quaker again? He looked solemn, and mon-
strous pale, and I wondered who he could be.
Over the branch, I looked back, but he
wasn't in sight."

Mr. Coan was severely cross-examined,
but his evidence was not shaken. The
State's attorney looked worried and puzzled.
He could not understand the thing at all, and
seemed to suspect a plot against him. The
spectators were now in a fine state of excitement, and I could see the most intense
interest on the part of the jury.

"Call Rufus Gorsuch."

"Mr. Gorsuch, where were you on *Friday
morning*, early, of August 7th?"

Mr. Gorsuch proved, unmistakably as
Coan, that on Friday morning at 5 o'clock
he was crossing Potts' Level branch, on his
way to a "meet" of fox-hunters, when he
saw the Quaker, whom he most graphically
described, sitting on the fence. "He beckoned to me, and I tried to ride up to him,
but my mare shied and cut up so I couldn't
do it; and when I did get her quiet, the old
chap had got out of sight."

The State's attorney only asked Gorsuch a
question or two; and now, witness after witness, school-children, old people, neighbors
and strangers, to the number of more than a
dozen, came in one after another, and testified to seeing the strange Quaker, at various
intervals from Friday noon back to Thursday
morning; but none had seen him except
upon the fence, pale and beckoning, or else
entering or departing from Jake Moore's door.
The crowded audience was fairly electrified
with excitement and wonder; the jury looked
both puzzled and concerned; and even Jake
Moore, rousing out of his stolid indifference,

showed an eager interest in the testimony. Evidently, he was as much perplexed as any one else. Dr. Beard was recalled; and, when he had carefully repeated his testimony, a distinguished surgical expert told us that, upon that showing, it was impossible for death to have taken place so late as Friday morning or Thursday evening.

I glanced at Grandison. He cast a searching eye towards the jury, then nodded his head.

"Call Sarah Moore."

And Sally took the stand, and, in her plain, simple, quiet, unreserved way, told the same story she had told before, softening the recital of her father's faults, and giving emphasis to the interview with the Quaker. Every word of her narrative told; and I saw that all the jury believed it, where none of them would have placed the slightest faith in it had it not been prefaced by the mysterious confusion in the testimony.

"Do you want to argue it?" asked the State's attorney. "I'll submit it if you say so, for I can't make out a Chinese puzzle."

"I've only a word to say," I said, glancing at a line which was tossed to me by Grandison as I rose. ("Give 'em the supernatural,—all juries believe in ghosts,—and this judge does," was the skeptic's admonition.)

"I have only a word to say, gentlemen. As I warned you in advance, the evidence on both sides can neither be controverted nor reconciled. There is a doubt as to the murder; a certainty that it was not committed by Jacob Moore. You cannot doubt that little girl's frank blue eyes and untripping tongue. I told you the defense had no theory as to this case; but I, as an individual, have a theory. I believe that the unknown deceased went to Jacob Moore's and took that knife, as represented, with the purpose of committing suicide. I believe that he walked to that dreadful ravine, on that Wednesday afternoon, and there and then cut his own throat, and died, and his body rested there until it was found as you have heard. I believe, nevertheless, gentlemen of the jury, and I know that in your secret hearts you believe with me, that the dead man, in his living image, either that or his specter, or a shape assuming that image, appeared as has been testified by the various witnesses. Why, gentlemen of the jury? Why should that unquiet ghost have returned from the regions to which it had just now fled in despair?"

"He came back to fix it on Jake Moore, I guess," said the prosecutor, laughing.

"Ah, gentlemen of the jury," I said, "we may not go beyond the grave in search of motives—it boots us little to vex the inscrutable with our questions, but that, at least, did not bring the unhappy specter back. Jake Moore was already convicted, by the knife and the purse, before that shade came back. May we not rather assume"—I put it timidly —"that, in the new-born prescience of another existence, it was seen that by taking the knife and leaving the purse an innocent man's life was put in peril? May not the dead man's spirit have dragged itself wearily back to the world of troubles, not to convict, but to acquit; not for vengeance, but in mercy and justice; not to follow up a criminal, but to save the hunted life of the innocent and unfortunate man before you? Gentlemen of the jury, ask yourselves that question, and bid your own hearts furnish the answer!"

Well, Jake Moore was acquitted, of course. The jury declined even to leave their seats. When the applause that welcomed the verdict had ceased, Mr. Grandison arose and said: "May it please your Honor, while I should be sorry to see the evidence of ghosts taken often, in this or any other court, against the evidence of hard facts, I am happy in being able to show, in the most satisfactory manner, that the conclusion to which the jury has come, in the present instance, is the right one. Since we have been sitting here, I have seen an officer from Canada, who has given me the history of the unfortunate deceased. He was a member of the Society of Friends, a person of consequence and property, Philip Dingle by name, and a most amiable gentleman, but, unhappily, subject to occasional attacks of mental aberration. It was in one of these fits he wandered off and destroyed his own life in the manner described to you. That he himself committed the deed we know from a letter written by himself, in the neighboring city, and there mailed a day or two previous to his appearance in Humberg, in which he avows his intention in unmistakable language. That letter was sent to his nephew and heir, living in Australia, and it has been the means of tracing up Mr. Dingle and establishing his identity in an undoubted way. I knew these facts before the case was given to the jury, may it please the Court," concluded Mr. Grandison; "but I was confident the prisoner would be acquitted, and I had not the impudence to interrupt the brilliant and ingenious defense contrived by my young associate, who, as I need not say to your Honor, has this day shown himself an ornament and a light to our profession."

"Well, the ghost was of no use, after all," said Lightbourn ; "the man would have been acquitted without his interposition."

"But how could I have got into practice without his invaluable aid?" rejoined Knox.

"What became of Moore and little Sally?" asked Bertha.

"Moore never drank a drop afterwards ; it was enough to be warned by a ghost, he said ; and he is now an owner of some land, and doing well. Sally is a buxom farmer's wife, with a houseful of children. I see her often."

"There !" cried Bertha, "say the ghost did no good! But for him, Jake Moore would have died a drunkard ! I believe in ghosts myself !"

PROFESSOR MORSE AND THE TELEGRAPH.

SAMUEL F. B. MORSE.

In the year 1811, Benjamin West, the President of the Royal Academy of Fine Arts, and then past seventy years of age, was enjoying the noontide splendor of his fame as the great historical painter of England.' During his presidency the Academy had a high reputation, for he was an eminent instructor, and young men from many lands went to it to learn wisdom in Art.

On a bright autumnal morning in the year just mentioned, West's beloved American friend, Washington Allston, entered the reception-room of the venerable painter, and presented to him a slender, handsome young man, whose honest expression of countenance, rich brown hair, dark magnetic eyes and courtesy of manner, made a most favorable impression upon the president. This young man was SAMUEL FINLEY BREESE MORSE. He was then little more than nineteen years of age, and a recent graduate of Yale College. He was the eldest son of Rev. Jedediah Morse, an eminent New England divine and geographer. Rev. Samuel Finley,

D.D., the second president of the College of New Jersey at Princeton, was his maternal great-grandfather, from whom he inherited the first portion of his name. Breese was the maiden name of his mother.

At a very early age young Morse showed tokens of taste and genius for art. At fifteen he made his first composition. It was a good picture, in water colors, of a room in his father's house, with the family—his parents, himself and two brothers—around a table. That pleasing picture hangs in his late home in New York, by the side of his last painting. From that period he desired to become a professional artist, and that desire haunted him all through his collegiate life. In February, 1811, when he was nearly nineteen years of age, he painted a picture (now in the office of the Mayor of Charlestown, Mass,) called "The Landing of the Pilgrims at Plymouth," which, with a landscape painted at about the same time, decided his father, by the advice of Stuart and Allston, to permit him to visit Europe with the latter artist. He bore to England letters to West, also to Copley, then old and feeble. From both he received the kindest attention and encouragement.

Morse made a carefully-finished drawing from a small cast of the Farnese Hercules, as a test of his fitness for a place as a student in the Royal Academy. With this he went to West, who examined the drawing carefully, and handed it back saying, "Very well, sir, very well; go on and finish it." "It is finished," said the expectant student. "O, no," said the president. "Look here, and here, and here," pointing out many unfinished places which had escaped the undisciplined eye of the young artist. Morse quickly observed the defects, spent a week in further perfecting his drawing, and then took it to West, with confidence that it was above criticism. The president bestowed more praise than before, and with a pleasant smile handed it back to Morse, saying, "Very well indeed, sir; go on and finish it."—"Is it not finished?" inquired the almost discouraged student. "See," said West, "you have not marked that muscle, nor the articulation of the finger-joints." Three days more were spent upon the drawing, when it was taken back to the implacable critic. "Very clever indeed," said West, "very clever; now go on and finish it."—"I cannot finish it," Morse replied, when the old man, patting him on the shoulder, said, "Well, well, I've tried you long enough. Now, sir, you've learned more by this drawing than you would have accomplished in double the time by a

dozen half-finished beginnings. It is not numerous drawings, but the character of one, which makes the thorough draughtsman. Finish one picture, sir, and you are a painter."

Morse heeded the sound advice. He studied with Allston and observed his processes; and from the lips of West he heard the most salutary maxims. Encouraged by both, as well as by the veteran Copley, he began to paint a large picture for exhibition in the Royal Academy, choosing for his subject "The Dying Hercules." Following the practice of Allston (who was then painting his celebrated picture of "The Dead Man restored to Life by touching the Bones of Elijah"), he modeled his figure in clay, as the best of the old painters did. It was his first attempt in the sculptor's art and was successful. A cast was made in plaster of Paris and taken to West, who was delighted. He made many exclamations of surprise and satisfaction; and calling to him his son Raphael, he pointed to the figure and said: "Look there, sir, I have always told you that any painter can make a sculptor."

This model contended for the prize of a gold medal offered by the Society of Arts for the best original cast of a single figure, and won it. In the large room of the Adelphi, in the presence of British nobility, foreign ambassadors and distinguished strangers, the duke of Norfolk publicly presented the medal to Morse, on the 13th of May, 1813. At the same time his colossal painting, made from this model, then on exhibition in the Royal Academy, was receiving unbounded praise from the critics, who placed "The Dying Hercules" among the first twelve pictures in a collection of almost two thousand. So began, upon a firm foundation, the real art-life of this New England student.

Encouraged by this success, Morse determined to contend for the highest premium offered by the Royal Academy for the best historical composition, the decision to be made late in 1815. For that purpose he produced his "Judgment of Jupiter," in July of that year. West assured him that it would take the prize, but Morse was unable to comply with the rules of the Academy, which required the victor to receive the medal and money in person. His father had summoned him home, and filial love was stronger than the persuasions of ambition. West and Fuseli both urged the Academy to make an exception in his case, but it could not be done, and the young painter had to be contented with the assurance of the President afterwards, that he would certainly have won the prize (a gold medal and $250 in gold) had he remained.

West was always specially kind to those who came from the land of his birth. Morse was such a favorite with him, that while others were excluded from his painting-room at certain times, he was always admitted. West was then painting his great picture of "Christ Rejected." One day, after carefully examining Morse's hands, and observing their beauty and perfection, he said, "Let me tie you with this cord and take that place while I paint in the hands of the Saviour." It was done, and when he released the young artist, West said to him, "You may now say, if you please, that you had a hand in this picture."

Fuseli, Northcote, Turner, Sir Thomas Lawrence, Flaxman, and other eminent artists; and Coleridge, Wordsworth, Rogers, Crabbe, and other distinguished literary men, became fond of young Morse, for with an uncommonly quick intellect he united all the graces of pleasant manners and great warmth and kindliness of heart, which charmed the colder Englishmen. And when in August, 1815, he packed his fine picture, "The Judgment of Jupiter," and others, and sailed for his native land, he bore with him the cordial good wishes of some of the best men in England.

When Morse reached Boston, he found that his fame had gone before him, and the best society of that city welcomed him. Cards of invitation to dinner and evening parties were almost daily sent to him. He was only in the twenty-fourth year of his age, and was already famous and bore the seal of highest commendation from the President of the Royal Academy. With such prestige he set up his easel with high hopes and the fairest promises for the future which were doomed to speedy decay and disappointment. The taste of his countrymen had not risen to the appreciation of historical pictures. His fine original compositions and his excellent copies of those of others (among them one from Tintoretto's marvelous picture of "The Miracle of the Slave"), which hung upon the walls of his studio in Boston, excited the admiration of cultivated people; but not an order was given for a picture, nor even an inquiry concerning the prices of those on view.

Disappointed, but not disheartened, Mr. Morse left Boston, almost penniless, and in Concord, N. H., commenced the business of a portrait-painter, in which he found constant employment at $15 a subject, cabinet size. There he became acquainted with a Southern gentleman, who assured him that he might find continual employment in the South at four fold higher prices for his labor. He appealed to his uncle, Dr. Finley of Charleston, for advice, who cordially invited him to come as his visitor and make a trial. He went, leaving behind in Concord a young maiden to whom he was affianced, promising to return and marry her when better fortune should reward his labors. That better fortune soon appeared. Orders for portraits came in so thickly (one hundred and fifty, at $60 each) that he painted four a week during the winter and spring. In the early summer time of 1818, he returned to New England with $3,000 in his pocket, and on the 6th of October following his friends read this notice in the *New Hampshire Patriot*, published at Concord:—

"MARRIED, in this town, by Rev. Dr. McFarland, Mr. Samuel F. B. Morse (the celebrated painter) to Miss Lucretia Walker, daughter of Charles Walker, Esq."

Four successive winters Mr. Morse painted in Charleston, and then settled his little family with his parents, in a quiet home in New Haven, and again proceeded to try his fortune as an historical painter, by the production of an exhibition-picture of the House of Representatives at the National Capital. It was an excellent work of art, but as a business speculation it was disastrous, sinking several hundred dollars of the artist's money and wasting nearly eighteen months of precious time. No American had taste enough to buy it, and it was finally sold to a gentleman from England.

Morse now sought employment in the rapidly-growing commercial city of New York. Through the influence of Mr. Isaac Lawrence he obtained the commission, from the corporate authorities of that city, to paint a full-length portrait of Lafayette, then in this country. He had just completed his study from life, in Washington city, in February, 1825, when a black shadow was suddenly cast across his hitherto sunny life-path. A letter told him of the death of his wife. There is a popular saying that "misfortunes seldom come single." The popular belief in the saying was justified in Mr. Morse's case, for in the space of a little more than a year death deprived him of his wife and his father and mother. Thenceforward his children and art absorbed his earthly affections, and he sought in a closer intimacy with artists the best consolations of social life. By that intimacy he was soon called upon to be the valiant and efficient champion of his professional brethren in a bitter controversy between two associations, in this wise :—

The American Academy of Fine Arts, then under the presidency of Colonel John Trumbull, was in a languishing state, badly managed and of little use to artists. Indeed, the artists complained of ill usage by the directors, a majority of whom were not of the profession ; and Thomas S. Cummings, a spirited young student with Henry Inman, drew up a remonstrance and a petition for relief. Morse took a great interest in the matter, and called a few of the artists together at his rooms to discuss it. At that meeting he proposed as a remedy for the fatal disease of which the old Academy was dying, the formation of a society of artists for improvement in drawing. This was done in November, 1825, at a meeting held in the rooms of the New York Historical Society, at which the now venerable Asher B. Durand presided. The new organization was named "The New York Drawing Association." Mr. Morse was chosen to be its president. Its members were immediately claimed to be students of the Academy, and Colonel Trumbull endeavored to compel their allegiance. The artists were aroused, and the subsequent action of the Academy determined them to cut loose from all connection with it.

At a meeting of the Drawing Association in the following January, Mr. Morse, after a short address, proposed by resolutions the founding of an association of artists, far wider in its scope than the one over which he presided. He foreshadowed in a few words its character. The resolutions were adopted, and on the 18th of January, 1826, the new association was organized under the name of THE NATIONAL ACADEMY OF DESIGN. Mr. Morse was chosen to be its president, and for sixteen successive years he was annually elected to that office. Mr. Durand and General Thomas S. Cummings (the latter for forty years the treasurer of the new association) are the only survivors of the founders of that now flourishing institution.

The friends of the old Academy were very wrathful, and assailed the new association with unstinted bitterness, in which personalities were indulged. A war of words in the public press was carried on for a long time, which Mr. Morse, as the champion of the new society, waged with the vigorous and efficient weapons of candor, courtesy, and dignified, keen and lucid statements and arguments, which finally achieved a complete victory. *

Mr. Morse inaugurated a new era in the history of the fine arts in this country, by calling public attention to their usefulness and necessity, in a series of lectures on the subject before the New York Athenæum, to crowded audiences. These were repeated before the students and academicians of the National Academy of Design.

In 1829 Mr. Morse made a second professional visit to Europe. He was warmly welcomed and duly honored by the Royal Academy in London. West had been dead nine years, and Fuseli was no more ; but he found an admirer in Sir Thomas Lawrence, West's successor, and many friends among the younger academicians. During more than three years he made his abode in various continental cities. In Paris he studied in the Louvre, and there he made an exhibition picture of the famous gallery, with beautiful miniature copies of about fifty of the finest works in that collection. It failed as a speculation, and finally went to Hyde Hall, the seat of Mr. George Clarke, on Otsego Lake.

In November, 1832, Mr. Morse landed in New York, enriched by his transatlantic experience and full of the promise of attaining to the highest excellence in his profession. Allston, writing to Dunlap in 1834, said : "I rejoice to hear your report of Morse's advance in his art. I know *what is in him,* perhaps, better than any one else. If he will only bring out all that is *there,* he will show powers that many now do not dream of."

A higher revelation than art had even given it was now vouchsafed to the mind of Morse through Science, its sister and coadjutor. For several years his thoughts had been busy with that subtle principle, by whatever name it may be called, which seems to pervade the universe, and "spreads undivided, operates unspent." The lectures on electro-magnetism by his intimate friend, J. Freeman Dana, at the Athenæum, while he (Morse) was giving his course there on the Fine Arts, had greatly interested him in the subject, and he learned much in familiar conversations with Mr. Dana. Even at that early day, Dana's spiral volute coil suggested to Morse the electro-magnet used in his recording instruments.

While on his second visit to Europe, Mr. Morse made himself acquainted with the labors of scientific men in endeavors to com-

---

* A record of this controversy, with the newspaper articles of the combatants, may be found in that rare and valuable work, *Historic Annals of the National Academy of Design,* by Professor Thomas S. Cummings, N. A.

municate intelligence between far distant places out of the line of vision by means of electro-magnetism, and he saw an electromagnetic *semaphore* in operation. He was aware that so early as 1649, Strada, a Jesuit priest, had in fable prophesied* of an electric telegraph; and that for half a century or more, philosophers had been, from time to time, partially succeeding in the discovery of the anxiously-looked for result. But no *telegraph* proper—no instrument *for writing at a distance* —had yet been invented.*

In the ship *Sully*, in which Mr. Morse voyaged from Havre to New York in the autumn of 1832, the recent discovery in France of the means for obtaining the electric spark from a magnet was a fruitful topic of conversation among the cultivated passengers; and it was during that voyage that a revelation was made to the mind of Morse, which enabled him to conceive the idea of an electro-magnetic and chemical *recording* telegraph, substantially and essentially as it now exists. Before the *Sully* had reached New York, he had elaborated his conceptions in the form of drawings and specifications, which he exhibited to his fellow-passengers. This fact, proven by the testimony of those passengers given in a court of justice, fixes the date of the invention of Morse's electro-magnetic recording telegraph at the autumn of 1832.

Circumstances delayed the construction of a complete recording telegraph by Mr. Morse, and the subject slumbered in his mind. During his absence abroad he had been elected to the professorship of the Literature of the Arts of Design in the University of the City of New York, and this field of duty oc-

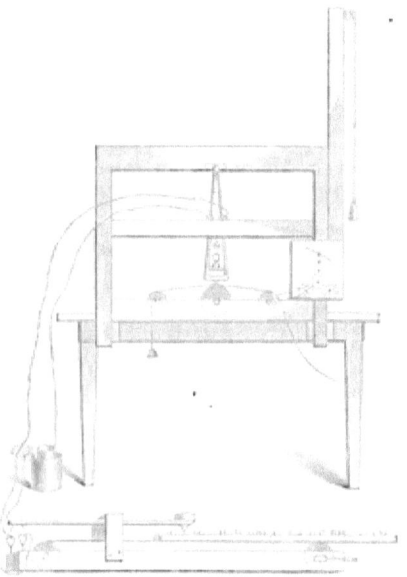

MORSE'S FIRST RECORDING TELEGRAPH.

cupied his attention for some time. Finally, in November, 1835, he completed a rude telegraphic instrument—the first recording apparatus—which is now in the library of his country-seat near Poughkeepsie. It embodied the mechanical principles of those now in use in every quarter of the globe. But his whole plan was not completed until July, 1837, when, by means of two instruments, he was able to communicate from as well as to a distant point. In September, hundreds of people saw it in operation at the University, the larger portion of whom looked upon it as a scientific toy constructed by an unfortunate dreamer.

In the following year Mr. Morse's invention was sufficiently perfected to induce him to call the attention of the National Congress to it, and ask their aid in the construction of an experimental line between the cities of Washington and Baltimore. Late in the long session of 1838, he appeared before that body with his instrument. Before leaving New York with it he invited a few friends to see it work. The written invitation ran thus, —I copy one now before me:

"Professor Morse requests the honor of Thomas S. Cummings, Esq., and family's company in the Geolo-

* In 1774, Le Sage constructed an electric semaphore with twenty-four wires corresponding to the 24 letters of the alphabet. In 1793, Claude Chappé established an aërial line of electric semaphores. From 1780 to 1800, German, Italian, and Spanish philosophers made interesting experiments in this direction. In 1810 Schweiger discovered the multiplying power of the magnet by an electric coil, and in 1819 Oersted perfected the discovery of electro-magnetism. Ronalds constructed an electric semaphore, which made signals at a distance of eight miles, in 1816. In 1825 Sturgeon invented the electro-magnet. In 1830 Professor Henry applied Schweiger's coil to Sturgeon's magnet, and wonderfully increased the magnetic force which Morse subsequently used. Arago, Faraday, Ampère, Gauss and Weber, and Steinheil had made many valuable advances towards the great discovery, and Wheatstone very nearly reached it.

gical Cabinet of the University, Washington Square, to witness the operation of the electro-magnetic telegraph, at a private exhibition of it to a few friends, previous to its leaving the city for Washington.

"The apparatus will be prepared at precisely 12 o'clock, on Wednesday, 24th instant. The time being limited, punctuality is specially requested.

"NEW YORK UNIVERSITY, *June 22, 1838.*"

One of the first messages on that wire was given to Mr. Cummings (yet in his possession) in these words : " Attention the Universe—By Kingdoms, right wheel—Facetiously." It may be explained by the fact that Mr. Cummings had just received military promotion to the command of a division. It is probably the first message by the recording telegraph now extant, and how prophetic!

Professor Morse found very little encouragement at Washington, and he went to Europe with the hope of drawing the attention of foreign governments to the advantages, and securing patents for the invention, having already filed a caveat at the patent office of his own country. His mission was a failure. England refused to grand him a patent, and France gave him only a useless *brevet d'invention*, which did not secure for him any special privilege. So he returned home, disappointed but not discouraged, and waited

patiently four years longer, before he again attempted to interest Congress in his invention.

The year before he went to Europe, Professor Morse suffered a severe disappointment in the way of his profession. He was an unsuccessful applicant for a commission to paint one of the pictures for the eight panels in the Rotunda of the national Capitol, which a law of Congress had authorized.

Morse was greatly disappointed. His artist friends showed their sympathy in the practical way of giving him an order to paint a historical picture, raising funds for the payment for it in shares of $50 each. The first intimation the Professor had of their generous design, was when two of his professional brethren called upon him and gave the order, and at the same time informed him that $3,000 had already been subscribed. " Never have I read or known of such an act of professional generosity," exclaimed Morse. He agreed to paint for them the picture he had projected for the Government—" The Signing of the First Compact on board the Mayflower "—and addressed himself to the task. But the telegraph soon absorbed his attention, and so won him from painting that he

almost abandoned its practice. In 1841 he returned to the subscribers the amount in full, with interest, which had been paid to him, and so canceled the obligation. "Thus," wrote General Cummings, " while the world won a belt of instantaneous communication, the subscribers lost the pleasure of his triumph as an artist. The artist was absorbed in the electrician."

While Professor Morse was in Paris, in the spring of 1839, he formed an acquaintance with M. Daguerre, who, in connection with M. Niepce, had discovered the method of fixing the image of the camera obscura, which was then creating a great sensation among scientific men. These gentlemen were then considering a proposition from the French government to make their discovery public, on condition of their receiving a suitable pension. Professor Morse was anxious to see the photographic results before leaving for home, and the American Consul (Robert Walsh) made arrangements for an interview between the two discoverers. The inventions of each were shown to the other ; and Daguerre promised to

W   h   a   t

This sentence was written from Washington by me at the Baltimore Terminus at 8.h 45 min. A.M. on Friday, May 24th 1844, being the first ever transmitted from Washington to Baltimore, by Telegraph and was indited by my much loved friend Annie G. Ellsworth.

Saml. F. B. Morse. Superintendent of Elec. Mag. Telegraphs.

send to Morse a copy of the descriptive publication which he intended to make so soon as the pension should be secured. Daguerre kept his promise, and Morse was probably the first recipient of the pamphlet in this country. From the drawings it contained he constructed the first daguerreotype apparatus made in the United States.

From a back window in the New York University Professor Morse obtained a good representation of the tower of the Church of the Messiah, on Broadway, and surrounding buildings, which possesses a historical interest as being the first photograph ever taken in America. It was on a plate the size of a playing card. He experimented with Professor J. W. Draper in a studio built upon the roof of the University, and succeeded in taking likenesses from the living human face. His subjects were compelled to sit fifteen minutes in the bright sunlight, with the eyes closed, of course. Professor Draper shortened the process, and was the first to take portraits with the eyes open. Some of the original plates so photographed upon by Professor

Morse were presented by him to Vassar College, of which he was a trustee.

On the preceding page will be seen an engraving of part of one of these plates (which originally contained three figures), in which the costumes almost mark the era of its production.

Again Professor Morse appeared before Congress with his telegraph. It was at the session of 1842–3. On the 21st of February, 1843, the late John P. Kennedy of Maryland moved that a bill in committee, appropriating $30,000 to be expended, under the direction of the Secretary of the Treasury, in a series of experiments for testing the merits of the telegraph, should be considered. It met with ridicule from the outset. Cave Johnson of Tennessee moved as an amendment, that one-half the sum should be given to a lecturer on Mesmerism, then in Washington, for trying mesmeric experiments under the direction of the Secretary of the Treasury. Mr. Houston thought Millerism ought to be included in the benefits of the appropriation. After the indulgence of much cheap wit,

h   *a*   *t*   *h*

Mr. S. Mason of Ohio protested against such frivolity as injurious to the character of the House, and asked the chair to rule the amendment out of order. The chair (John White of Kentucky) ruled the amendment in order, because, as he said, "it would require a scientific analysis to determine how far the magnetism of Mesmerism was analogous to that to be employed in telegraphs." His wit was applauded by peals of laughter, when the amendment was voted down and the bill laid aside to be reported. It passed the House on the 23d of February, by the close vote of 89 to 83, and then went to the Senate. The efficient friends of Professor Morse in procuring this result were J. P. Kennedy of Maryland, S. Mason of Ohio, David Wallace of Indiana, C. G. Ferris of New York, and Colonel J. B. Aycrigg of New Jersey.

The bill met with neither sneers nor opposition in the Senate, but the business of that House went on with discouraging slowness. At twilight on the last evening of the session (March 3, 1843) there were 119 bills before it. As it seemed impossible for it to be reached in regular course before the hour of adjournment should arrive, the Professor, who had anxiously watched the tardy movements of business all day from the gallery of the Senate chamber, went with a sad heart to his hotel and prepared to leave for New York at an early hour the next morning. While at breakfast, a servant informed him that a young lady desired to see him in the parlor.

There he met Miss Annie Ellsworth, then a young school girl — the daughter of his intimate friend, Hon. Henry L. Ellsworth, the first Commissioner of Patents — who said, as she extended her hand to him : " I have come to congratulate you."

" Upon what ? " inquired the Professor.

" Upon the passage of your bill," she replied.

" Impossible ! Its fate was sealed at dusk last evening. You must be mistaken."

" Not at all," she responded. " Father sent me to tell you that your bill was passed. He remained until the session closed, and yours was the last bill but one acted upon, and it was passed just five minutes before the adjournment ; and I am so glad to be the first one to tell you. Mother says, too, that you must come home with me to breakfast."

The invitation was readily accepted, and the joy in the household was unbounded. Both Mr. and Mrs. Ellsworth had fully believed in the project, and the former, in his confidence in it and in his warm friendship for Prof. Morse, had spent all the closing hours of the session in the Senate chamber, doing what he could to help the bill along, and giving it all the influence of his high personal and official position.

Grasping the hand of his young friend, the Professor thanked her again and again for bearing him such pleasant tidings, and assured her that she should send over the wires the first message, as her reward. The matter was talked over in the family, and Mrs. Ellsworth suggested a message which Prof. Morse referred to the daughter, for her approval ; and this was the one which was subsequently sent.

A little more than a year after that time, the line between Washington and Baltimore was completed. Prof. Morse was in the former city, and Mr. Alfred Vail, his assistant, in the latter ; the first in the chamber of the Supreme Court, the last in the Mount Clare dépôt, when the circuit being perfect, Prof. Morse sent to Miss Ellsworth for her message, and it came.

" WHAT HATH GOD WROUGHT ! "

It was sent in triplicate in the dot-and-line language of the instrument to Baltimore, and was the *first message ever transmitted by a recording telegraph.* A fac-simile of that first message, with Professor Morse's indorsement, is here given.

The story of this first message has been often told with many exaggerations. It has roamed about Europe with various romantic material attached to it, originating mainly in the French imagination, and has started up anew from time to time in our own country under fresh forms, but the above story is simply and literally true. An inventor in despair receives the news of his unexpected success from his friend's daughter, and he makes her a promise which he keeps, and

thus links her name with his own, and with an invention which becomes one of the controlling instruments of civilization for all time.

The first public messages sent were a notice to Silas Wright, in Washington, of his nomination for the office of Vice-President of the United States by the Democratic Convention, then (May, 1844) in session in Baltimore, and his response declining it. Hon. Hendrick B. Wright, in a letter to the author of this sketch, says: "As the presiding officer of the body, I read the despatch; but so incredulous were the members as to the authority of the evidence before them, that the Convention adjourned over to the following day, to await the report of a committee sent over to Washington to get *reliable* information upon the subject."

Such were the circumstances attending the birth of the Electro-Magnetic Recording Telegraph. The ingenuity of man had fashioned a body for it; but there it lay, with all its perfections undreamed of, excepting by a few prophetic philosophers,—its mighty powers all unknown,—almost as lifeless and useless as a rock in the wilderness, until Morse, divinely inspired, as he always believed, endowed it with intelligence. The poet said concerning the discoveries of Newton, which dispelled so much of the darkness which hung around the truths of science:

"God said, Let Newton live, and all was light."

With equal truth may Morse be ranked among the creative agencies of God upon the earth.

The infant of his conception, so ridiculed and distrusted, immediately gave signs of its divinity. The doubters were soon ready to bring garlanded bulls to sacrifice to it as a god; and a prophet wrote:

"What more, presumptuous mortals, will you have?
Sir Franklin seize the Clouds, their bolts to bury;
The Sun resigns his pencil to Daguerre,
And Morse the lightning makes his secretary?"

He stood before the world as the peer of Kings and Emperors, for the application of his thought to exquisite mechanism revolutionized the world. And kings and emperors soon delighted to pay homage to his genius by substantial tokens.

The Sultan of Turkey was the first monarch who recognized Professor Morse as a public benefactor, by bestowing upon him the decoration of the *Nishan Iftichar*, or *Order of Glory*. That was in 1848, the same year when his Alma Mater conferred upon him the honorary degree of Doctor of Laws. The Kings of Prussia and Whurtemberg and the Emperor of Austria each gave him a *Gold Medal of Scientific Merit*, that of the last named being set in a massive gold snuff-box. In 1856, the Emperor of the French bestowed upon him the *Cross of a Chevalier of the Legion of Honor*. The next year the *Cross of Knight Commander of the First Class in the Order of the Danneburg* was presented to him by the King of Denmark, and in 1858 the Queen of Spain gave him the *Cross of the Knight Commander de numero of the Order of Isabella the Catholic*. The King of Italy gave him the *Cross of the Order of SS. Maurice and Lazarus*, and the Sovereign of Portugal presented him with the *Cross of the Order of the Tower and Sword*.

In 1858, a special congress was called by the Emperor of the French to devise a suitable testimonial of the nation to Professor Morse. Representatives from ten sovereignties convened at Paris under the presidency of Count Walewski, then the French Minister for Foreign Affairs, and by a unanimous vote they gave, in the aggregate, four hundred thousand francs ($80,000) as "an honorary gratuity to Professor Morse," a "collective act, to demonstrate the sentiments of public gratitude justly excited by his invention." The States which participated in this testimonial were France, Austria, Russia, Belgium, Holland, Sweden, Piedmont, the Holy See, Tuscany and Turkey.

Like all useful inventions, Morse's recording telegraph found competitors for honors and emoluments. Its own progress in securing public confidence was at first slow. In 1846 House's letter-printing telegraph was brought out, and in 1849 Bain introduced electro-chemical telegraphy. Rival lines were established. Costly litigations ensued, which promised, at one time, to demand more money than the income from the inven-

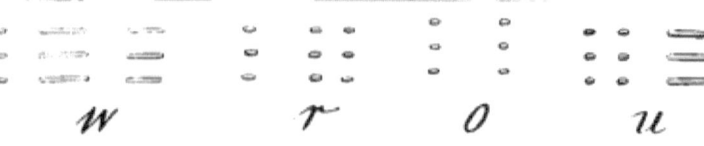

w r o u

tion. Finally, in 1851, the rival lines were consolidated, when different companies were formed to operate under the same patent. Since then other consolidations have taken place, and the Western Union Telegraph Company now controls a greater portion of the business in this country. According to a statement made by its able electrician, George B. Prescott, in January, 1871, that company was then operating 56,000 miles of line, 125,000 miles of wire, 4,600 offices, and was transmitting over 10,000,000 messages annually. The remaining companies were then operating about 10,000 miles of line. At about the same time there were in round numbers 175,000 miles of line and 475,000 miles of wire in operation in Great Britain, Ireland, and on the European continent. At the same time also there were over thirty-six thousand miles of submarine lines laid under the waters of the Atlantic and German Oceans; the Baltic, North Mediterranean, Arabian, China, Japan and Red Seas; the Persian Gulf; the Bay of Biscay; the Straits of Gibraltar and Malacca, and the Gulfs of Mexico and the St. Lawrence, by which the civilized world is put into close mental communication.

Of marine telegraphy, Professor Morse was the originator. So early as 1842, he laid the first marine cable across the harbor of New York, which achievement won for him the gold medal of the American Institute; and in a letter to John C. Spencer, then Secretary of the Treasury, in August, 1843, concerning electro-magnetism and its powers, he

wrote: "The practical inference from this law is, that a telegraphic communication on the electro-magnetic plan may with certainty be established across the Atlantic Ocean. Startling as this may now seem, I am confident the time will come when this project will be realized." That prophecy was fulfilled in 1858, when Professor Morse had yet fourteen years of life before him, and the most wonderful achievements of his marvelous invention were yet unrevealed. Among these was the long-worked-for result, accomplished only a few weeks before his death, namely, *the transmission of messages both ways over the same wire at the same instant.* This is the last great triumph of electro-magnetic telegraphy.

Very soon the almost sentient electro magnetic nerve will convey instant intelligence through every ocean to every continent of the globe. May we not liken that nerve, throbbing with its mysterious essence, to the voice of the angel in the Apocalypse, who stood with one foot upon the *land* and the other upon the *sea* and proclaimed that *time* should be no longer?

Professor Morse enjoyed the full fruition of his great discovery, and received during his life the honors and emoluments which were justly his due. In addition to the attentions paid to him by governments, he was made the recipient of public honorary banquets in London, Paris, and New York. At the latter, given at the close of 1868, the Chief Justice of the United States presided, and many of the dignitaries of the republic and the British minister at Washington were in attendance.

In 1871 a statue of Professor Morse was erected in Central Park, New York, at the expense of the telegraph operators of the country. It was unveiled on the 10th of June with the most imposing ceremonies, in which leading men of the nation participated. There were delegates from every State in the Union, and from the British provinces. In the evening a public reception was given to the venerable inventor at the Academy of Music, at which Hon. William Orton, President of the Western Union Telegraph Company, presided, assisted by scores of the

MORSE'S RESIDENCE AT LOCUST GROVE.

leading public men of the nation as vice-presidents. Impressive speeches were uttered. The last scene was most impressive of all. It was announced that the telegraphic instrument before the audience was then in connection with every other one of the 10,000 instruments in America, when Miss Cornell, a young telegraphic operator, touched its key and sent this message to all: "GREETING AND THANKS TO THE TELEGRAPH FRATERNITY THROUGHOUT THE WORLD. GLORY TO GOD IN THE HIGHEST, ON EARTH PEACE, GOOD-WILL TO MEN." Then the venerable inventor was conducted to the instrument, touched the key, and the sounder struck "S. F. B. MORSE." A storm of enthusiasm swept through the house for some moments, as the audience arose, the ladies waving their handkerchiefs, and old men and young men alike cheering as with one voice.

Professor Morse appeared in public for the last time on the 22d of February, 1872, when he unveiled the statue of Franklin erected in Printing House Square, in New York. After that his health rapidly declined, and on Tuesday, the 2d of April, 1872, his spirit passed out peacefully from its earthly tabernacle to the bosom of God. On the 5th his remains were carried in a casket to the Madison Square Presbyterian Church, when the glorious Anthem, "I heard a voice from Heaven," was sung, a funeral discourse was pronounced by Rev. William Adams, D.D., and a concluding prayer by Rev. B. F. Wheeler, pastor of the church at Poughkeepsie, of which the deceased was a member. Then the remains were taken to Greenwood Cemetery. Just before his death, Professor Morse's physicians, uncertain as to the exact nature of his disease, raised him up and sounded his chest with finger tappings. The Professor roused from the stupor in which he had

been lying, when one of the physicians said, "This is the way we telegraph." The dying man comprehended the point, and replied, "Very good—very good." These were his last words.

Professor Morse was twice married. His first wife, as we have seen, died in 1825. His second wife (still living) was Sarah Elizabeth Griswold, a grand-daughter of the late Arthur Breese, of Utica, and Catharine Livingston, of Poughkeepsie, to whom he was married in the summer of 1848.

The Professor's private life was one of almost unalloyed happiness. After his last marriage, his summer home was on the banks of the Hudson just below Poughkeepsie, called "Locust Grove," and his winter residence was in New York City. His presence was always sunshine to his family, and his influence in society was benign. He was, in the highest sense of the term, a Christian gentleman, a faithful disciple of the Redeemer, and a fine exemplar of dutiful obedience to every law in all the relations of life, domestic and social.

The invention of Professor Morse is a gift to mankind of immeasurable value. It has already widened the range of human thought and action, and given to literature a truer catholicity and humanity, whilst more than any other agency it is binding the nations of the earth in a brotherhood which seems like the herald of the millennial era. Its silent forces are working with awful majesty in the realm of mind, reducing the ideals of the old mythologies to practical and beneficent results.

Has inspiration ceased? Have revelations come to an end? Was that first message a chance communication, or a direct inspiration of the Almighty? "WHAT HATH GOD WROUGHT!"

FOLK-LIFE IN GERMAN BY-WAYS.

THE TOILER OF THE VOGELSBERG.

THE highways of the Fatherland have, of
late years, become common property of the
average tourist; and he who would not repeat
an oft-told story must seek a more retired field
for his observations. And thus we turn from
the plains of Northern Germany, the smiling
vineyards of the Rhine, the charming landscapes of the Neckar, the towering summits
of Alpine peaks, or the calm bosom of eme-
rald lakes, to penetrate into hidden retreats,
where we shall have the opportunity to observe and study the whims and ways, the
walk and talk of peasant life.

And these opportunities are manifold and
manifest, for in scores of instances the high
road of European travel leads within an hour's
ride of some of the most unique and peculiar
phases of the German peasantry. Many of
the landings along the Rhine are at the mouth
of some little stream whose windings would
soon bring us into a new world. Follow its
tortuous path, or clamber the rocky heights
that form its sides, and in a short time you
will, most likely, come into a region whose
inhabitants bear quite a different stamp from
those we meet in places where travelers most
do congregate.

The German peasants form the most con-
servative communities in the world. Within
a stone's throw of all the habits and customs
of modern civilization, they will persistently
maintain their speech, their costume, and
their notions, both at work and at play.
These differ also greatly in different regions,
so that one can stand on a mountain summit,
and look into valleys right and left, whose inhabitants wear different garbs, speak different
dialects, and who, quite likely, may be of
opposite faiths. These peculiarities are so
marked that one well versed in folk-lore can
divine among a score of men of different
origin, the valley or the mountain range to
which each one belongs.

Some of the greatest of German philolo-
gists—like the brothers Grimm—have devoted
many years to the study of their various dialects and legends, and thus unraveled many
a riddle as to their probable origin, and the
part which their fathers played in the emigration that finally settled among all these hills
and vales. The study of German folk-life is
therefore well-nigh exhaustless, and one who
would do justice to it must choose some particular region, that its manners and customs
may be considered apart. In this view we
will ask our readers to accompany us to the
heart of the Grand Duchy of Hesse, whose
mountain range, known as the Vogelsberg, is
famous for the hardihood and quaintness of
its peasantry.

The Vogelsberg, some thirty miles in length
and twenty in breadth, if we include its slowly
receding sides, forms the watershed between

AN AGED HELPMATE.

the Rhine and the Weser. It is a bald basaltic region rising to the height of about three thousand feet, and its rocky soil gives but a scanty support to the peasantry who here fight the sharp battle of life. But this very struggle for subsistence has developed a remarkable energy of character and tenacity of purpose, which have also left their physical imprint in the personal appearance of the population. The Vogelsberg peasantry are known far and wide as a community that can work harder, obtain more from a given area, and live on less, than perhaps any other in the Fatherland.

The whole mountain range is pretty well settled, and the principal occupations in the summer are husbandry, the dairy, and cattle-raising. But the season is short, on account of the elevation, and the winters are extremely severe. Popular humor affirms that in a village near the summit, it takes three men to wear one fur cap during a wind storm, viz., one whose head it covers, and one on each side of him to help hold it on. The snow often lies so deep in this same village that it frequently reaches to the second story windows, out of which the boys slide on the frozen snow with their sleds. But the Vogelsberger learns to fight the snow as the sailor does the stormy waves, and this strife helps to make him the strong man that he is.

As a mere child of six or seven years he is sent out to tend the cattle, and when a little older he will go in harvest-time to earn a few dollars at reaping or threshing in a neighboring valley, and when he has acquired a field and a cot of his own he is industrious beyond most toilers, for the rising sun finds him at his labor, which is frequently prolonged late into the evening, when he is favored by the moon. This hard service gives him a tough constitution and a wiry frame that makes him a capital soldier, capable of enduring the sternest exposures of war. He is therefore a great favorite in the grand-ducal army, and many of the peasants of the Vogelsberg were in former times recruited by their ruler to be hired as mercenaries to foreign powers. And in this way the famous Hessians were sent to this country during the Revolution, the innocent victims of a rapacious monarch.

The few hundred dollars that a Vogelsberger may thus obtain in a campaign will enable him to procure a little home for life, and thus he willingly for a period becomes a soldier for the purpose of being able to obtain a cot of his own. His life is in this way a continuous battle, and by the time he is

well through with it few men present a harsher or more weather-beaten frame and face than he. But in this line we believe that our artist can tell a better story than can we; and we have presented two portraits, taken from life, of an aged pair, man and wife, whose toils and struggles are now nearly over. The husband was a famous soldier in his early days, and did good service in the battles of Jena and Wagram. In this last battle he was wounded and taken prisoner, but was finally exchanged, and discharged with a little pension that he still receives. His hair is yet dense and not entirely gray, and covers the forehead in Vogelsberg style, but his back is pretty well bent by the weight of four-score years and more. It would be hard to find a sterner face than his or that of his aged wife, who still tarries with him. She is from the highest village on the mountain, and commenced early her career as a toiler in the field and the cabin, aiding by her industry and economy to support the household that has grown up around them.

These families often come in groups to this country, to wander out on our fertile prairies, and we are not alone in wondering at their prosperity, for the surrounding peasants have a saying that where these Vogelsbergers prosper, other men would die.

Yet these incessant toilers must have their pleasures to counteract the stern severity of labor, and as these are mostly social, they give rise to many peculiar customs. As soon as winter comes, the spinning-wheel is the accompaniment of nearly every gathering. Old and young, male and female, all spin, and the winter evenings are generally thus spent, either in company or at home. The peasant girls have their spinning-parties, to which the lads are invited in the evening, which generally close with a frugal supper and a dance. They are also great singers, and in this respect without their equals

THE BROADWAY OF WILLINGSHAUSEN.

from the mouth of Luther, as for instance: "A peasant without the fear of God is no better than his god-father, the ox."

Their food is plain, and ordinarily sparse; oatmeal gruel often takes the place of coffee, though the latter, with bread, is their favorite breakfast. Milk and eggs they have in abundance, but meat not more than once or twice a week, usually on Sunday. Their national vegetable is the potato. This appears in the form of broth, dumplings, pancakes, etc., on every festive occasion. On Sundays a piece of salt beef or pork, with sourcrout or sausage or smoked bacon, is considered quite a treat. Butter is seldom eaten by them; this, with cheese and eggs, goes to pay the taxes, or the little expenses of the week.

In no part of Germany have the peasants clung so tenaciously to their old costumes as in the Vogelsberg. These have not changed for centuries. And in some instances, here, the Catholics can be immediately distinguished from the Protestants by their dress, as a few Catholic villages on the east side of the mountains have maintained their identity until the present time, though surrounded by a Protestant community. In the matter of costumes it is observable that the Catholics retain them more strictly than the Protestants, and the women everywhere more so than the men. And it is an interesting fact that in this region the young peasant girls still wear their blonde hair precisely as Tacitus described it eighteen hundred years ago; a bunch is first collected on the top of the head, and round

among the German peasantry. They sing in the house and in the meadow, and especially over the plough and the flax. An ancient saying affirms that the flax is sure to turn out well that has been planted, pulled, and spun with song.

As a community they are deeply imbued with a religious spirit, as is well shown by a number of their quaint adages. "Sunday makes the week," they say; that is, it is by far the most important day of the week. "A peasant that does not go to church is no better than the other cattle." "He is a bad peasant who can relish his sourcrout on Sunday without a sermon." Many of these crude proverbs are handed down directly

this are coiled rich braids of hair fastened to it with a wooden pin.

Their family festivals, such as marriages, baptisms and funerals, always take place in the church, and there are consequently many of these scattered over the Vogelsberg; every village has its shrine, of which we give an illustration in "The little Church of Busendom." This is the scene of many a merry marriage festival, and the wreath-crowned pole indicates that preparations for one are making at the inn to-day. There are always two marriages—the first makes the "bride" and the second the wife. The betrothal generally occurs on Sunday at the house of the prospective bride. Hither the relations repair in procession, and in their presence are drawn up the papers of agreement, stipulating distinctly what the young people are to receive respectively from their parents, in fields and meadows, cattle, money, and household utensils. When these matters are all amicably settled, the papers are signed, the parties are declared bride and groom, and the company makes merry in feasting and dancing; the bride and groom dancing together alone at the opening of the festival, and then eating together from one plate.

At the second or actual marriage, great pride is taken in having a stately wagon bearing the principal gifts to the young pair. Part of the load is composed of flax, which the bride's parents have been collecting for her during all the years of her girlhood; to this are added chairs, table, bureau, bed, and

VOL. V.—39

kitchen utensils, but above all a beautiful new spinning-wheel covered with the whitest flax and decked with ribbons. The train to the church is headed by the bridal pair, adorned with wreaths, that of the bride trimmed with white ribbons in case her character for chastity is unsullied, but should she not be free from imputation, these would be indignantly torn from her during the march. As they pass to the church the bridal pair are to walk close together and in silence, and are not to look backward; this precaution is considered necessary, that witches may not slip in between them.

"WE TRUSTED IN GOD, AND BUILT THIS HOUSE IN 1832."

THE PEASANT OF WILLINGSHAUSEN.

When the ceremony is over, each one lays his gift on the altar, and the new wife gives to the pastor her white handkerchief and rosemary bud. A gift of some kind every invited guest is expected to bring. The event of course closes with an abundant feast, music and dancing. Sometimes the whole company will partake first of coffee and cake at the parental house, and then start off for a procession through the village, while the home is being prepared for the substantial meal. In this ceremony the men all have in their mouths long clay pipes bound around with red and blue ribbons.

The next family festival is that of the "christening." The anxieties of child-birth are scarcely over before this begins. The new-born child must be baptized as soon as it is possible to take it to the church. The superstitious feeling that death without this ceremony would result in the eternal suffering of the infant soul impels them to be absolutely cruel at times in hurrying the little innocent out into cold or storm:—for again this must if possible take place in the church, and be attended with great ceremony. A score of god-parents are to be chosen, and the father pays each one a visit of etiquette to announce the happy event and extend the invitation. These, then, in their turn must, according to their circumstances, on an early visit to the mother, present her a small sum of money and a quarter of a pound of coffee and sugar. This is with the view to enable every family to have a Christian supper. It is the duty of the persons thus chosen to be present at the ceremony, and promise their special care and protection to the child should it lose its parents. The men adorn their hats and coats with ribbons and flowers, and the women add to these other ornaments of beads and pearls that are the common property of the community. The christening feast is always a famous entertainment of the best things that the people can afford, so much for each guest, and what he cannot eat he wraps up and takes home with him,—paper being provided specially for that purpose. Parties living far from the village frequently hold the festival at the baker's, that the good things may be in abundance and near at hand.

These festive occasions, however, are about the only ones when the Vogelsbergers may be called good livers, and their reputation with the peasants of the surrounding regions is not at all desirable, for these indulge in many sharp thrusts at the lofty mountains with nothing to eat on them, and the spacious vessels filled with sour wine. And indeed the whole land of Hesse is the butt of rustic wits in this regard, but somewhat unjustly. For if we leave these bold and rugged regions by way of the valley of the Schwalm, and wend our course towards the south, we shall meet with many fruitful plains covered with rich harvest-fields and luxuriant meadows. On either side rise lovely hills planted with extensive vineyards, which yield a favorite wine. Here the people are proud of their stately herds and noble horses, and live in large and smiling villages, handed down by their forefathers, whose good old ways and customs the children retain with passionate pride. Some of these peasant villagers are of quite an aristocratic caste, from the fact that their estates revert to their eldest sons, while the other children are sent out into the world to make their fortune as they best can. This custom produces comparative wealth among those who remain, and such villages scarcely contain a really poor peasant. And such a community is so proud of its possessions, and so desirous of retaining them, that if one of their number by neglect or bad management allows his patrimony to become endangered by debt, they appoint a guardian to take care of him, or they force him to sell his property to one of them, that it may not fall into strange hands, for they seem to be strongly opposed to the introduction of strangers. These peasants of the wealthier villages of the Schwalm valley seldom even marry a wife from any other region.

These are not, however, the best spots to study folk-life, for the aristocratic pride of caste deters them from indulging in many of the peculiar customs that mark poorer and genuine peasant life. For this purpose we select one of the homelier villages of a side valley, known as Willingshausen, which is but two or three miles from a prominent station on the road leading from Cassel to Frankfort. As it is so accessible by rail, it has been quite a place of resort for some of those famous Düsseldorf artists, one of whom has tried his pencil on nearly every quaint and humble object in the vicinity. We open the panorama with his view of a street in Willingshausen—its Broadway, indeed, where may be seen all the life and gayety of the old village. Its peculiar frame-work architecture of wood, filled in with stone and mud or mortar, with the lofty pointed roofs, forms a striking contrast with the style of building in the Saxon villages. In these latter the houses are generally low and set back from road or street, with yard inclos-

ed by a wall for wagons, ploughs, and other agricultural implements. But in Willingshausen the street is free to all and everything, and thus presents a motley though not picturesque group of cows and carts, peasant women and children, and whatever else of man or beast may chance to gravitate to this center.

Though the reader may fail to perceive the evidences of a lively town by the illustration which we give, there are seasons when these avenues are thronged with the peasants of all the region around, and ring with jest and rustic merriment. The annual "Kirmess" or church-mass, a festival supposed to be instituted in honor of the dedication of the church, occurs here in October, and generally lasts three days, and affords an opportunity to witness folk-life in all its peculiarity of deed and costume. And though it is a so-called church-festival, there is now nothing church-like about it but the name, whatever it may have been in the beginning. It is now a sort of harvest-home rejoicing, after the heaviest labors of the year are over, and the gains, if any, are in the peasants' pockets. They now feel that they deserve a merry-

"MAY AND DECEMBER."

making, and none but a cynic can blame them, after their long and fatiguing toil. We will therefore look on and enjoy it with them.

The Kirmess is a period from which to reckon what is to happen or what has passed. It is so many weeks before or after Kirmess. Everybody must then have a little money for clothes and pleasure, though at other times he may be poor unto rags. A few days before the rustic fair begins, the young fellows of all the region meet in the village inn, and inscribe themselves as contributors to the festival, with the names of the peasant girls with whom they have the exclusive right to dance. Their choice has generally been made at the .May festival in the spring, at a sort of public auction, when the town-crier, surrounded by all the lads and lasses, mounts a wagon and demands what maiden shall be allotted to the gallant fellow at his side, when by public acclamation is awarded the fairest lassie to the bravest lad, and thus the pairing goes on until every Jack has his Gill, even to the humblest and most unseemly. By this generous proceeding all are mated for the dance and attendance on public occasions for the year, and though it seems simply adopted as means to secure to all the pleasure of these occasions, the coupling on May-day frequently results in better or for worse through life.

The evergreens are then planted around the village inn, and profusely adorned with flags and ribbons, during which the boys and girls, now free from work or school, have a merrymaking on the dancing-floor. The day is opened with church service, which is more festive than devotional, and when this is over, the young men, with music and banners, go from house to house in procession, each one calling on and taking with him the maiden whom he is to protect. When the band is thus fully formed, and all in gala dress, they march around to serenade the parson, the schoolmaster, the burgomaster, or civil chief of the community. This being over, the festival is fairly begun at the inn with music, song, and dance. The first three rounds are always danced by the pairs as coupled on May-day, then the lads step into the background and invite all strangers to try their skill, — and the more of these the better for the pockets of the boys, for all who dance contribute a fixed trifle to the expense, and thus lessen the cost of the entertainment.

The first day is largely given up to visitors, and the second belongs more especially to the inhabitants of the place. In the morning the band serenades the most influential families, and by noon they all appear with song and jest ready for a jovial time during afternoon and evening, when there seems to be a special demand for rustic wit, and pranks which savor more of sensuous exuberance than of good taste. Then, with great gusto, they always execute the national dance which

"CHERRY-BOYS."

overflows with odd, ungraceful ges-
ticulations and contortions of the
body, and closes with a measured
striking of the heels, accompanied
with time-honored strains declaring
that to-day the peasants forget all
care and drown all sorrow. In the
evening the married pairs have exclusive right to the dance, when the
young people step respectfully aside,
or perhaps wander away farther than
the dancing parents might think judicious. And finally, when the
weather permits the festivities in the
open air, under the favorite lime-
trees, the closing scenes do not
occur till nearly morning, when with
sad songs and funereal marches the
Kirmess is buried in an old pot until
the following autumn.

The frivolous and worldly character of these so-called church festivals might lead us to infer that there
was an utter absence of religious
feeling among the Hessian peasantry, but this is far from being the
case, for nearly every celebration is
introduced by some religious ceremonies. The trouble is that these
are too common, and thus give their
name to what is not now intended
to have any churchly relation.
Their religion runs into superstition
rather than indifference, and they
seldom undertake any enterprise without in
some way invoking the blessing of God.
Nearly every house in Willingshausen bears
some testimonial of this on the outside, to say
nothing of the pious or wise proverbs that
crown the doorposts of nearly every room.
We have given a quaint specimen of one on
a house at the corner of one of the principal streets, that will aid us in studying the
architecture and adornments, while illustrating
our remark. Over the door will be noticed
what is apparently a sign, but is really the
pious inscription : "We trusted in God, and
built this house in 1832." It will also be
observed that the head-dress of the family circle is such as we have described, while the
general appearance will testify that there are
no backdoors in Willingshausen—pigs, chick-
ens, cows, and horses all having the same
playground and entrance as the family. But
the little platform for flowers at the window will also indicate that these peasants
have a certain love of nature that rather
strangely contrasts with their other arrangements.

THE UNDERGROWTH OF WILLINGSHAUSEN.

The costume of these peasant women on
holiday occasions is often quite tasty and attractive. Their peculiar coiffure is crowned
with a neat red cap, in case the wearer is a
maiden, but if married this must be of black.
The neck is nearly always adorned with strings
of red coral, which are quite often a costly heir-
loom. The chest is protected by a tight corsage embroidered with gold, and in front el-
aborately worked with beads and silk. But the
strangest part of their costume is their dozen
kirtles, of which they are always proud, and
which give to them at times an ungraceful
rotundity. The innermost and longest reaches
only to the knee, and exposes nothing but its
broad white embroidered edge ; then they rise
gradually one above the other, the edge of
each exposed to discover its color and workmanship, until finally the corsage closes by
what is little more than a broad silken band,
bordered with some deft handiwork of the
wearer. Long white stockings and high-
heeled shoes complete the picturesque outfit.

The men have also their peculiar dress,
which we present in illustration, and exactly

as there seen; they mostly have tall, stalwart figures, with pleasant face and blue eyes. The hair is usually blonde, and falls in waves or curls over neck and shoulders. The costume of the men is much like that seen in lower Saxony or Swabia; their head in summer and winter is usually covered with a velvet cap trimmed with fur and gold braid. On grand occasions, or when they leave home, these have an enormous broad brim, fastened up behind and before with a cord. In winter they wear the long blue coat all buttoned down before, which in summer is exchanged for one of dazzling white. As will be seen in the cut, they delight in buttons; these are sometimes nearly as large as a Mexican dollar, and in rare cases, for a grand display of wealth, they are actually silver coins. The waistcoat is mostly of the deepest red, adorned with large, round brass buttons. Buttoned leggings extend from the foot to the leather or velvet breeches at the knee.

The artist has rightly given us the peasant beside his plough, for the men of the valley of the Schwalm are as diligently industrious as those of the Vogelsberg. In the laboring season they allow themselves but a few hours' repose in the twenty-four. One wonders how their bodies can stand such unremitting toil. To be known as a sleeper is a great disgrace, and the greatest honor is accorded to him who is the first to leave his couch in the early morning. This sometimes becomes a jealous rivalry. Thus in the summer the honor belongs to the man who is the first to have finished his harvest; and therefore no part of Germany presents a more industrious and busy population in the months of summer and high harvest than the valleys of this region.

And to industry they join a stern economy; few know better how to save a penny as well as earn it, than the peasantry of these quiet retreats. Their very speech is full of adages showing this to be the ruling passion, and they are thus taught in early life to be almost covetous. But though saving to a fault, they are strictly honest in all their dealings. Their word is their bond, and a bargain is seldom closed in any other way than by the shake of the hand. If a document is demanded, it is generally considered a sign that the credit of the debtor is not very good, and the demand would in many cases be considered an insult, and lead to the retraction of the bargain.

After the "Kirmess," the very best opportunity of observing and studying these people is afforded by their annual fairs for the

VINTNER OF THE NECKAR.

sale of their products and the purchase of their necessary supplies. These are held in the different villages at stated seasons, and nearly every center is celebrated for some special trade—in one it is cattle, in another grain, in another cheese or butter, and so on. At all of them nearly everything that they need is supplied in return by the wandering traders, so that they have but little need of stores in the villages, and usually do not have them. During these fairs the surrounding villages are very nearly deserted, because the inhabitants all flock to the fair to sell or buy, to meet friends, or to learn what is going on in their region. Young and old, "May and December," crowd in to see and be seen; some in the most ancient and humble costumes, as shown in our cut, and others all afloat with waving ribbons, blue or white coats with fancy buttons, or deep red vest, and corsage with a host of parti-colored skirts. Occasionally the towering white caps of the women from other valleys are seen, or the short bobtail coats of the men, the corn

WEAVERS OF THE NECKAR.

pany presenting an ever-varying panorama of odd outfits that seldom come so far from home under any other inducement than to sell their wares. But from whatever district they may come, they all seem to feel that the honor of said region is in their keeping, and thus they appear in what seems to them the most attractive array, which gives the stranger the fairest opportunity to study all local costumes.

In Willingshausen, as, indeed, everywhere in the Fatherland, the children of the peasantry, very nearly as soon as they can walk, adopt the national garb and enter the rank of the workers. They thus all appear prematurely old, and sometimes extremely ludicrous as they toddle about in skirt and bodice, in long coat and breeches. The distinctive mark of the little girls are the long braids of hair that hang over back or breast until they are quite advanced into maidenhood, as they enter which they have strong desires to see it coiled around their heads, and when this is

attained they begin to feel like young women. Our artist has by no means neglected the claims of childhood in the valley of the Schwalm, and his cunning pencil in "Cherry-ripe," and the "Undergrowth of Willingshausen," does the little ones far more justice than we could hope to attain to in any rivalry with the pen.

And now we propose to turn from the stern severity of life, look, and deed of the peasants of Northern and Middle Germany, to the more genial and kindly ways and appearance of the dwellers in the valleys and on the hillsides of the sunnier lands of the south. The smiling vineyards seem to exert a kindlier influence on those who cultivate them and live among them, and to offer a more generous return for the labor that makes the battle of life a little less severe. And we can for this visit scarcely choose a more interesting region in all Swabia, as the principal land of Southern Germany is called, than the fertile and smiling valley of the

Neckar. The inhabitants of all these lands receive in contempt from the Northern Germans the appellation of "Schwabs," which it will be seen is a corruption from the Latin name of their territory. To be a Schwab is to be an easy, good-natured personage, but a decidedly "slow coach," and therefore the Northerners say that the Schwabs do not arrive at the age of maturity till forty, and are not much wiser than children then. But a great deal of this talk springs from sectional rivalry and petty jealousy, and the tarrying tourist finds more generous hospitality, undisguised welcome, and frankness of nature here than elsewhere. A proof of this is found in the fact that thousands of foreigners, and especially of Americans, are now finding temporary homes for a few years of pleasant stay, or the education of their families, in some of the South-German cities.

We will make a little trip to one of the vintners' villages on the banks of the Neckar, which we shall find, in many respects, calculated to remind us of home. The comfortable little houses grouped in the valley below the vine-bearing hills bear more the appearance of cottages than most of the rural homes in the Fatherland; they are frequently painted white, with green blinds to the windows, to protect the inmates from the heat of the mid-summer sun. The grape is cultivated, all around the houses, in running vines which ever and anon intrude their welcome presence into doors and windows, and in the autumn offer rich treasures of purple clusters to the diligent inmates. But the labor is of course expended on the terraced vineyards that creep step by step up the hillside above the village, and year after year repay in undiminished quantities the steady diligence of the workers. For the vintner's life is no holiday affair, though it is seldom the fearfully slavish toil by which the Northern peasant is forced to wring a scanty subsistence from the soil.

The season of labor during almost night and day is that of the vintage, when everything else must for a time make way for the exigencies of the moment. For many circumstances can occur which make it absolutely necessary to gather the juicy harvest in half the ordinary time, to save it from disease or unpropitious weather. Then every woman and child of the village is picking the grapes from the stalks, and every able-bodied man or boy is doing severe duty in carrying on his back, in large wooden vessels, the gathered grapes to the wine-press. Some of these stalwart men will bear away hundreds of pounds in one burden and carry it long distances. What is gathered during the day is often pressed out at night, and even after this labor is performed they find time for a little recreation and rest before daylight again calls them to the welcome toil.

This work requires broad shoulders and heavy frames, which are developed by labor and nourishing food; and it needs also a large degree of intelligence for competent judgment regarding the treatment of the vine, the gathering of the grapes, and the manufacture of the wine. These qualities we believe the artist faithfully depicts in the three vintners of the Neckar, whose frank and kindly faces are portraits of living and acting personages. We need scarcely call attention to the marked contrast here offered to the stern and weather-beaten faces with which we began our story of folk-life. It is plain to be seen where it would be most easy to find or form warm-hearted friends. This trio are man, wife, and brother, who live, and work, and pray in harmony. For we are among a community that possesses a deep religious feeling, which fashions their daily lives. The men carry on the vineyard, while wife and daughters care for the household, the dairy, the meadow, and even cultivate a field large enough to supply them with the ordinary wants of the table.

These brothers are members of a praying-band, that on Sundays and twice during the week hold their meetings, in which a sermon is delivered, or an exhortation made, accompanied with singing, discussion of religious matters, and prayer. Now this pious fervor among laymen is no ordinary occurrence in Germany, and therefore is worthy of notice.

These are some of the members of quite a wide-spread body in Wurtemberg that derives its tenets and its zeal from a pious peasant of the early part of the present century, who believed in the early coming of Christ, and wrote much concerning this subject, which has found believers and adherents. These keep their relations with the church, and usually attend it in the morning, holding its ordinances in honor, and enjoying them with sincerity. When the duties of the church have been faithfully performed, these pious members feel that they have still a personal responsibility, which they practically execute by leading the devotions at these special meetings for prayer and praise. The elder of these men is seventy years of age, and still performs cheerfully and easily all his labor in the vineyard, while he has growing up around him a numerous and happy family of well-trained and successful children and grandchildren.

He is a man of reliable judgment in all matters of deep interest to his community and his co-religionists, and has the advantage of quite extensive travel which he took r001 to the inducement. His sect seem to have the ordinary appreciation of Bible truth common to evangelical sects, with the exception of some peculiar doctrines regarding the early coming of Christ. They believe that the Saviour will soon appear again in person on earth, and that he will choose Jerusalem as the scene of his advent. They feel it therefore a religious responsibility that Palestine be prepared for his coming, and appreciate the advantage of being near the present scene of his appearance. To this end they have long been preparing for an extensive emigration to the Holy Land, with a view to rescue it from the hands of the unbelievers before the coming of the Lord. A few years ago Hofmann, their present leader, a most able theologian and historian, resolved to make a journey to the Promised Land to convince himself of the feasibility of emigration to that spot and settlement there. His aged friend accompanied the leader, with a view to judge of the adaptability of the land to the culture of the grape and the cereals, so as to be able to decide whether it would be judicious to encourage emigration thither.

The wise old man seems to have returned with the sage conclusion that it were better to remain at home, and tend his earthly vineyard where he began it, than to render to God what he knew not of. But his familiarity with the Bible from his youth up enabled him to make his journey to the Promised Land with great profit, and since his return to his village he is the oracle of his village in matters regarding this vast enterprise, and probably by his quietly staying where he is, has induced many to abandon a scheme which could only end in disaster.

Hofmann finally took a band with him to Palestine in the futile hope of being permitted to proceed to Jerusalem and settle there, but the Turkish authorities have hither to so persistently rejected all endeavors to obtain land and homes there, that they have settled down as industrious artisans in Jaffa or Beyrut, and have even, we believe, established a hospital in that port for the reception of sick travelers. They are said to be doing well on the borders of the Promised Land while waiting for a favorable opportunity to reach the capital. They hope that the intercession of the German government in a diplomatic way will finally bring them to their goal, but the German authorities do not seem to favor the enterprise, and would doubtless much prefer to keep at home so honest and thrifty a portion of their population; and well they may, for such a peasantry are the true jewels of the land.

SATISFIED

You question if her love have depths like mine
Under the fair gold calm of what it seems;
If beauteously an equal sun-ray shine
Down the still hidden cloisters of our dreams.

You question if I find not in her gaze
Reflex of glowing fervors from mine own—
If half the glad sweet music of my days
From shadow-realms of fancy be not blown.

Friend, do I cavil at the rich low star
That crowns yon roseate mistiness of sky,
Wanting its placid orb less vague and far—
One beam the tenderer, mellower? Not I

Always they fail who always would attain.
Wherefore I ask no costlier good than this:
Perfectly to accept the joys I gain,
Blind for a life time to the joys I miss!

NAPOLEON II.,

KING OF ROME AND DUKE OF REICHSTADT.

NAPOLEON II.

THE 20th of March, 1811, was a day of jubilee in Paris. As soon as it was rumored that the Empress Marie Louise was indisposed, the Tuileries were besieged by all classes, who regarded the event as one of the deepest national interest. At length the auspicious moment arrived, and the infant heir of Napoleon was brought to the light of day.

In a note to Chaboulon's Memoirs of Napoleon in 1815, vol. ii., p. 79, the editor writes, that when young Napoleon "came into the world, he was believed to be dead; he was without warmth, without motion, without respiration. Monsieur Dubois, the accoucheur of the Empress, had made reiterated attempts to recall him to life, when a hundred guns were discharged in succession to celebrate his birth. The concussion and agitation produced by this firing acted so powerfully on the organs of the royal infant, that his senses were reanimated."

No sooner had the feeble cry escaped from the infant's lips than Napoleon hurried to embrace him, and, bearing him into the presence of the great dignitaries of state, who had been assembled as witnesses to the event, proclaimed him *King of Rome*—the title which,

THE KING OF ROME—(BORN 1811, DIED 1832.)

it had been announced, would be conferred on a son. On the same day, the young king was privately christened in the chapel of the Tuileries.

So great was the delight of the Parisians that they kissed and embraced each other in the streets. Men, women, and children flocked to the Tuileries to obtain intelligence, and it was deemed necessary to issue bulletins, in order to inform them of the health of the mother and child.

Young Napoleon was intrusted to a healthy and robust nurse, chosen from the laboring class. She was neither suffered to quit the palace nor to converse with any man. In fulfillment of these regulations, the strictest precautions were adopted. She, however, rode out in a carriage for the sake of her health, but never without being accompanied by several ladies.

The public baptism of the young prince was celebrated at Paris, with the greatest pomp and magnificence, in the church of Notre Dame, June 9th, 1811. The ceremony took place at five o'clock in the afternoon, and the Imperial infant received the names of Napoleon-Francis-Charles-Joseph-Bonaparte. The baptism was followed by a grand dinner, given by the Prefect of the Seine and the municipal body of Paris to the Mayors of the large cities of the Empire, and of the Kingdom of Italy.

Shortly after his birth, the Emperor determined to surround his son with a guard in harmony with his age. Accordingly, on the 30th of March, 1811, a decree appeared, ordering the formation of two regiments, of six companies each, which were to bear the name of "pupils of the guard;" the decree further announced that there should be no *grenadiers*. On August 24th of the same year, the corps, which was formed of the orphans of those who had fallen in battle, consisted of 8,000 men; the uniform was green, with yellow embroidery. One day, when the Emperor was reviewing, in the Cour du Carrousel, a part of his grand army, a battalion of little foot-soldiers, in good order, was seen to advance, the oldest being scarcely twelve years of age. They drew themselves up in line of battle immediately opposite a battalion of the old guard. At the sight of these children, the veterans smiled. As soon as the Emperor appeared, "the pupils" were severely reviewed, and then, placing himself between them and the old grenadiers, he said: "Soldiers of my guard, there are your children! I confide to them the guard of my son, as I have confided mine in you. I require at your hands friendship and protection for them."

Turning to his pupils, he addressed them: "And you, my children, in attaching you to my guard, I impose on you a duty difficult to observe; but I rely on you, and I hope that one day it will be said, 'These children are worthy of their fathers.'" A deafening cry of "Vive l'Empereur" answered the address, and from that day "the pupils of the guard" were in the service of the King of Rome.

In the latter part of the year 1811, the young king was a marvel of beauty and good-nature. The Duchess D'Abrantes remarks that he resembled one of those figures of Cupid which have been discovered in the ruins of Herculaneum. The Emperor would sometimes take his son in his arms, with the most ardent demonstrations of paternal love, and toss him in the air, whilst the child would laugh till the tears stood in his eyes. The infant was brought to him every morning when he was at breakfast, and on these occasions the Emperor would give the child a little claret, by dipping his finger in the glass and making him suck it, and he seldom failed to besmear the little one with everything within his reach on the table.

Marie Louise, who had never been accustomed to young children, scarcely ventured to take her son in her arms or to caress him, lest she should do him some injury. She would repair at four o'clock in the afternoon to his apartment, and, busily engaged on a piece of tapestry, would look now and then at him, saying, as she nodded her head, "*Bon jour! Bon jour!*" At the end of a quarter of an hour, perhaps, she would be informed of the arrival of her dancing-master, and the

NAPOLEON FRANCIS CHARLES: AN EMBLEMATIC PICTURE.

afternoon visit would be over. Thus the child became more attached to Madame de Montesquiou, his governess, than to his mother. Madame de Montesquiou had taken charge of him from his birth, and it would have been difficult to have made a better choice. She was young enough to render herself agreeable to a child, and yet, at the same time, she had a sufficient maturity of years to fit her for the position to which she had been appointed by the Emperor.

After the retreat from Moscow, Napoleon, care-worn and dejected, sought in the companionship of his wife and child to dispel the busy thoughts of an active brain. The Emperor had for his son an almost inexpressible love. His countenance illumined with smiles when he held him in his arms or upon his knees. He caressed him, teased him, and carried him before the looking-glass, where he made faces for his amusement. But most frequently his affection would manifest itself by whimsical tricks. If he met his son in the gardens, for instance, he would throw him down, or upset his toys. On one occasion the Emperor took his son to a review in the Champs de Mars, and the features of the young king brightened with pleasure at hearing the joyful acclamations of the old guard, tanned by the suns of a hundred battles.

"Was he frightened?" inquired the Empress.

"Frightened! no, surely," replied Napo-

leon. "He knew he was surrounded by his father's friends."

Madame de Montesquiou took advantage of every opportunity to inculcate those principles of piety for which she herself was distinguished. Kneeling by her side every night and morning, the young king lifted up his little hands in prayer to the Great Creator. After the terrible losses in Russia, she caused the infant to address the following words to the Throne of Grace: "O Lord, inspire papa with the wish of restoring peace, for the happiness of France and of us all." One evening Napoleon happened to be present when his son was retiring to rest, but Madame de Montesquiou made no alteration in the prayer, and the child repeated the words already mentioned. Napoleon listened attentively, and, observing that it was his wish to restore peace, changed the conversation.

The supposition of the young prince being occasionally flogged is entirely erroneous. His governess adopted the most prudent and effectual means of correcting him. He was in general mild and docile, but he occasionally proved himself to be of the blood of Napoleon. He was, like his father, restless and impetuous, and sometimes gave way to fits of passion. One day when he had thrown himself on the floor, crying loudly, and refusing to listen to anything his governess said, she closed the windows and drew down the blinds. The child, astonished at this, immediately rose, forgot the subject of his vexation, and asked her why she had shut the windows.

"I did so lest you might be heard," replied Madame de Montesquiou. "Do you think the people of France would have you for their prince, were they to know that you throw yourself into such fits of passion?"

"Do you think any one heard me?" he inquired.

"I should be very sorry if they did."

"Pardon me, *Maman Quiou*" (this was the endearing name by which he always addressed her), "I'll never do so again."

The Emperor almost always, even in his most serious labors, wished to have his son with him. When the child was brought to him Napoleon hastened towards him, took him in his arms and carried him away, covering him with kisses. His cabinet, in which were planned so many wise combinations, was very often, also, the sole confidant of the tendernesses of a father. Napoleon had caused to be made for himself a number of small pieces of mahogany of unequal length and of different shapes, the tops of which were carved to represent battalions, regiments, and divisions. When he desired to try some new combinations of troops—some new evolution—he made use of these pieces, which were arranged upon the carpet to give a large field of action. Sometimes his son would enter the cabinet when his father was seriously engaged in the disposal of the pieces. The child, lying at his side, and charmed no doubt by the shape and color of the mimic soldiers, which recalled to mind his own playthings, would frequently disturb the whole order of battle, at the decisive moment when the enemy were about to be vanquished. Such, however, was the presence of mind of the Emperor, that he displayed not the least annoyance, but began again, with perfect coolness, to arrange his wooden warriors. It was not only the inheritor of his name and power that he loved in the person of his son. When he held him in his arms, all ideas of ambition and pride were banished from his mind. He was simply a fond and indulgent father.

The Emperor had conceived many novel ideas relative to the education of the King of Rome. For this important object, he decided on the *Institut de Meudon*. There he proposed to assemble the princes of the entire imperial family, and he intended that they should receive the attentions of private tuition, combined with the advantages of public education. Their teachings were to be founded on general information, extended views, summaries, and results. He wished them to possess knowledge rather than learning, and judgment rather than attainments. Above all, he objected to the pursuing of any particular study too deeply, for he regarded perfection, whether in the arts or sciences, as a disadvantage to a prince.

COAT OF ARMS OF THE KING OF ROME.

But, alas! all the Emperor's brightest hopes and expectations were dashed to the ground. The tocsin sounded the summons to war, and, on the morning of the 25th of January, 1814, Napoleon, having tenderly embraced his wife and child, whom he beheld for the last time, quitted the Tuileries to place himself at the head of the army. This campaign, as is well known, ended with the capitulation of Paris.

On the 28th of April, Napoleon embarked for Elba, and, on the 2d of May, Marie Louise and the King of Rome left France forever.

The reign of the little king was over. A change was to come over the spirit of his dream. The bright ideas of youth, the fairy fancies of his infant brain were to fade away, like mist before the rising sun,—the child was hereafter to be a prisoner rather than a prince.

On arriving at Vienna, the palace of Schönbrunn was assigned to Marie Louise and her son, as a royal residence. Towards the end of May, Madame de Montesquiou was formally requested to return to France. She was succeeded by a German lady, the widow of General Metrowski. Marie Louise soon after repaired to Aix-la-Chapelle for her health, and, during her absence, young Napoleon remained at Schönbrunn, where he was frequently visited by his grandfather and his aunts, who seem to have had for him a true affection. The other members of the Austrian family, with but few exceptions, failed to regard him with that interest which was due to his age and position. They conceived the idea of creating him a bishop, and this suggestion was carried so far, that, in the Congress of Vienna, September, 1814, some of the members argued that it was necessary for the safety of Europe to conceal under the garb of a priest this heir to so much glory.

On the 22d of June, 1815, Napoleon proclaimed his son Emperor of the French under the title of Napoleon II., but the battle of Waterloo had been too decisive to permit the French the choice of their own sovereign. The Duke of Wellington formally declared in favor of Louis XVIII., Bonaparte was banished to St. Helena, and the rights of Napoleon II. were disregarded.

Without being anything extraordinary as a child, young Napoleon was from the first precocious. His answers were as quick as judicious, and he expressed himself with great elegance of phrase. M. Foresti, who was his tutor for sixteen years, nearly the entire period of his Austrian life, remarks that "he **was** good-natured to his inferiors," but that "he only obeyed on conviction, and always began with resistance."

On the 14th of September, 1815, Marie Louise renounced for herself and her child all claims to the throne of France. She was thereafter to take the title of Archduchess of Austria and Duchess of Parma, and her son was to be called Hereditary Prince of Parma. She shortly afterwards gave her hand in marriage to Count Niepperg, and, leaving for Parma, many years elapsed before she again beheld the face of her son.

At the age of five years, young Napoleon was remarkably beautiful. He spoke with a true Parisian accent, and all his movements were full of grace and gentleness. His great amusement was mischievous practical jokes, such as filling his grandfather's boots with gravel, tying the skirt of his coat to a chair, etc. The first instruction attempted to be communicated to him was a knowledge of the German language. To this he opposed a most determined resistance, regarding all endeavors to teach him as an insult and an injury, but, finally, he learned the language so rapidly that he soon spoke it in the imperial family like one of themselves.

In July, 1816, Francis II., being on a visit at Schönbrunn with his two daughters and his grandson, wished to see a young lion, a present from the Princess of Wales. The lion, being very young, was nursed by two goats; on the approach of the Archduchesses, one of the goats came forward in a menacing attitude. Young Napoleon took hold of the goat by her horns and remarked to his aunt, "You can pass now; have no fear, for I will hold her." Francis II. was extremely pleased, and said to him, "That is well, my boy. I like you for that, for I see you choose the right way where there is danger."

Young Napoleon was far from being of a communicative disposition, and, consequently, he did not, like some children, talk himself out of his recollections. Ideas of his own former consequence, and the greatness of his father, were constantly present in his mind. One day, one of the archdukes showed him a little silver medal, of which numbers had been struck in honor of his birth; his bust was upon it. He was asked, "Do you know whom this represents?"

"Myself," answered he, without hesitation, "when I was King of Rome."

On another occasion, General Soumariva, military commandant of Austria, was relating to him the lives of three illustrious personages, whom he cited as the greatest warriors of their times. The child listened attentively, but, suddenly interrupting the general, he eagerly remarked, "I know a fourth whom you have not named."

"And who is that, Monseigneur?"

"My father," replied the child, as he ran rapidly away.

On the 18th of June, 1817, an international convention deprived him of the name of Napoleon, and substituted for it the more common one of Charles. The Emperor of Austria conferred upon him the title of Duke of Reichstadt, together with that of Serene Highness. At this early age he evinced a taste for a military life, and Count Diedrich-stein was accordingly intrusted with his education in that profession. In the prosecution of this design, and to divert his mind from another model, the example of Prince Eugene of Savoy was proposed for his imitation. At the age of seven he was indulged with the uniform of a private; after a time, in reward for the exactness with which he performed his exercise, he was raised to the grade of sergeant.

On the 22d of July, 1821, the young Duke was informed of the death of his father. He wept bitterly and shut himself up for several days. The next day he put on mourning, which he wore so long beyond the accustomed time, that an imperial order was issued to compel him to suppress all tokens of grief. Time rolled on, but every year, on the 22d of July, he retired to his apartment and prayed earnestly for the soul of his father.

The greatest care was taken with the Duke's education. He was taught the dead languages, at first by M. Collin and afterward by M. Oberhaus. His military studies alternated with his classical ones. Of all his Latin books, Cæsar's Commentaries seems to have been his favorite. In fact, he became so infatuated with this work, that he wrote a remarkable treatise upon it which has been published. He also edited a life of Prince Schwarzenberg, in which there were many passages relating to his father. From his fifteenth year, he was permitted to read any book on the history of Napoleon and the French Revolution. He seems to have known, almost by instinct, that it was only through war that he could ever rise to more than a mere subordinate of the palace, and this is probably the reason why he took the deepest interest in everything that partook of a military character.

About 1827 it was deemed necessary to initiate the young duke into the policy of the

Austrian cabinet. Accordingly, Prince Metternich, under the form of lectures on history, gave him the whole theory of Imperial government. These lectures produced the desired effect, and he was thoroughly imbued with the doctrines of absolutism.

From a book entitled *Le fils de l'homme*, published in France in 1829, we learn that the Duke of Reichstadt was a prisoner both in body and mind. No Frenchman was allowed to be presented to him; no communication could be made to him except through the medium of his jailers, and no word could be uttered in his hearing which might by possibility touch the chord of ambition. His life was measured out by the square and rule; the cabinets of France and Austria determined on what he should know, and what he should think. The risk which he was informed that he incurred of being assassinated by some crazy fanatic of liberty, was the talisman by which this enchantment of soul and body was effected. His orders were obeyed, his every wish anticipated; he had his books, his horses, and his equipages for promenade or the chase; but in relation to all that the heart holds dear, he was, with slight exceptions, a solitary prisoner.

The revolution of 1830 produced a startling effect on the young Duke, for he perceived at a glance the future which lay open before him. He heard with emotion of the events which were transpiring in France, but he abstained from all participation in them, for he was surrounded on all sides by the spies and emissaries of Metternich. It was about this time that the Countess Camerata, a daughter of Eliza Bacciochi, made an attempt to involve him in a correspondence. One evening, in disguise, she lay in wait for him on entering the imperial palace, seized his hand, and kissed it with an expression of the utmost tenderness. Monsieur Oberhaus, the Duke's tutor, who was alone with him, and had been struck with surprise as well as the Duke, stepped forward and asked her what she meant. "Who," cried she, in a tone of enthusiasm, "will refuse me the boon of kissing the hand of the son of my sovereign?" At the time, the Duke was ignorant who it was that had tendered him this equivocal homage, but her subsequent letters informed him that she was his cousin.

His first appearance in society was on the 25th of January, 1831, at a grand ball given at the house of Lord Cowley, the British Ambassador. It was there, also, that he became acquainted with Marshal Marmont, one of his father's generals, and, forgetting the treachery

NAPOLEON II. IN UNIFORM OF LIEUTENANT-COLONEL OF HUNGARIAN INFANTRY.

of the man who had delivered Paris to the allies, he informed him that there were many points relative to his father on which he would be happy to be enlightened. Metternich's permission was obtained; the marshal and his ancient master's son were mutually inclined. The young Napoleon had a thousand questions to ask, a thousand points to clear up. Marmont was finally engaged to give the Duke a whole course of military lectures, the text being Napoleon's campaigns. These lectures lasted for three months, and were then discontinued, as their frequency had begun to give umbrage.

On the 15th of June, 1831, he was appointed lieutenant-colonel of a battalion of Hungarian infantry. From this time his life was passed in the barracks and on the parade-ground. He felt that this was his first step to emancipation, as he called it, and he devoted himself to the duties of a chief officer with an ardor which quickly devoured the body that had been shaken by the silent struggles of solitude. His voice became hoarse, he was subject to coughs and attacks of fever, and his symptoms became so alarming that it was finally deemed advisable to send him to Schönbrunn to recuperate his strength.

The air and quiet at this imperial residence were extremely beneficial, but the first return to vigor was the signal for exertion. To enjoy the solitude and the contemplation of nature, he repaired daily to a little village near Vienna, and it was there that he became struck with the grace and beauty of a niece of the good woman who kept the inn in that out-of-the-way resort. Her picturesque costume and simple manners naturally attracted his youthful attention, and he soon became deeply enamored. To this girl it is said he unfolded the secrets of his heart, and the restraint which had been killing him was overcome at last. Finding his health and spirits much improved, he was seized with an irresistible desire to see the ballet of *Le Diable Boiteux*, in which the *Cachuca*, danced by Fanny Ellsler, had become the talk of the city. On beholding the dancer, he gazed first in terror, then in doubt, then in horror and amazement, and sank slowly down senseless on the floor of the box where he was placed. It was the dancer herself on whom his whole heart and soul had been bestowed. He went back no more to the village, and could never be persuaded to behold even once again the traitress who had so imposed upon his trusting heart. No one but himself ever suspected Fanny Ellsler of any base intrigue; the pastoral comedy had been played out in good part, and, it is said, with the entire concurrence of imperial relatives.

On his return to Schönbrunn, he commenced hunting in all weathers, which, together with exposure in visiting in a neighboring military station, soon occasioned a recurrence of the most dangerous symptoms of his disease, and, on the 22d of July, 1832,—the anniversary of the day whereon he had been informed of the death of his father,—the Duke of Reichstadt breathed his last.

At the time of his decease, many reports were circulated to the effect that foul means had been employed to hasten his death, that he had been poisoned, and that he had been permitted to indulge in every species of dissipation in order to bring about the desired result. On tracing these reports to their source, I find that these unworthy suspicions originated in the brains of a few French writers, who were desirous of beholding the young duke seated on the throne of his illustrious father. As a farther argument against these rumors, it is affirmed by some that the Emperor of Austria was greatly affected at the death of his grandson, and that he experienced for him a strong affection which was reciprocated on the part of young Napoleon. As a still farther argument, it was found, on the opening of the body, that one of the lungs was nearly gone, and that, while the sternum was that of a mere child, the intestines presented all the appearances of old age.

The Duke left no will and his mother accordingly inherited his property, the yearly income of which was nearly a million of florins imperial. He was buried in the Carthusian Monastery at Vienna, and his funeral, which took place two days after his decease, was attended with the same forms and honors as that of an archduke of Austria.

Whilst sojourning at Vienna in the winter of 1868, I determined on visiting the monastery in which the Duke of Reichstadt is sepulchered. On ringing at the little gate of a building adjacent the church, a capuchin, who discharged the functions of porter, desired me to wait a few minutes until another of his brethren, specially appointed for the guidance of strangers, should arrive. This was an old capuchin, who came at length, holding a large bunch of keys in one hand and a lighted lantern in the other. He opened a side gate, and, descending before me, illumined with his lantern the steps of a stair-case that had but little of royalty about it, and was completely dark at its upper end. We said not a word to each other. At length, having descended about sixty steps, I found myself in a vault, on the two sides of which were ranged a great number of bronze tombs of different forms and dimensions. A small gate, at the farther end of the vault, led into a little octagonal hall, lighted from above and inclosing some nine or ten tombs. Stopping suddenly before one of these funeral monuments, the old capuchin remarked, "There it is!" Nothing could be more simple than this receptacle of departed royalty. The vault, and the walls which support it, are covered with a color between rose and gray. No sculpture, no fresco, no ornament of any kind exists. The daylight falls from above through a glass covering, fixed in the middle of the vault. The ground is paved with yellow and violet-colored slabs. The tombs, supported on the ground by three round feet, are of bronze, and have no other ornament except three great bronze rings attached to their lower part. In one corner stood the coffin of the ill-fated Maximilian, covered with wreaths and immortelles, and a silver wreath of laurel, said to have been the gift of Carlotta, formed a pleasing contrast to the unfading green by which it was surrounded. Upon the tomb of Napoleon, which is near that of his mother, Marie Louise, was a Latin inscription.

The following is the English of the epitaph, which was placed on his sepulcher by the order of Francis II. :

To the eternal memory of

JOSEPH CHARLES FRANCIS,

DUKE OF REICHSTADT,

Son of Napoleon, Emperor of the French, and Marie Louise, Archduchess of Austria. Born at Paris, March 20, 1811. When in his cradle he was hailed by the title of King of Rome ; he was endowed with every faculty, both of body and mind ; his stature was tall ; his countenance adorned with the charms of youth, and his conversation full of affability ; he displayed an astonishing capacity for study, and the exercises of the military art ; attacked by a pulmonary disease, he died at Schönbrunn, near Vienna, July 22, 1832.

For years it has been universally believed that the direct line of the "Little Corporal" became extinct in the person of the unfortunate prince, and, although various rumors relative to a secret marriage were prevalent at the time of his decease, they were generally regarded as the creations of an idle brain. Events which have subsequently transpired give these reports a semblance of truth, and, to render them still more plausible, it is a well-known fact that the late Emperor of the French spared neither expense nor labor in forming a complete collection of the correspondence and private papers of "*le fils de l'homme.*"

It appears, however, that these writings were not the only links which united the present with the past ; for, in the summer of 1871, an individual, who bore an extremely striking likeness to the Bonaparte family, made his appearance at Ischl, and was fined by the district court and expelled from the Austrian dominions for having made an objectionable entry in his "wander-book"—a sort of journeyman's passport. He was a tailor by trade, and, for several years previous to this occurrence, had been living at Wurzen, in the kingdom of Saxony, and also at Stuttgardt, under the name of Carl Gustave Ludwig, and in both of these places he had distinguished himself by his diligence, skill, and modesty. His intimate acquaintances affirmed that, in spite of his humble occupation, he had always asserted his claim to

VOL. V.—40

the name and title of Prince Joseph Eugene Napoleon Bonaparte, and, according to his own account, it would seem as if he was an issue of a secret marriage of the Duke of Reichstadt with a Hungarian countess. He stated that, when quite young, his mother was induced by Prince Metternich to apprentice him to a tailor in Wurzen named Ludwig, as a means of getting rid of him, and in order to facilitate her second marriage in Saxony. As a further proof of his origin, he declared that there was an author then living at Leipsie, but formerly a Hungarian officer, who had been a witness to the marriage, and who would, if it ever became necessary for him to make known his rank and title, supply him with the requisite documents in order to compel the countess to recognize his birth and parentage. After leaving Stuttgardt, he traveled through Germany, Switzerland, and a part of Austria, earning his livelihood as a tailor, and maintaining his claim to a princely rank, but never attempting to obtain money or credit by it. On returning to Stuttgard, in November of the same year, he found that his conviction and punishment had been mentioned in the papers of that place, and he accordingly published an explanation in the *Burger Zeitung*, in which he affirmed that he was not punished for claiming his name and title, his right to which the court at Ischl had in no wise disputed, but merely for writing it of his own accord in his passport before he had succeeded in establishing his identity before a court of law. The reputed prince is still living, and the *Cross*,—one of the leading newspapers of Germany,—in an article written at the time, states that not only does he bear a good character for his steadiness and general good conduct, but he also produces a very favorable impression by his manners.

Napoleon I. has a natural son still living, named Count de Léon, who bears a striking resemblance to Prince Napoleon, but he is not ambitious, and resides at L'Isle Adame. He never claimed any favor from Napoleon III. He is the son of a Polish lady with whom Napoleon intrigued at the time of the Russian war, and who looked upon him as a sort of Messiah—a liberator of Poland. Napoleon I. had also another son, the well-known Count Walewski.

A SPIRITUAL SONG.

FROM THE GERMAN OF NOVALIS.

EARTH'S Consolation, why so slow?
Thy inn is ready long ago;
Each lifts to thee his hungering eyes,
And open to thy blessing lies.

O Father, pour it forth with might;
Out of thine arms, oh! yield him quite;
Innocence only, love, sweet shame,
Have kept him that he never came.

Oh! hurry him into our arm,
That he of thine may yet breathe warm;
Thick vapors round the infant wrap,
And lower him into our lap.

In rivers cool send him to us;
In flames let him glow tremulous;
In air and oil, in sound and dew,
Resistless pass earth's framework through.

So shall the holy fight be fought,
So come the rage of hell to nought;
And, ever blooming, round our feet
The ancient Paradise we greet.

Earth rouses, breaks in bud and song;
Full of the Spirit, all things long
To clasp with love the Saviour-guest,
And offer him the mother's breast.

The winter fails. A year new-born
Clasps now the manger's altar-horn;
'Tis the first year of a new earth
Which this child claims in right of birth.

Our eyes they see the Saviour well,
Yet in them doth the Saviour dwell;
With flowers his head is wreathed about,
From which himself looks gracious out.

He is the star; he is the sun;
Life's well that evermore will run;
From herb and stone, light, sea's expanse,
Glimmers his childish countenance.

In every act his childish zest,
His ardent love will never rest;
He nestles, with unconscious art,
Divinely fast to every heart.

To us a God, to himself a child,
He loves us all, self-undefiled;
Becomes our drink, becomes our food—
His dearest thanks, to love the good.

Our misery grows yet more and more;
A gloomy grief afflicts us sore;
Keep him no longer, Father, thus;
He will come home again with us.

CHRIST'S MIRACLES SCIENTIFICALLY CONSIDERED.

CONSIDERED, as it will be throughout this discussion, wholly apart from its object, a miracle as defined by Strauss is "an event which, inexplicable from the operation and co-operation of finite causalities, appears to be an immediate interference of the supreme, infinite Cause, or of God himself;" and by Renan, "the special interposition of Deity in the physical and psychological order of the world, deranging the course of events."

Thus regarded, a miracle may be disallowed, first of all, on the supposition that there is no personal God to perform it. This would be a common ground of denial, whether for the atheist, materialist, or pantheist. But either of these is to-day a *rara avis* in the higher mental circles. Indeed, to be classed with such is now regarded by the leading skeptics as a mingled travesty and insult. "This lamentable observation of mine," says Strauss, for example, "according to Olshausen, has its source in something worse than intellectual incapacity, namely, in my total disbelief in a living God." So also Renan says: "Persons unfamiliar with subjects of thought often affect an air of lofty wisdom by falsifying and exaggerating. . . . By their leave, one is pantheist or atheist without knowing it. They create schools on their own authority, and often one learns from them, with some surprise, that he is the disciple of masters he never knew." The truth is that Strauss explicitly places "the belief that the world is governed by a spiritual and moral Power" among "the indispensable, imperishable parts of Christianity." And Renan, with an equal emphasis, avers: "If your faculties, vibrating in unison, have never rendered that grand, peculiar tone which we call God, . . . you are wanting in the essential and characteristic element of our nature." And thus unequivocally also, Herbert Spencer says: "By the persistence of Force, we really mean the persistence of some Power . . . The manifestations do not persist, but that which persists is the unknown Cause of these manifestations."

The reason, therefore, why nearly all the skeptics of the day deserving notice deny a miracle, is not because they are either atheists, materialists, or pantheists. "The absolute Cause," according to Strauss, "never disturbs the chain of secondary causes by single, arbitrary acts of interposition, but rather manifests itself in the production of the aggregate of finite causalities, and of their reciprocal action."—"What we deny to the miracle," says Renan, "is the exceptional state. . . . We acknowledge heartily that God may be permanently in everything, particularly in everything that lives; and we only maintain that there has never been . . . any particular intervention."

But no matter whether it be affirmed that no personal God exists to work a miracle, or that, although existing, he is yet, like the law of gravitation, always uniform and constant, never exceptional in action, and so performs no miracle. What we wish specifically to decide by this investigation is, whether all theories of denial to the contrary, the miracles of Christ in particular are not scientifically proven ones.

"Inevitably," says Froude, "the altered relation in which modern culture places the minds of all of us toward the supernatural, will compel a reconsideration of the grounds on which the acceptance of miracles is required."—"Discussion and examination," says Renan, "are fatal to miracles." "We do not say a miracle is impossible; we say there has been hitherto no miracle proved." "None of the miracles with which ancient histories are filled occurred under scientific conditions."—"And if any one is able to make good the assertion," says Huxley, "that his theology rests upon valid evidence and sound reasoning, then it appears to me that such theology will take its place as a part of science."

This, therefore, is that imperious requisition which is now abroad among the master minds, namely, either that miracles must be established by what is tantamount to a scientific demonstration, or else they must be abandoned as mere illusions of the past.

From such a test as this no real miracle will care to shrink. And if those of Jesus do not fully bear it, henceforward they must look for credence solely to believers of the lower mental orders, or at least to those by whom they are received without a thought about the why or wherefore.

"In support of the reality of miraculous agency, appeal is made," says Renan, "to phenomena outside of the course of natural laws, such, for instance, as the creation of man." Nor, until comparatively recently, would any believer in a personal God, however anxious to deny the supernatural, have thought to challenge the concession made by Strauss, even in his final *Life of Jesus*, that "of the first origin of organic beings, or the beginning of the human race, it is impossible to explain the difficulty without assuming an immediate interference of the Divine Power of creation." But now, doubtless, this remark of Strauss will be considered by many scientists almost absurdly antiquated. "Science demonstrates," says Renan, as their mouthpiece, "that on a certain day, by virtue of natural laws, which so far had presided over the development of things, without deviation or external intervention, the thinking being appeared, endowed with all his faculties, and in all his essential elements perfect." "He who is not content," says Darwin, "to look, like a savage, at the phenomena of nature as disconnected, cannot any longer believe that man is the work of a separate act of creation."

A theory of the origin of man, however, which, though held by a large number, especially of the younger and rising naturalists, is yet "opposed," as even Darwin owns, "in every form by many of the older and honored chiefs in natural science," can scarcely be said, as Renan claims, already to have attained to the dignity of a scientific demonstration. It would be more accurate to speak of it as a theory not without a vast array of scientific data in its favor, and as becoming more and more largely an accepted opinion in certain of our highest scientific circles.

"Besides," says Darwin, "I see no good reason why the views given in this volume [*The Origin of Species*] should shock the religious feelings of any. . . . A celebrated author and divine has written to me that he has gradually learned to see that it is just as noble a conception of the Deity to believe that he created a few original forms capable of self-development into other and needful forms, as to believe that he required a fresh act of creation to supply the void caused by the action of his laws."

Unquestionably, however, Darwin here concedes too much to the supernaturalists, that is, too much to suit the present temper of the evolutionists. "Looking back," says Huxley, "through the prodigious vista of the past, I find no record of the commencement of life, and therefore I am devoid of any means of forming a definite conclusion as to the conditions of its appearance. . . . But . . . if it were given me to look beyond the abyss of geologically-recorded time, . . . I should expect to be a witness of the evolution of living protoplasm from not living matter." Indeed, the entire existing tendency of the anti-supernaturalistic schools of science is utterly, and at all prehistoric epochs, to exclude all thought of a special divine intervention from alike the origin and the history of things.

This, then, is what we wish to say. Only to the satisfaction of certain scientists has the evolution theory of the first origin of organic beings been at all established. Others, equally competent to form a judgment in the case, steadily reject the theory in every form, and still adhere to that of the special-creationists. And even Darwin himself feels the intellectual need of admitting—though he prefers to say it through a clergyman—that God did at least specifically create "a few original forms capable of self-development," before organic life could either begin, or begin to evolve itself into other and higher forms. Nor is it by the compulsion of any scientific demonstration, any more than it is by a wholesale concession solely to the present temper of the anti-supernaturalists, that we herewith and henceforward argumentatively assume in this discussion, that, in order adequately and undeniably to explain, both in their origin and development, all phenomena peculiar to the field of science, in no case is it essential to resort to the hypothesis of a special intervention of Divinity.

And now what? In the first place, there doubtless is a supposition, current in sundry scientific circles, that the entire subject of the supernatural may be summarily dismissed as one of simple science;—we use the term as distinguished from that of history. For instance, one of the most brilliant of the younger skeptics, solely in his capacity as cosmist, assures the writer, in a private letter, that "while the miracles of Jesus are still matters of interest for the theologian, they are of no more interest for the scientific thinker than the oracles of Apollo."

But manifestly, if the entire field of science should vainly be explored for any trace or sign of miracles, it by no means follows that the same would be the case did we enter upon a thorough investigation of the history of Jesus Christ. Indeed, simply as the scientist, one might precisely as well undertake to dogmatize whether Alexander ever fought a battle, as whether Jesus ever wrought a miracle. By the same impartial historical processes employed in any other instance, it must first of all be determined, and that beyond a question, what events really figure in the life of Christ. Then the scientist will of course be at perfect liberty to cast those events into his crucible, to see if they will stand the test of miracles or not.

Turn we, therefore, to the gospel record of the life of Jesus.

"Criticism," says Renan, "has two modes of attacking a marvelous narrative . . . It may admit the substance of the narrative, but explain it by taking into consideration the age, the persons who have transmitted it to us, and the forms adopted at such and such an epoch to express facts. . . . It was in 1800 that Dr. Paulus put out under full sail on this new sea. . . . The gospels, according to Paulus, are *histories*, written by credulous men under the action of a vivid imagination. . . . To arrive at the truth, we must place ourselves at the point of view of the epoch, and separate the real facts from the embellishments which credulous faith and a taste for the marvelous have added to it. . . . When they tell of Jesus as walking on the sea, they mean to say that he rejoined his disciples by swimming, or walking along the shore. Another time he calmed the tempest by seizing the tiller with a firm hand. The multiplication of the loaves is explained by secret magazines, or by provisions which the auditors have in their pockets. . . . The insufficiency of such a shabby method of interpretation was not long in making itself felt."

In 1835 appeared the famous *Life of Jesus* by Dr. Strauss, driving with a scourge of intertwisted argument and ridicule the school of Paulus out of every subtilty and subterfuge, far from the presence of every scholar and logician, and triumphantly establishing that "if the gospels are really and truly historical, it is impossible to exclude miracles from the life of Jesus."

But criticism has this second "mode of attacking a marvelous narrative," which Renan mentions, namely, that it may "cast doubt on the narrative itself, and may account for its formation without conceding its historical value."

There are at present two leading lines of assault, or of "casting doubt," upon the Bible, the scientific and the critical.

And first, the scientific. "The account of the creation of man and the world which is given in Genesis," says Froude, "and which is made by St. Paul the basis of his theology, has not yet been reconciled with facts which science shows to be true."—"All theologies," says Huxley, "which are based upon the assumption of the truth of the account of the origin of things given in the book of Genesis, being utterly irreconcilable with the doctrine of evolution, the student of science, who is satisfied that the evidence upon which the doctrine of evolution rests is incomparably stronger and better than that upon which the supposed authority of the book of Genesis rests, will not trouble himself further with these theologies, but will confine his attention

to such arguments against the view he holds as are based upon purely scientific data." Nor does it require the slightest penetration to perceive that these remarks of Huxley only need the formality of a specific application in order to lie with equal force, as against the truthfulness of Genesis, so also against that of all those other portions of the Scripture, wherein the correctness of the Mosaic account of the origin of things is asserted or implied. Indeed, Froude has already pointed out to us their fatal bearing on certain underlying features of the theology of Paul; and we shall not be long in learning how they stand related to the entire New Testament doctrine of Jesus as the Creative Logos, and the like.

Two courses here present themselves. One is to pause and endeavor to clear the Bible, not only from the doubts suggested above, but from all others of whatever nature cast upon it by the scientists. The other is argumentatively to leave the Bible resting under all these doubts, however manifold and vital, and so proceed with our investigation. The latter is the course decided on.

The chief attack of modern times upon the Scriptures, however, is the critical. This attack of course makes full account of all that science urges for their invalidation. Speaking also with reference to the gospels in particular, Renan says : "The four principal documents are in flagrant contradiction the one with another; Josephus, moreover, sometimes corrects them." But this latter objection, namely, that the gospels are not in harmony with general history, the critics urge with very feeble voices. The great clamor is about their variations and their contradictions. And here Strauss is, and ever must remain, their chosen mouthpiece. As Renan has it : "The criticism in detail of the text of the gospels . . . has been done by M. Strauss in a manner which leaves little to be desired."

Concerning this assault of Strauss upon the gospels, the time will come to speak before the sequel. Just here suffice it to say that, if it were not for a single thing, the most hostile of their critics would be perfectly content if they could only reduce these Christian writings from the rank of an inspired history to that of an ordinary human composition of the like antiquity.

What, therefore, is that one element in the gospels which, in the estimation of the modern skeptics, not merely sinks them below a Tacitus or Livy in point of their historical value, but converts them, according to

Strauss into mythical productions, according to Renan into legendary biographies?

That element is—the supernatural. "It is not because it has been beforehand demonstrated to me," says Renan, "that the evangelists do not merit an absolute credence, that I reject the miracles which they relate. It is because they recount miracles that I say the gospels are legendary." So also Strauss avers that "the gospels, or even one of them, could not be taken as truly and fully historical, for the simple reason that they contain supernaturalism."

Renan accordingly adopts "this principle of historical criticism, that a supernatural relation cannot be accepted as such;" and Strauss maintains that "such an account, in so far as it either expressly states or even implies the supernatural, is to be considered as not historical."

The first thing imperatively requisite for the anti-supernaturalists is, in accordance with the above principle of historical criticism, to set aside the gospel of John almost entirely. "In presence of this gospel," says Strauss, "it was incumbent upon criticism either to break in pieces all her weapons and lay them at the feet of her antagonist, or force it to disavow all claim to historical validity."

Attempts have indeed been made to separate this gospel into historical and non-historical fragments, and thus save as much of it as possible. "While Weisse assumed the reflections and longer speeches of Christ in the fourth gospel to be apostolical," says Strauss, "rejecting, on the other hand, the narratives as a late compilation, Renan, conversely, takes offense at the abstract metaphysical lectures, as he calls the speeches of Jesus in John, and, on the contrary, considers the narrative portion of the gospel as extremely important." "Now," continues Strauss, "it will be from the speeches most immediately that every one, with a sound understanding and capable of appreciating historical truth, will get the first rays of light as to the late origin of the fourth gospel, but still it is the common ground of its divisibility, upon which Renan places himself with his German predecessor, which also makes his hypothesis untenable from first to last. The narrative part of the fourth gospel is only tolerable to him, because from the very first he takes no accurate notice of the miraculous narratives in it. The raising of Lazarus, indeed, he cannot well pass by; and as he will have nothing to do with miracles, he makes of it a mystification."

In the thirteenth edition of the *Life of Jesus*, Paris, 1867, Renan, smarting under such stings as these, inserts a lengthy Appendix, the aim of which, says he, "is to show that in recurring so often to the fourth gospel to fix the woof of my fabric, I have had good reasons."

Into the merits of this dispute we have neither the desire nor the occasion to inquire. All that we wish is to point out and emphasize the fact that, whether the fourth gospel be accepted in part as history, or be rejected *en masse* as mythical or legendary, either hypothesis is only tolerable to him who makes it in so far as it will not compel him to take any accurate notice of the supernatural features of this gospel. Once convinced that to deny *in toto* its historical character is the only method to get rid of its supernaturalism, no critic will hesitate an instant to say it is a simple fiction.

It is needless to add that the canon of historical criticism in question has been applied to the synoptics as well as John, and that everything in them seeming to the special critic, or to the special school of critics, to support the supernatural, has been duly set aside as not historical.

But the question now arises, whether the four documents referred to are unqualified inventions. "At first sight it would appear," says Row, "to have been the easiest course to assert that they are simple forgeries. . . . But this is what no unbeliever of the present day who regards his literary reputation ventures to propound as the alternative to their historical credibility. Why is this simple course abandoned, and an infinitely complicated theory substituted in its place? The answer is, that their entire phenomena negative the supposition that they could have originated in directly conscious fraud."

Accordingly the task which the modern skeptics have imposed upon themselves is not to prove that the gospel is an absolute invention, but, according to Renan, "to seek what portion of truth and what portion of error it may contain;" or, as Strauss has it, "to see what, after the severance of foreign and baser elements, would remain as historical gold."

It has already been seen that, in order to satisfy the extremest demands of anti-supernaturalistic criticism, the fourth gospel must "disavow all claim to historical validity."

Of the three remaining gospels, both Strauss and Renan accord to Luke in all respects the lowest rank as history, and so we herewith pass it by in silence.

"The narrative portions in the first gospel," says Renan, "have . . . in them many legends . . . spring from the piety of the second Christian generation. The gospel of Mark . . . is much less cumbered with fables of later insertion."—"On the contrary, we, as well as Baur," says Strauss, . . . "consider the gospel of Matthew as the most original, and, comparatively speaking, the most trustworthy." In quoting which our only object is to say that inasmuch as Renan regards the narratives of Matthew as being so largely fraught with fables, and Strauss those of Mark, compared with those of Matthew, as having even a less historical value, the narrative parts of both the first and second gospels may therefore as well be at once dismissed from any further notice.

Which leaves us only the discourses of Jesus in Matthew and Mark to ask ourselves about.

So far as Mark has any of the speeches of Christ in common with Luke and John, they have already been set aside. If those speeches which Mark has in common with Matthew also be deducted, the residue of its speech-element becomes so inconsiderable, that, for all the practical purposes of this debate, as above in its narrative portions, so now in its discourses also, this gospel likewise may as well be altogether remanded from our presence, as a common basis of investigation.

The only final fragment of the gospels, therefore, which is left us to consider, is the Logia of Matthew. And concerning this Strauss remarks: "As regards the speeches of Jesus in particular, notwithstanding all doubt upon individual points, every one must admit that we have them in the first gospel, though not unmixed with later additions and modifications, still in a purer form than in any of the others."

In connection with these "later additions and modifications," Strauss would specifically call attention, first, to the "prophetical pragmatism of Matthew," and secondly, to his "tendency to combine traditional utterances of Jesus with larger groups of speeches." "We have therefore to take away," says he, "many a Jewish feature from the figure of Christ as given by Matthew," and also to bear in mind that he "represents Jesus as saying at one time what he obviously said at different times and on different occasions." This done, the discourses of Jesus in Matthew come out even of the crucibles of Strauss as a pure, historical residuum of the gospels.

Renan also pronounces "Matthew the Xenophon of nascent Christianity." Elsewhere more in detail he remarks: "Matthew clearly deserves our unlimited confidence as regards the discourses ; he gives . . . actual notes from a clear and living memory. . . . He who attempts the task of forming a regular composition out of the gospel history possesses in this respect an excellent touchstone. The real words of Jesus will not be concealed ; as soon as we touch them in this chaos of traditions of unequal value, we feel them vibrate ; they come spontaneously and take their place in the narration where they stand out in unparalleled relief."

If it should now be inquired, therefore, to what extent the anti-supernaturalistic criticism can lay claim to having "cast doubt" on the miraculous narratives of the gospels, the foregoing analysis develops, first, that, allowing in undiminished force all that can possibly be urged against them, on the score of their conflict with the discoveries of modern science, their discrepancies with each other and Josephus, their contradictions, and the like, though no longer to be regarded as inspired, these documents would still, at the lowest supposition, maintain as high an historical rank as any other works of the same historical epoch. Beyond this point the entire onslaught upon the gospels must be waged solely in the name of the anti-supernatural. And after this onslaught has been pushed to the uttermost extreme, and we have boldly thrown away as unhistorical every fragment of these Christian records which any critic questions, even then, with unimportant limitations and exceptions, the discourses of Jesus reported by Matthew remain to us confessedly authentic.

Argumentatively, therefore, from this point forward it will be assumed that these Logia of Matthew are, as Renan says, "the basis of all that we know of the teachings of Jesus."

But after the anti-supernaturalistic criticism has thus thoroughly finished the task of "casting doubt" upon the gospel narrative of miracles, it must then take up the still more difficult task of "accounting for the formation of this narrative without conceding its historical value." "And that no one may say"—we quote from Renan—"that such a manner of proposing the inquiry implies a begging of the question, let us suppose *a priori* that which is to be proved in detail, namely, that we know that the miracles related by the gospels have not had any reality."

I.—THE METAPHYSICAL OR MYTHICAL HYPO-
THESIS OF STRAUSS.

"In my former work," says Strauss, "I offered the idea of the Myth as the key to the miraculous narratives of the gospel. . . . It is in vain, I said, in the case of stories like that about . . . the miraculous feeding, and the like, to make them conceivable as natural events; but . . . all narratives of this kind must be regarded as fictitious. If it were asked how, at the time to which the appearance of our gospels is assigned, men came to invent such fictions about Jesus, I pointed, above all, to the expectation of the Messiah current at the time. When men, I said, . . . had come to see the Messiah in Jesus, they supposed that everything coincided in him which, according to the Old Testament prophecies and types, and their current interpretations, was expected of the Messiah. . . . Jesus might have uttered words of severe reproach against the desire for miracles, . . . and those words might be still living in tradition; but Moses, the first deliverer . . . had worked miracles, therefore the last deliverer, the Messiah, and Jesus of course had been he, must likewise have worked miracles. Isaiah had prophesied that at the time of the Messiah the eyes of the blind should be opened and the ears of the deaf should hear, etc. Thus it was known in detail what sort of miracles Jesus, having been the Messiah, must have performed. And so it happened that in the earliest church narratives might, nay, could not fail to be invented without any consciousness of invention on the part of the authors of them."—"But when we thus point out that an unconscious invention of such accounts was possible far beyond the limits within which they are generally considered admissible, we do not mean to say that conscious fiction had no share at all in the evangelical formation of myths. The narratives of the fourth gospel, especially, are for the most part so methodically framed, so carried out in detail, that if they are not historical, they can apparently only be considered as conscious and intentional fictions."

This, therefore, is what Strauss is pleased to call his "peculiar apparatus for causing the miracles of the evangelical history to evaporate into myths."

Only it must not be supposed that he designs to draw his materials for its practical operation solely from the sources specified above. He draws them in fact from every quarter of the compass. If a given feature of the gospel narratives of miracles did not originate traditionally in some Messianic type or prophecy, then it did in some doctrine, faith or notion current with the early Christians; or if in none of these, why, then in something else. Besides, when the case is very desperate, it always remains for him to fall back upon "the unconscious poetry of legend, such as prevails in the first three gospels," or, "the more or less conscious fictions, the existence of which we cannot overlook in the fourth gospel." And with such an apparatus, and with such a vast variety of resources and resorts, what more facile mode of proving the miracles of Christ not historical could possibly be conceived or wished for?

The problem, however, which Dr. Strauss proposes by his mythical hypothesis to solve, is this, namely, how, though Jesus personally disclaimed performing any miracles whatever, and was not believed by his contemporaries to perform any real miracles, he yet became accredited with performing them in the tradition which arose about him after he was dead, but prior to "the time to which the appearance of our gospel is assigned" by the critic to suit his said hypothesis.

But that Jesus personally disclaimed performing miracles, is, of course, too much for Strauss to take for granted; and so, though not until the issue of his final *Life*, he makes the feint of seeming to prove the point, by citing the summary refusal of Christ to show to certain Scribes and Pharisees a sign from heaven. But even here he is driven to say that "Luke, as compared with Matthew, has preserved the more original account," not to mention other subterfuges.

It so happens, however, that when he has thus far, and after such a fashion, proceeded, to his unalloyed delight, our critic has then exhausted all the evidence even appearing to look in the direction of his desires. Accordingly, he is forthwith compelled to say: "It is true, indeed, that the answer which Jesus gave to the messengers of the Baptist . . . appears to stand in the sheerest contradiction to this refusal to perform signs and wonders."

From this dilemma, how does Strauss propose therefore to extricate himself? Why, in this very simple manner: "To this detailed account," says he, "of the miracles which any one might see him perform, Jesus adds: 'And blessed is he who shall not be offended in me.' . . . These words seem . . . to have been uttered against those who were offended at his not performing the miracles expected of the Messiah, and then the miracles to which he appealed are to be understood in a spiritual sense of the moral effects of his doctrine. 'How,' he means to say, 'you do not see me perform the miracles which you expect from the Messiah? And yet I am daily opening, in a spiritual sense, the eyes of the blind, the ears of the deaf, making the maimed walk uprightly, and giving new life to those who are morally quite dead. He who sees of how much more worth these spiritual miracles are, will take no offense at the want of material ones.' "

Now this is indeed a certain way of putting things, but let us see how it will stand inspection.

And, first of all, we must demand why Dr. Strauss ever presumed to dismiss this whole question as to whether Christ disclaimed working miracles, after glancing at only the merest item of the evidence. It was well indeed for him to notice the words of Christ about "the sign," and also those before us now. But why should he so strangely forget to notice—only these? If it was all along his intention thus conveniently to ignore the evidence almost *en masse*, he would have immeasurably more deserved the respect of scholars had he ignored it altogether. As it is, we must insist that he likewise pay some specific attention to those other pertinent words of Christ of which he has chosen to seem so perfectly oblivious; words with which, according to all the most rigid canons of historical criticism ever yet invented to reduce and destroy the speeches of Jesus in our possession, he yet may not refuse to grapple; words not found in the fourth gospel, but in the synoptics; words not peculiar to Mark or Luke, but vouched for by the almost unquestioned Matthew.

Let us begin, however, by rejecting in a body, first, all the words of Christ in question of a Judaizing tendency, as when he says: "Show thyself to the priest, and offer the gift that Moses commanded for a testimony unto them;" and, secondly, all those others in the case of which the precise phraseology of Jesus himself is not given, as when it is merely asserted that he "rebuked the wind and the sea," though in exactly what terms we do not know, unless we accredit Mark that his language was: "Peace, be still." That this process will leave us only well authenticated words of Jesus for the purposes in view, M. Strauss, even in his most fastidious moments, reluctantly must own.

To remove this matter even still farther, however, from any future question, even of those undeniably authentic discourses of Jesus thus remaining to us in the first gospel,

we will now also discard that entire mass which depends upon the narrative portions with which they are interwoven, to render it certain that they relate to miracles. Thus: "Believe ye that I am able to do this?"— "Be it unto thee even as thou wilt," and so on to the end of the catalogue. Perhaps here also should be included, as being in themselves somewhat ambiguous, such further words as these: "Stretch forth thine hand;" "Let no fruit grow on thee henceforward forever;" and the like.

And yet, after all this is done, Jesus still continues his discourses thus in Matthew: "I will come and heal him."— "I will; be thou clean."— "Whether is easier to say, Thy sins be forgiven thee, or to say, Arise and walk? But that ye may know that the Son of man hath power on earth to forgive sins. . . . Arise, take up thy bed and go unto thine house."— "But if I by the Spirit of God cast out devils, then the kingdom of God is come unto you."— "Woe unto thee, Chorazin, woe unto thee, Bethsaida; for if the mighty works which were done in you had been done in Tyre and Sidon, they would have repented long ago in sackcloth and ashes."— "They need not depart; give ye them to eat. . . . Bring them hither to me."— "I have compassion on the multitude, because they continue with me now three days, and have nothing to eat; and I will not send them away fasting, lest they faint by the way . . . How many loaves have ye?"— "Why reason ye among yourselves because ye have brought no bread? Do ye not remember the five loaves of the five thousand, and how many baskets ye took up? Neither the seven loaves of the four thousand, and how many baskets ye took up?"

These words of Jesus in Matthew alone, therefore, detached entirely from the context and picked up anywhere on a slip of paper by themselves, would abundantly establish, and that beyond a question, that whoever took such language on his lips professed, and in the most decided sense of supernaturalism professed, to be a worker of miracles.

And in the light of this, consider now these further words of Christ in Matthew also, "Go and show John again those things which ye do hear and see: the blind receive their sight, and the lame walk, the lepers are cleansed, and the deaf hear, the dead are raised up." Assuredly, when Strauss endeavors to make Jesus here enter into a sort of apology for not performing the expected Messianic miracles, and to appear in the *rôle* of a Messiah, seeking to palm off upon the Jews the moral effects of his doctrine in lieu of proper miracles, he only deserves to have it retorted upon him that by no means a Paulus is the only skeptic who is "fond of lending to the hallowed personages of primitive Christian history the views of the present age."

Indeed, upon this whole question as to whether Christ disclaimed working miracles, there is, on the part of Strauss, such ineffable condescension, first, in his special pleading about the solitary text which even seems to suit his purpose; secondly, in his imputing to the only other text he presumes specifically to notice, a meaning in utter contradiction to the thought of Christ himself; and, thirdly, in his wholesale suppression even of his own evidence at large in Matthew;—such an ineffable condescension on the part of Strauss is here evinced, we say, that his entire argument deserves no further notice than barely the exposure given it above.

But the question still remains, how Christ succeeded in his *rôle* of wonder-worker. In the proper and the highest sense, did his contemporaries receive him in this character or not?

On this point, however, Strauss has ventured to commit himself much more fully to the central current of the truth than on the former one. There he did not dare to wet his feet; but here we find him wading almost beyond the shallows.

"Meanwhile," he says, "however Jesus might disclaim the performance of material miracles, it was supposed, according to the mode of thought of the period . . . that miracles he must perform whether he would or not. As soon as he was considered a prophet, . . . miraculous powers were attributed to him; and when they were attributed to him, they came of course into operation. From that time, wherever he showed himself, sufferers regularly crowded around him in order only to touch his garments, because they expected to be cured by doing so."

From which it is apparent, even according to the critic, that Jesus was regarded by his contemporaries as the performer of not spiritual, but material miracles. What they thronged him for was not to be spiritually profited by "the moral effects of his doctrines," but to be physically healed of their diseases.

So far as these material miracles can be accounted for by the mere "force of excited imagination," Strauss is ready not merely to admit that Christ was believed by his contemporaries to have worked them, but that

"in many cases the account given in the gospels may have exactly corresponded with the fact." The secret of this concession is that afterward, in attempting mythically to account for "the origin of the evangelical narrative of miracles," the critic finds it exceedingly convenient to declare: "First, there are the miracles produced by faith, perfectly natural, and which we have not disputed."

But after Strauss, in order to reach this helpful goal, has thus unguardedly allowed himself to be swept so far down the stream of proof as to admit that Jesus was accredited by his contemporaries with working miracles at all, his doom is fixed. Beyond help or hope, he must now be swept onward to confess that as well as with those to be accounted for by the force of excited imagination, so also with those to be accounted for only by the exercise of supernatural power, Jesus was accredited with performing miracles by the sufferers who thronged him day and night. As Jesus, for instance, professed to cleanse the leper and raise the dead, so the entire tenor of the testimony establishes he was believed to do.

Wherefore have we written this? Most assuredly not still more absurdly to swell the list of formal refutations of the mythical hypothesis of Strauss, as it concerns the miracles of Christ. When even Renan says: "The book of Strauss, in spite of its somewhat exaggerated fame, has been laid aside, and has satisfied nobody," the day is surely past when formal refutations of this aspect of *Das Leben Jesu* are in place.

But our point is this. The mythical hypothesis of Strauss, as it concerns the miracles of Christ, has never called for, and never can call for, a formal refutation. Whatever the fact may be, and whatever the fact may over and over again have been demonstrated to be, no one has ever needed to inquire whether it is satisfactory or unsatisfactory. The simple truth is, that, despite all the countless essays and volumes written for its explosion, it has always been utterly irrelevant; it has never had the slightest bearing on any actual issue about the miracles in question. It was contrived, as we saw above, solely to solve the problem how, though Jesus while living personally disclaimed performing any miracles whatever, and was not believed by his contemporaries to perform any real miracles, he yet became converted into a miracle-worker by traditions arising after he was dead, but prior to the time to which the appearance of our gospels is by Strauss assigned. But historically the critic never had, and never could fairly get before him, any such problem for solution. Christ while living professed to perform, and was believed to perform, not spiritual but material, not imaginary but actual miracles. Posthumous traditions never had the remotest opportunity originally, and in the fullest sense, to foist upon him his character as miracle-worker, because he both claimed and attained that character long before he died. In other words, the very question about the miracles of Christ which the mythical hypothesis of Strauss attempts to solve, itself is mythical. The same brain that contrived the apparatus, contrived the problem also.

If *Das Leben Jesu* should therefore be compared to a man-of-war, whenever its constructor and commander runs out his guns before a paper fort of Paulus, death or flight is sure to follow. Whenever he directs a broadside against the gospels,—at their contradictions and the like,—whoever may doubt that he breaches through and through the theory of their inspiration, no one who knows the facts can question that his missiles smite a thousand times against the view as with a clap of thunder. But when he gives the order utterly to annihilate the miracles of Christ, discharge after discharge results in simply nothing, except in noise and smoke, and for the simple reason that his fire has not been directed against any possible scholarly issue about the miracles in question, but has merely been emptied at a target put up to seaward for his own private practice. He commits the blunder of trying to storm the city by throwing away his shot and shell directly out to sea.

On the question now before us, therefore, we do not need specifically to inquire whether any one either ever has or ever can dismount or spike a single gun of Strauss. Conversely, suppose that, on this especial side, *Das Leben Jesu* should continue in full force and fire until its gallant captain has filled up with wasted scholarship and subtlety the very ocean of his conjectures as to how tradition posthumously converted Jesus into a wonder-worker of the very highest order. It will be time enough for those within the walls to think about replies, when he launches forth with quite another kind of cruiser, whose guns, instead of being forever fastened to the seaward, are brought immediately to bear upon the citadel itself, namely, upon the question how Christ came so successfully to play the part of wonder-worker, if he did not do his miracles in truth.

And now for vital and real aspects of our subject still remaining.

II.—THE SCIENTIFIC, OR LEGENDARY, HYPOTHESIS OF RENAN.

"We venture to affirm," says Renan, "that if France, better endowed than Germany with practical perception, and less inclined to substitute in history the action of ideas for the play of passion and the force of individual character, had undertaken to write scientifically the life of Christ, it would have employed a more rigorous method, and, avoiding the error of transferring the problem, as Strauss has done, to the domain of abstract speculation, would have come much nearer the truth." Of which presaging remarks we now have before us in the since famous *Vie de Jésus* the detailed exposition.

Renan, then, in comparison with Strauss, is far too penetrative even to make the effort to have Jesus converted for the first time into a miracle-worker by the posthumous traditions which arose about him. He cannot, indeed, concede that Jesus ever worked a miracle. But he does "admit unhesitatingly that acts which would now be considered traits of illusion or of hallucination figured largely in the life of Jesus." Not that he thinks Jesus had any direct complicity with all such acts narrated of him in the gospels. Conversely: "It is impossible," says he, "among the miraculous stories, the wearisome enumeration of which the gospels contain, to distinguish the miracles which have been attributed to Jesus by popular opinion, from those in which he consented to take an active part." "In most cases," he alleges, "the people themselves, from the undeniable need which they feel of seeing in great men and great events something divine, create the marvelous legends afterwards." Besides : " Who knows whether the celebrity of Christ as an exorcist did not spread about without his knowing it ? Persons who reside in the East are sometimes surprised to find themselves, after a little time, possessed of great renown as physicians, sorcerers, or discoverers of treasure, without being able to discover any satisfactory account of the facts which have given rise to these strange imaginings."

But after all the marvelous acts thus unhistorically foisted on him have been deducted, there still remain *some* miracles of Christ narrated in the gospels "in which he consented to take an active part." And what of these ? Why, according to M. Renan, to the contemporaries of Jesus these acts were miracles, but to us moderns they are merely "traits of illusion or hallucination."

Precisely what he means by which we now proceed to see.

"Miracles," says he, "only occur in periods and countries in which they are believed in, and before persons disposed to believe in them. No miracle was ever performed before an assembly of men capable of establishing the miraculous character of an act. Neither men of the people nor men of the world are competent for that. Great precautions, and a long habit of scientific research, are requisite. In these days have we not seen nearly all men the dupes of gross prestiges or puerile illusions? . . . Is it not probable that the miracles of the past, all of which were performed in popular assemblages, would present to us, were it possible for us to criticise them in detail, their share of illusion? . . . Let a thaumaturgist present himself to-morrow with testimony sufficiently important to merit our attention; let him announce that he is able. I will suppose, to raise the dead; what would be done? A commission composed of physiologists, physicians, chemists, persons experienced in historical criticism, would be appointed. This commission would choose the corpse, make certain that death was real, designate the hall in which the experiment should be made, and regulate the whole system of precautions necessary to leave no room for doubt. If, under such circumstances, the resurrection should be performed, a probability, almost equal to certainty, would be attained. However, as an experiment ought always to be repeated, . . . the thaumaturgist would be invited to produce his marvelous act under other circumstances, upon other bodies, in another medium. If the miracle succeeds each time, . . . supernatural acts do come to pass in the world. But who does not see that no miracle was ever performed under such conditions? that always hitherto the thaumaturgist has chosen the subject of the experiment, chosen the means, chosen the public? . . . Till we have new light, therefore, we shall maintain . . . that a supernatural relation always implies credulity or imposture."

If now a commission of modern scientists should be selected by M. Renan, and they should start upon an exploration of the past, at the utmost what sort of a resurrection from the dead would he expect them to witness on the part of Christ?

"It seems," says he, "that Lazarus was sick, and that it was indeed in consequence of a message from his alarmed sisters that Jesus left Perea. . . . Perhaps Lazarus, still pale from sickness, caused himself to be swathed in grave-clothes as one dead, and shut up in his family tomb. . . . Martha and Mary came out to meet Jesus, and . . . conducted him to the sepulcher. The emotion which Jesus experienced at the tomb of his friend whom he thought dead, may have been mistaken by the witnesses for that groaning, that trembling, which accompanies miracles. . . . Jesus . . . desired to see once more him whom he loved, and the stone having been removed, Lazarus came forth with his grave-clothes and his head bound about with a napkin. This apparition must have been regarded by all as a resurrection."

It is indeed true that, as a substitute for the above, Renan subsequently declares: "The hypothesis which I propose in the present [the thirteenth] edition reduces all to a misapprehension." Thus: "Wearied out by the ill reception which the kingdom of God found in the capital, the friends of Jesus, it appears, sometimes desired a grand prodigy which should have a powerful effect upon the Hierosolymite incredulity. A resurrection must have seemed to them as that which, more than anything else, would be convincing. It may be supposed that Mary and Martha suggested this to Jesus. Popular report already attributed to him two or three works of this kind. 'If,' doubtless said these pious sisters, 'one of the dead were raised to life, perhaps the living would be brought to repentance.' 'No,' Jesus would reply, 'when even a dead man should be raised, they would not believe.' Recalling then a history which was familiar to him, that of the good beggar covered with ulcers, who died and was carried by the angels into Abraham's bosom: 'Should Lazarus return again,' he said, 'they would not believe him.' Afterward there arose on this subject strange mistakes. Hypothesis passed into assertion. They spoke of Lazarus resuscitated," etc.

All of which is very acutely surmised, indeed, by way of a change of base, about this narrative of John. But Renan must still remember that not only had popular report attributed to Jesus two or three resurrections from the dead prior to the episode in question, but that Jesus himself, in Matthew, places works of this kind among the Messianic miracles which the messengers of John might see him do. And if he is at all, intelligibly to himself, to conceive how Christ could play a conscious part in working wonders of this order, our present critic has no choice, according to his theory, but substantially to fall back upon the expression given of the matter at the very outset. Even if Christ had never historically claimed to raise the dead, even if John had never put the incident of Lazarus on record, even if it should now for the first time merely be hypothecated that Christ appeared proclaiming he could effect a resurrection, still it inheres in the very principle of his legendary hypothesis of miracles at large, that Renan must depict Jesus as able to raise the dead only after some such a fashion as, in all the earlier editions of the *Life of Jesus*, he does depict him doing at the ancient town of Bethany. For if the thaumaturgist, Christ, should present himself to-morrow with testimony sufficiently important to merit our attention, announcing he could raise the dead, what would be done? Why, a commission composed of physiologists, physicians, and the like, would be appointed. But why a commission of scientists, rather than of men of the people or men of the world? Because men of the people and men of the world are not competent to sit in judgment in the case of miracles. In fact, nearly all men, and even in our enlightened age, have in such matters been the dupes of gross prestiges or puerile illusions. Doubtless at the bottom of all these pretended prodigies is either credulity or imposture. To detect this, however, great precautions and a long habit of scientific research are requisite. Scientists should be the ones to conduct the whole affair, choose the corpse, make certain that death is real, designate the hall in which the experiment is to be made, demand to see the prodigy repeated under other circumstances, upon other bodies, in another medium. But who does not see that no miracle was ever performed under such conditions? that always hitherto the thaumaturgist has chosen the subject of the experiment, chosen the means, chosen the public? And to this the case of Christ is no exception. If he ever did perform a conscious part in the *rôle* of one who could raise the dead, the thing to be on our guard against is, first, credulity on our own part; secondly, intrigue on the part of the special friends of Jesus; and thirdly, imposture on the part of Christ himself. "A miracle, in other terms," says Renan, "supposes three conditions: 1, the credulity of all; 2, a little compliance on the part of some; 3, the tacit acquiescence of the main author."

Now it must of course be admitted, first of all, that the miracles of Christ only occurred in a period and a country in which they were believed in, and before persons disposed to believe in them; and that, in addition to being over-credulous, the popular assemblages before whom they were performed undoubtedly did not possess that long habit of scientific research which would have been requisite to take the proper precautions against being the dupes of Christ and his disciples, in case the latter did propose to dupe them.

Nor is it, in the second place, essential to inquire whether the disciples of Jesus were, or were not, morally capable of playing any such compliant part in getting up a miracle for Christ, as Renan, in the first twelve editions of the *Vie de Jésus*, pictures them as doing, when they would have him work a resurrection at the grave of the beloved Lazarus. Let us the rather proceed upon the supposition that they were so.

But what of the compliant Christ himself, in case M. Renan is correct in his proposed solution of his thaumaturgy?

Before responding to this painful question, however, it will be essential to make some explanatory remarks as to the reason why we must nerve ourselves up to probe this legendary view of the miracles of Jesus to the very bottom.

The first reason, therefore, is this: that the volume in which it occurs, by a powerful and permanent impression, has everywhere been, as it were, branded on the minds of men throughout the Christian world. "The reception of Renan's *Life of Jesus*," says Hurst, "was most hearty throughout France. . . . Over an hundred thousand copies were soon sold, and translations were made into all the European tongues."—"It marks," says Schaff, "an epoch in the religious literature of France, and found an unparalleled circulation on the continent of Europe, and even in England and America." Froude also speaks of it as "the now notorious work which is shooting through Europe with a rapidity which recalls the era of Luther." This was indeed all written soon after the first appearance of the book in 1863. But even so recently as 1870, Dr. Rigg, of England, pronounces "Renan undoubtedly one of the most distinguished leaders among men of learning and culture."

A second reason why we must not pause until we have probed the legendary hypothesis of the miracles of Christ advanced by Renan to the very bottom, is this, namely, that when the whole question of the miracles of

Christ comes eventually to be decided, Renan, from the very nature of the problem, ever must remain the last man to represent the world of scholars on the anti-supernaturalistic side of the investigation; and this we now proceed to show.

"Science," says one of our highest American authorities on all such subjects, in a private letter, with kind consent to cite in this connection,—"science knows nothing of miracles, or of events which are not explicable as the consequents of finite, knowable antecedents. The hypothesis of a personal God does not form a part of science, but is added to science by theology. If one begins by accepting the hypothesis of a God extraneous to the Cosmos, and acting upon it as a man acts upon a machine, the controversy about miracles becomes a legitimate one. But so long as we stand upon purely scientific ground, discarding all the extra-scientific theories furnished by theology, the controversy about miracles is not legitimate. Hence, in my articles on the 'Jesus of History' and the 'Jesus of Dogma,' I have omitted the subject entirely. And in my projected work on the 'Founding of Christianity,' I shall probably recognize the existence of the question only in the preface."

Before making a single comment on this extract, we must, however, do its gifted author the simple justice of saying that, despite anything in his language which looks in that direction, he is yet neither an atheist, materialist, nor pantheist. Conversely, after giving his detailed reasons, he has expressly stated in the public prints, that it is "the final outcome of a purely scientific inquiry, that the existence of God—the supreme truth asserted alike by Christianity and all inferior religions —is asserted with equal emphasis by that Cosmic philosophy which seeks its data in science alone."

But what we wish to say is this. No matter whether the position taken by the investigator be that no personal God exists to act upon the Cosmos from without, and as a man acts upon a machine; or that, although confessedly existing, no personal God, or if it be preferred, no Persistence of Force, no Divine Dynamis, ever acts upon the Cosmos in the manner mentioned. What of this? When we come specifically to speak of the miracles of Jesus Christ, all this is simply irrelevant. Let it be supposed no personal God exists. Still a personal Jesus Christ unquestionably has existed. Says Renan of Strauss, and very truly: "Most people know him only through the abuse of his adversaries, and from the re-

port that a visionary of that name had denied the existence of Christ, for it is in terms as absurd as these that the *Life of Jesus* has been summarily spoken of."

So also let it be hypothecated that no personal God, no Persistence of Force, no Divine Dynamis, though existing, ever has acted, ever does act, or ever will act, extraneously upon the Cosmos, as a man acts upon a machine. Still Jesus Christ has undeniably been in this world, extraneous to this world, and has acted upon it, so far as the mere principle is concerned, precisely as a man acts upon a machine. Did he do this after a merely human fashion; or that,—and something more?

While, therefore, and for very obvious reasons, the demonstration that Jesus was in truth a worker of miracles might possibly be the first step towards establishing the views of God which Jesus held, as contra-distinguished from those of the atheist, materialist, pantheist or modern anti-supernaturalistic scientist, we must emphasize and never forget the fact that the question of the miracles of Christ is by no means dependent for its settlement upon the prior establishment of either of the views of God referred to. In other words, the atheist, the materialist, the pantheist, and the modern anti-supernaturalistic scientist, in common with the Christian theist, must alike concede that a personal Jesus Christ has existed, and that he has performed certain actions in this world, and it only remains to be determined whether among those actions miracles can be proven to the satisfaction of the scientist.

A second remark above suggested by our distinguished Cosmical philosopher is this. We have already noted the fact that there is a supposition current in certain scientific circles that the whole question of the supernatural may be summarily dismissed as one of simple science. "Not from our line of reasoning, but from the whole mass of modern science," says Renan, "comes this immense result: Nothing is supernatural." And our correspondent but carries this supposition to its extremest logical results when he proposes, *ex cathedrâ*, to assume that to the modern scientific thinker even a controversy about the miracles of Christ is not legitimate, and then, having merely recognized the existence of the question in his preface, proceed to write a formal treatise on the Founding of Christianity, in the body of which the whole matter of those miracles is most steadily ignored. But we must here be permitted to reiterate what we have said before, that, as the simple scientist, one might precisely as well undertake to dogmatize whether Alexander ever fought a battle as whether Jesus ever wrought a miracle. Renan may, or may not, be perfectly correct in saying that "by so much as one admits the supernatural he is outside of science; he admits an explanation which is in no sense scientific; an explanation ignored by the astronomer, the physician, the chemist, the geologist, the physiologist, and which the historian also should ignore." But what we wish here to insist on and emphasize is this, that because the scientist has concluded that he can, as such, ignore the supernatural, it does not therefore and of course result that the historian can conclude the same. In other words, when it was above argumentatively assumed that, in order adequately and undeniably to explain, alike in their origin and development, all phenomena peculiar to the field of science, in no case is it essential to hypothecate the supernatural, the question still remained, if the same were true about all the phenomena peculiar to the field of history. When the astronomer, the physician, the chemist, the geologist, the physiologist, and every other scientist, has announced that nothing is supernatural in his especial sphere, altogether they must yet explore that other field of facts referred to, and see if they can there announce the same. It would indeed be perfectly legitimate altogether to dismiss the supernaturalistic view of the miracles of Christ, after only a brief reference to it in the preface of a formal discussion of the Founding of Christianity, because, in the estimation of the writer, that view had already been exploded by certain predecessors in this department of historical investigation, as by a Renan, Strauss, or even Paulus. But thus to dismiss the supernaturalistic view of the miracles of Christ, on the simple ground that "science knows nothing of miracles, or events which are not explicable as the consequents of finite, knowable antecedents," is carrying the logical results of modern anti-supernaturalistic tendencies, as opposed to demonstrations, not merely to a most illogical extreme, but almost beyond the calm respect of scholars. The first thing to be done, as we remarked above, is, by the same impartial historical processes employed in any other instance, to determine, and that beyond a question, what events really figure in the life of Christ. After that, the scientist will of course be at perfect liberty to cast all such events into his crucibles, and satisfy himself completely whether they survive the proper tests of miracles or not.

But no sooner does the scientist attempt to explore the records of the life of Christ, than, on the supposition of the historical reality of those records, he is in the midst of miracles on every hand. Men who do not quail before the problem of accounting, in a purely natural way, not only for the fact of the descent, but for the manner of the development of man — intellect, conscience, religious sense, and all — from some pre-existing form, must yet falter before the problem of healing lepers and raising dead people by a word, aside from the hypothesis of something supernatural. Here there is for the scientist, indeed, no choice, except either, first, to say we have to deal with miracles in truth; or, secondly, to drop the character of scientist and play the part of Paulus; or, thirdly, to deny that the records of the life of Jesus with which we have to do are in the proper sense historical; or, fourthly, and as a last resort, as we shall see hereafter, adopt the views of Renan.

Of these four alternatives, the third, of course, will be the one first considered by the scientist.

But so soon as the work of "casting doubt" upon the gospels has progressed to the full extent to which they can be asserted to be in conflict with the settled facts of science, the scientist then must pause, and leave the rest of the task to be completed by the proper gospel critics.

Accordingly, when it has argumentatively been conceded to the scientist, first, that within his special province there is no trace or sign of the supernatural, and, secondly, that to the extent above mentioned the historical validity of the gospel record of the life of Christ has been by him impugned, he is thereafter and forever left behind in his capacity of simple scientist, and can be permitted henceforward to participate in our deliberations about the miracles before us, only on condition of his turning the critical historian; until we come, in conclusion, to sift and test the hypothesis of Renan, when he may don again his character of scientist. But first the field of history.

"Paulus," says Renan, "was a theologian who, admitting the least possible of the miraculous, and not daring to treat the Biblical recitals as legends, tortured them to explain them in a purely natural way. Paulus pretended with this to maintain all the authority of the Bible, and to enter into the real mind of the sacred writers." — "All the features of the recital were thus accepted as real, but explained without miracle. The new interpreters did not for a moment think of asking if the narration in question might not be a fiction."

But after a few preliminary suggestions on the part of other critics, Strauss, plainly perceiving, as he has already told us, that "if the gospels are really and truly historical, it is impossible to exclude miracles from the life of Jesus," instituted and organized that attack upon the gospels which is still raging throughout the Christian world, thus hoping that it would be possible to exclude miracles from the life of Jesus, as a matter of fact in which we moderns must believe. For it was not merely at that time, but it has continued until the present day to be the current supposition among the skeptics and the orthodox alike, that, as Christians,—to quote again from Froude,—"the inspiration of the Bible is the foundation of our whole belief, and it is a grave matter if we are uncertain to what extent it reaches, and how much it guarantees to us as true ;" and that, specifically on the subject now before us, "nothing less than a miraculous history can sustain the credibility of miracles."

Starting out upon this supposition, the objective point which Strauss had in view is stated very clearly by himself, where he says, " that the external evidence, far from proving these writings to have come from eye-witnesses, or those who were near to the date of the gospels themselves, or to the events narrated in them, have, on the contrary, an interval open between that date and the composition of these writings, during which very much that is unhistorical may have been introduced ; and that the internal character and relation of the gospels to each other are altogether those of writings which, having been written in succession at this later period, from different points of view, record the facts not purely as they were, but metamorphosed by the ideas and struggles of this later period and its various tendencies."

The reader who has made himself familiar with the preceding stages of this investigation, perceives how very neatly this conclusion of Strauss about the late origin and manner of the unhistorical development of the gospels is adjusted to his proposed mythical solution of the miracles of Christ. Whether it is a conclusion which can be legitimately drawn from the external and internal evidences about these documents or not, it surely is precisely that conclusion which Strauss devoutly wished for. For then he could assume that, though Jesus never personally professed to perform any miracles whatever, but rather the reverse,

and was never believed by his contemporaries to perform any real miracles, still, between the death of Jesus and a certain indefinite period afterward, when our present gospels are alleged by the critic to have been reduced to writing,—could assume, we say, that between the death of Jesus and this imagined later date, we have an interval open during which Jesus, metamorphosed by the ideas, and struggles, and various tendencies of the times, became unhistorically converted, both in his personal pretensions, and in the popular belief about him, into a wonder-worker of the very highest order.

Now, after he has thus neatly brought out his conclusion about the late origin of the gospels, and the precise manner of their unhistorical development, so precisely to suit his proposed mythical hypothesis of the miracles of Christ, we do not need to be so unceremonious as Renan is, and flatly say : " M. Strauss is mistaken in his theory of the compilation of the gospels."—" Upon the whole, I accept the four canonical gospels as authentic. All, in my judgment, date back to the age that follows the death of Jesus." On the other hand, we can well afford to allow this much-belabored Titan of the modern gospel critics such poor consolation as there may be afforded him in supposing that, so far from being mistaken, he is undeniably correct in his theory of the compilation of the documents in question.

No matter, then, at how late a period our present gospels were reduced to writing ; and no matter, also, how much of the unhistorical may have been introduced into them by reason of this supposed tardy composition. We must still—for this we cannot possibly avoid—be so unfeeling as to ask our critic how all this will help him onward, even by a trifle, towards success in his peculiar effort unhistorically to solve the miracles of Christ. Whatever else may have been unhistorically admitted into our gospels, whenever they were composed, the speeches of Jesus, as we have them now in Matthew, are still confessedly authentic. But, as has already been proven, those speeches at once, forever and unalterably, fix upon Jesus in person the responsibility of professing to perform, and of being believed to perform, not spiritual but material, not imaginary but real miracles. And thus all the peculiar apparatus invented by our critic to evaporate the miracles of Christ into myths, on the assumption that Jesus personally disclaimed performing miracles, and that the problem to be accounted for is how posthumous tradi-

been themselves established by their own independent and proper proof, then very legitimately employ those miracles to attest the Bible as the Word of God. But some one now steps forward and demands that the miracles by which we would attest the Bible as the Word of God, be themselves not *supposed*, but *proven* to be established. And then what? Why we then very *naïvely* turn about and say, *ex cathedrâ*, that the Bible *is* the Word of God, and that the scriptural evidence to the miracles recorded in the Bible *therefore* is the evidence of God, and *hence* that the miracles therein narrated are *of course* established! "*O Sancta Simplicitas!*" A given miracle may, if proven, attest a given miraculous history, but that same miraculous history cannot, in turn, be used to attest its own attesting miracles. So, though all else in the Bible should be regarded as under the ban and seal of a divine authority, the miracles of the Bible must, even from the stand-point of the strictest orthodoxy, ever remain without the pale, and freely open to a fearless scrutiny.

Or take the special case of Christ himself. Suppose he were in person to appear on earth to-day in the character of a divine revelator. Upon being asked for his credentials, he professedly and apparently performs a miracle. But we are incredulous, and demand of him to know how we are to be assured beyond a doubt that his offered credential is not a thaumaturgic trick. Would we be content to have him merely turn around and say, *ex cathedrâ*, that he *is* a divine revelator, and that it is therefore sufficient for us to know that he, a divine revelator, *asserts* his miracle is true? Manifestly, on any such principle as this, any pretender or enthusiast or charlatan whatever can be a self-asserted messenger from heaven, and can attest himself at pleasure also in these pretensions with his self-asserted prodigies.

No, what we wish to know about the miracles of Christ is not in what sort of a book they may have happened to be, or not to be, recorded. On the contrary, all we need the Bible or the very gospels for is merely this, namely, to determine primarily,—as we have already said,—whether Jesus professed to be and was believed to be a real wonder-worker; and, secondarily,—and this is all we need to say about our uses for the gospels,—whether there exists to-day sufficient reason for us to believe the same.

Upon the former point it has already been seen that the Logia of Matthew, or any other fragment of our gospels, indifferently selected, is perfectly conclusive. What will yet be our answer to the second portion of our problem remains to be determined.

Meanwhile we must, first of all, point out this further mistake of Froude, namely, that "the gospels themselves tell us why M. Renan's conditions were never satisfied. Miracles were not displayed in the presence of skeptics to establish scientific truths." But no matter for that. Jesus displayed his miracles to establish his supernatural mission. And if he expects them to establish his supernatural mission to the satisfaction of a modern scientist, he has no right whatever to shrink from displaying them before the party to be convinced. So the direction in which Jesus now must go is not to take shelter under the attestation of a certain alleged miraculous record of his life, to sustain the credibility of his miracles. But the only proper thing for him to do is frankly and fearlessly to appear before our congregated *savants*, and then and there submit his prodigies to the most searching tests that modern science can demand.

Renan, therefore, after all, is right. The same "common-sense principle which we apply to all supernatural stories of our own time, which Protestant theologians employ against the whole cycle of Catholic miracles," *ought* to be "carried to its logical conclusions" in the case of Christ as well. If he cannot stand before the same searching scientific scrutiny before which any other wonderworkers fall, then he must fall as well as they. For this there is no help; nor should there be.

But precisely what is the point about his thaumaturgy which a modern scientific commission needs determine? It is not whether the prodigies which he professedly performed with such astonishing success before his contemporaries, if actually done, were real miracles. Healing lepers by a word, raising the dead,—these are surely superhuman acts enough to satisfy any modern scientist, if only Jesus ever did them.

Did Jesus ever do them? If not, then precisely the thing to be detected is the very matter raised by Renan, namely, how he not merely professed to do them, but deluded his contemporaries into believing that he did them.

It is utterly impossible, however, for Jesus now to appear in person before our modern *savants*, in order that they may not only see his miracles, but see them under those conditions of a perfect scientific scrutiny which would be forever exclusive of any future question, in case his miracles were invariably successful.

But, in the unavoidable absence of the thaumaturgist, Jesus, it will answer equally as well, if it can only be demonstrated to the satisfaction of a scientific commission, that both mentally and morally he was utterly incapable of professing to perform any prodigies at all, unless he did in fact perform them.

Once for all, therefore, let us look this matter in the face, frankly, fully, fearlessly, and see with what results.

In a general way, therefore, Renan's position here is this : "Fraud shall yet come to be regarded as an inseparable element of religious history."—" Christianity is the grandest and the noblest of facts of that order, but it has not escaped the common laws which govern the facts of religious history. There is not a single grand religious creation which has not been implicated a little in what would now be called fraud."

With regard to miracles in particular, his language is: "There is no religious movement wherein such deceptions do not play a part." And from this remark, as we are already well aware, he does not propose to make the miracles of Christ the least exception. They, like all other miracles, are yet to find their true solution, not in the hypothesis of a supernatural order of facts, but rather in the hypothesis of credulity on the part of the witnesses, and of imposture on the part of Christ and his disciples.

Planting himself upon this position boldly in the *Life of Jesus*, Renan tells us, and tells us truly, that "the first task of the historian is to depict well the surroundings in which the events which he records took place;" that "we must not attempt to reconstruct the past according to our fancy ;" that "Asia is not Europe ;" that, in the case of the miracles of Christ, we must recollect that we have to deal with "a tradition conceived by another race, under another sky, in the midst of other social needs."

Then,—putting us especially on our guard against "mutilating history to satisfy our poor susceptibilities ;"—exhorting us to remember here that "the essential condition of true criticism is to comprehend the diversity of periods, and to lay aside those instinctive repugnances which are the fruit of a purely national education ;"—cautioning us not to forget that "by our extreme scrupulousness in the employment of the means of conviction, by our absolute sincerity and disinterested love of the pure idea, we all, who

have devoted our lives to science, have founded a new ideal of morality ;"—thus cautioned and guarded against rejecting what we shall see, merely because to us the whole affair is most supremely "shocking," we are duly introduced by M. Renan into the midst of the Oriental scenes of Jesus's thaumaturgy.

Here we find ourselves at once "transported into a world of women and children, with minds ardent and wandering ;" into a world where "passion is the soul of everything and credulity has no limits ;" where there is, in short, "no grand movement produced without some deceit ; . . . where natures, absolute after the Oriental fashion, once having embraced an opinion, never draw back ; and where, if delusion becomes necessary, it requires no effort."

Renan, however, tries to conduct the exposition of his hypothesis of the miracles of Christ always within these limits. "Must we sacrifice," says he, "to this unpleasant aspect of such a life its sublime aspect? Let us beware of it. . . . So the exorcist and the miracle-worker have fallen, but the religious reformer shall live forever." Accordingly, we forthwith find him endeavoring to clear Jesus from the charge of being a common "charlatan," and the like. And thus indeed throughout it will be discovered by him who reads the *Life of Jesus* with this thought in view, that M. Renan is forever at his very wit's end how to represent the case of the Christ of his hypothesis so as to keep the implications cast upon his mental and his moral character always at the very lowest.

But M. Renan here has upon his hands a most delicate and often a most desperate affair to keep within control. So long as he can have "the people themselves, who, from the undeniable need which they feel of seeing in great men and great events something divine, create the marvelous legends afterwards" for Jesus ; so long as he can say, "Who knows whether the celebrity of Christ as an exorcist did not spread about without his knowing it ?"—on the principle that "persons who reside in the East are sometimes surprised to find themselves possessed of great renown as physicians, sorcerers, or discoverers of treasure, without being able to discover any satisfactory account of the facts which have given rise to these strange imaginings ;" so long as he can continue in this strain, we say, all goes forward "as merry as a marriage bell." The only misfortune to Jesus is that the people will, unhistorically, foist upon him his thaumaturgic character.

But no sooner do we begin to inquire about those miracles "in which Jesus consented to take an active part," than the waters begin to deepen. The lowest form of suspicion that instantly begins to cling to Jesus is that after "some one, not himself," had become "responsible for the first rumor of his miracles," he merely "did not reject the reputation given him," though he knew full well that he ought in honesty to do so.

The next unavoidable query suggested is whether, after all, Jesus was a common charlatan. We begin to reply in the negative. "Not a charlatan," we confidently assert, for "a charlatan is detestable; he performs miracles without believing in them." And this all goes on very well so long as we proceed no further than to say: "The most of the miracles which Jesus thought he performed were miracles of healing. The disorders were very slight—a gentle word often sufficed to drive away the demon." His only misfortune here is not being a modern *savant.* "Ignorant," as he was, "of a rational medical science," he could not have suspected that his prodigies of healing were but psychical effects. What we moderns would put down to the "force of excited imagination" in his patients, he very artlessly passed over to the credit of himself, as a person of supernatural powers.

But when we come to ask ourselves how about those other instances of healing which he professedly performs, such as curing the leper by a word, we find ourselves in —deep water.

Possibly, however, in all such deeply suspicious instances the adoring friends of Jesus may have prepared his thaumaturgy ready to his hand? Thus Lazarus, still pale from sickness, might have caused himself to be swathed in grave-clothes, as one dead, and shut up in his family tomb. Martha and Mary might then have sent for Christ, and conducted him to the sepulcher. Responsively to the command of Jesus, Lazarus only needed to come forth with his grave-clothes, and his head bound about with a napkin, and the resurrection was complete. In view of which, as Jesus is supposed *not* to "be a party to the deception," Strauss only cares to ask whether "*he* was blinded by so coarse a trick." But, unfortunately for this view of the matter, it will cover only certain portions of the evidence, not others. Cases of leprosy, and of feeding thousands of people with a few loaves of bread and a few small fishes, are miracles, for example, which could not have been successfully

manufactured for Jesus. At least we are already beginning to be confronted with the question whether this Jesus of Renan's hypothesis is to be taken for a lunatic, or—*worse.* Less than a lunatic he cannot be, if, whether because of his own ignorance of nature's laws, or of the imposition of his friends, or for any other reason, he really believes he performs such prodigies as we now find he professes to do, and does not do so. And if he is not a lunatic, and does not do these prodigies in truth, it is the mildest thing that we can assert when we say, that in professing to do them, and in deluding people into supposing he does them, he is one of the most detestable charlatans possible to imagine.

But really this unpleasant feature in the life of the Jesus of Renan's hypothesis is becoming so excessively unpleasant, perhaps it can in some way at least be palliated. It may be that "he was a miracle worker only in spite of himself." Perhaps, "as always happens in great and divine careers, he suffered the miracles which public opinion demanded of him, rather than performed them." They may have been "a violence done him by his time; a concession which the necessity of the hour wrung from him." But here again the facts in the case of the Jesus of Matthew are very far from being covered. After all the evidence looking in this direction in his favor has been exhausted, we still find him deliberately taking the entire initiative and conduct of his miracles; as when he refuses to let his disciples send the multitude away to buy victuals, and persists in personally feeding them in a superhuman manner.

But was not all this done at a "late period?" Not by the Jesus whose discourses we have in Matthew. It might as well be said that *that* Jesus began to talk only at a late period, as that he began to discourse about miracles only at a late period. It is a matter of daily conversation with him to profess to work miracles, to appeal to his prodigies in proof of his divine mission, and the like. Or, if it be preferred to say that Matthew, whose characteristic is supposed to be massing together into long speeches the cognate discourses which Jesus in fact delivered on many diverse occasions and at remotely different periods of his preaching, as in the instance of the Sermon on the Mount,—that Matthew has here exactly reversed his custom, and broken up certain long discourses which Jesus delivered only late in life concerning miracles, and has distributed them in fragments throughout his gospel.—the matter for Renan's Christ would even then scarcely be mended. Con-

openly, we should then have a Jesus, during the last few days of his career, crowding his pretensions as a miracle-worker for the first time upon his contemporaries after such a sudden and overwhelming fashion, that he would forthwith appear before us in the double character of a most detestable charlatan and lunatic combined.

But when we now raise the question why, late or early, *unless reason*, Christ performed his prodigies at all, Renan's ready answer is: "It was the received opinion that the Messiah would perform many. . . . Jesus therefore had to choose between two alternatives, either to renounce his mission or to become a wonder-worker."

And after we have waded out so far as this from shore, deeper and deeper the waters with a surprising swiftness. Now Jesus has introduced into his life "the page that wounds us." Now he has fully entered upon that career of "grievous acts" by reason of which "his worship" is already beginning to "grow feeble in the heart of humanity." In order "to succeed," he has begun "to make sacrifices." He has entered, in short, upon that "desperate struggle" for the triumph of his mission, out of which he never can emerge "immaculate." "Believing that all great things are achieved by the people," and that "the people are led only by yielding to their ideas;" "taking into consideration each day the weakness of men;" and laying it down as a settled line of policy "not always to give the true reason for truth," he "adopts the baptism of John," announces that "the Baptist was the old prophet Elias resurrected for his precursor;" "accepts the title Son of David," or calls himself "the Son of Man," or "Son of God," to suit his auditors; "spares himself too precise declarations;" pretends, like another "Joan of Arc," "to reveal the secrets of the heart or life;" works a miracle, or does anything beside, either "in his own direction" or "not in his own direction," does all this, we say, to help him onward in his divine career. And if all this begins to wear a very threatening aspect for every sublimer feature of his life, we must still wait until "we can accomplish by our scruples what he did by his falsehoods," before we shall acquire "the right to be severe upon him."

Meanwhile, let us now for a moment see how our critic will depict this tricky thaumaturgist of his hypothesis in action.

"Antipater heard of his miracles," we are told, "which he doubtless supposed were cunning tricks, and he desired to see some

of them. With his ordinary tact Jesus refused. He took good care not to wander forth in to an irreligious world, which desired of him nothing but a vain amusement; he aspired only to gain the people; he reserved for the simple means good for them alone." — "Thus far he had always avoided great centers, preferring for his field of action the countries and towns of small importance."— "Behold what is of the greatest moment. That Jesus should have acquired a great renown as thaumaturgist in an ignorant, rural country, favorably situated as Galilee, is quite natural. Had he not even once countenanced the execution of marvellous acts, these acts would still be done by him. His reputation of thaumaturgist would be spread abroad independently of all co-operation on his part and without his knowledge. A miracle explains itself before a well-inclined public; it is then in reality the public that makes it. But before a disaffected public, the question is entirely changed. This is well seen in the relapse of miracles which took place five or six years ago in Italy. The miracles which were produced in the Roman State succeeded. On the contrary, those which dared to appear in the Italian provinces submitted immediately to an inquest and were quickly stopped. Those whom they pretended to have cured acknowledged never to have been sick. The thaumaturgists themselves, upon being interrogated, declared that they did not comprehend anything, but that the noise of their miracles being spread abroad, they had believed to have done them. In other words, for a miracle to succeed a little compliance is necessary. The spectators not aiding, then it must be that the actors aid." — "Jesus was a stranger at Jerusalem. . . . Instead of that unlimited facility of faith . . . which he found in Galilee, . . . he encountered here at every step an obstinate incredulity, upon which the means of action which had succeeded so well in the north produced little effect."— "So that if Jesus had done any miracles at Jerusalem, we come to suppositions very shocking."— "One cannot for years lead the life of a thaumaturgist without being many times cornered; without having the hand forced by the public. He begins with ingenuousness, credulity, absolute innocence; he ends with embarrassments of every kind, and to sustain the divine power, in default of its possession, he extricates himself from these embarrassments by desperate expedients. . . . Ought he to let the work of God perish because God delays to reveal himself?"

Wherefore, in the case of Renan's Jesus, we come eventually to read: "We must remember that, in this impure and oppressive city of Jerusalem, Jesus was no longer himself. His conscience, by the fault of men, and not by his own, had lost something of its primitive pureness. Desperate, pushed to extremes, he no longer retained possession of himself. His mission imposed itself upon him, and he obeyed the torrent.' Death, moreover, was in a few days to restore him to his divine liberty, and to snatch him from the fatal necessities of a character which each day became more exacting, more difficult to sustain."

And all this M. Renan is fairly driven to say in order merely to account for the fact that Jesus "played a conscious part" in the resurrection of the beloved Lazarus, even according to the "mere misapprehension theory" of the matter given in the final casting of the *Life of Jesus ;* and played a conscious part therein only to the extent that will enable us to conjecture that it is "not impossible that even a report of this kind should be noised abroad in the lifetime of Jesus, and have had fatal consequences for him."

Does not the reader now perceive what a perfectly fearful hypothesis of the miracles of Jesus Renan has to hold in hand? If he should for a single instant dare to let this hypothesis dart onward, goaded at full speed only by the Logia of Matthew, to its legitimate goal, so far from leaving a solitary aspect of the sublimer sides of the life of Jesus unaffected, it would at once and forever shatter the entire mental and moral character of Jesus into a thousand hopeless fragments. If he should only once honestly and fully give free reins to his theory of Jesus's thaumaturgy under the full whip and spur of his own historical proofs, instead of ever being able to announce: "So the exorcist and the miracle-worker have fallen; but the religious reformer shall live forever;" he would inevitably be obliged to exclaim: "So the religious reformer has fallen in an utter and eternal ruin, and only the detestable and tricky thaumaturgist stands forever." Thus says Strauss: "Jesus cannot, as the evangelists report, have rebuked the wind and the sea, unless he was either conscious of unconditional power over nature, or a miserable braggart and impostor." Again: "If, according to Matthew, Jesus said to the captain, 'Go thy way, and as thou hast believed, so be it done unto thee,' . . . he must either have been . . . a performer of miracles in the sense of the most decided supernatural-

ism; or, if he attributed to himself such miraculous power as this without any good ground, he was a wild enthusiast; while, if he ascribed it to himself with the consciousness that he did not really possess it, he was an audacious cheat and impostor. . . . No one but either an impostor, who was as inconsiderate as he was shameless, or a man who was conscious that he could put an end to illness, would declare that a sick person at a distance, represented as dying, would not die."

Now it is indeed no sufficient reason for rejecting this last scientific word against the current Christian view of the miracles of Christ, simply because it is supremely "shocking." No more is it any sufficient reason for adopting it, simply because it is to the very last degree revolting. Is it true or is it false ? is it tenable or is it not tenable ? This is all we, who have been duly put upon our scientific "guard against mutilating history to satisfy our poor susceptibilities," either seek or wish to know.

And regarded as a hypothesis of the miracles of Christ which merely casts the gravest implications upon his mental status, little need be said about it one way or the other. For suppose it should be conceded, for the mere sake of scientific shortness, that Jesus *could* have been "blinded by so coarse a trick," as either one of his major miracles doubtless would have been, in case they were only foisted on him by his adoring followers. We must still soon leave this region altogether, and pass onward into that other region where Jesus is always himself the prime mover and actor in every cardinal feature of his thaumaturgy, as when, be it here repeated, he deliberately refuses to let his disciples send the multitude away to buy victuals, and persists in personally feeding them by a prodigy. So, as ultimate scientific thinkers, we herewith cease to have the slightest interest in the question how great a fool the hypothesis of Renan requires his thaumaturgic Christ to be ; and all our interest centers in the single final question— how great a knave it would require that wonder-working Christ to be whose words remain to us in Matthew. And this Strauss just now has very plainly told us.

But is it historically possible, is it even historically conceivable, that this Jesus of Matthew could have been so very great a knave as this?

M. Renan here, however, to the extent of the needs of his hypothesis, would prefer to speak with the utmost scientific guardedness. Thus, concerning Christ, his question is:

"What was his moral character?" and this his answer : "Those who wish in history only what is unquestionable, ought to keep silence in all this." Again his subtle query runs: "Does not Jesus seem to us devoid of human frailties simply because we look at him from a distance and through the mist of legend? Is it not because we lack the means to criticise him that he appears to us in history as the solitary sinless person?" Or thus, in general: "What prophet could hold out against criticism, if criticism followed him into his closet? Happy they whom mystery covers, and who fight entrenched behind the cloud!" Indeed, M. Renan not merely holds, but plumply says : "Jesus was not sinless ; he conquered the same passions which we combat."

But, first of all, is it indeed true that we have been left by history in such a very great incertitude about the moral character of Christ? Strauss at least does not think so. "If Jesus," says he, "omitted to do this, his conduct places him in an equivocal light, in which he by no means appears in the other evangelical narratives." Again : "This view of the matter would place the character of Jesus in the most equivocal light . . . . We cannot ascribe such conduct to him, because it would be in direct contradiction to his general conduct, and the impression which he left on his contemporaries."

Or suppose we turn from Strauss to the final test, *i.e.*, the words of Christ in Matthew. "Blessed are the pure in heart." "Blessed are they which do hunger and thirst after righteousness." "Blessed are they which are persecuted for righteousness' sake." "If thy right eye offend thee, pluck it out . . . If thy right hand offend thee, cut it off." Do these indeed appear to be the key-note to the moral teachings of a Christ whose very moral character is itself in doubt?

Our second remark is this : Renan's hypothesis of the miracles of Christ does not lead the purely scientific investigator into any comparatively trivial question about the absolute sinlessness of the thaumaturgist. Wholesale fraud, and open, shameless charlatanry are the real things wherewith we have alone to do. And where can we find such a Christ as this, even by suggestion, in the Logia of Matthew?

The truth is, that the farther this chase to get away from the purely supernaturalistic view of the miracles of Christ is indulged in, the farther away we get, as simple scientists, from all the facts and figures. Thus, Paulus only needed to invent a suitable private interpretation of his own to get rid of the real meaning of the gospels, in order to bring his so-called rational solution of these miracles into requisition ; and Strauss only needed to create a purely imaginary issue about these miracles themselves in order to make his mythical hypothesis of them available ; but Renan must arbitrarily contrive his very thaumaturgist, and that in all the essential features of both his mental and his moral character, before his theory can find any sort of Christ to fit it.

Men of science, what do you say, therefore, *i.e.* in view of this final outcome? Was Jesus Christ either "a miserable braggart," "an audacious cheat," or "an impostor who was as inconsiderate as he was shameless"? Or was he "conscious of unconditional power over nature"? was he, in fine, "a performer of miracles in the most decided sense of supernaturalism"? At least, in the light of this discussion, we are not merely shut up to these alternatives, *but shut up to them as scientists.* In other words, though we should flee again and again from destructive gospel criticism to Cosmic philosophy ; and from Cosmic philosophy to all the anti-supernaturalistic schools of science ; and from all the anti-supernaturalistic schools of science to materialism ; and from materialism to pantheism ; and from pantheism to atheism ; still, when the race is ended in either and all these directions, the goal always reached must be that Jesus has lived and done something in this world, and that if *he did not do real miracles, then he was—precisely as he is depicted in the words of Strauss above.*

The Christian world accordingly awaits to hear from the anti-supernaturalistic schools of science on this very vital question. Who will now step forward to demonstrate the necessary proposition resulting from the denial that Jesus was a wonderworker of the very highest order? Will it be Darwin? Will it be Huxley? Will it be Tyndall? Will it be Herbert Spencer? Will it be our own Fiske of Harvard?

At least the scientific schools of thought in question ought in honor here to rally to the rescue of their Renan. Not only is he the only truly scientific thinker who has thought their side of the subject to the very bottom ; he has also had the rare moral courage to bring the Christian world fairly confronted with the final shocking issue. Men of science, to your Renan's rescue! Either prove that the Christ of history was at once an arrant knave and fool ; or else frankly confess that the Christ of history worked miracles, just as actually as the Cæsar of history led armies.

GEORGE P. PUTNAM.

At the funeral services of George P. Putnam, when, as is the custom, an attempt was made to sum up the character of the life that had closed, Mr. Elder, his pastor, called it "pure, patient, gentle, self-sacrificing." No words could have been more fitly chosen, and not one could have been spared. The purity of his nature was so perfect, so child-like, that I think he was hardly ever called upon to resist a temptation, for many things that would have seemed such to other men, were regarded by him as simple impossibilities. I remember, however, one vanquished in his boyhood. He was hardly twelve years old, a fatherless lad, trying to make his way in commercial life as youngest clerk or errand-boy in a Boston store. He was living with very strict relatives, whose religious principles forbade the indulgence of any "worldly" amusements. The little fellow, however, whose imagination was hungry and craved nourishment, contrived two means of satisfying it. He carried a volume of Miss Edgeworth's tales about with him, and read them whenever sent on an errand; afterwards, stimulated to greater daring by this first nibble at forbidden fruit, he managed to make several secret visits to the theater. But this last concealment was too serious a strain upon his conscience, and one evening a sudden self-reproach arrested him in what then seemed a "mad career,"—on the road to the theater. He turned round, walked home, and voluntarily renounced the enticing pleasure; even the innocent dissipation of Miss Edgeworth's stories was for a while given up, under the pressure of remorse. I do not know that he ever suffered remorse again in his life.

Mr. Putnam's judgments of things were formed from their sunny and kindly, but also superficial aspect. Worldly superficiality is common, but unworldly superficiality is rare. The reason is, that most men who escape from the world, do so in virtue of a profounder reflection that pierces its illusions and seeks more solid ground than its sham supports. But he escaped, even to the end of his life, by the same instinctive purity and naïveté of feeling that we fancy we detect in a child who prefers flowers to diamonds. He had indeed a naïve delight in the sheen and glitter of certain worldlinesses, but this always took one shape,—the sense of pleasure of belonging to a social institution, or a group, or an individuality wider than his own. He was so completely destitute of

arrogance or self-assertion, that he habitually thought of what he was or what he did as quite insignificant, but attached a rather whimsical importance to the occasions which had brought him in contact with notable things, events, or men. I have heard him relate many times, and with the utmost glee, the account of some public banquet to which he was invited in London, which was graced by the presence of many eminent men, and over which Prince Albert presided.

Early in life, when Mr. Putnam was principally associated with men of letters and of the world, he never forgot to lend his share of support to the church. During the last fifteen years, when religious belief had become a matter of profound personal experience with him, and he was associated with many who dreaded the world, he entered with even more earnestness into schemes for the general improvement of society by means of political reforms in cities, or the establishment of reading-rooms and lecture associations in country places—of innocent enjoyment everywhere. Within my recollection of him, though now long ago, he did active battle for Fremont, in the great campaign of '56, that virtually forbade the extension of slavery into the Territories; and during the last year of his life he was an active though unostentatious member of the council for political reform, that he helped to found. As a young man, hewing a way for himself in London, he wrote his volume of American Facts, proud to vindicate the reputation of his country in Europe. And it is well known to many of his fellow-citizens, that almost his latest and most enjoyed efforts were in behalf of their Metropolitan Art Museum, in which seemed to him foreshadowed European glories for New York, which opened an illimitable vista to his imagination, and about which he dreamed fondly, in the quaint, shy, reticent manner in which he always dreamed.

His interest in Art was indeed chiefly the expression of his general interest in the moral welfare of society. He had, as has been said, an almost human fondness for pictures and books, such fondness as we sometimes have for dumb animals, for their own sake, and not for what they cannot say to us. He never received the intellectual training requisite for the thorough study of any one thing, and his was not a powerful concentrated nature, able to dispense with such training and grasp a subject for himself. But without the knowledge requisite for real intellectual culture, his innate refinement and natural taste gave him a love for beautiful things, that he desired to see propagated as a humanizing influence. He had that craving for harmony and orderly fitness which, carried further, becomes an artistic faculty, but which with him predominantly suggested his love of peace and good-will. He was so thoroughly gentle himself, that he always believed that men only had to be soothed in order to be purified ; and his desire for purity gave a latent enthusiasm to his social efforts, and tinged many things for him with a certain romantic ideality. By the side of the restless activity that distinguished his youth was another nature, quiet and dreamy, such as characterizes men who have spent their lives as custodians in the cloistered libraries or great museums of the Old World. It was this that gained ground as he grew older (for he did not live to grow old), and when those who stood nearest to him could mark that the pulses of his life were beating with greater stillness. He was looking forward, I think, to a quiet old age, to an afternoon of beneficent leisure, filled with social plannings, such as is the legitimate reward of a broad and sympathetic and reverent life. It seems hard that this should have been denied him.

His beneficence, however, did not wait for old age or for leisure ; it was so spontaneous with him that it imitated none other, but was always characteristic of himself. He made no researches, he originated no missions,— he shrank from those departments of philanthropic work that unmask depths of wretchedness and degradation. He left to others the task of digging painfully at the roots of things, but devoted himself all the more earnestly to his own work of diffusing brightness, and pleasantness, and sunniness on the surface. It has always seemed to me rather whimsically typical of him, that the one general mission among the poor with which I knew him to be connected, was an enterprise for establishing public baths and wash-houses. He used to laugh over this himself. He perfectly illustrated the rather subtle distinction that exists between a thoroughly public spirited man and a philanthropist. Both are good, but few men can be everything.

His public spirit was the result both of instinct and principle ; his kindness was always personal, and so natural that it seemed scarcely to require the intervention of principle.

It was both in social beneficence and in individual kindness that he habitually sought refuge from personal care. I remember once, when some financial crisis had just inflicted upon him losses that he could ill afford to sustain, and when he might be well supposed to be absorbed in the future of his own family, he took a poor widow with her children from a wretched tenement house in the city, found a home for them in the country near his own, and for months watched over them with unforgetting solicitude. He believed very practically in the doctrine, "As ye do unto them, so also will your heavenly Father do unto you."

Other kindnesses, however, he did not recognize to be such. His business brought him into frequent relation with a class for whom he always had the most profound and chivalrous sympathy,—poor and solitary women, struggling to maintain themselves by the uncertain profits of the pen. I do not know that anything ever touched him so much,—and this never failed to touch him. To refuse the manuscript of such an one, when he had once made personal acquaintance with her, was a positive pain to him; and the care with which he tried to soften such refusal and render it "less ungracious," has certainly been appreciated by many with whom he has had to do. This word "ungracious" was very frequently on his lips, and one of his strongest expressions of disapproval. I think the idea of showing indifference or rudeness to the personal presence of another human being, struck him as something like blasphemy, of which indeed he was literally incapable. He would sometimes say at a distance, "So and so is a queer genius,—I should like to give him a piece of my mind ;" but, once brought in contact with the offender, the suavity which was the literal expression of the goodness of his heart, and never disguised his independence, always prevented the threatened verbal retribution.

He theorized so little, that it was easy for him to be consistent. His philosophy was wonderfully homogeneous, and stood the test of every trial, great or small. He believed in the first place in the most absolute liberty for every human being, and had a perfect horror of every kind of coercion or tyranny, temporal or spiritual, social or domestic. The large indulgence that outsiders noticed in his treatment of his children from infancy upward was regarded by himself as a matter of simple justice. He disclaimed all right to interfere with the individuality of another human being, which seemed to him sacred, though it were that of his own children. He always showed a fastidious delicacy in regard to speech with them on topics of intimate personal experience, and his rare words of counsel and admonition were generally conveyed by letter, and with an eloquence unsuspected by those who knew the hesitation with which he spoke.

His general elastic confidence in the integrity and good intentions of mankind, was absolute in regard to those in whose veins ran his own blood. Whatever the disagreement, either in theoretical belief or in practical preferences, he never allowed it to become a cause of separation or of distrust ; but with a rare sweetness and magnanimity of feeling himself set it aside, and acted as though it never had been. He really dreaded imposing his own opinions even upon those who were naturally bound to be guided by them ; and was always ready to further their plans because they were theirs, even when in themselves they crossed his wishes, or seemed to him absurd.

He was thus endeared to his children by the very things that so often introduce alienation and discord into families, and he had the satisfaction in many cases of seeing the final triumph of his own wishes, whose silent weight he had not deigned to enforce by command or exhortation.

His second fundamental belief was certainly in Providence. Even in the space of my recollection of him, I can trace the gradual evolution of this belief from the general conviction "that everything would turn out for the best," conviction at first originating in the constitutional elasticity and animal spirits of his youth and younger manhood. When he was young, he looked persistently on the bright side of things because it attracted him ; when he was older, he kept his eyes steadily fixed in the same direction, because he would have esteemed it a wicked unthankfulness to have done otherwise. The name of God was rarely upon his lips, but it was frequently in his heart, and his constant watchword in any trouble or misfortune was, "We have had so many mercies, we have no right to complain." He was indeed spared a long catalogue of the worst misfortunes that fall so thickly on many, and which never even menaced him ; but a man's judgment of his own fortunes depends more upon his own nature than on theirs. And into minute daily affairs, —those that often torment people as by a rack of pins, so unnecessarily, we think, yet so inevitably,—he carried the same patience with which he confronted greater trials. It was touching to see in later years how his patience gained upon his hope,—to learn to recognize by a certain look that crossed his face at times, that the vivacity of his enjoyment had begun to lessen and his sensitiveness to pain to increase. This transition is the common fate of all ; its details may seem trivial, yet they are not so, for according to their nature they foretell the approach of a genial and loving, or of a selfish and querulous old age. This last never could have been his, whose sympathies continually widened and deepened as he grew older,—with whom one amiable instinct after another became converted into a fixed principle, and who could thus be rightly ranked with those just men whose light shineth more and more unto the perfect day.

This was moral light. Intellectually he accomplished his best work long before he died. Perhaps his period of greatest mental activity was the two years of his boyhood from fifteen to seventeen, when, after working as a clerk until nine o'clock in the evening, he then studied till two, arranging material for *The World's Progress*, whose publication gave him a just title to precocious authorship. On account of its precocity, of the disadvantages in regard to leisure and previous education under which the boy labored, this book affords proof of a certain originality and boldness of mental conception which could not be fairly inferred from it were it the work of a mature man, or of one professing to be a *ripe* scholar. It is a proof too of the patient persistency that characterized him, and which was rather moral than intellectual. He had no capacity for intellectual research or analysis ; he had a great deal for the grouping of things together in a manner to be most effective—that is, to convey the most intelligible meaning to some one else, and I consider this preference another proof that his interest in literature as in art was, unconsciously to himself, chiefly moral. While he loved refinement, he hated subtleties ; he admired a pithy sentence, even though it contained a loose thought, and, it must be acknowledged, frequently failed to comprehend a pithy thought, especially if clothed in vague language. Associated with so many books, he really, after the one great effort of his boyhood, read few, and his taste lay very definitely in one direction—for the calm, even, harmonious style that we associate with Addison and Goldsmith and Irving.

His association with the latter writer has been so intimate, and is so well known, that to many it is perhaps the principal fact suggested by the mention of his own name. The association is not fortuitous, but, I think, really means all that it seems to imply. It has been said that one peculiar charm in Irving's life of Goldsmith arises from the evident kinship that exists between the persons of the author and that of his hero. The devotion of one life to the interpretation of another always implies the consciousness of some such kinship between the two, even when the mode of expression of the genius be quite different, as in the case of Turner and Ruskin; or when the genius is all on one side, and on the other belongs only what Carlyle has well called "the genius of appreciation" in Boswell for Johnson. To this latter class of appreciative friendship belongs that which for so many years existed between Mr. Putnam and Washington Irving. This was much more than the ordinary relations between a publisher and author who share each other's success. Mr. Putnam was one of the first to appreciate Irving, and immediately devoted himself to the task of hewing out a road for his future reputation, with a zeal and generous confidence that was certainly to its generously recognized, and has been amply recompensed.

But this early divination of Irving's possibilities for success, to whose external conditions he largely contributed, was not the mere foresight of a man of business trained to detect what will succeed. It was rather that joyful perception of a person who meets in another the full and graceful and adequate expression of what he would like to say himself, and glad to find the way in which he would wish to say it.

The serenity, the openness, the freshness, the limpid clearness of Irving's style and of Irving's not too deep thought, no less than the gentleness and geniality of his character, with its quaintness, its shy delicacy, its fastidious reserve, its unspoken depth of sentiment, its stainless honor, irresistibly attracted a nature that, though intellectually inferior, was morally akin. A sketch of Irving that Mr. Putnam wrote for *Harper's Weekly*, about two years ago, shows distinctly the points at which he had attracted himself to him; the details upon which he most loved to dwell. Irving was indeed his hero, his ideal in the world of letters in which he lived, his type of the region of that world which he most preferred.

Irving has a national fame which will last, at least for a while; that of his friend, in the hurry of events, and in the urgent proportion of other things, must be sooner forgotten. It is for that very reason that I, as one of his nearest and dearest friends, have tried to gather up into an imperfect portrait these few traits of a man that I loved, not merely from habit and association, but because his character has always impressed me as winning and touching and lovely. He was nearly always inadequate to fairly express himself; who is not that as worth the expression? He lacked grace and presence, so that his real depth and force were frequently concealed or misunderstood. But it was these had once been felt, they were not easily forgotten. Nor, in a world thronged at once with louder merit and with vices yet more loud, can pass unnoticed and unmissed this life, whose, though so concrete in action, possesses of its greatest power in silence; and which, though so voracious in worldly activity, yet through singleness of purpose and sincerity of belief ever kept itself at least unspotted from the world.

TOPICS OF THE TIME.

The Reading of Periodicals.

IT is lamented by many that the reading of periodicals has become not only universal, but that it absorbs all the time of those who read them. It is supposed that, in consequence of these two facts, the quiet and thorough study of well-written books—books which deal with their subjects systematically and exhaustively—has been forsaken. As a consequence of this fact, it is farther supposed that readers only get a superficial and desultory knowledge of the things they study, and that, although their knowledge covers many fields, they become nothing better than smatterers in any.

We think these conclusions are hardly sustained by the large army of facts relating to them. We doubt whether the market for good books was ever any better than it is now. We have no statistics on the subject, but our impression is, that through the universal diffusion of periodical literature, and the knowledge of books conveyed and advertised by it, the book trade has been rather helped than harmed. It has multiplied readers and excited curiosity and interest touching all literature. There are hundreds of good books which would never reach the world but for the introduction and commendation of the periodical; and books are purchased now more intelligently than they ever were before. The librarians will tell us too that they find no falling off in their labors ; and we doubt whether our scholars would be willing to confess that they are less studious than formerly. Science was never more active in its investigations than now; discovery was never pushed more efficiently and enthusiastically, and thought and speculation were never more busy concerning all the great subjects that affect the race.

No, the facts do not sustain the conclusions of those who decry the periodical; and when we consider how legitimately and necessarily it has grown out of the changes which progress has introduced, we shall conclude that they cannot do so. The daily newspaper, in its present splendid estate, is a child of the telegraph and the rail-car. As soon as it became possible for a man to sit at his breakfast-table and read of all the important events which took place in the whole world the day before, a want was born which only the daily paper could supply. If a man, absorbed in business and practical affairs, has time only to read the intelligence thus furnished, and the comments upon it and the discussions growing out of it, of course his reading stops there ; but what an incalculable advantage in his business affairs has this hasty survey given him! If he has more time than this, and has a love of science, the periodical brings to him every week or month the latest investigations and their results, and enables him to keep pace with his time. If the work of the various active scientists of the day were only embodied in elaborate books, he would never see and could never read one of them. In the periodical all the scientific men of the world meet. They learn there just what each man is doing, and are constant inquirers and correctors of each other, while all the interested world studies them and keeps even-handed with them. A ten-days' run from Liverpool brings to this country an installment of the scientific labor of all Europe, and there is no possible form in which this can be gathered up and scattered except that of the periodical. In truth, we do not know of any class of men who would be more disastrously affected by a suspension of periodical literature than those who have particularly decried it—the scholars and the scientists.

Within the last twenty years, not only have the means of communication been incalculably increased, but the domain of knowledge has been very greatly enlarged, and the fact is patent that periodical literature has been developed in the same proportion. It has grown out of the new necessities, and must ultimately arrange itself by certain laws. At present it is in a degree of confusion ; but at last the daily paper will announce facts, the scientific journal will describe discoveries and processes, the weekly paper will be the medium of popular discussion, the magazine and review will furnish the theater of the thinker and the literary artist, and the book, sifting all—facts, processes, thoughts and artistic fabrics, and crystallizations of thought—will record all that is worthy of preservation, to enter permanently into the life and

literature of the world. This is the tendency at the present time, although the aim may not be intelligent and definite, or the end clearly seen. Each class of periodicals has its office in evolving from the crude facts of the every-day history of politics, religion, morals, society and science those philosophic conclusions and artistic ... izations that make up the solid literature of the country ; and this office will be better defined as the years go by.

We do not see that it is anything against the magazine that it has become the medium by which books of an ephemeral nature find their way to the public. The novel, almost universally, makes its first appearance as a serial. Macdonald, Collins, Reade, George Eliot, Mrs. Stowe, Mrs. Whitney, Trollope—in fact, all the principal novelists—send their productions to the public through the magazines; and it is certainly better to distribute the interest of these through the year than to devour them *en masse*. They come to the public in this way in their cheapest form, and find ten readers where in the book form they would find one. They are read, too, when serials, mingled with a wider and more valuable range of literature, as they always should be read. Anything is good which prevents literary condiments from being adopted as literary food. If the fact still remains that there are multitudes who will read absolutely nothing but periodical literature, where is the harm? This is a busy world, and although our country is prosperous, the great multitude cannot purchase large libraries. Ten or fifteen dollars' worth of periodicals places every working family in direct relations with the great sources of current intelligence and thought, and illuminates their home life as no other such expenditure can do. The masses have neither the money to buy books nor the leisure to read them. The periodical becomes, then, the democratic form of literature. It is the intellectual food of the people. It stands in the very front rank of the agents of civilization, and in its way, directly and indirectly, is training up a generation of book-readers. It is the pioneer ; the book will come later. In the mean time, it becomes all those who provide periodicals for the people to take note of the fact, that their work has been proved to be a good one by the growing demand for a higher style of excellence in the materials they furnish. The day of trash and peddling is past, or rapidly passing. The popular magazine of to-day is such a magazine as the world never saw before ; and the popular magazine of America is demonstrably better than any popular magazine in the world. We are naturally more familiar with this form of periodical literature than any other, and we make the statement without qualification or reservation. That it is truly educating its readers is proved by the constant demand for its own improvement.

Professional and Literary Incomes.

THE clergyman, the lawyer, the physician, the editor, the teacher, and the writer of books, in order

do not know. The physician has some apology for getting high fees of those that can pay, because he is obliged to do so much for the poor who cannot pay; but the lawyer, as a rule, does not undertake a case which promises him no remuneration. He goes in for money; and there ought to be some law which will enable the poor man to get justice without financial ruin. There is at least no good reason why one set of professional men should half starve while another gorges itself upon fees that bring wealth and luxury. That fees are too large and salaries too small has become a popular conviction, which can only be removed by a reform in both directions, that shall bring literary and professional men equivalent rewards.

The Complicity of Justice with Crime.

It is not to be denied that our city of New York is gaining a most unenviable notoriety as a theater of crime. Those who would explain and apologize for the condition of things that exists, are fond of saying that it is attributable to the fact that the city is the gathering place of criminals of all nations—that crime is not bred here, but that it comes here. There is something in this, without doubt; but why do they come here? Simply because New York is an easier and safer place for them than the places they come from. Authority is more lenient and justice more uncertain here than where they were bred. At any rate, native or imported, there are multitudes of dangerous men here, and almost every morning-issue of the newspapers spreads before a public, hardened to such reading, the details of some new and astounding crime. A man kills his paramour; a mistress shoots her lover; a wife murders her husband; a husband beats out his wife's brains; an unoffending man is waylaid in the streets, knocked down and robbed; pickpockets throng the street-cars and omnibuses; robberies occur at mid-day; and turn appropriate the revenues of the city to feed their own luxuries and to hold the services of their hirelings, or steal railroads and sweep the boards in the Wall street gambling-hells.

It is not a pleasant picture of society to spread before the country, and were it not that New York is just as remarkable for its churches, its charities, its social and religious culture, and its men and women whose whole lives are devoted to works of benevolence as it is for crime, it would be a very hopeless one. The real trouble is that the laws are not executed. The men who have the law in their hands are influenced by other considerations than those of justice. We do not mean that all the judges are corrupt, for there are many ways by which justice may be cheated of its dues. A notorious character was arrested a few weeks ago for a murderous assault, of whom it was freely said that, although he had engaged in similar affrays before, he had escaped arrest on account of his political influence. At the time of this present writing, there are, we believe, nearly thirty men in the Tombs under arrest for murder. They are mostly notorious men, of whose guilt there is no

doubt; but who supposes that these men are to be hanged? The public have become entirely faithless in the matter, notwithstanding the recent conviction and sentences of some of them. They have ceased to have confidence in juries. They know that every trick and quibble will be resorted to by a set of ingenious lawyers to save the murderers' necks. They know that some of their judges are not to be trusted. They know that if these men are convicted and sentenced, there will be determined efforts for commutation of punishment or for pardon. They feel that nobody is as much in earnest to secure justice as multitudes are to defeat it. They feel that the drift of power is for the protection of the criminal, and not for the protection of society.

It is but a short time since New York was entirely in the hands of those who are denominated "the dangerous classes." The men of power in the city were a set of gigantic thieves. They fattened on public plunder, and intrenched themselves behind the votes of pimps, panders, thieves, murderers, whoremongers, dram-sellers, and drunkards. They bought votes; they stuffed ballot-boxes; they hired ruffians to do their bidding. They polluted the politics of the city and the State. They demoralized every man that came within their influence. There happened a great uprising, and the men were thrust from power, but still their foul influence lingers. Some of their tools are still in office, and it will be many years, under the most favorable conditions, before the city can recover its moral tone. In the meantime, every newspaper and every good man and every possible good moral influence should array itself on the side of the law, and demand its faithful execution. Let it be fully understood and hoisted on that the dangerous classes include all those officers of justice who are derelict in duty, and who, in any way, try to shield criminals from the consequences of their crimes.

Neither human life nor property can be any safer than they are at present until it becomes less safe to make depredations upon them. So long as it is legal to sell unlimited rum, so long as theft and swindling and burglary and murder go unpunished, so long as flagrant crime is sure of sympathy and determined effort to free those who are guilty of it, so long as influential names are easily procurable in the attempt to shield the criminal from the legal consequences of his misdeeds, so long will crime go on unchecked. We feed the flames of anger and lust and malice with poisoned liquors, and hold up our hands in horror over the results. We keep men in power who will not do their duty, and walk the streets at night with bludgeons in our hands and revolvers in our pockets. We shut up criminals, and then submit to any mockery of justice by which they are released. And then, when the crime and the criminal are too outrageous to permit them to be ignored, we sign papers begging for commutation of punishment or for pardon. Let it be understood, then, that every man, high or low, who seeks for the release of the criminal from the legal consequences of his crime unites himself to the dangerous classes, and becomes an accomplice in their deeds. Crime will cease, or greatly diminish, just as soon as official and popular justice cuts off its complicity with it; and it will not cease or diminish until that event occurs. Crime thrives because the officers of the law do not do their duty, and because the popular voice does not demand those safeguards of social and political order that are essential to its maintenance. The

ignorant brute, maddened by alcohol and degraded by the example of those whom he helped to place in power, can be reached by no motive but fear; and so long as that motive does not exist, we may expect to see in every newspaper we take up the record of a new crime, and to bow our heads in shame for our city, the while we examine anew the defences we have spread around our goods and our lives.

THE OLD CABINET.

My mind has been strangely drawn of late **to the** subject of statistics. I suppose the recent census has had something to do with it. There are certain friends of mine who take a singular delight in that census. They pore over it as a child pores over Gulliver or books of African travel. They come away from its pages with a glow in their eyes and a flush upon their cheeks and a wonderful story upon their lips. "According to the recent census, it appears that in Rhode Island alone the number of adult males, of Portuguese descent, who died from spinal meningitis during the first half of the last decade, was just twice the number of Ashburere goats imported during the succeeding five years by the entire state of New York." They not only say it, but if I am in a hurry to go anywhere, they pause it by figures, and they write communications to the newspapers, consisting mainly of tables and maps, in order to promulgate ideas like that.

While I acknowledge that there is a sphere in which statistics are useful as well as entertaining, I am sure that it would be well for the world if their limitations were better understood. The number of periodicals that have been started on statistics in the United States, and have miserably perished of them, is lamentable. A corrected list would make an interesting chapter in our mart errors. A young friend of my own started one of these papers. He took a sheet of foolscap and two or three lead-pencils, and the then recent census, and began in this fashion: Here is a community with a population of so many thousands; I may calculate, on general principles, that at least twenty persons in every thousand will take the paper the first year—which gives a handsome paying circulation to begin with. Then so many columns of advertisements will come to so much per week, and pretty nearly all of this may be put down to account of profit. So the second year will open with an increase of say—to be moderate—one third in circulation and the same in advertisements.

I tried to wean him away from his populations and his confounded sums in arithmetic. But it was of no use. He went around town for about three weeks in a hectic condition with his pockets full of lead-pencils, and little note-books containing all sorts of deceitful calculations based on the recent census. At the end of that time the *Morning Magnifier* made its appearance. I caught occasional glimpses of the editor's haggard countenance as he flitted home for his night's repose at eight o'clock in the morning. But why prolong the melancholy tale? Enough to say that my young friend has long since gone West.

And then I have another friend who believed in the doctrine of the annihilation of the souls of the wicked. In fact, he was generally acknowledged to be the foremost expounder of that doctrine in the country. Well, what does he do but write a novel of society,—with little or nothing to it concerning his pet doctrine. That is not so pathetic as the fact that he became a slave to statistical delusions. He had taken some sort of a private census of his own, by which he had determined that there were in the United States—I forget how many millions of people, who believed with himself as to the matter of annihilation. There were the avowed believers—so many millions; and there were the believers who dared not avow—a great many millions more; and he was the celebrated Expounder—and so many thousands out of every million (it was quite a low estimate, I thought) would buy the novel, of course. I myself was fresh in the faith of statistics in those days, and I remember how I envied that man his copyright—till six months after the date of publication the publishers sent in their bill for stereotype plates.

When statistics are wrenched from their proper sphere in connection with nations, cereal crops, areas, immigration and the like, they not only prove financially delusive and dangerous, but they manifest a tendency to corrupt good morals. The man who first proclaimed the relation between the corn-crop and the number of matrimonial proposals in any given year, struck a blow at the foundations of society. He is of kin to that disagreeable person in Washington, who has pretty nearly succeeded in doing away with what used to be known in conversation as the weather. He is of kin to all people who account for things on general principles, who are always ready with their classifications and "I told you sos,"—your abominable social botanists.

Suppose an editor says to a young poet that he can tell in advance not only how many poems will be sent in during the next year, but just about how many of them will relate to horticultural subjects; how many will refer to an infinite longing of the soul; and how many will be descriptive of the subtle charms of certain young ladies (real name not given) in whose arms, etc., owing to their grace of face; and duty of beauty (or beauty of duty); to say nothing about gladness and gladness, or fire and desire, etc., etc., etc. Or suppose he says to a lackling novelist that he—the editor—is sure to receive, within a certain space of time, in the neighborhood of so many stories in which something or other will come into the heroine's life; and so many in which the hero will cast a half-defiant glance at a person standing conveniently near,—what, I say, will become of the young poet's or the young novelist's vim, or verve, or fizzle, or whatever it is that makes composition spontaneous and sparkling, and life something more than a dreary submission to the inevitable, a melancholy dance of destiny, a column of figures in a census report?

It is only carrying the thing a little farther when a man in the blues ponders over the statistics of suicide till he considers it quite the natural and inevitable thing that he should help along the count of those who take fatal doses of laudanum between the hours of 2 and 4 A.M.

Rather than that affairs should come to such a pass, let us have a little uncertainty—yes, downright, reckless hap-hazard if you please! Where is the fun of throwing dice after you find they are loaded? What is more uninteresting than eating straight down through a pile of buckwheat-cakes? Remove the pile from the sordid restaurant to the family circle; the element of chance is at once introduced, and true enjoyment begins. You are no longer sure that the batter will be mixed aright, and getting the top cake becomes, as it should be, a piece of good luck.

It makes no difference in my feelings toward him that the sum of statistics is apt to be right in the long run. In fact this rather aggravates the matter. He hasn't the subtlety to discern, nor will he ever

acknowledge, that my exceptions are just as good as his rule.

. . . I shall fight my enemy as long as I have life; but I confess to a mortal fear lest he should triumph over me dead by classifying my poor life and untimely departure under the heading of "Obituary." O gentle friends! if any deed of mine should be worthy recited outside of the funereal column where the last act is curtly chronicled, and if that record has over it the hateful word I have just written—a word that would snatch from death the pang of surprise, the accident, the individuality, and the awe—then remember this my protest, and let me be avenged even in the grave!

The Poet to his Poem.

O BLESSED babe of my brain,
Outwrought in bliss and pain !
I may not hold thee mine,
I may not beckon or call thee,
By word or look enthrall thee,—
Like Mary, chief of mothers,
And least, with her Child Divine.
For thou art not mine, but another's ;
He loves and understands thee,
His service sweet demands thee.

Go forth, O son, God-sent,—
In thy innocent young eyes
The ancientest mysteries,—
Go forth to spend and be spent ;
Go forth to reap and to sow,
To lose and labor and grow,
To carry a curse and to bless.

I can sit in my silent room
And hide my face in my hands,
Till, all in a solemn morrow,
Over the seas and the lands,
Over the lands and the seas
Come thy loving messages,—
(For I know that at last they will come)
Like thy first dear baby cares,—
And I rise and forget my sorrow.

HOME AND SOCIETY.

Household Art.

" THE back is soon fitted to the burden," says the pathetic old proverb ; pathetic, not because it means that men learn to carry heavy loads cheerfully, but because it means that men, coming to forget their loads, cease trying to be rid of them. Hence the perpetuity of some terrible burdens—among others, and in our country chief of all, the burden of ugliness.

With many religions and a good deal of religiousness we have fought vice; ignorance, too, we have

fought with such fury, that even the smallest child has now hardly a chance for his life if he be found ignorant.

But ugliness, which is as vicious as vice, and is the sum and substance of ignorance, we have left so undisturbed in its reign that one might almost fancy we believed it a deity to be propitiated. And this is not so far from the truth, after all ; for the trouble is rooted in an old antagonism to superstition ; and as the bitterest of all feuds are feuds between brothers, to this very antagonism was, and is, of next kin to the thing it hated and fought and left behind. We are paying, and must continue to pay high charges for that we've no arbitration can ever settle the importance for all, and have it paid and done with. We shall have helious pictures in America for years to come, because good Roman Catholics have built before for ages; and our saints will sit for centuries in their hearts, instead of in us.

But of late things have begun to brighten. Many an leisure and journeying have opened a few eyes. Art, whose name is Beauty, and who cannot forsake her children, is beginning to have some worship among us. To be sure, most of the altars might well bear the old Athenian motto; but to have the altar at all is significant that the god will not always be "unknown."

One of the good signs of the present year is the publication, and with some the welcome, of two such books as Faulkner's *Hints on Household Taste*, and Walter Smith's *Art Education.* Such books as these are an education of art in every home into which they go. Another sign of the better time coming is the establishment in Boston of the "Household Art Company."

The modest little pamphlet of this firm gives brief suggestion of its ends and aims. "Rooms or houses can be furnished complete, with antique and artistic furniture, carpets, mirrors, etc., etc." This is the only promise set forth in its pages; the rest are filled with a catalogue of antique furniture and objects of household art, already on exhibition in the rooms. Many of these articles are of great beauty and interest.

Here are old cabinets, tables, secretaries, and chests, from Spain, Italy, France, and Holland; ancient chairs from Amsterdam and Spanish; a Friesland desk, name of boy owner unknown, but if he were alive now he would be about two hundred years old; and a settle from the same country—perhaps the owner of the desk was rocked in it; it belonged to a burgomaster of Purmerend, a little town twenty miles north of Amsterdam, and is of wood, painted from stem to stern, from rocker to rocker, with Scripture scenes in blues and reds as dull and solid and quaint as the Dutch worthies they color. A more picturesque and suggestive old relic is seldom seen.

Then there are tables of old Delft ware, rare old Nankin china, Sgraffito and Wedgewood wares, brass sconces for walls, large dishes from Minton's art studios, hand-painted tiles for mantel-pieces and fire-places, candlesticks, door-knobs, stair-rods, hinges and nails, upholsterers' cloths, altar-cloths, stained glass, standard and pulpit lights for churches, brackets, lecterns.

The collection of majolica is small, but contains some very choice styles. In decorated glass also there are some exquisite things; and in terra cottas some of the articles are set on tables draped with matrons-

colored cloths; some are hung against walls of a delicious gray; and the carved and gaily painted antique furniture is tastefully disposed in the rooms. Simply to walk through them is a pleasure, and will no doubt be a lesson of color and arrangement to many persons.

The company has agents abroad, who are to be constantly on the lookout for rare things in Europe, Asia, and Africa. The passion for this sort of collection is now so strong, that the best relics are fast being accumulated in rich men's houses and in museums in England and France, and we have no time to lose if we would not be left destitute of them. But the furnishing of choice antiques and interesting relics to the few who have money and taste for them is not the chief aim of the Household Art Company. It is to introduce true ideas of beauty, harmony, and fitfulness in the appointments of houses. Average householders, men and women, need education on this point more than any other. They will make sacrifices to secure skilled service in the preparation of all they eat and all they wear, but ignorant carpenters, upholsterers, and cabinet-makers may create their houses. To supply to people destitute of which they are not conscious, is a task as difficult as thankless; but the true lover of beauty is a missionary by instinct, and a proselyte in spite of himself, and when this instinct allies itself to systematic and professional purpose, results cannot but follow.

Co-operative Marketing

A GENTLEMAN living in one of our large Eastern cities, whose a good table is always a heavy expense, recently made an experiment which was certainly very satisfactory. In connection with two or three friends, he ordered a barrel of meat and game from a town in Indiana. The provisions arrived in due time and in excellent condition, and the following table will exhibit the comparative cost of the articles in the Eastern markets and in those of some of the older Western states:—

	Western Prices.		Eastern Prices.
6 doz. quails	@ $1.50 ...$9.00.	@ 3.00 $18.00
2 doz. prairie chick-			
ens	@ $4.20 .... 8.40	@ 9.00 $18.00
5 turkeys, 42 lbs.	@ .13 cts. 5.88	@ .28 $11.76
16 lbs. venison	@ .25 cts. 4.00	@ .30 $ 4.80
68 lbs. beef (steaks & roasts)			
	@ .15 cts. 10.20	@ .25 $17.00
Barrel	.25	
Expressage	7.70	
	$45.43	69.36
		45.43
Difference in favor of Western market		$23.53

The various articles were all of the best quality and carefully packed. The turkeys were fat and sound, and came without heads and with the useless portions of legs and wings cut off—these weighty appendages not being charged for. The beef, which was tender and fat, came in three enormous roasts and five great steaks, neatly boned and skewered. The meat and game was fresh, and in as good condition as it can be had in the markets of our great Eastern cities. As to the saving of expense, it may be said that Eastern prices are very often much higher than those quoted, beef being often thirty-three cents per pound instead of twenty-five, and other things in proportion. A few families, tired of paying the high prices asked in our large cities, might readily club together and obtain from a Western dealer excellent meats and game, and have them brought to their doors at a saving of one-third the price charged in the Eastern city markets. Even in our large city markets, co-operation of this kind, by enabling families to purchase at wholesale, would certainly be economical, and might result in other advantages.

Ladies at Sea.

It almost always happens with ladies who go to sea for the first time, that in spite of the advice of friends and their own personal care and foresight, they find their outfit lacking in something essential to comfort,—something whose lack presses so heavily on a half-sick condition, that all the journey through there is a reiterated lament of " Why did I never think?" or " Why did not some one tell me?" It is useless to attempt universal rules for experiences which must differ with each individual, but in the following simple suggestions, somebody new to the sea may find comfort.

1st. State-room baggage should be compact. A small hat-box, or a valise which can be pushed under the berth, are least in the way. A trunk which must stand in the middle of the state-room becomes a serious affliction when the vessel pitches and throws you upon its sharp corners.

2d. By all means provide yourself with one or two linen bags, made with pockets like a shoe-bag, and carry a hammer and tacks with which to nail them against the side of the state-room. These convenient little catch-alls, into which your watch, slippers, brushes, etc., can be crammed when not in use, are indispensable to comfort at sea.

3d. Let your traveling dress be old and warm. Finery is useless at sea. However clean the ship, there is something at every turn which rubs off and soils—fresh paint, newly oiled wood-work, newly greased chains. The brasses spot you with verdigris. Sprinkles of salt water visit you now and then. Soup will spill when the table stands at an angle of forty-five degrees; it may even chance of a stormy evening that a goose or a leg of mutton, flying from under the carving-knife, shall alight in your lap! Under these circumstances it is comforting to have on a gown whose spoiling is of no consequence.

But whether of choice fabric or of hodden-gray, it is above all essential that the garment be warm. The ocean climates are cool even in the heats of summer. You want woolen under-garments, thick boots and gloves, wraps of all kinds, and a hood to tie over your hat. With these precautions you can be comfortable for many hours each day on deck, and where there is the least disposition to nausea, fresh air is the surest and speediest remedy.

4th. We would advise all persons whose sailing qualities are untested, to carry with them to sea a cane-bottomed reclining chair with a long back, also a warm rug to wrap round the feet while using it. Some of the steamships provide deck chairs for their passengers, but they are not of this comfortable kind, and many vessels carry none at all. A person of steady head does very well cuddled into corners of the deck, against the sails, etc.; but to many of us, the command of a comfortable chair makes all the difference between being able to keep in the air or being forced to retreat to the close cabins below. There are arrangements made for storing these chairs in Liverpool, so that they shall be ready for the journey back.

5th. It is unnecessary to carry many stores to sea, nor indeed does any one know, until the moment of actual experiment, what is or is not likely to be acceptable in his or her particular case. Fruit, especially grapes, is almost always grateful; a box of Albert biscuits may serve a good turn, and a few fresh lemons are almost sure to do so, as the lemonade on ship-board is usually made of concentrated lemon, and lacks the acid freshness which is so reviving. Another thing which every sea-traveler will like to have is a box or bottle of good fresh French prunes. They are so very grateful and wholesome, that if your fellow-travelers know you have them they will probably be gone before the end of the voyage. It is well to be provided with a little good brandy in case of extreme exhaustion, and persons who can bear champagne sometimes find that a small quantity, made very cold with ice, is the only thing that will stay down after extreme illness, and that it seems to restore the tone of the stomach and prepare it for the reception of food. It may be well for such to provide themselves with a few half-pint bottles, as the steamer people have a habit of being out of everything but quart bottles, and so little is generally taken at a time, that the wine spoils before it can be used. Champagne, however, cannot be universally recommended. Indeed, nothing can. There is no predicting what will or will not suit anybody. With sea-sickness more than any other phase of mortal experience the adage holds true, that what is one man's meat is another man's poison.

Smelling-salts should be remembered. Cologne and aromatic vinegar are often excessively disagreeable to persons who are ill. A warm woolen wrapper and knitted slippers should be provided for use at night, and an india-rubber bottle to hold hot water and keep the feet warm in bed.

We would advise all persons going to Europe to select a ship which has the reputation of a *stay deck*, and which has saloon or deck state-rooms. Nobody who has not tried it can appreciate the increase of freedom in comfort of being able to keep the port-hole of the state-room open in tolerable weather. Nothing but fresh air enables one to forget the ship's smell, and to do this is the great *desideratum* at sea.

Some people ask their friends, and some friends are so thoughtful as moved to write a note or two to be read at intervals during the voyage. The captain or the stewardess takes charge of these billets, and their unexpected reception, five days or eight days out, make a pleasant break in the monotony of the transit.

Lastly, do not expect any pleasure at sea. Prepare your minds for the worst, for ten or eleven or twelve miserable days, and go resolved to endure all with patience. Then each day free from illness, each meal swallowed with relish, each calm morning or smooth moon-lighted evening, will become the aspect of an agreeable surprise, something not counted on or hoped for, even by the kind farewell voices which wished you "*Bon voyage.*"

Hyper Gentility.

We remember reading of three unfortunate ladies who were entertained one summer day at the house of a country friend, and whose consequent sufferings were so remarkable that they will serve to point a little moral. These ladies were very high-toned, so to speak. They were so very genteel and so extremely proper in their manners, that if society conferred degrees they would have been Mistresses of Social Arts and Doctoresses of Social Law.

So these three high-toned ladies sat down to dinner in the house of their country friend, and there were peas on the table. "Peas," said one of the immaculate trio, "such as we never see in town—fresh, green, plump, and luscious, and so delightfully hot and tempting! But as the forks had only two prongs, making it quite useless to try to eat peas with them, we were obliged to leave the delicious things on our plates. The family ate their peas with their knives, but of course we could not do that."

Now our opinion may be worth little, but we certainly believe that a true lady would have eaten those peas with her knife. She would have done so simply because she would have known that the laws of true politeness made it imperative upon her to use her knife in such a case. But this genteel trio did not appear to understand that politeness requires a greater attention to the feelings of others than to mere forms; that what is very genteel in one place is often quite boorish in another, and that there is a hyper gentility and a pho propriety which is offensive to the nostrils of a true gentleman or lady.

The Games of Children and the Gambling of Men.

As our elderly and middle-aged readers recall their childhood, they can remember but few games of chance or skill that were considered legitimate to the fruits, and these were such games as *Checkers*, *Fox and Geese*, and *Twelve men Morris*, played with red and yellow kernels of corn on designs scratched on the opposite sides of a plain pine board. The various games of cards were generally considered contraband, and hence had wonderful charms for the boys who keenly enjoyed the stolen fruit in back garrets, wood-sheds, and hay-mows. In the youthful days of the younger of our adult readers the games of *Dr. Busby* and the *Man who may Happiness* were added to the list recognized by the heads of most families, and we well remember our doubts concerning the propriety of reporting at home the fact that we had been exceedingly fascinated with the game of *Dr. Busby* at the house of a playmate, and also our happiness when the game, after becoming a little known in the neighborhood, was introduced to our fireside by parents who had the good sense to believe in making home pleasant to the youngsters.

From these small beginnings a few other games came into general use, and parents began to learn that it was not beneath their dignity to devote a part of their evenings to making home interesting and attractive to the children.

The word "games" is at present used to denote a wide range of amusements and recreations adapted to the home circle, such as charades, parlor magic, fortunes, wax figures, pantomimes, etc., as well as games of chance and skill played with various kinds of cards, or on boards with dice and men, all of which we believe are each year becoming more popular in American homes.

But while this is so, we would not have a parent forget for a moment that the line should be drawn between innocent home amusements and what we understand as gambling. Many are unable to see where this line is and in what it consists, and while they admit the necessity of making home the most attractive place to the children, argue that games played at home in childhood tend to gambling in manhood. This is not so; it is the use of the game that decides which side of the line it must be placed. That delight of every boy, the game of marbles, is as innocent as any other childish recreation, and yet many boys have received their first lessons in gambling when playing marbles for *gains*, and many parents have allowed their sons to count over the contents of their marble-bags at night in their presence, who would have held up their hands in holy horror at a game of *Bezique* around the evening lamp. Here is just the line we would draw. Never countenance any game played for a permanent gain, or in which money or its equivalent is the object played for.

That this must be the one and only distinction between innocent recreation and harmful gambling must be seen from the fact that the same recreation or amusement of chance or skill may be used for gambling purposes, and hence no dividing line can be drawn between two games unless, indeed, one of them involves vicious habits or practices in itself.

But if all games are made simply matters of amusement, it is not likely that those boys who stay at home in the evening to play them with their parents and sisters will be attracted in their manhood by the temptations of the gaming tables.

On the other hand, a boy who has been encouraged to be proud of his constantly-increasing bag of marbles, as the reward of his shrewdness and skill in playing, will be apt enough to consider it legitimate in after years to keep his purse filled in the same manner, although ivory balls and pieces of card may be substituted for the marbles. It is a matter of satisfaction to all who have given the subject thought, that innocent games and home amusements are fast becoming a prominent feature in our homes, thereby establishing counter-attractions to those of the saloons and haunts of vice that crowd so closely to our doors, not only in the larger cities but in every country village in the land.

CULTURE AND PROGRESS.

Büchner's "Man."[*]

MR. DALLAS, the English translator, clears himself of responsibility for the opinions in this book, but gives a cue to the reader and comforts himself at the same time with the thought that it will prove instructive, especially to opponents, as showing to what results the principles maintained by the school of thinkers to which Dr. Büchner belongs necessarily lead. A follower in the paths of severe scientific induction has no business to falter in view of possible results. The hint might seem an improper one, but there are so many wild speculations which are boldly put upon popular audiences as if they had the authority of inductive science, that the caution will not prove without reason if the reader is thereby moved to the closer scrutiny of facts and reasonings.

Dr. Büchner treats of Man's Position in Nature, and "proposes to present to the general public an exposition of the results attained by inductive science for its elucidation, and for the refutation of the old-world errors and prejudices." His presentation is not only professedly scientific, but sharply and decisively polemic. His positiveness of speech in the name of science is great, his scorn of "prejudices" greater. As in a glass of his own national beverage, it is difficult at times to tell where the froth of scorn ends and the true lager of Science begins.

Whence are we? What are we? and Whither are we going? are the three great questions over which men have been blundering for ages under the dominion of religious prejudice. Science now sloughs off the effete body of the old philosophy by thrusting out, at a blow, the religious conception as unscientific, and by announcing, as therefore the sole master of the situation, the greatest discovery of all time—the natural origin of man. As the great astronomers Copernicus swept away the former geocentric conceptions of the universe, so now the great naturalists, Darwin, Lamarck, Lyell, have forever banished the anthropocentric idea which has been so long embarrassing human thought by representing man as in the image of God, and having a special endowment in the shape of a soul. Our ancestors, the Doctor allows, were little to be blamed, seeing that, *prima facie*, there is so vast a distance between man and nature that they might readily mistake him for a superior being. But it is only bigotry now that can persist in regarding man as anything more than a highly-refined animal.

The elements of this greatest of discoveries **are** fully set forth, together with the leading data and processes of reasoning by which it is sustained. While there is no novelty in these, except in his own bold handling, we may take the argument from an apostle so competent, and so thoroughly in earnest, as at its best estate, and the more confidently test its value in the name of "strict inductive science."

In brief, the case of this prosecutor of bigotry and old prejudice stands thus :—

Human remains, such as flint axes and weapons, with a limited number of bones, have been found associated, chiefly in caves, with bones of extinct mammals, the mammoth, cave-bear, etc. Add to this the facts that the long bones of these creatures were split, apparently for the marrow, and that certain rude attempts at figuring the mammals in question have been found, and the proof culminates towards showing that primitive man was contemporary with those beasts in the Diluvial age. Therefore, Dr. Büchner says, primitive man must be referred to a very high antiquity, say, not less than one hundred thousand years. Or, if some more recent discoveries in the Tertiary are sustained, then the time must be reckoned by the hundreds of thousands of years. He fondly hopes they will be. Curiosity must linger a moment, to wonder how a professor of inductive science can so far share the spirit of a religious enthusiast as to hope for one result rather than another.

The next principal step in the argument is that the cranial bones which have been found, and associated facts, indicate absolutely that primitive man was of

[*] *Man in the Past, Present, and Future.* Philadelphia : J. B. Lippincott & Co.

a low, beastly type. The author admits that he here treads "an uncertain and dangerous course," that he must "depend rather on assumptions, conclusions from analogy and the like, than on direct knowledge, and thus fancy must more or less lend its aid to reason in testing and arranging the evidence." One could look on this passage as pre-eminently fair-minded and just, but for the surprise of finding no abatement of positiveness, as if inductive science were still the authority, nor any "let up" of wrathfulness against the bigots who, unmindful of "assumptions, analogies and the like," still believe in a special endowment of soul. Just about here the reader may as well be warned that if he do not call in aid some of that "fancy" which bears the author easily along, there is a pit of difficulty into which he may fall. Man began "as a rude savage scarcely above the grade of animality." Miserable altogether were the conditions of life; and yet, "*armed only with his wretched stone wedges*" (the italics are the author's), "this savage or primitive man had to maintain an almost unceasing struggle with the overpowering forces of nature which surrounded him, and with the powerful animals of the Diluvial or Tertiary period. Out of this contest he certainly would not have come as a conqueror, if he had not been supported by his comparatively great intellectual power." The author emphasizes this by a citation: "Those must be blind who cannot recognize the traces of this long, hard, desperate, bloody, and diabolically cruel contest between the first men and all the adverse forces of the air and the earth, a contest in which all the advantages were on the side of nature, and in which nevertheless man conquered because the powers of mind and reason came to his assistance." But the man who conquered in that struggle was physically diminutive in stature, and intellectually as low as, if not lower than, the lowest savage known in our times, and to rise from that semi-idiotic, "perhaps dumb," state of being to the present has taken enormous time. The first weapons were of the crudest shape and rough hewn. It took ages on ages to develop the ideas of shapeliness and smoothness, or to conceive the thought of pottery. Ages more passed before metals came into human hands; and through these successive stages we have the whole pre-historic time variously divided into epochs. The Darwinian solution admirably covers the whole development. Huxley, Carl Vogt, Lyell, Lubbock, with a score of other distinguished evolutionists come in to help.

Through the testimony of these it is shown that man is essentially ape-like, with not a characteristic to separate him in origin, in structure, in mode of life, or in endowments from the brute creation. He came by natural descent from some creature who was progenitor alike of man and monkey. To imagine, as certain "*soi-disant*" great thinkers" ("called thinkers on the *lucus a non lucendo* principle") do, that a man received a supernatural gift, is to break a

law of development, and to break a law of development is intolerable to right reason and science.

Proceeding on this basis, the author, flush with the grandeur of the discovery, and with the perfect assurance that every opponent is extinguished, grasps almost every problem of human life with the gripe of a giant. We can only catalogue. Government, finance, labor, capital, communism, woman, education, morality, religion, Paulinism, which is his name for Christianity; over all, with no slightest fear, he flings his scepter as an autocrat. Huxley renders him splendid service; but poor Huxley must take a two-page sermon of great severity, because he quails before the "bigotry" of his countrymen, and dares not be materialistic to the end, and that end is this: At death man loses *personal consciousness*, but still lives on in nature, in his race, in his children, in his deeds, in his thoughts—in short, in the entire material and psychical contribution which, during his short personal existence, he has furnished to the subsistence of mankind and of nature in general. He lives as does the water-drop,—a glorious immortality for the inductive philosopher to sit down at the end of his toil and contemplate in ecstasy. Dr. Büchner, at least, makes no secret of his delight.

The brilliant audacity of this book may abash some reader into the feeling that it would be an impertinence, or a piece of bigotry, to doubt this all-knowing German. It is quite within the scope, however, of an ordinarily intelligent man, especially in these days when scientists are so freely kind in popularizing their various studies, to take the place of juryman and pass upon the arguments which are drawn out at length. Certainly it will take no profound knowledge to discover how little inductive science has to do with this book, and how greatly the author depends on "assumptions, conclusions from analogies, and the like," together with "fancy," to maintain a theory which rules him with a despotic bias scarcely to be paralleled. He addresses the public as a pure inductive reasoner. He insults the public by calling them bigoted on almost every other page, and worse by imagining that they cannot see the difference between inductive proof and the assertions of a dogmatist, and then trying to daze them by the brilliancy of great names of the same school. It may be very interesting to study the theories of Huxley, Lyell, Darwin, Vogt, and Büchner, but these men, as to their solutions of grave problems, are only *prophets*. They have unbounded faith that their theories are at last to be justified. The confidence of some of them is sublime—it grows on them as they grow old; but were there ten thousand of them, all without an inharmony raising the same voice, the gift of prophecy is no part of inductive science. And yet whenever an opinion is put to test, the prompt recourse is to great names, quite as the Church appeals to the Holy Fathers.

The high antiquity of man has by no means been proven. If he began in the age of mammals, it is quite as likely that the mammals survived more recently as that man existed more anciently than has been supposed. The stress of proof falls on the data which geology has to give as to the deposits in which these bones have been found. Nothing is regarded by prudent geologists as more doubtful than any calculation of positive time in the deposition of alluvium, in erosions, in uplifts, in coral or peat growth, or in the accretion and the dispersion of ice-masses. Dr. Büchner supplies an example. A mound near Lake Geneva was cut through twenty-three feet by a railroad, uncovering remains of three civilizations, the Roman, Bronze and Stone ages. It was calculated that this must have taken ten thousand years in decomposition, but a more recent American calculator sets it down at five thousand, and the Doctor troubles himself little with the exact figures. Only he relegates the geological argument to Sir Charles Lyell. Sir Charles has had long war as an "*uniformitarian*" with the "*catastrophists*," and with him the long-time side of any question has ever had the preference. Yet by a singular carelessness in just those things wherein a scientific man should never fail—actual measurements—he has done much to destroy his own authority as an expert in time calculations. One surveyor's measurement instantly cut down his figures in a certain calculation from twenty thousand to two thousand years. Time estimates founded on the rate of progress in art must take their cast from the theory with which the reasoner starts. The transition from the rough-hewn flints to the smooth and shapely would naturally depend on the amount of leisure, and might readily be the work of a few generations. If boys played with mud pies—a relic of barbarism which has not been cast off—or if men cemented ovens with clay, the art of pottery could come in at any time between father and son. Metals brought to light by accident, rather than as the result of processes of reasoning, might very suddenly introduce a bronze age. The postulate of enormous ages to accomplish such progress is only the assumption of men who are predetermined by their theories as to the origin of man. From one interesting epoch of history, at least, we learn a different story. "Picture," says M. Taine, "in this foggy clime, amid hoar-frost and storm, in these marshes and forests, half-naked savages, a kind of wild beasts, fishers and hunters, even hunters of men, these are they, Saxons, Angles, Jutes, Frisians." Thus in Jutland, afterward in Britain, "they must have lived as before, as swineherds and hunters, brawny, fierce, gloomy. Here the barbarian, ill-housed in his mud-hovel, who hears the rain rustling whole days in the oak-leaves, what dreams can he have gazing upon his mud-pools and his somber sky?" From such as these, and inside of two thousand years, has sprung the Anglo-Saxon race! To assert that man developed body and soul from an ancient beast by natural and very slow processes, and then to turn around and argue that the time was very great because the process was slow, as Dr. Büchner does, is very much like reasoning in a circle. One would gather from him that there could be no dispute

as to this animal origin. The steps of the great evolution are worked out with undoubted genius, but it is by the use of analogies, assumptions and fancies, and these playing with evidences of the crudest kind. It is claimed, for example, that man was anticipated by the animal in the idea of agriculture. Turning with no little curiosity to the proof, we find that some one person reports an *agricultural ant* in Texas which builds a storehouse, plants around it a sort of grass which bears a small seed, which seed is harvested into the storehouse. This *proves*, says Dr. Büchner, that animals sometimes practice agriculture. It proves nothing as it stands unsupported, or if it did, only the most distant analogy can give it any bearing on the question of man's origin. In the same style of reasoning, when he finds that the beginnings of individual human life are beyond the reach of his microscope, he exclaims: "Who can venture to speak of *brute* matter, or to deny its ability to produce mental phenomena?" We can now understand readily what he means in another place by saying: "Nothing is more ridiculous than the *pride of not knowing*, with which so many respectable men of science are at present fond of acting."

As the culmination of his efforts, he reaches the "probability" that we shall some day find the immediate creatures between man and his brute ancestor somewhere in the Malay Archipelago. These intermediate types in the evolution are just what inductive science waits for, in the "pride of not-knowing" what is only *a priori* theorizing. M. Quatrefages, than whom no one is better conversant with all the facts, says: "With regard to the simial origin of man, it is nothing but pure hypothesis, or rather nothing but a mere *jeu d'esprit* which everything proves utterly baseless, and in favor of which no solid fact has yet been appealed to." Dr. Büchner does not cite Quatrefages, nor hardly gives a hint of the very strong school of scientific men who differ from himself. As for the cranial bones which are brought in evidence, they really are so few and so fragmentary as to shed but little light. The whole subject of craniology is so difficult that Prof. Rolleston tells us that no expert with a given set of unnamed skulls before him could be trusted to name their race, unless it might be the Esquimaux or the Australian. A German expert is making a collection at Berlin, in which he expects to include every known type of skull on earth, and yet all from the heads of his own countrymen! The Neanderthal skull Huxley pronounces the most bestial and ape-like in existence. On the other hand, Pruner-Bey claims to prove that it is a fair specimen of the Celtic. But the Neanderthal skull was not found in any close association with other bones, and its age is utterly in doubt. Inductive science can manifestly make but little out of this relic, however lovingly Büchner cherishes it on his rosary.

The want of space forbids further sifting of that style of reasoning which the Büchner school adopts, and which is legitimate enough, provided it is not

"Mrs. Skaggs's Husbands."

"Middlemarch."

ONE hardly takes in its full significance the remark of Macaulay, in his Essay on Lord Bacon, that in the time of Henry VIII. and Edward VI. (he might have added, during nearly the whole of Elizabeth's reign as well) there was no such thing as an English literature—until he bethinks him what life would be if we were cut off from the stream of delightful entertainment that has flowed to this generation from the pens of a few great novel-writers. Walter Scott, Miss Edgeworth, Miss Martineau—whose *Deerbrook* was the worthy pioneer of the modern novel of domestic life—made bright the youth of the generation that has just turned the middle point of life. Then came Dickens, Thackeray, Charlotte Brontë, Mrs. Gaskell, and now one of the greatest is still in her prime, the author of *Adam Bede* and of *Middlemarch*.

Middlemarch * has not the charm of plot, of story to tell, that made a large part of the delightfulness of *Adam Bede* and *The Mill on the Floss*. It has not the intensity of passion that bore the reader along through the picturesque and tragic pages of *Romola*. It is a quiet study of life in an English village; and though its interest is concentrated upon one woman, the heroine of its pages, yet, as we close the book, a half-dozen other portraits, no less clearly and cleverly drawn, if not so well worth the putting forth of the author's power as that of Dorothea, long continue to give pleasure in the recollection. Of these minor characters Mr. Brooke is the principal, and the most freely drawn. The scene at the hustings is inimitable, the only drawback being that we cannot make up our minds to enjoy the actual maltreatment of a man toward whom we are forced to feel so kindly. Still, we do not see how such a speech as is put into Mr. Brooke's mouth could have been more appropriately greeted. In a bit of writing such as is this speech, and in the conversations throughout the book, George Eliot shows her dramatic power more than in her situations. These people talk as naturally and as put to the purpose as Shakespeare's. To find how real their talk is, compare it, first, with the stilted or farcical talk of Dickens's people,—funny as much of the farcical is, it is never natural; and then with that of Thackeray, a great master, but mannered in his method, and the merit of George Eliot's dialogue will come out in a strong light. Then turn the full blaze of Shakespeare upon it, and it will be found to bear the trial well. Nature is the standard by which each has worked.

Mrs. Cadwallader is another character who lights up the book; she and her husband are equally well drawn, but the lady says the better things. Mr. Farebrother is perhaps not made so clear to the mind as his mother and aunt, but the whole group is one, it is wholesome to meet. Lydgate is rather an aimless portraiture, yet he serves well to bring out the

character of his wife, who, of all the personages in the book, makes the most striking contrast to Dorothea. For a person of infinitely small nature, she is drawn with great power, and George Eliot shows her skill in handling her with so cool and contained a temper. She may madden Lydgate, and make us wish her all manner of evil, but the author will see that she has justice done her, and will not allow her hand to shake as she paints her, or her brush to take up a bit more color than belongs to her. Rosamond for a decent bad woman shall be painted as carefully as Dorothy for a saint. We do not like Mr. Bulstrode as a piece of art, but the end of his career is well painted, and there are few more striking scenes in the book than the interview between him and his wife. Indeed, this scene makes amends for the melodramatic air of much of Bulstrode's story—George Eliot is not clever at melodrama. Dorothea's sister Celia and her good-natured husband Chettam, with the dowager Lady Chettam, are pretty pieces of *genre* painting, and stand well for what we mean when we use the expression "thoroughly English." Within a certain narrow circle, these people (and Mrs. Farebrother belongs to the same order of human beings) show a hundred good traits, but their narrowness is of a miraculous quality, confined to England, let us hope, a curiosity of the soil, as ancient and intimate a possession as the tin of Cornwall. As we recall the minor characters of this remarkable book we feel the impossibility of doing justice to them in this skipping way. Fred Vincy is nicely drawn, but better, it seems to us, when he first appears than later. Mary Garth is as refreshing and cordial a draught as fair spring water met with in the heat of a summer walk, and her father is as tonic, but more medicinal. Mary is of that crystal clearness and beauty, she seems as much a part of nature as the blue sky or the daisied turf. If only Lydgate had been mated with her! Not, however, that we wish poor Fred the ill luck to have been chained to Rosamond. Too hard a fate that to be lightly thought of for any man, least of all for one so estimable and high purposed as this young doctor, who is going to wash the world clean of its medical errors, washing it as men wash a dish, wiping it and turning it upside down. Old Mr. Featherstone with his relatives, Mrs. Waule and Mrs. Cranch and Solomon, make another group of humorous characters, but the humor of the book is not confined to them—it is perhaps George Eliot's most pervading quality, and she knows how to mingle it so deftly with the elements of human character that it never usurps an undue place, but remains in her portrayal as it is in nature, a delicate aroma, a grateful flavor, not the rank offense it becomes in the hands of the professed "humorist."

Among those who have read *Middlemarch* with full enjoyment, we often hear it said that the first half of the book, the first volume, is the more interesting. But is not this simply because in the first volume we are struck with the vigorous and skillful way in which the author moves her pieces about the board, setting

* *Middlemarch: A Story of Provincial Life.* By Geo. Eliot. In two volumes. Harper and Brothers.

subjects and fields of labor except precisely the one necessary for a good society novel. Statisticians, and scientists and economists—poets, historians, and abstract or mystic thinkers—we have had them all. But the one department of *social observation* is ill represented among us.

Never Again (Putnam) is a fluent and discursive story of a good young man—a sort of second Whittington—who comes up from the country to seek his fortune, saves an old French lady from the hands of desperate villains who are trying to wrest her fortune from her, and is, by the grateful old lady, enabled to aspire to the hand of his wealthy employer's daughter. The personages are in the main thin, sketchy, and conventional, the story improbable and rambling, and the language verbose and often slangy. But there is some vigor and nature in such personages as Whoppers, the editor, and old Planly, the inventor; while, on the other hand, the hero is a mere stage figure, the heroine a nullity, and the old sea-captain a fair exaggeration of the worst type of Bowery sailor. But some bits of dialogue and Dr. Mayo's side dissertations, though they seriously break the course of the story, are bright, shrewd, and amusing. If we could pick them out, referring the usual school-girl method, and throw away the story, our enjoyment of the book might be the greater.

"The Brook, and Other Poems."

THE title of the minor poems in this volume, "Songs and Studies," indicates that they spring from one common thought, which is more delicately fashioned and wrought into manifold relations in the principal poem. (*The Brook, and Other Poems*, by William B. Wright. New York: Scribner, Armstrong & Company.) The links of the latter within itself are distinct, though subtle; but while the harmonious effect of a whole is produced, it is not easy to define what that whole is intended to be. Its design is felt as the result of impressions from many slight indirect touches, rather than formally stated and methodically developed. Much of the highest modern poetry—Browning's may be instanced—addresses itself in such unsystematic ways to subjects that seem indefinite only because their range is vast and their connections multifarious.

One of the commonplaces of literature is the allegorical representation of human life under the image of some progressive movement, like that of a day, a journey, a stream, followed through its sequence of opening, course, and end. Other more vivid and ingenious illustrations of the stages in man's existence appear in poems like the "Song of the Bell" and the "Song of the Ship," choosing the history of some material object, picturesque in itself, to frame descriptions of human hopes and trials, and to point apt moralizing upon them. A curious reversal of this illustrative process is common enough with Shelley, who uses a kind of intellectual refinement on mythology in numberless passages, and definitely in such

verses as the "Sensitive Plant" and the "West Wind," to describe inanimate objects as sharing in man's emotions and possessed with a part of his spirit. And Emerson's short poems are full of sudden glimpses of the thought that there is a pervading life of which man's life is but one manifestation. But our author's work seems to us unique in the boldness of its motive and the skill of its management. Taking the Brook as his subject, he conceives it in a much more subtle mode than that of merely humanizing it, by lending to it the emotions and the vicissitudes which man undergoes. He sets it before his fancy rather as having its own peculiar reason for existing and part to fill in the general plan of things, and, endowing it with consciousness, seeks to enter into that consciousness and express its working. Of course this expression can only be uttered in terms of human experience, and hence the difficulty, almost reaching impossibility, of success in the attempt. Translation of such alien imaginings there is none, and only symbol and similitude must take its place. Both the method and the language of the effort must be those suggested in the passage that comes nearest to an explanation of the design.

"Yet I, though many forms of being,
Intent to find the steadfast soul,
Catch often type with type agreeing,
To point to an unchanging goal:
Fixed firmly released in a part
The features of the perfect whole."

This is the confession that the essence of the subject is intangible to conception, irresponsive to speech—the confession of the finite poet's incapacity to measure and unfold the infinite order.

A moment's reflection will serve to show that such purpose and treatment in poetry are not only exclusively modern, but are also an inevitable growth from the expansion and complexity of modern ideas. Ancient thought, absorbed in humanity as the center of all things, busied itself with the forms of man's work and passion, more than with the solution of human problems. How, not why, was its question; and if Plato philosophized or Lucretius poetized beyond those limits, blind conjecture led their futile excursions. Modern science has unfolded to the poet of to-day new and ever-receding horizons. How much farther it may widen the range of his vision without tempting his faculty beyond the borders of the intelligible, it is of course impossible to predict. It has already opened boundless fields for new combinations of thought. It has proved that man's world in space, instead of being a pivot, is a mere outlying fleck in the great drift; and as to his world in time, that the life of his race scarcely fills a measurable instant in the incalculable succession of life. It has suggested the bold hypothesis (and whether that be true or only plausibly conceived, the effect as a mental stimulus is the same) that man, in kind, instead of having always been what he is, is only the present phase of an ascending series.

We have not here to deal with the truth or falsity of such speculations—the point in question is that the mere fact of their arising in the modern mind necessarily transforms all poetic conceptions. Whether the poet adopt them as new realities, or combat them as errors, he must soar far enough and poetize deep enough to meet them in the regions from which they spring. Regarding man's spiritual nature as always the same, poetry will draw grander inspiration from this wider scope and finer complexity of his relations to the universe. Its very nature forbids the narrowing of its theme to man as he is known to be. It must account also for man as he supposes himself to be, since the power that impels to such supposition is itself a part of his being. And while retaining its reverence for his spiritual nature and its dependence, poetry must follow the most daring flights of inquiry if it would perform that which it would not be unfaithful to prove a part of its task, to reconcile religion and science.

These poems are suffused with such reverence, which is not the less real because it is expressed in freer forms than those of a past fashion. They depict man neither in the wrong old way, as the center of all things, nor in the wrong new way, as sufficient in his own strength. They are full of fine intimations, plainer in the shorter poems than in the longer one, that the alternations of labor and rest, joy and pain, which perplex his life, rule everywhere, and that a power works more for good to him than harm throughout the unseen net of circumstance in which he is unconsciously bound. The loose movement and scattered rhyme of the short, quick verse fit very well the wayward indirectness of its suggestions; while bits of sketch and miniature pictures are set in the neatest conciseness of primitive words. The best pastorals give no lighter touch than that of the morning landscape on page 53, nor shape any clearer figures than those of the mill-interior on page 57. We catch an echo of Emerson in

"Treaties knit with dead and son,
That never will their bond outrun"

and here a trace of Shelley, in

"And winds like down the cloudy aisles
The moon slipped from the morning's eye"—

but nowhere is there intentional imitation. Every page gives line after line of rare fancies and finest humor, dressed in pure, quaint, original English. It is long since so fresh and inspiriting a book has appeared, of poetry thoroughly healthy in sentiment, and philosophy free from irreverent dogmatism.

The New Volume of Lange.

For obvious reasons, the Book of Psalms is, of all the books of Holy Scripture, one of the most difficult of exposition, and submits itself to the labors of the commentator with the most reluctance. For the commentator is almost necessarily, in virtue of his office, a student rather of scientific than of poetic temper,

occupied with rules of grammar and minute details of exegesis, more than with the spirit of the inspired lyrics with which he has to do. Or if he escapes the peril of too dry and prosaic an interpretation, he is liable to fall into the easy snare of a deeply doctrinal and theological interpretation,—forgetting that the Psalms are essentially emotional rather than didactic, expressive of religious sentiment and purpose, of prayer and praise, of confession and of trust, rather than impressive of religious truths. It is because the commentators will not, or by nature cannot, escape these perils, that commentaries on the Psalter are apt to be so painfully unsatisfactory and inadequate.

It would be too much to expect that the new volume of Lange, which has just been published by Messrs. Scribner, Armstrong & Co., should wholly have escaped these dangers. But it is not too much to say that it has probably come nearer to escaping them, and to furnishing to English readers a satisfactory commentary on the Book of Psalms, than any other work to which they can have access. The introduction is especially learned and able; and the "Homiletical and Practical" department is very rich and valuable. It abounds in full and free citations from Mr. Spurgeon's yet unfinished Treasury of David. Great use is also made of Luther's admirable commentary, extracts from which, full of strong, good sense, and of manly and hearty devoutness, may be found on almost every page.

It is easy to appreciate the "strong desire" of the American editor (the learned and excellent Dr. Schaff), "to prepare the commentary on the Psalter" himself. But as this was impossible, the work was distributed among competent scholars (the Reverend Dr. John Forsyth, of West Point, the Rev. James B. Hammond, and the Reverends Charles A. Briggs and J. F. McCurdy, of New Jersey). The King James version, arranged in parallelisms, is made the text of the Commentary; but a new and revised translation, by the learned Dr. Conant, is appended to the volume.

In some of the American churches there is, just now, a revival of interest in the liturgical uses of the Book of Psalms, and a growing belief that we are not making sufficient use of it in our public worship. The intelligent study of the book, with such useful help as this volume of Lange will render, both to ministers and to laymen, will do much to deepen and to extend that interest, and to promote a wise and devout use of what should be regarded as an inspired liturgy for the Church throughout all ages.

A Volume by Dr. William M. Taylor.

The new pastor of the Broadway Tabernacle Church (who has already become so widely known and beloved that it is hard to think of him as a new pastor), has published, through Messrs. Scribner, Armstrong & Co., a little volume of simple and devout evangelical teaching, founded upon the three beautiful parables of the fifteenth chapter of St. Luke's Gospel.

(*The Lost Found and the Wanderer Welcomed*, by William M. Taylor, D.D. Scribner, Armstrong & Co.) It is not difficult to discover, even upon a hasty examination of the book, what those rare gifts are in virtue of which Dr. Taylor has at once taken his position among the foremost men in the American pulpit. A simple and reverent acceptance of the Scriptural revelation, a deep and earnest love for the Divine Saviour whom that revelation makes known to us, and a hearty humanity which puts him on the level of all sinful and needy souls, whom, with his Scotch fervor of entreaty, he would almost compel into the Kingdom —these are the characteristics of this volume, as they are of the preaching to which so many hundreds give earnest heed as they listen to it from the Tabernacle pulpit. One may look long to find the persuasive stories of our Lord, in the chapter on which the book is founded, urged home with more simple and practical force than here.

Williams' "Window Gardening."

Now that it seems as proper to have flowers in our houses in winter as it is to have them in our gardens in summer, a very natural interest is excited in the subject of the culture of plants in windows. We cannot all have a conservatory and an imported gardener; but our windows may be filled with every kind of floral loveliness. We have seen windows of which Spenser might have said:

> "No daintie flowre or herbe that growes on ground,
> No arboret with painted blossoms drest
> And smelling sweete, but there it might be found
> To bud out faire, and throwe her sweete smels al around."

It requires a certain skill to produce an effect of this kind; and if we be not well grounded in horticulture, or cannot have a gardener to teach us, we must buy a book on the subject, and there is no better book to buy than Henry T. Williams' *Window Gardening* (*Horticultural* Office, New York). From this really excellent volume we may learn everything about the management of window gardens in general, and the management of the various flowers in particular; how to keep our plants alive and to deal out death to our insects; how to plant, propagate, and prune; what to do with hanging baskets; how to train climbing vines; how to grow Roses, Camellias, Heliotropes, Lilies, Myrtles, and all those other lovely things that our hearts ache for in winter (we mean those of us who have no gardens—in windows or anywhere else). Besides being so complete, this work is reliable. When such men as Thomas Meehan of the *Gardener's Monthly*, and Dr. Thurber of the *Agriculturist*, indorse an author, we may plant, trim, water, fertilize, pull up and set out by his directions in a spirit of absolute confidence.

NATURE AND SCIENCE.

The Chemical Rays of the Spectrum.

THE second memoir of Dr. John W. Draper's Researches in Actino-chemistry is published simultaneously in the *London and Edinburgh Philosophical Magazine* and in the *American Journal of Science and Art*. His first memoir was on the distribution of heat in the spectrum; the present one is on the distribution of chemical force. In the former he showed that all the rays of the spectrum possess equal heating power. In this, he shows that every ray can bring about chemical changes. Hitherto it has been supposed that the actinic force—the force that brings about chemical decompositions—is restricted to the violet of the spectrum, and in all the books treating on this subject, figures are introduced illustrating this view. In this memoir, the error of this is shown by an analysis of several decompositions brought about by the agency of radiation. The following paragraph furnishes a summary of the evidence:—

"At this point I abstain from adding other instances showing that chemical changes are brought about in every part of the spectrum. The list of cases here presented might be indefinitely extended, if these did not suffice. But how is it possible to restrict the chemical force of the spectrum to the region of the more refrangible rays, in face of the facts that compounds of silver, such as the iodide, which have heretofore been mainly relied upon to support that view, and in fact originated it, are now proved to be affected by every ray from the invisible ultra-red to the invisible ultra-violet? how, when it is proved that the decomposition of carbonic acid, by far the most general and most important of the chemical actions of light, is brought about, not by the more refrangible, but by the yellow rays? The delicate colors of flowers, which vary indefinitely in their tints, originate under the influence of rays of many different refrangibilities, and are bleached or destroyed by spectrum colors complementary to their own, and therefore varying indefinitely in their refrangibility. Toward the indigo ray the stems of plants incline; from the red their roots turn away. There is not a wave of light that does not leave its impress of ferments and resins, some undulations promoting their oxidation, some, their deoxidation. These actions are not limited to decompositions; they extend to combinations. Every ray in the spectrum brings on the union of chlorine and hydrogen."

He adds, in conclusion: "The figure so generally employed in works on actino-chemistry to indicate

The Electric Spark.

English Country Labourers' Houses.

Fossil Man at Mentone.

An Extraordinary Surgical Operation.

Decay of Fruits.

delicate filamentous tubes, which are the parts first to appear and form the buds, as it were, of the fungus, are called the Mycelium, and are found in almost all fungi.

Sea-Sickness.

In discussing M. Bessemer's saloon steamer a writer says: Persons suffering from sea-sickness complain not only of giddiness, arising from themselves and everything about them being continually in motion, but also in particular of a qualm which comes over them every time the ship or the part of it on which they are standing, is descending, sinking as it were from under their feet. An approach to this qualm is commonly felt in a garden-swing during the descent, and also in jumping from considerable heights. There can be very little doubt that this is due to the fact that the intestines are then wholly or partially relieved from their own weight, and therefore exercise an unusual pressure against the stomach, liver, and diaphragm. This pressure produces the qualm, and its rapid and frequent alternations cause sufficient irritation to produce in most people sea-sickness, and in some persons more serious effects. Physiologists are by no means agreed as to how much of sea-sickness is due to this cause, and how much to the reaction upon the stomach of the brain-disturbance.

Floriculture.

ALL lovers of flowers must remember, that one blossom allowed to mature or "go to seed" injures the plant more than a dozen new buds. Cut your flowers then, all of them, before they begin to fade. Adorn your rooms with them; put them on your tables; send bouquets to your friends who have no flowers; or exchange favors with those who have. You will surely find that the more you cut off the more you will have. All roses after they have ceased to bloom should be cut back, that the strength of the root may go to forming new roots for next year. On bushes not a seed should be allowed to mature.

The Lost Comet.

THE comet of Biela was first recognized in 1772, and rediscovered by Biela in 1826. During its visit in 1846 it was noticed that it had undergone division, and was separated into two portions which were gradually receding from each other, and at the time of its disappearance they were about 157,000 miles apart.

On the next reappearance, in 1852, the space between the two portions had increased to 1,250,000 miles. The parts were of nearly equal brilliancy and moved side by side, the interval between them gradually increasing until they disappeared.

Though carefully searched for in 1859 and 1866, the comet failed to make its appearance; but Mr. Hind expected that it would make its nearest approach to the earth in the latter part of 1872, and its positions for successive nights were calculated and foretold to assist in its detection, but with the same want of success as on previous occasions.

The comet having disappeared, it is found by the directors of the observatories at Vienna and Copenhagen that its orbit is marked by a considerable meteor stream, and it becomes a matter of the greatest interest to determine the relations between the comet and this meteor stream.

Original Investigations in England and America.

Nature says: "The Journal of the Chemical Society, of which the original and proper function was to print the investigations of English chemists, now appears to exist simply to inform us of what is accomplished elsewhere. The volume for the year 1874 is a stout octavo of 1,224 pages; of these, however, not more than 154 are occupied with original communications read before the Society, while the rest of the volume is filled with innumerable abstracts of the investigations of the chemists of Germany and France. Ten years ago the same Journal contained on the average at least 400 pages of original matter."

From the above quotation, it would appear that the dearth of original investigation which Professor Tyndall deplores so much as being the crying deficiency of this country, is also felt to an equal if not greater extent in England, since there there is a great falling off in the amount, while here we are at least advancing.

So seriously is the deficiency in this respect felt in England that it has become a matter for discussion at public meetings. At one of these the following resolutions were passed, which support a plan well worthy of our consideration on this side of the Atlantic:—

1st. That to have a class of men whose lives are devoted to research is a national object.

2d. That it is desirable, in the interest of national progress and education, that professorships and special institutions shall be founded in the Universities for the promotion of scientific research.

3d. That the present mode of awarding fellowships as prizes has been found unsuccessful as a means of promoting mature study and original research, and that it is desirable that it should be discontinued.

Testing the Endurance of Stone.

AT a recent meeting of the Philosophical Society of Manchester, Dr. R. Angus Smith said that he had observed that the particles of stone most liable to be in long contact with rain from town atmospheres, were most subject to decay. Believing the acids in the air to be the cause, he supposed that the endurance of a silicious stone might be somewhat measured by measuring its resistance to acids. He proposed therefore to use strong solutions, and thus approach to the action of long periods of time. He tries a few specimens in this way and with the most promising results. Pieces of about an inch cube were broken by the fall of a hammer, and the number of blows counted. Similar pieces were steeped in weak acid; both sulphuric and muriatic were tried, and the latter pre-

Thanatophidia of India

Restoring Waste Places

Memoranda

A WINTER'S TALE.

1. Which her name is Horace May.　2. (Need we conceal it:—Clara?) . . . . . and he loves.　　3. On a winter's day, he mounts his steed and rides to tell her so.

4. The snow soon forces him to lead his noble courser.　　5. After a while, progress becomes difficult.　　6. Curtain falls : music by the chorus.

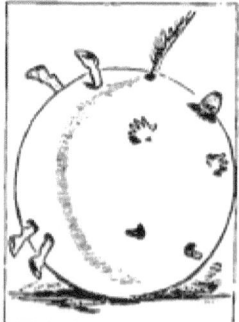

7. Clara looks forth frequently, expecting Horace Morris.　　8. But the boys, who do not expect him, make a big snow-ball.　　9. Which melts as Spring approaches, and the end of the tale is obvious.

AMONG THE ELGIN WATCHMAKERS.
BY EDWARD EGGLESTON.

FATHER PERRELET, THE FRENCH WATCHMAKER.

In the office at the factory of the National Watch Company, at Elgin, one finds hanging the portrait of the patriarchal French watchmaker, Perrelet, sitting at his work at ninety-three years of age. Since the day of the skillful Père Perrelet, "the father of modern watchmaking," a new era has come in his trade, and if he could have gone with us through that great, busy factory, and could have seen what we saw,—how all his tedious processes are performed now by tireless and errorless fingers of steel,—he might have believed himself indeed in some land of enchantment as wonderful as any ever dreamed of by the visionary Princess Scherezade. Some things which the old Perrelet forty years ago achieved with infinite pains, even after a life-long training, are now performed ten times as well, and more than ten times as rapidly, by curious, infallible little machines, watched by young girls. These inanimate punches, dies and lathes mock the skill acquired in a patient lifetime, nearly a century in length, by surpassing Perrelet's most perfect work.

But there must be brains somewhere. Whatever people may say of Paley's argument from the design to the designer, as applied to the Universe, it certainly holds good as applied to a watch. There may be no thought in a machine, and the steady-fingered workman who feeds it may not even know the use of the piece his machine is helping to perfect ; but back of the machines and the workmen there must be a calculating intellect somewhere. Let us, therefore, go first into the Draughting Department. Let us take things in their logical order for an Elgin watch is the concrete result of logic,—it is as much the fruit of logic as Holmes' "One Hoss Shay." All the wonderful little pieces that compose your watch must go on paper before they can be realized in metal. And, before they can be drawn, they must be devised, and their elements calculated. Think of calculating the angle of an escapement or the precise shape of the leaf of a pinion where the unit of measurement never exceeds the one twenty-five-hundredth of an inch ! Such wisdom is too wonderful for me. Here is devised, calculated and drawn the machine for turning a thread on screws so small that you cannot detect the fact that they are screws except by the use of the microscope. Bear in mind that nothing is done by guess work,—it is not "cut and try ;" each change in the construction of a watch is settled by a mathematical calculation as careful, thorough and exhaustive as that by which an engineer settles the elements of such a work as the East River Bridge. The microscopic pieces are not half so wonderful to me as the microscopic mathematics by which their size, shape and adjustment are fixed.

This exceeding smallness of the scale is one of the most curious things in watch-making. Here are gauges for measuring accurately the size of a pivot. They will show a difference of size in the points of two fine needles. In the Steel and Screw Department is a girl who sits watching a lathe that turns out screws so fine that they look like filings till you see their heads and threads under a powerful glass. In a box half an inch deep and two and a half long, by one and a half inches in width, she had twenty-five thousand screws, and the box lacked a full ten thousand of being full. That is to say, thirty or forty thousand screws in a small "hook and eye" box. Did she count them ? That is just the question I asked. Screws are estimated by the length of wire used. Some small pieces, however, as jewels, are of great value and are counted carefully, one by one. In the Train Room I saw jewel-pins made of garnet. A workman made a statement which seems sufficiently incredible, that one hundred and twenty-five thousand (125,000) of these little stone pins weigh an ounce! And yet, I insist that the strangest thing of all is, that every dimension of these little pieces is a matter of calculation, foreordained in the construction of the series of machines by which it is made.

Charles V, may yet come to be realized in some great democratic watch factory like this at Elgin.

In the Punch and Die Department is a punch that strikes out a brass wheel every second. It punches out the inside of the wheel, leaving the rim supported by arms,

TRAIN ROOM, ELGIN WATCH FACTORY.

The Watch Factory has its own machine shop. The men who make steam-engines and other machinery, even of the most delicate sort, could not be trusted here, where the 1-2500 of an inch of error, or even the 1-10000 of an inch too much or too little, might mar the whole production of this vast factory. There are traditions of single errors in altering machinery in watch factories—errors so slight that they were not perceptible to any but a practiced eye—having cost, though corrected at once, half a hundred thousand dollars. The machinery must do its work with infinite exactitude; there must be no patching, pinching, twisting or fixing afterward. Every particle of hand-work is an element of uncertainty, and the end and aim of watchmaking by machinery is to eliminate the element of uncertainty, and every improvement has for its purpose the attainment of something like infallibility. That dream of two time-pieces absolutely and invariably together, which was attributed to the royal clockmaker,

and it cuts the outside of the rim from the strip of brass with so fine a blade that the wheel is unconscious of its separation and stays in its place until the boy alongside the machine pushes it out with his thumb. After a while it is placed under a finishing punch that takes off two and a half one-thousandths of an inch from the inner side of the rim and the arms. The taking off of this homœopathic shaving serves only to give it polish—a nicer finish than could be produced by the use of the first punch alone. It used to be that one man could finish twenty-five a day; but now one man can finish three thousand in a day. I say finish, though the wheel is far from finished when it goes from this room. In the die cupboard here are a great variety of punches for making all sorts of wheels, or at least beginning to make them. It is yet a long road to completion, for it will be six months before wheels punched here to-day can be running in watches ready for the pocket of the buyer, and the Company has continually nearly half a million invested in incomplete work.

Nowhere was I more impressed with the curious infinitesimalness of these operations than when I saw a drill making screw-holes in the edge of a plate. So delicate is the drill that a larger one has to make a "center" for it first—a hole started as a guide to keep the little drill from deflecting in boring its way into the edge of a plate. But I cannot tell you why it is that, instead of the delicate little drill revolving, it is the plate that turns—much as though a wheelwright, wishing to bore a hole in the tire of a very large wheel, turned the wheel round instead of the auger.

SETTING JEWELS.

But when it comes to settling such questions as those of "side-shake" and "end-shake," I confess that I am lost in amazement. How much larger must the aperture of a jewel be than the pivot that plays in it? You suppose that they should be of the same size; and so did the first Yankee who undertook to make watches by machinery. But he found that when the pivot filled the hole exactly there was no room for oil, and there was so much friction that the watch was stopped by a grain of dust. It will no more do to have a pivot exactly fitted to its aperture than to have an axle-tree fit tight in its hub. A series of investigations has proven that a pivot must have 2-2500 of an inch "side-shake;" that is, that the hole in a

jewel must be 2-2500 of an inch larger than the pivot. The difference is, of course, too small for the eye to detect. But here is a young woman measuring the jewels by slipping them on a tapering needle connected with an index which indicates their size exactly by showing how far down each jewel slips before the thickness of the needle arrests it. And lying by her we see a gauge—a pair of nippers with a watch-dial arrangement on which the ten-thousandth of an inch of variation can be detected, and on which the twenty-five-hundredth is plainly marked. This nipper-gauge is for measuring the pivots.

The "end-shake" is the space left at the end of a pivot for oil and for the play of the pivot. How much is it? I did not learn, and it doesn't matter. The difference between two-twenty-five-hundredths of an inch and three is not thinkable to you or to me. It does not matter to me for purposes of thought whether the pivot of a watch-wheel is 2-2500 of an inch or only 1-2500 short, any more than it matters to me whether the sun is ninety-three millions of miles away or ninety-five. When a thing gets too big or too little for my comprehension, it does not matter whether it is a little larger or a little less.

But this painstaking in minute operations fascinates me. If you will look at the dial of an Elgin watch, you will read in letters hardly visible to the naked eye the words: "National Watch Company;" and I have one of these trusty time-pieces that was given me some years ago by a company of generous friends as a souvenir, on the face of which the entire presentation inscription is painted in these miraculously perfect little capital letters—only legible by people of sharp eyes. But here we see the master of Lilliputian sign-painting, working without die or stencil to guide him. Nothing but the human fingers—the most wonderful of mechanical devices after all—can make these graceful little inscriptions. Looking through a powerful glass, the painter steadies his hand against his cheek and works very delicately and cautiously with the finest of brushes. He cannot do this work constantly, —human eyesight could not bear the strain,— so he rests himself by painting the figures on the dials. This minute painting reminds one of what Agassiz says of certain microscopists who abstain from food in order to reduce their blood and acquire steadiness enough for their most difficult operations.

For it really seems that heart-beats would be sufficient to make this painter's hand mar letters so delicately small.

Not only are these lathes and drills of incredibly minute workmanship, but they attain incredible speed as well. The little screw holes in the rim of a balance-wheel are bored by a little auger that "revolves on its axis" at the lively rate of forty-eight hundred revolutions a minute, or eighty revolutions a second. These screw-holes are so small that they have to be tapped out afterward by hand, the tap is too delicate to trust it to automatic machinery. An automaton may be very much more exact than the hand, but there are operations that must be modified by human sense detecting changed conditions. And the hard, inevitable steel arms can neither feel nor modify. Here then we have reached a limitation of machinery. It has no nerves.

But in the Balance Room we saw a curious machine—a set of automatic hammers for hardening the brass rim of a balance-wheel. They not only pound with incredible velocity, but they know when their work is finished. They rattle away at a revolving wheel until they have hammered it just thirty seconds; then they stop and wait for a new piece to

CUTTING PINIONS.

pound. Pity that some ministers and lecturers could not be arranged on the same self-stopping plan, to keep them from pounding away at a subject after they have done with it!

You laugh at me for seeing something human in these automata? Here is this strange and powerful little machine for cutting the "leaves" of pinions; it utters a piteous, half-human cry as it plows its way through the hard steel. Surely some subtle Ariel is shut up in it, doing his work, but sighing for release. Just alongside is a noiseless apparatus for cutting teeth in brass wheels, which makes one tooth in each of thirty wheels at a single motion, and it is so arranged that every tooth in every wheel is just like every tooth in every other wheel of the same kind—an end not attainable without machinery.

These last operations are in the Train Room; for, with all my good beginning in writing logically of watchmaking, I find that I have hopped and skipped about from room to room, following my vagabond association of ideas rather than any right order. In truth, there are more departments in this great building than I can pretend to remember; a department for draughting plans, one for making machinery, one for punching wheels and rolling steel, one for making screws, one for plates, and one for dials, and a room devoted to balances and hair-springs, another to making the "train" or running gear of a watch, one to gilding the brass work, another to jewel-cutting, and a setting-up department, where the watch is put together and tested. How many other departments there may be, I cannot say. I saw a blacksmith's forge in the basement, though what a blacksmith can have to do with a watch I do not know. Doubtless he works about the machinery. I am sure he does not make hair-springs.

Watchmaking, indeed, is not one trade, but a hundred; it has its affiliations with almost every other handicraft. All sorts of work in brass, and all sorts of work in steel, and all the arts of the goldsmith, and all kinds of work in precious stones, find some place in the manufacture of a watch. Even the followers of Palissy, the makers of enameled porcelain, are represented in the men who stand in that hot little room baking the dials, taking infinite pains that this fine enamel, by repeated processes, shall be brought out at last without a defect. Some idea of the multiplicity of operations may be formed from the fact that the foreman of the Train Department alone has to look after nearly seven hundred different processes.

One of the most curious automatic arrangements is the profile machine, by which the edge of a plate is cut irregularly after a model. It almost directs itself, and is, indeed, about as intelligent a machine as you ever saw.

PROFILE MACHINE.

I have read that there is a clock just completed for the Cathedral of Beauvais which contains a trifle of ninety thousand wheels, and indicates the days of the week, the month, the year, the signs of the zodiac, the equation of time, the course of the planets, the phases of the moon, the time at every capital in the world, the movable feasts for a hundred years, the saints' days, and ever so much else that is of no consequence to anybody. It is arranged so as to show the additional day at Leap Year. It has a dial twelve feet in diameter, and cost forty thousand dollars—with no discount to the trade! But the clock at Beauvais, if considered in comparison with the Watch Factory at Elgin, indicates one thing not intended by its inventor and not marked on its dial, and yet of much greater consequence than the movable feasts or the signs of the zodiac. It indicates the difference between the Old World and the New. At Beauvais the ingenuity of lifetimes is wasted on a toy with ninety thousand wheels. Here mechanical genius devises machinery which puts into the pockets of people of moderate means a watch

whose hands give all the really useful information supplied by the costly trifle in the Cathedral tower at Beauvais. There is more than the Atlantic Ocean between Europe and America.

I mentioned a while ago that the Company have continually nearly half a million of dollars invested in incomplete watches—that is, in human labor, for it is human labor that makes a watch so valuable. Many of these little steel bits are worth ten times their weight in gold, and this value is chiefly the usury of human life and skill.

Everything about a watch must not only be done well, but done artistically, for watches are keepsakes, jewels, precious ornaments, as well as articles of use. So there is everywhere here a burnishing, polishing, finishing, a striving after elegance as well as after mechanical perfection, which comes nigh to making it a fine art. It lies between the two sorts of art somewhat as the goldsmith's calling did in the Middle Age. Every screw head and every plate is brightened and finished to the last degree.

You will see the train—or, as it is popularly called, the works of a watch—all set up and running, but looking dingy and miserable. This is called a "gray watch." When once the Setting-up Department is satisfied that a watch keeps good time, under all sorts of tests, it is taken apart and all the brass work sent to the Gilding Room. Here the plates are scrubbed—I cannot call it anything else—by rotary brushes of fine wire. It is related that the Superintendent of sales in the Company's Chicago office, a famous Sunday School man, was not a little scandalized on his first connection with the Company to find bills for several barrels of beer coming in for payment each month. He could hardly see the necessity for keeping workmen supplied with beer while they were engaged in work so delicate. But he was relieved to find that the beer was for the watches and not for the watchmakers. While these rotary brushes of fine brass are scouring away at the plates, a constant stream of sour beer is kept pouring upon them, by way of mellowing them, perhaps. Whatever may be thought of the mental effects of beer, a certain

helps to make watches bright. When the plate is thoroughly cleaned and rendered frosty in appearance, it is ready for gilding, and is put into the bath and gilded by the galvanic process. It is then returned to the Setting-up Room, where it made its first appearance as a gray watch, and is now bright with gold. But this galvanic process is quite as minute as the mechanical ones. The cheap foreign watches sold as galvanized or plated have their cases treated in the same way, and the simple countryman buys a watch for gold or "oroide" which is a delusion as "thin" as a galvanic process can make it. Of course, the reputable American Companies put nothing but solid gold and silver into their cases. Gold being unfit for the running gear, and the plates which hold it, the brass portions are gilded to save them from the dingy look of the "gray" watches and to prevent corrosion.

The jewels used are garnet, ruby and aqua marine. The Jewel Room is one of the most interesting of all. The stones are sawn into "planks" by a curious saw-mill. These thin planks are then cut into joists—it seems a joke to call these ruby sticks joists—and the joists are then broken into bits which are by many curious processes fitted for the places they are to occupy. Where there is needed a peculiarly firm resistance to friction

MAKING HAIR SPRINGS.

in a fine watch, jewels are used, and no part of the work of the watchmaker is more vital than the preparation and setting of these jewels.

Theodore Parker said that he was not half so much interested in the fine arts as he was in the coarse ones by which men and women earned their bread. Here is an art that is *fine* enough, and, aside all play upon the word, this highest of the mechanic arts is in some sense an æsthetic one. I have already said that a watch is not alone an article of use, but a thing of beauty—an ornament and a souvenir. George Macdonald loves to represent the enthusiasm of an imaginative boy for old relics, and the relics which appear in his different books are fiddles, swords and watches. Not only is an old watch precious, but a new one is often used as a gift intended for a perpetual memento of the tenderest affection. So that this art is in some sense a fine art, though it is also one by which a great multitude of men and women get their bread. I could not but fancy that the introduction of watchmaking of the highest grade into this Illinois country has had a refining influence upon the population. There is a neatness, orderliness, cleanliness, and an extreme quietness not often seen in a factory, and which I could not but attribute to the influence of the art. The very best trained artisans were imported from the East by the Company at the beginning, but the great majority of the five or six hundred now employed in the shops have learned the art here. That girl who is cutting screws, and whose hair is, like the Blessed Demozel's, "yellow like ripe corn," is without doubt a native of this Illinois country; indeed, very many of these deft-handed girls are the daughters of neighboring farmers, and

BAKING DIALS.

to them the factory has been a great boon.

If watchmaking is a fine art on one side, it has its analogies with scientific investigations also. The determining of such nice questions as those of "side-shake" and "end-shake" is in reality a scientific process of no mean order. The factory has had a wonderful influence on jewelers. Very many letters are received by the Company from country watchmakers, some of them very ingenious and valuable, suggesting new devices. And in the factory investigations are always going on, looking to the devising of new and better methods of accomplishing the different ends which have to be kept in view. Inventions in watchmaking are of two sorts—the one an improvement in the mechanism of the watch itself, the other in the machinery by which some part of the watch is made.

Where the twenty-five-hundredth part of an inch is of consequence, there grows naturally a sense of responsibility which gives a quietness and steadiness to the atmosphere of the place. And watches have much to answer for, if, indeed, it is true that the worst railway accidents are attributable to errors in time-keepers. The Pennsylvania Railroad has set a good example in this regard. It owns the watches carried by its engineers; there is an Elgin watch belonging to each locomotive, and, when the locomotive is sent out, the watch which belongs to it is given to the engineer in charge. When he returns and reports, his watch is hung up in the office, where it is carefully regulated, so that there can be no variation in the time-pieces carried by the employes of this great road.

"Time is money," says the old adage, and doubtless the force of the saying is felt by the Elgin stockholders, who began with the expectation of investing a hundred and fifty thousand dollars, but who have now about three-quarters of a million in time-keepers. It is pleasant to know that the corner has been turned, and that these weary years of patient and courageous enterprise have at last been rewarded with success. The excellent reputation the watches have gained is the foundation for this prosperity. When we were at the factory, the demand was in excess of the production, and the higher grades, such as the "B. W. Raymond," could not be supplied fast enough. Notwithstanding the accuracy of the watches, the factory was a little behind time.

The principal office of the Company is in Chicago, and, of course, was burned in the fire, but their vault resisted the heat so well that a live mouse of a horological turn of mind was found in it—the sole survivor of the burnt district, having made a timely escape to rejoice in the untimely winding up of the life of every cat that ever watched his wary steps or tried to force him to paws. With his tale our story ends, and his portrait shall be the tail-piece.

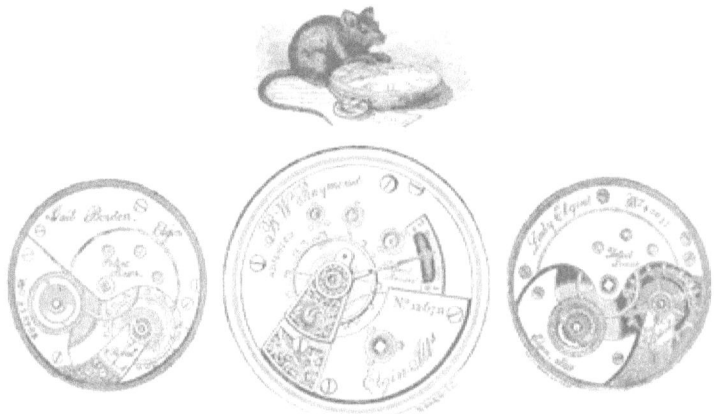

10 P. M.—ELGIN TIME.

"Methought I heard a voice cry :
'Sleep no more!'"

11 P. M.—ELGIN TIME.

"Sleeping I dream, love,
Dream, love, of thee."

ONE MINUTE AFTER ELEVEN.

"That bright dream
Was his last!"

MIDNIGHT.—"What charm can soothe her melancholy, What art can wash her guilt away."

ONE SECOND AFTER MIDNIGHT.—"Can such things be,
And overcome us like a summer's cloud, Without our special wonder?"

1 A. M.—ELGIN TIME.

"If it were done, when 'tis
done, then 'twere well
It were done quickly."

ONE SECOND AFTER ONE.

"If the assassination could tram-
mel up the consequence."

2 A. M.—ELGIN TIME.

"Bloody instructions, which being taught, Return to plague
the inventor."

3 A. M.—ELGIN TIME.

"Things without all remedy,
Should be without regard :
what's done is done."

PUBLISHERS' DEPARTMENT.

Letters from the People.

SAXE HOLM'S STORIES.—A lady writes to us:

"I think Saxe Holm's stories are as nearly perfect as any compositions I have ever read. There is literally never a word too much, or a sentence that could be improved. The exquisite pictures, the flowers, landscapes, descriptions, the tenderness of the scenes, and the tenderness of the situations, and, above all, the satisfying completeness, leaving nothing to be desired—instead of the usual uncomfortable wondering how they did really get along, are beyond praise. They are the only short stories that absolutely satisfy one."

Saxe Holm has written a new story for us: THE ELDER'S DAUGHTER, a sequel to DRAXY MILLER'S DOWRY, which will begin in the April number.

The Great South

From numerous letters in relation to this series of Illustrated Papers, to be commenced in the Monthly early next summer, we copy the following:

I rejoice heartily that Mr. Edward King has been employed by you to travel through the South, and write a series of papers for SCRIBNER'S MONTHLY. My object in writing this note is simply to say that Dr. ——— ———, who is a geologist, and myself will give him a hearty welcome, and one or the other of us will try to accompany him in his tour of observation. Both of us have traversed more than once our beautiful State, not on railroads alone, but on foot and on horseback, and we shall be able to point out the objects of greatest interest in every county. We shall be glad to aid in the effort to let the world know something more of our immense resources, our great variety of soil, and climate, and our magnificent scenery, etc., etc."

We have received similar letters from almost every portion of the South; we do not answer all of them, but we forward them to Mr. King, who with Mr. Champney, the artist, is, at the time of writing this notice, somewhere in Texas, en route for New Orleans. The party will work south at the season advances. We invite special attention and aid in this effort to illustrate, by pen and pencil, this vast region—nine times larger than all of Great Britain, possessing agricultural and mineral resources almost boundless, and commercial and industrial possibilities scarcely yet begun to be appreciated by the world.

These letters from the people are not only full of interest to us, but they are also full of information, and we invite further communications on the subject.

Mr. King writes as follows: "SCRIBNER'S is growing rapidly in the South. In several towns that we have visited the sale is one to every eighty or eighty-five inhabitants!"

The Magazine is growing throughout the entire country in the same way. In some places the sale by the dealers has more than doubled within a few months.

Remember, friends, that we aim to do nothing less than to make SCRIBNER'S MONTHLY "the best in the world."

THE NEW YORK EVENING POST says the February SCRIBNER is the best number we have yet issued. We were ourselves inclined to award the palm to the January number, but we defer to the opinion of our neighbor the Post. An English critic says that "SCRIBNER'S is the best magazine we have ever come across."

American Silks.

We have received from Cheney Brothers, Hartford, and South Manchester, Conn., a specimen of silk of their own manufacture, which seems to equal in beauty and finish the famous silks made at Antwerp. Accompanying this dress pattern was a sample yard of colored silks, which were in every way a surprise. Those who have only seen specimens of silks made in this country two or three years since, should send for one of these sample cards.

Diamonds and Precious Stones.

We desire to call the attention of all our readers, who are coming to New York this spring, to the establishment of TIFFANY & CO., on Union Square. It is literally a palace of gems and gold.

Fire, and Accident, and Life Insurance.

AMONG the FIRE INSURANCE COMPANIES that have survived the great and disastrous conflagrations of the past year, and still present unimpaired claims to the public confidence, we note THE HOME, of New York, THE HANOVER, of N. Y., THE NIAGARA, of N. Y., and THE FRANKLIN, of Philadelphia. We insure in all these companies. Among the brood of accident companies that started up a few years ago, we believe "THE TRAVELERS," of Hartford, Conn., under the leadership of Mr. J. G. Batterson, the first in the field, is the only survivor. Of the solvency of this company there is not the slightest question. The MUTUAL LIFE INSURANCE CO., of New York, and THE CONNECTICUT MUTUAL, of Hartford, Conn., if not the best Life Insurance Companies in the United States, are certainly among the best, and any man is fortunate who holds a paid-up policy in either of these companies.

A Word to Invalids.

WE know so many chronic invalids who have been benefited at the CURE of Dr. Geo. H. Taylor, in this city (No. 67 West 38th Street), that we cannot refrain from calling attention to it. Dr. Taylor's modesty is only equalled by his skill. His system, "the movement cure," without medicine, and without the debilitating effect of the water cure, is certainly a specific in the treatment of all the varied forms of loss of muscular or nervous power. We know parties who have been cured at his establishment after half a lifetime of suffering.

"Window Gardening"

Ladies who love Flowers will be delighted with this handsome new volume. It is devoted to Flowers for parlor use and house decoration. Superbly illustrated; 250 engravings; 300 pages. Inquire for it at any book store, or order direct by mail of the publisher. Price $1.50. Prospectus free on receipt of stamp. The Ladies' Floral Cabinet. A beautiful paper devoted to Flowers. Charmingly illustrated. $1.00 per year. Specimen free. Address, HENRY T. WILLIAMS, Publisher, Box 2445, New York.

7

8

10

11

The Nation.

VOL. XVI.—Nos. 392-443.   THURSDAYS.   {FIVE DOLLARS PER ANNUM / TWELVE CENTS PER COPY}

TRIAL, 50 CENTS.

12

14

New Standard Books

FOR THE OPENING SEASON OF 1878,

NOW READY, OR SHORTLY TO BE ISSUED BY

Scribner, Welford & Armstrong, 654 Broadway,

NEW YORK.

---I.---

Manual of Mythology.

FOR THE USE OF SCHOOLS, ART STUDENTS, AND GENERAL READERS.

Founded on *the* Works *of* Petiscus, Preller, and Welcker,

BY

ALEXANDER S. MURRAY,

DEPARTMENT OF GREEK AND ROMAN ANTIQUITIES, BRITISH MUSEUM.

With thirty five plates on toned paper, representing seventy six mythological subjects. 12mo, cloth extra................ $3 00

PROSPECTUS.

With the view of making the subject of ancient mythology accessible to the higher classes of schools, to art students, and to general readers, the plan, and, to a great extent, the substance of the present book, have been taken from the German work of Petiscus, entitled "Der Olymp," which has proved how well it is adapted for such a purpose by the fact of its having already reached a seventeenth edition. At the same time, while endeavoring to imitate the simple style of narrative to which the success of that work has mainly been due, it has been found necessary to reject many of the observations made by its author, and to adopt in their place the results of more recent research. This is particularly the case in regard to the Introduction, in which it is attempted to show how the belief in the existence of the gods originated, and to point out the influence of such belief with special reference to the ancient Greeks. The legends of the Greek heroes have also been given at a greater length, and in a manner, it is hoped, more worthy of the subject.

In addition to the mythologies of Greece and Rome, the present work will be found to contain an account of the Scandinavian and Old German, the Indian and Egyptian mythologies.

---II.---

MISCELLANEOUS AND POSTHUMOUS WORKS OF

Henry Thomas Buckle.

Edited, with a Biographical Notice, by HELEN TAYLOR.

Three vols. 8vo, pp. 1,184, cloth... $22 50

---III.---

ILLUSTRATED LIBRARY EDITION OF THE

Life and Works of Charlotte Bronte

(CURRER BELL)

And her Sisters, EMILY and ANNE BRONTE (Ellis and *Acton Bell*).

In Seven Monthly Volumes, large crown 8vo, handsomely bound in cloth. Price per volume............................ $3 00

The descriptions in "Jane Eyre" and the other Fictions by Charlotte Bronte and her Sisters being mostly of actual places, the publishers considered that Views would form the most suitable illustrations of the Library Edition of the novels. They are indebted for a clue to the real names of the most interesting scenes to a friend of the Misses Bronte, who has thus enabled the artist, Mr. G. M. Wimperis, to identify the places described. He made faithful sketches of them on the spot, and has also drawn them on wood. It is therefore hoped that these Views will add fresh interest to the reading of the stories. The following are the principal illustrations:

Vol. 1. JANE EYRE.—Gateshead Hall—School at Cowan Bridge—Thornfield—Moor House—Ferndean Manor. (*Now Ready.*)
Vol. 2. SHIRLEY.—Nunnely Wood—Hollow's Mill—Yorke's House—Fieldhead—Briarfield Church. (*Now Ready.*)
Vol. 3. VILLETTE.—The Park, Brussels—Pensionnat of Madame Beck—Garden in Rue Fossette—Grand Place, Brussels. (*Now Ready.*)
Vol. 4. THE PROFESSOR and POEMS.—Portrait of Rev. Patrick Bronte—Rue Royale, Brussels—Protestant Cemetery, Brussels View on the Moors. (*Ready in March.*)
Vol. 5. WUTHERING HEIGHTS and AGNES GREY.—Wuthering Heights—View on the Moors—Distant View of Haworth Church—Snow Scene.
Vol. 6. TENANT OF WILDFELL HALL.—Wildfell Hall—Grassdale Manor—Horringby Hall.
Vol. 7. LIFE BY MRS. GASKELL.—Portrait of Charlotte Bronte—Casterton School—Roe Head—Haworth Parsonage and Church—The Bronte Waterfall.

☞ *Any or all of the above works sent, free of charge, upon receipt of the price by the publishers.*

15

www.ingramcontent.com/pod-product-compliance
Lightning Source LLC
Chambersburg PA
CBHW021122020726
47500CB00003B/885